Upon the Mountains

OTHER BOOKS AND AUDIO BOOKS
BY GALE SEARS:

Autumn Sky

Until the Dawn

Upon the Mountains

a novel

GALE
SEARS

Covenant

Top image: *Woman in Lace* vintage postcard 1912.
Bottom image: *Battle of the Somme* photography by Richard Caton II Woodville.© 2007 The Bridgeman Art Library. Courtesy of www.gettyimages.com

Cover design copyrighted 2007 by Covenant Communications, Inc.

Published by Covenant Communications, Inc.
American Fork, Utah

Printed in Canada
First Printing: August 2007

11 10 09 08 07   10 9 8 7 6 5 4 3 2 1

ISBN 978-1-59811-443-0

To my father,
Norman Johns Kamp.
A good man.

Acknowledgements

Heartfelt thanks to the following individuals whose help has kept me looking forward.

Teri Boldt, my first reader. George Sears for a ton of reasons. Nola Sears, Roxanne Glassey, Margot Kimball, and Nancy Tullis for offering insights and encouragement. Vicki Ragsdale for her love and knowledge of flowers. Dawn Bates for walks on the long and winding road. Shauna Chymnboryk for wanting not to edit. Dr. Jarad Tjadge for his medical expertise. Steven Kimball, Celina Robinson, and Grethe Hughes for translation help with German, French, and Danish respectively. The many librarians, history museum docents, and archive directors who patiently point me in the right direction. Kerry Blair for her example, writing prowess, and friendship. And lastly to my great editor, Angela Eschler, who is so very wise.

Central Characters

In San Francisco (Originally from Sutter Creek, CA)

Elizabeth Lund (mother to Alaina, James, Eleanor, and Kathryn)

Kathryn Lund (youngest child, 13)

In Salt Lake City

Lars Erickson (grandfather)

Patience Erickson (mother)

Nephi Erickson (son)

Alaina Lund Erickson (wife to Nephi)

Eleanor Lund (living with her sister's family to attend medical school)

In Sutter Creek

Philomene Johnson (teacher/mentor/confidante for the Lund sisters)

Rosemund Family

Robinson Family

Serving in the Great War

James Lund

Daniel Chart (stepson, Robinson family)

In Belgium

Hannah Finn (great aunt to Philomene Johnson)

How beautiful upon the mountains are the feet of him that bringeth good tidings, that publisheth peace; that bringeth good tidings of good, that publisheth salvation; that saith unto Zion, Thy God reigneth!

Isaiah 52:7

1

The soldier was running from death—running in the cold moonless night from the menace of fixed bayonets and slaughter. His lungs seared with fire as he sucked in the winter air. He willed his muscles to work, to move him forward over the frozen ground. If he could just make it to that grove of apple trees, the leafless branches might offer him some protection from the inevitable bullets.

Run!

Into the barren field behind him came waves of dark forms hunkered low to the ground and moving at great speed. Expertly maneuvering around shell craters and cutting through barbed wire, the enemy came growling and cursing like demons from a pit.

The soldier was twenty feet from the edge of the grove when he fell—fell over a putrid corpse onto the frozen mud. He frantically crawled forward on his hands and knees, but it was too late—the dark forms were advancing without fear and without pity.

"James!"

Alaina Erickson sat straight up in bed.

"James!" she called out in a sob. She reached over in the pale morning light to grasp some part of her husband's clothing. "Nephi?" She turned to look, but he was not beside her. *Where is he?* He'd been going off to work earlier this past week, but surely not this early. It couldn't be much past six o'clock.

Alaina brought her knees up to her chest and laid her head on them, speaking to her husband as though he were present. "It was James. I saw him running from the German soldiers. I saw him running and the soldiers were coming after him, and he couldn't run fast enough. He couldn't get to the trees. He fell, and he . . ."

Her heart was pounding. She threw back the covers and struggled out of bed.

Stop Alaina. Stop. It was just a dream. Just one of your stupid dreams. She calmed her breathing and walked to the water closet to splash water on her face. She chided herself as she went. "It's the first day of a new year, Alaina Erickson, and you're not going to start off with troubled dreams."

The house was cold and she shivered.

"You have a busy day ahead of you. Think of that." She turned to dress, her hands aching from the cold, her body aching from the terrifying run through the French countryside.

* * *

As Alaina put up the new calendar for 1918 in her mother-in-law's kitchen, she was amazed that four years had passed since her arrival at her husband's family home in Salt Lake City. *Four years? How is that possible?* Seven hundred miles separated her from her home in California, but she still remembered every minute of her life there. *Enough of those thoughts.* She retied her apron strings and forced her mind back to the kitchen. Come March, her daughter Katie would turn three. *But wasn't it only yesterday that their little daughter was in her cradle?* Nephi's grandfather, Lars Erickson, had set his gnarled arthritic hands to make one last piece of precious furniture for the family. The burly Dane had brought his woodworking craft with him from Denmark, and traces of his genius could be seen in many of the homes he built in the Salt Lake Valley. His own cottage was a place of enchantment with porch railings and posts festooned with woodland creatures and flowers, and though Katie's cradle was of simple make and embellished with only one iris on the headboard, Alaina knew its value.

She turned from the calendar and went to drag out the flour can and heavy bread bowl in an attempt to distract her mind from somber thoughts. She'd had unsettling dreams in the night—dreams of apple trees standing dormant in a ghostly winter frost, of dark-suited men lowering her father's coffin into the ground, of her brother James running through a blasted waste-land, of German soldiers, and death. She set the bowl down on the kneading board and worked at prying the lid from the flour can. She wouldn't think of James. She couldn't. She had tried for years to avoid emotional involvement in the horrific events of the Great War embroiling more and more of the European nations. The pompous heads of state had prophesied victory in six months, and now, almost three and a half years later, the youth and blood of all the combatants were seeping through the sieve of political ferocity.

Nephi and his brother Elias talked of little else when they were together, poring over newspaper articles and debating the strategies, ethics, and portent of battles won and lost. They attended war rallies and wrote letters to President Wilson encouraging him to join the fray. As of April 1917, their hopes had been realized. Along with the blatant sinking of more American merchant ships by German U-boats, there was the discovery of a secret anti-American document sent from Germany's foreign secretary Arthur Zimmermann, to the president of Mexico. The Zimmermann Telegram promised a return of New Mexico, Texas, and Arizona to Mexico if that country would join on the side of Germany.

Wilson, the great believer in isolationism, had had enough. On April 2, 1917, he made an impassioned speech to Congress, and on April 6 war was declared. The United States began at once to focus its strength and resources on military preparedness. Part of that preparedness was a call for men—a call that Alaina's brother James had answered with little hesitation.

Alaina measured out the cups of flour, added the lard, warm water and yeast, mixing the ingredients with her hands and trying unsuccessfully to keep James's face out of her mind. His letter had come in June, addressed to both her and their younger sister Eleanor, as Eleanor had been living in Salt Lake City for several years now.

June 4, 1917

Dear Alaina and Eleanor,

I'm writing to let you know that I will soon be leaving for France. I have enlisted in the army, and due to my knowledge of horses, they're attaching me immediately to a British unit somewhere near the front line. Mr. Regosi has been very understanding, and I've left a young man by the name of William Trenton to help out on the ranch while I'm away.

Don't worry about me. Once us Americans get over there we'll clean things up in no time. I'll probably be back in Sutter Creek for Christmas.

Your brother,
James

Oh! By the way, the Rosemunds are taking good care of the farm. They're bound to bring in another record crop this season.

Alaina worked the dough into a ball, picked it up, and threw it hard into the bowl. Hadn't they had enough grief in their lives with the death of their father and the selling of their beautiful apple farm? James was already separated by distance—she didn't need him separated by something more cruel.

She heard a scraping noise behind her and turned to see Katie dragging a step stool over to the wall. "Katie, what are you doing?" Alaina asked, pausing with her hand on the rim of the bowl and watching her daughter's determined progress.

Katie didn't answer, but pointed at the light switch.

"We don't need the light," Alaina said simply, not surprised when Katie continued her advance. The agile little girl climbed up on the stool, put her fingers on the small round knob, and clicked the light on, off, then on again, a look of wonder and delight fixing itself onto her cherub face.

"That's enough now," Alaina said, her voice more commanding. "Turn the light off and jump down."

Katie looked at her mother and turned the switch off. There was a moment's hesitation and the light came on again.

"Katie Eleanor Erickson! If you turn that switch one more time I will have to put you into the corner!" Alaina's voice was taut and tired. Her nerves were ragged from lack of sleep, and the usual patience she had with her daughter's precocious temperament was absent.

"But, it's New Year bufday!" Katie complained, "and I want the yight on."

"It is a bright morning and we don't need it," Alaina explained, moving to turn off the light.

Katie's hand went immediately to twist the knob, bringing a stern look from her mother. "Ah," Alaina warned. "Don't touch it."

Katie grunted, jumped down from the stool, and stamped her foot.

Alaina understood her daughter's fascination with the electric lights, a miracle of modern invention that had been installed in her mother-in-law's home just before Christmas. Electric lighting systems had been part of major and midsize cities for over a decade, but in more rural areas the benefits were just now being appreciated.

Katie was watching her mother with a practiced eye. She crept her fingers up the wall toward the switch as Alaina frowned. "I mean it," Alaina said darkly. She was too tired to tolerate any more disobedience from her daughter.

"Why don't you go out and help Grandma feed the chickens?" Alaina suggested hopefully, returning to the kneading of the bread dough. "You can wear your warm red coat."

Katie shook her head, causing the puff of pale blond hair to stick out in several places. "Don' yike chickens. Dey twy an peck me."

"Only because you chase them."

Katie ran around in circles. "Too cold. Too cold. Too cold."

The back porch door opened, and Alaina heaved a sigh of relief. Katie squealed and headed toward the back of the kitchen. "Grammy!"

Alaina pondered anew Katie's pet name for her grandmother, as no one had been able to figure out where she'd come up with it. Of course, Katie had her own distinct name for a lot of things, and often it was like trying to decipher a foreign language to figure out what she wanted. Grammy was the best at interpretation, which created a further bond of comradeship between the two.

Alaina loved her mother-in-law. Eleanor Patience Erickson was a short, round woman with a perfect tenderness and humor. Patience had been a polygamist wife of Alma Erickson. In 1890 when the prophet Wilford Woodruff issued the Church's Manifesto, ending the practice of plural marriage, Alma and Patience reluctantly secured a temporal divorce, and Patience and the boys moved into a comfortable little home on the outskirts of the city. While Alma continued to support his family financially, Patience prided herself in taking the least amount of money possible and supplying most of their needs through her seamstress business.

Alaina remembered her feelings of shock and apprehension when Nephi had first told her of his family's unusual genealogy, but as she lived among the people whose lives had been affected by both the practice and the prohibition, she chided herself for her once-narrow thinking. Alma Erickson was devoted to his first wife Eunice and their children, but he was also solicitous of Patience, Elias, and Nephi—the family he had been forced to abandon.

Alaina smiled as she thought of Mother Erickson's jovial demeanor. She was not refined or disapproving like the first wife, Eunice, which made her more endearing, and as Alaina thought back over the years that she and Nephi had lived with Mother Erickson, she had never known the woman to lose her temper. Patience was clear in her displeasure when a situation demanded it, but the wrongdoer could be assured that love would always follow the reprimand.

"Good morning, little muffin!" Alaina heard Mother Erickson's cheerful voice from the back porch. Alaina looked over from her task to see the dear woman hanging her well-worn coat on a wall peg and gathering Katie into her arms.

Katie put her hands on her Grandma's face. "Grammy, you face is cold."

"I expect it is, pumpkin," she said rubbing her nose on Katie's nose. "I think we're in for more snow."

"I don' yike snow," Katie said, frowning.

"You do when your daddy pulls you in your sled," Mother Erickson reminded, sitting Katie down well away from the hot stove. "So, did you wake up on the wrong side or the right side of the bed this morning?" she asked her granddaughter lightly as she drew on her apron and moved to the icebox to put away the freshly gathered eggs.

"The wight side," Katie answered assuredly.

Alaina raised her eyebrows and Mother Erickson smiled. "Good, then you can help us with the morning chores."

"I will be yiking dat!" Katie answered, hopping up and down.

Mother Erickson pulled Katie's high chair up to the table and lifted her into it. She placed a breadboard in front of her and sprinkled it with flour. Katie reached out to grab the powdery substance, but Mother Erickson stopped her. "Ah, don't touch it yet," she commanded gently. "We forgot your apron." She opened a drawer filled with kitchen linens and found Katie's apron. As she slipped it over her granddaughter's head and tied the back, Katie ran her hands over the soft fabric and smiled at her mother.

"I yook yike Mommy!" she said happily.

Alaina smiled. She would store this tranquil moment to remember later when she fell into bed exhausted and weeping from dealing with her daughter's strong-minded exuberance.

"What I doing, Grammy?" Katie asked, watching her grandma intently as she reached into Alaina's bread bowl.

"Helping us make bread," Mother Erickson replied in a matter-of-fact tone.

"Scrimmy!" yelled Katie as Mother Erickson put two small lumps of dough in front of her.

"Scrimmy?" Alaina questioned, looking at her mother-in-law for interpretation.

"I think it's her new word for hooray," Mother Erickson replied, patting Katie's head. She sat down in a chair next to her granddaughter. "Now, first we flour our hands," she instructed, "and sprinkle a little flour on the top of Mr. Dough Man's head." Katie giggled and followed her grandmother's example. "Then we work the dough like this."

"We push in him's head?" Katie asked, her eyes dancing.

"We do." Mother Erickson chuckled.

The back door opened, and Katie looked up expectantly. "Daddy's home!"

The two older Erickson women shared a look of concern, and then softened their expressions as Nephi Erickson came into the kitchen.

"Daddy!" Katie squealed. "Yook, Daddy, I mashing Mr. Dough Man's head," she said proudly, showing off her new ability.

Nephi smiled at her, but Alaina could see he was not really paying attention, and the smile was only show.

"Yook, Daddy, yook! Watch me!" Katie insisted, but Nephi merely ran a finger across her cheek and turned to his wife.

"In a minute, sweetheart, I need to talk to Mommy first."

Alaina stood mutely, her hands covered in flour and dough. Mother Erickson stood up immediately and came to her.

"Not to worry," she said lightly. "Katie and I can take care of this, can't we little muffin?"

Katie punched Mr. Dough Man's head again. "We do it, Mommy."

Alaina looked guiltily at Mother Erickson. "But, it's my job."

"Tell ya what—I'll let you make dinner tonight. Now, you two get. Why don't ya bundle up and walk down by Westminster school? Pretty place."

Nephi stood watching his daughter enjoy breadmaking as Alaina cleaned her hands and went to put on her boots. She tried to keep worried thoughts from her mind, but the expression on Nephi's face did not indicate good news. When she came back into the kitchen, he was already on the back porch holding her coat. She slipped into it, along with a knit hat and a pair of mittens.

"Shursha," Katie said, waving to them.

"Shursha," Nephi said back.

"Whatever that means." Alaina replied with a grin.

"Take your time," Mother Erickson called after them. "I'll put her down for her nap."

"No nap!" Katie declared.

Nephi and Alaina moved outside, away from the sound of a disagreement over naps. The sky was brilliant blue, but the air was dry and cold. Alaina shoved errant wisps of dark hair under the snug-fitting cap and pulled the hat lower over her ears.

They walked south from the house down 12th East, one shouldering the weight of concealed bad news, the other the fear of it. Alaina noted the dejected look on Nephi's handsome face. Being at his mother's home for so many years had been difficult for him. She and Nephi were grateful for Mother Erickson's kindness, and the first few years had been good. Nephi had found work in the building of the state capitol and was saving every extra penny to buy land for their own home, and the two of them had deepened their friendship and discovered love—as well as experienced the joy of having Katie come into their lives. But the work at the capitol had finished two years ago, and Nephi had found it difficult to keep a steady job. He wasn't trained for anything, and even though he and his father's relationship had mended, Nephi refused to work at the family hardware store. He could not abide Eunice Erickson, his father's first wife, and she was at the store daily, scrutinizing every transaction. Besides, Nephi's older brother Elias held the job of manager, and Nephi would have found it hard working under him.

Alaina sighed and gripped her husband's arm as they walked over an icy spot on the sidewalk. She also knew her reluctance to move forward in the gospel was a worry to her faithful husband and that it placed a strain on their relationship. She knew the Book of Mormon was a true book of scripture. She'd known that from the time she'd finished reading the final verses in Moroni. That knowledge had taken her into the waters of baptism. In fact, she and her sister Eleanor had been baptized on the same day, and Alaina cherished the memory: Nephi standing with her in the font at the Tabernacle, trembling as he held her wrist, and raising his arm to the square. She thought about the joy on his face as he brought her up out of the water, of standing, dripping wet, on the steps as he baptized Eleanor. She felt her throat tighten with emotion as she remembered Grandfather Erickson laying his gnarled hands on her and Eleanor's heads and performing their confirmations. It was a good day. And now, years had passed, and as Eleanor had moved forward in her commitment and testimony, Alaina knew that she held back and pondered. She supposed it was her way. She remembered many times when her father would call her by her pet name and say, "Fancy, you have to beat an idea near to death to see if it will live."

"Are you warm enough?" Nephi asked.

Alaina pulled her thoughts to the present and looked over at him. "Fine."

"I think we're supposed to get more snow later today."

Alaina stopped walking. "Nephi, what is it?"

Nephi didn't look at her. "Mr. Stewart had to lay some of us off."

"But I thought the project was going to last . . ."

"Yeah, so did I."

Alaina pulled her hat farther over her ears. "So, you have a couple of weeks . . ."

"No. He laid us off a week ago. Just after Christmas."

"But, you've been going to work."

"No, I've been looking for work. I thought I'd have something by now."

Alaina heard the bitter edge to Nephi's voice and stopped her next question. She took his arm and started walking. She was too agitated to keep still. *It isn't his fault. It isn't his fault,* she kept saying over and over again in her mind. *But, how will we live?* They paid their own way for food, and clothing, and doctor bills, and even tried to save a little, but the jar in their dresser drawer only held eleven dollars, and that wouldn't last long.

"I thought you told me if we paid our tithing we'd be all right," Alaina said suddenly.

Nephi stopped to stare at her. "I . . . we . . ."

"Never mind," Alaina said shaking her head. "It doesn't matter."

"It does matter. Do you regret paying tithing?"

Alaina didn't answer.

"Alaina?"

"No. It's just that I thought there'd be more blessings," she lied.

"It doesn't work that way," Nephi said quietly.

"Obviously another one of those principles I'm not faithful enough to understand." She watched pain settle into Nephi's eyes, and she turned away, ashamed of her bitter words. She had a choice to make. She turned back to him. "I'm sorry. That was awful."

Nephi put his arms around her. "No, I'm sorry. I'm not a good provider."

Alaina stepped back. "Nephi, stop."

He hung his head. "Well, I'm not."

Alaina took her husband's hands. "It's just that we're not where we should be. We should be on a farm picking apples."

Nephi looked at her. "Alaina, we can't keep going back to that."

Alaina shook her head. "I'm not pining, Nephi. I'm just saying that it's the kind of work we're good at . . . that you're good at. We're not meant to live in a city. We should be living on a farm somewhere.

"So, what do you suggest?" he asked slowly.

She stopped, the light draining from her eyes. "I don't know. Isn't there a farm that would hire us?"

She could tell that his next words came at a cost. "A single man, maybe, but not a family."

Nephi turned and walked onto the grounds of Westminster College. *This is funny,* he thought. *Me, walking around a school . . . a place I should go to make something of myself. A place I can't go.*

Alaina came up beside him and took his arm. "We've always been all right before. We'll think of something."

They walked together down a small pathway.

Nephi cleared his throat. "Actually, I have thought of something."

"You have?" Alaina questioned, surprised by his ready reply.

He nodded. "I've enlisted in the army. The marines, actually."

She pulled him to a stop. "What?"

"I've enlisted in the marines."

A slight smile touched her mouth. "Nephi, that is not funny."

He looked away from her.

"You have not enlisted," she pressed.

He held her by the shoulders. "Listen to me. It solves everything."

She could not reply.

"I'll make good money, and you can live off of it and put some away in the jar."

She stared at him.

"Look, America needs to get over there and stop this war. I can be a part of that. I want to be a part of that."

Tears pressed into Alaina's eyes. "I see."

Nephi rubbed her arms as if to warm her. "I probably won't even see any fighting. The Germans will hear we're coming over and run their tails back to Düsseldorf or wherever."

"And what about me and Katie?"

"What? Well . . . you'll be fine. You'll be here with Mother and Eleanor . . ."

Alaina's voice hardened. "You can't really expect me to say yes to this. My brother James is over there! And you want me to worry myself sick over the both of you?"

Nephi was quiet.

"I see. So, there's no changing your mind."

He folded his arms across his chest. "I've already signed the papers."

She did not answer.

"Alaina, I prayed about it, and it seemed . . ."

"Don't!" she said sharply. "You know I don't understand that."

"Yes, you do. You've had dreams and feelings before about a lot of things."

"Yes, and the dreams I'm having now are of chaos, and graves, and death!" Tears jumped into her eyes. "How could you do this to me?"

Nephi looked as if she'd slapped him. "I'm doing this *for* you," he answered, his voice husky with emotion. "For you and Katie. We might be able to save enough for a little piece of land." He reached out to touch her, but she stepped back.

"I need time to think, Nephi. You go on ahead of me and tell your mother what you've done. I need you to just leave me alone for a while."

"Alaina, I . . ."

"No. You really need to give me time to think." She turned and walked down the path alone. She turned back once and saw Nephi heading for home, his hands in his pockets, his shoulders slumped. Her thoughts tumbled over themselves. He wasn't actually going to the war. Tomorrow he'd come to her and say he'd found another job. How could he tell her something like this on the first day of a new year? She should have been angrier—told him he had to go back and rip up those enlistment papers. She needed to talk to Eleanor, but her younger sister had enough of her own concerns taking care of Grandfather Erickson and going to medical school. *I need to talk to my father, but he's dead and his grave is seven hundred miles away in Sutter Creek.* She kicked hard at an icy snow pile, ignoring the pain that shot into her foot. She hated distance and separation.

She stopped abruptly in front of a large bulletin board. It was covered with notices of school activities: a reading of *She Stoops to Conquer,* a performance by the Westminster String Quartet, a lecture on Freud. There were also ads for things to be sold: a used rosewood bed frame—five dollars; a first year English book (excellent condition)—fifty cents; kittens—free. Alaina smiled. She could just imagine what Katie would do with a kitten.

She had forgotten for a moment about the war when her eyes slid over to a recruiting poster at the edge of the board. The scene depicted a drowned woman holding her baby in her arms. The greenish sea enveloped the two figures in horrifying helplessness. There was only one word at the bottom of the poster: ENLIST.

Alaina stood for a moment glaring at it, knowing it dramatized an actual occurrence, the sinking of the *Lusitania.* A sob caught in her throat as she took off her glove, gripped the center of the poster, and pulled. A large, jagged piece came away in her hand.

"I don't care," she mumbled, her voice full of tears. "I don't care! I don't care about you!"

She crumpled the paper into a ball and threw it down onto the sodden path. A young man walked by, his arms laden with a stack of books. He gave Alaina a critical look.

Alaina turned and walked quickly toward home, muttering under her breath. "Elly, I have to talk to Elly."

2

It was the first day of January, and while other professors had given their students the day off, Dr. Thorndike had arranged for a session in the cadaver lab for any student bright enough not to waste a day.

Eleanor Lund pushed the annoying strands of dark hair back from her face and sat forward in her seat. It was her first observation of work on a cadaver, and she didn't want to miss a thing. She glanced quickly at the few other students who had taken the professor's invitation seriously. Smug Ernest Grant was looking a tad green around the gills, while Shawn Burbage and several others were trying to adopt a nonchalant demeanor. Eleanor felt no such desire to mask her enthusiasm. She was a medical student, and she marveled again at being accepted so young. It was January 1918, and she wouldn't be twenty until August, yet here she sat, a woman, surrounded by ten men—her peers. Eleanor knew it was a wonder for a young woman to be attending medical classes. She also knew that much of her acceptance had to be attributed to her mentor, Dr. Lucien. He'd spoken to colleagues, arranged tests, and—she was sure—twisted a few arms to secure her enrollment. And even if it were on a limited, probationary trial, Eleanor didn't care. She would prove herself.

When she'd written to her former teacher in Sutter Creek about her acceptance, she'd received a telegram in return:

My Dearest Eleanor,

Maladies tremble.
Patients rejoice.
Women take heart.

Philomene Johnson

She'd also written to her friends in San Francisco—Mr. Palmer, Bib, Kerri, Ina Bell, and Mrs. Todd. Though servants that worked in her Aunt Ida's home, in the nine months Eleanor had lived there, they'd become family. To her little sister Kathryn and her mother, who still resided in the austere Victorian mansion on Beacon Street, those delightful people understair would always be servants and nothing more.

She smiled every time she thought about the return letter, written unmistakably by Miss Kerri McKee.

Dear Miss Eleanor,

Me and Ina Bell are forever busy sewing on the buttons we all keep bustin' off our uniforms. Now, aren't you the brightest thing in a month of Sundays? Mr. Palmer called for the bottle of raspberry cordial and we all had a toast in your honor. He keeps sayin' it's all his doin' because he insisted you take that doctor book with you when you left. Bib still laughs about the time you showed Ina Bell a picture of somebody's brain matter and she fainted. What fun we had together.

Dear, shy Mrs. Todd tells me to say hello from her. Mr. Glassey, our Mormon butcher, still comes around. I told him that you and your sister had joined his church and he was well pleased over it.

Sad to hear that your brother James is in the war. Me and Ina Bell are sayin' our prayers for him. Ina Bell is much better at prayin' than me, but I'm thinkin' the Lord takes pity on my meager efforts.

Now, I don't want to be spoilin' this celebration letter, but Mr. Palmer says we need to let you know that your mother is havin' her struggles. We're all keepin' a close watch on her, so don't fret. Mr. Palmer thinks it's the dreary time of year that's got her so melancholy, but me, Bib, and Ina Bell think it's the medicine the doctor's givin' her. Mr. Palmer doesn't know I slipped in that last part, so don't let on.

Well, I've got to go. The cream needs separatin', and me and Ina Bell are washin' windows today.

We're so proud of ya. Become a brilliant doctor and help the world. As me da used to say, "the noble climb the ladder first then reach down for the rest of us poor strugglin' souls."

We remain your friends,
Kerri McKee, Ina Bell Latham, Bib Randall, Mr. Palmer, and Mrs. Todd

"As you can see, the liver sits under the protection of the lower ribs . . ."

Dr. Thorndike's commanding voice focused Eleanor's mind on the scene in front of her. She chided herself for lack of attention and began diligently taking notes as the brilliant man continued.

". . . on the right-hand side of the upper abdomen. It is the heaviest single organ in the body, weighing about three and a half pounds in the adult."

When Dr. Thorndike reached into the abdominal cavity and brought out the large organ for closer inspection, Ernest Grant headed for the door with his hand clamped firmly over his mouth. Mr. Burbage found the departure funny, and Eleanor imagined the mocking that Ernest would receive at lunch later that afternoon. That was *if* Mr. Grant fancied lunch.

Eleanor was grateful that she'd never felt queasy concerning any part of anatomy or secretions or sickness. As a youngster on her family's farm in California, she had always been fascinated by animal births and deaths, by injuries, and the symptoms associated with illness. She loved diagnosing animal and human maladies—a skill at which she'd proven competent. Her father Samuel viewed this talent with amazement, while her mother Elizabeth found it foolish nonsense. The only medical condition that had eluded Eleanor's keen observation was the failing heart that eventually took her father from them. He had been gone a little over four years, yet Eleanor could see the place where he'd died, within the grove of apple trees, as vividly as if it were yesterday.

"Miss Lund, would you please repeat the last sentence I spoke?"

Eleanor snapped her mind to attention, noting the disapproving look in Dr. Thorndike's eyes. Luckily she had been listening with one ear, and she was grateful for the uncanny ability she had of thinking two things at once. She hoped the gift did not abandon her at this crucial moment. She took a deep breath. "The liver is attached to the diaphragm—the muscle which separates the chest and abdominal cavities—by a series of folds of membrane called the falciform, triangular . . ." she hesitated, "and coronary ligaments."

Dr. Thorndike studied her without smiling, nodded, and went on. "The liver is also joined to the stomach and duodenum by . . ."

As she left the medical building an hour later, Eleanor's mind was filled with wonder and so many questions that she walked into a slushy ice puddle before being aware of it.

"Hey! Hen medic!" a voice called out behind her. "Going swimming?"

Eleanor turned to scowl at the tall young man and his companion. They had both been in the lab with her, but she couldn't, at the moment, think of their names or a biting reply. In fact, she nearly dropped her carry sack into the pool of water. The two young men laughed.

"Go home and darn your husband's socks," the second fellow said tersely.

The first one laughed. "Husband? Who would marry someone immodest enough to appear with men in a medical lecture room?"

Eleanor stepped out of the puddle and continued on her way, ignoring the laughter which followed her departure. *Why can't they be more encouraging?* Eleanor fumed. She knew that she was an oddity because female medical students were rare, but as her peers, they understood the difficulty of the course work. They should admire her tenacity. *Huh! I should know better than to expect acceptance.* She stopped and shook water out of her boots, laughing when she realized she was not thinking of cold wet feet but of inferior extensor retinaculum, metatarsals, and peroneus brevis.

"Now, what is there funny about wet feet, Miss Lund?"

Eleanor gasped and looked up into the elegant face of Shawn Burbage.

"You could catch your death, and that would be tragic."

"Don't mock me, sir. I have just as much right to be in those classes—"

Mr. Burbage grinned.

Eleanor scowled at him. "What? Why are you smiling?"

"I wasn't mocking you. The loss of such a fine mind would be tragic."

Eleanor stammered, "I—I—"

He held out his hand to her. "Shawn Burbage," he said with a nod. "And we are not all buffoons, Miss Lund. To prove it, let me carry your sack to your next class?"

Eleanor straightened and tried to compose her "fine" mind. "That is kind of you, Mr. Burbage, but I think our only class today was Thorndike's."

The polished young man was momentarily flustered. "Of course. You're right. How silly of me."

Eleanor smiled at him. "Besides, I'm only enrolled in Thorndike's class and a lab, Mr. Burbage. I am here on limited trial."

"Hmm," Shawn said, buttoning the top button of his coat. "Cox and Williams should be the ones on trial. If either of them ever succeeds in getting a medical degree, it will be a crime."

Eleanor laughed. "You're funny, Mr. Burbage. I like you." She could tell by the look on his face that he was surprised by her candor. "I tend to be straight-forward," she said, hefting her carry sack over her shoulder. "Another of those unwomanly qualities that plague me."

The disarming young man smiled broadly this time, and Eleanor found she liked the way his eyes crinkled when he did so. She took a few steps back to gather her equilibrium and slow her heart rate. "So . . . off I go for home . . . well, Grandfather Erickson's, actually." She took several more steps back.

Mr. Burbage followed. "You live with your grandfather?"

"He's my brother-in-law's grandfather. Since coming from California . . . well, being booted out, actually . . ." Words began to trip on themselves. "Not booted out of California, but out of my aunt's home in San Francisco . . . which was entirely my fault, I guess . . . disobeying my auntie's wishes. Anyway . . . I needed somewhere to stay and something to do . . . so, since my sister was here in Salt Lake City, I came here, and I take care of Grandfather Erickson."

"Really?" he smiled. "That's quite a story."

"Anyway, I . . ." Eleanor stopped. "Mr. Burbage, do you plan on walking with me to the trolley depot? It's eight blocks, you know."

Now it was his turn to stammer. "I—I would love to accompany you, Miss Lund, but I have an appointment with my chemistry partner."

Eleanor nodded. "Well, off you go then, Mr. Burbage. And off I go to home and a nice pair of warm socks."

He laughed. "Good idea." He tipped his hat. "See you in Thorndike's class."

Eleanor sneezed. "If I don't catch my death." She turned and started walking.

"Hot chamomile tea, lemon, and honey!" he called after her.

"Not very scientific, Mr. Burbage," she called back.

"The best things in life usually aren't, Miss Lund."

Eleanor sneezed and laughed at the same time.

* * *

By the time she reached Grandfather Erickson's enchanting little house, Eleanor was stiff with cold and her nose was running. Nephi's sister-in-law Sarah sat with Grandfather Erickson at those times Eleanor had class, and would normally leave as soon as Eleanor arrived. Today Eleanor hoped Sarah would stay an extra hour so she could take a nice hot bath. But it was not Sarah who greeted her when she came in the front door. She was shocked to see her sister Alaina standing pale faced and crying in the front entry.

A knot of fear dropped into Eleanor's stomach. "Alaina, what is it? Is it James? Have you heard something about James?"

Alaina shook her head. "No, it's not James. I haven't heard anything about James. It's Nephi."

"Nephi?" Eleanor dropped her carry sack and took Alaina's arm. "Is he hurt?"

"No . . . no . . . he's . . ." Alaina started crying.

"Is Sarah here?" Eleanor asked, looking around.

"No. I sent her home. Grandfather's sleeping."

Eleanor maneuvered her older sister into the living room and sat her down on the divan—her cold feet and sneezing forgotten for the look of devastation on Alaina's face.

"Laina, what is it?" Eleanor asked softly. "What is it?"

"He's going off to war, Elly. He's going to be in the war, just like James."

3

The dead soldiers were unaware of the turning of the year. In darkness, 1918 crept its way onto the battlefield inside a ghostly fog, crawling into open mouths with silent mockery, whispering to the lads . . . *another year . . . another sunrise coming . . . another morning of voice and command.* But the mud-encrusted schoolboys had shut their ears to tutelage and muster. Hands fixed on grenade and bayonet, their final groans were carried off on tendrils of mist.

On both sides of the line the cease-fire engendered resignation and dread. Was the word good? Could each enemy venture safely into the muddy boundary land searching for chums and countrymen now dead or dying? Was it worth the risk when snipers watched like rabid dogs from camouflaged locations?

"Matthews, Lund, MacDonough, Clune!" the lieutenant yelled, his voice raw from smoke and overuse. "Bring on the stretchers!"

The four young men jumped from the trench, each team awkwardly hauling a canvas stretcher over the slick, uneven ground.

"Get out there, men, and bring 'em in. Standard procedure."

Standard procedure meant finding first the wounded and bringing them to the triage station, and, if there was time, bringing the bodies of the dead to the pit.

The cold January fog was lifting, but the landscape was blurred and eerie in the predawn light. James Lund stumbled over a blasted knot of tree limbs, righted himself, and pushed ahead; his face was caked with dirt, his eyes red-rimmed and angry. He yanked the stretcher hard and ran.

"Ey! Slow down there, Lund, or I'll be breakin' my legs and ya'll have ta carry me out on yer back!" Private Wheaten Clune called from the back end of the stretcher.

James glanced at the big Englishman and shook his head. "It would take an elephant to break one of those blocks you call legs."

Wheaten laughed.

The lieutenant yelled at them to hold to the task, and the laughter died.

James clenched his jaw as they moved around a dead horse, its guts torn out on grounding spikes. *Oh, please Lieutenant, let Private Clune and me keep talking while we do our work. Give us that amount of grace.* They walked over a dead soldier shot in the neck, eyes fixed and looking for the sunrise.

"Over there!" Clune yelled, motioning with his head.

James turned and saw an arm raised for an instant, then dropped. The two carriers headed immediately for the location. Clune swore when they reached the side of the pit. The British officer was pinned to the edge of the trench by a bayonet, the weapon held in place by a weeping German lad of no more than fifteen. His body shook as he turned his pale smooth face to glare at them—words of gibberish pouring from his mouth.

Clune dropped the stretcher and went to jump at the boy when the impaled officer yelled, "No! He has a grenade!"

Clune stopped.

The manic young German pushed the butt of his gun with his shoulder, bringing a scream of agony from the officer, while he raised his free hand to threaten with the grenade.

Clune swore again but held his body motionless.

James slowly lowered his side of the stretcher. The young man yelled something at him in his rough tongue, shaking the bomb and hissing.

James smiled and the boy blinked.

"What are ya doin'?" Clune whispered out of the corner of his mouth. "Yer gonna get us killed."

But James continued smiling as he sat down at the edge of the trench. He slid his hand into his pocket and brought out two dirt-smudged carrots. Carrots were a rare commodity, but as James was in charge of the ambulance unit's horses and mules, he was often given a supply of vegetables to keep the animals working. James gently held out his hand with the offering of carrots. The German soldier didn't move, but James saw some of the fear drop out of his eyes.

James spoke softly—the low tenor of his voice pushing aside the gasping moans of the wounded officer. "Seems we've gotten ourselves into quite a dilemma here, young man."

Clune stared at him. "Are ya daft? He's not understanding a word you're sayin'."

James kept on in the same soothing tone, never taking his eyes from the German boy's face. "It doesn't matter if he understands the words, he only needs to get the feeling that I'm not going to hurt him." He held out the peace offering of carrots. He'd heard rumors that the German troops were existing on turnip mash, and judging by the gauntness of the soldier's face, he figured it was true. Fresh carrots would be a banquet.

"Now, I know you're scared. Actually, we're all scared right along with you." James slid down into the trench, but the German didn't move. He spoke some words in a frightened whisper, but he held his ground. James softened his voice even more, remembering a time he'd calmed an unbroken cinnamon stallion enough that it took an apple out of his hand.

"Truth is, we all just want this fighting to stop so we can go home to some clean sheets and a bowl of our mama's homemade soup."

Tears slid down the German lad's cheeks. "Mamma?"

James smiled at him. "Yep, we all have those, now don't we? And even though mine might not be the kindest of women, I'm figuring by the look on your face, your mama is somebody to go home to."

The soldier slumped, and James grabbed the grenade out of his hand. Clune jumped down and pinned the boy's arms behind his back as James held the rifle.

"Get me out of here! Get me out of here!" the officer screamed.

"Sir!" James said sharply. "Don't move."

The officer clenched his teeth as James slowly unfixed the bayonet from the rifle.

"Just pull it out frontways!" the officer screamed.

"I can't do that, sir. This is a German bayonet and it would bring a lot of flesh with it if I did it that way." James leaned the officer forward against him, and pulled the serrated blade out of the shoulder from the back. The officer fainted.

James looked over at Clune. "I'll take the boy," he said, putting the carrots back into his pocket, "and you can carry the officer."

"Deal," the big Englishman answered, looking at James with an awed expression. "We haven't seen many of you Yanks in the war as yet, and I heard the pack of you were crude braggarts." Clune pushed the officer onto the lip of the trench and scrambled out.

"Really?" James said, tying the German soldier's wrists together with his boot lace. "And I heard all you Englishmen were dainty gents who only drank tea and were terrible at cards."

Clune laughed so hard that he fell to his knees while trying to hoist the unconscious officer.

James pushed the docile German out of the trench, and gave him one of the carrots. The young man struggled to keep from crying, and James turned to Clune. "Yeah, dainty gents, that's what I heard. So I guess you'd better not judge another man until you've known him for a while."

"Fair enough," Clune said, smiling as he pulled the officer onto his back. He nodded at the German. "Think ya might be needin' ta keep a piece on him? Just fer show?"

James shrugged and took out his field pistol. The young prisoner straightened and started walking in the direction James pointed him.

"Then again," Clune chuckled, "you could always lead him out with them carrots."

As they trudged back to the center receiving point, James's thoughts drifted to Sutter Creek and the Regosi horse ranch. He saw Mr. Regosi standing by the paddock watching the movements of some beautiful Appaloosa or chestnut thoroughbred. James knew that even at seventy-four years old the scruffy Italian was the best horse handler in the state of California, and during the years James had worked on the ranch, he'd absorbed every bit of wisdom the man so kindly offered—not just about horses, but about the honor of hard work and being a person of character.

As a young man of nineteen, Emilio Regosi had served in the Union army cavalry during the War between the States, and James carried many of Mr. Regosi's cautionary tales with him. *I'll have my own war stories to share when I get back to the ranch,* James thought, smiling. Coaxing a German to surrender with carrots would make the old man laugh. Emilio would laugh, and his wife Rosa would shake her head and make James a dinner of herb bread and ravioli.

A bomb exploded and a horse screamed somewhere in the distance. James was immediately alert. "Move!" he yelled, pushing the German toward the receiving area.

The men ran.

"Where'd that come from?" James yelled again.

"Triage station," Clune spit out, grunting with the exertion of carrying the unconscious officer while trying to keep on his feet over the slick, uneven ground.

The German boy stumbled a few times, but James kept him up and moving.

The lieutenant met them at the edge of no-man's-land. He was hard-faced and agitated. He took charge of the prisoner and sent Clune off with his patient to the dressing station, barking orders to James throughout. "Horse. Stepped on an unexploded grenade. Fifty yards north of the triage station. Find it!"

James ran. The horse's screams intensified with each yard he gained. In a clearing he spotted the magnificent black Percheron, its back leg dangling at a horrid angle—its belly covered in blood. Several doctors and two soldiers stood unmoving, transfixed by the gruesome sight. One of the soldiers had his hands over his ears to block out the agonizing sound of the animal's death squeals. James grabbed the man's rifle off the ground, ran forward twenty feet, and killed the horse with one shot.

For several moments, no one moved, then James fell to his knees and screamed. A doctor came over and stood by him as everyone else stoically resumed their tasks. James bit down on his anguish. The quiet after the chaos was deafening. It was quieter than James had experienced in months. He kept to his knees, breathing in the cold air and wishing for the sweet scent of hay and apples, not the stench of mud.

"You're a noble man, Mr. Lund," a voice said reverently.

James looked up into a face covered by a bushy brown beard and mustache. "How do you know me, sir?"

"By reputation, young man," the doctor answered.

James stood, looking more closely at the man's features. He could tell the face was accustomed to laughter by the deep laugh lines around the eyes, but at the moment the expression was reserved and even a bit melancholy.

James held out his hand, and the British doctor shook it.

"Dr. Joseph Robbins."

"James Lund . . . and I don't know that I deserve a reputation."

A slight twinkle animated the doctor's eyes. "Ah, yes. We've heard much about the American equine expert from California who works on our ambulance detail."

James shook his head. "No expert, I assure you. Just well trained."

The doctor sobered as he looked over at the carcass of the Percheron. "What a hellish nightmare for us all."

The soldier came timidly to retrieve his rifle, and James relinquished it without comment. He turned back to the doctor. "How long have you been here, sir?"

"Two years. All up and down the western front . . . Two years." The man's eyes drifted to the horizon—the red sun shimmering in a smoky sky. "So many of God's magnificent creatures taken before their time."

James knew that the healer's grief was for man and beast alike, as James felt the same sentiment. It tied them. *Precious lives wasted for greed and power.*

Birdsong pierced the melancholy moment and both men looked for the source. The doctor pointed. "There, on the top of that abandoned barn." The bird trilled again and the doctor smiled. "To me it means life will go on."

James nodded. "Yes, sir." He liked this man and wanted to sit and have a long conversation with him about his life in England, his family, his profession—but urgency called them both back to duty.

"Well, lad," the doctor said, laying his hand on James's shoulder, "I need to get back to the injured."

"Yes, sir, so do I."

"God watch over and protect you, James."

James smiled and watched the man move to the triage station, where he was accosted by a rush of worried medics before disappearing into the tent.

James went back to find Clune and continue their work. He knew that for the next several hours he would have to look upon the most heart-wrenching sights that evil could conjure—once-vigorous men with missing limbs and mangled bodies—and on the faces of the dead, a look of surprise that seemed to say, *Is this truly my time? Am I to die now before I've loved my first love?* But it was the smell of blood and putrid flesh that made a lesion on his soul. A wave of nausea ran through him, and James leaned over, placing his hands on his knees and sucking air into his lungs. His body was taut with emotion, and his spirit was weary. He gritted his teeth and moved forward, listening hopefully for birdsong as he walked, but the shout of commands and the sound of supply wagons moving along the rutted road were all that assaulted his ears.

4

Philomene Johnson, newly appointed headmistress of the Sutter Creek Primary School, was running. None of the teachers had ever seen her perform this particular activity, as she was a woman of propriety, but they well understood the breech of conduct—the middle-aged educator was attempting to save the life of a child. Of course, the child in question, Samuel Rosemund, was not aware that his life was in need of saving. When the bell had sounded for afternoon recess, the almost-ten-year-old raced with his classmates into the yard to enjoy the rare occasion of a hefty snowfall. This was not the normal January precipitation, which left Sutter Creek with a skiff of frosty white; through the night and into the early morning hours, this storm had laid down six good inches.

When Samuel had awoken to the enchanting sight, he'd begged his father to let him hitch his little toboggan to the back of the wagon and ride into town like a genie on a magic carpet. Samuel's father Edward, not being a very practical man, had seen no harm in the boy's enthusiasm, and indulged his wish, but as Samuel's mother, who was a woman of considerable common sense, watched them leave the farm in the pale morning light, she anticipated trouble ahead—trouble that had manifested itself at afternoon recess. On reaching the snowy wonderland of the activity yard, Samuel concluded that the best use of his outdoor time would be flying on his toboggan down the big hill next to the school. There had been no trouble securing his sled from the empty classroom or dragging it to the side of the schoolhouse, where cautious teachers couldn't see. His only blunder was in forgetting that Miss Johnson routinely made rounds of the yard to discourage mischievous behavior. She'd come around the corner of the building to discover Samuel and his toboggan teetering on the lip of the slope. She'd stood stunned for a moment until adrenaline helped her find her voice.

"Samuel Rosemund! Stop!"

But it was too late. Gravity tugged at the wooden sled and pulled it onto the incline. Samuel, not a disobedient child, would have liked to obey Miss

Johnson's command, but physics had taken over and he was no longer in control. He found himself excited and alarmed by the speed at which he was traveling but figured he could hang on until the hill leveled. What he did not know, but what Miss Johnson knew with perfect clarity, was that after a brief level area, this portion of the hill ended with a ten-foot drop into a rocky, dry creek bed.

Samuel could hear her frantic cries and turned quickly at one point to see her running after him. What was she yelling? Was it *fall off*? He didn't like that idea as he figured he might break an arm or a leg at this speed, but Miss Johnson's voice was persistent—not only persistent, but forceful. On her last command to FALL OFF, his body seemed to obey without thinking, and as he tumbled sideways he caught a brief glimpse of his toboggan before it disappeared. *Where did it go?* Samuel wondered as he slid forward another five feet. Suddenly his legs flipped over the embankment, and instinctively he grabbed at the snow, the air, anything! His hand found purchase on a scrawny bush, and he held tight. He heard below him the crack and splinter of wood on rock. "Help! Help me!" he cried out in panic as he heard labored breathing and the crunch of snow.

"I'm here, Mr. Rosemund." Two hands grabbed his upper arm. "Right here to help you."

He was yanked away from the precipice. He scrambled onto his haunches and looked back to gape at the pit into which he'd almost fallen. He looked around to discover Miss Johnson sitting in the snow, the effort of hauling him out of danger having thrown her off balance.

"Miss Johnson! Are you all right? I'm . . . I'm sorry."

"I'm fine, Mr. Rosemund," she answered, catching her breath. "Are you all right?"

He felt bruised and shaken, but there weren't any sharp pains to indicate broken bones. "I think I'm fine, Miss Johnson . . ." He hesitated. "You saved my life."

Miss Johnson looked at him kindly. "Only because you were smart enough to listen to my command."

Samuel's freckled face broke into a sheepish grin. "Well, you were yelling pretty loud."

"Loudly," she corrected his grammar. "If you would be kind enough to help me up, Mr. Rosemund."

Samuel jumped to his feet and moved quickly to his principal, his hand outstretched. He suddenly wondered how she had managed to run down the hill at all. Miss Johnson leaned to one side and rolled up onto her knees, placing one foot under herself for leverage. Samuel pulled as hard as he could, trying not to look at her awkwardness—borne of wounds from the war—as she struggled to her feet. All the students knew about Miss Johnson's brush with death in the summer of 1914, having been caught in Belgium at the beginning of the Great War. Her secret escape to Antwerp, and almost getting blown up by German bombs, was a thrilling tale told and retold by every student in Sutter Creek. Because of injuries suffered during the war, the stoic educator walked with a limp and often found it necessary to use a cane. She'd given up her cherished summer wanderings to Europe, citing the unsettled condition of the world as sufficient reason. But many of the old-timers, especially those with nightmares secured during the Civil or Spanish-American wars, tipped their hats to her and understood the depth of her need to stay home.

As Miss Johnson steadied herself on her feet, a throng of students and teachers surrounded the twosome. Miss Tullis, one of the youngest of the teaching staff, reached them first.

"Miss Johnson? Mr. Rosemund? Are you all right?" she gasped. She turned abruptly to Samuel, her normally sweet features pinched in a shocked reproach. "You! You were nearly smashed on those rocks!" Samuel flinched. "If it weren't for Miss Johnson, you could be lying in a heap on those rocks down there!"

Miss Jonson laid a calming hand on Miss Tullis's arm. "I believe Mr. Rosemund is acutely aware of his folly."

Samuel hung his head. "Yes, ma'am."

But Miriam Tullis was not to be deterred. "And I hope you know that we will be speaking to your father about this."

Samuel nodded. "Yes, ma'am, I do."

Miss Johnson looked around at the staring faces. "All right, everyone, back to school. Recess is nearly at an end."

The majority of onlookers followed Miss Johnson's command, but several boys gathered at the edge of the pit to take a momentary look at the smashed toboggan. Two thin boys elbowed each other silently, and one older lad whistled through his teeth. Samuel's best friend Robert Cupp ignored the exciting scene of devastation, choosing instead to give his chum a gentle punch on the arm. Samuel looked over at him sheepishly, and then smiled when Robert rolled his eyes and shook his head. "Your ma is gonna give you the dickens."

"Yep, that's a fact," Samuel answered, starting his way up the hill. "The dickens and then some."

Philomene chuckled as she watched the boys move off. She turned to make sure stragglers were safely away from the precipice when a knife point of pain struck her side. She gasped as old scar tissue around her rib cage pulled and twisted. Philomene chided herself for running, but she'd had no choice. She stood with her eyes closed, leaning over slightly and rubbing her side with her free hand.

"May I help you, Miss Johnson?" Miss Tullis asked softly, a note of concern in her voice.

Philomene slowly opened her eyes and discovered, much to her relief, that she and the young teacher were alone at the bottom of the hill. "Yes, Miriam, a strong arm would be a help." Philomene took a few more moments to breathe out the last of the sharp pain, then steadied herself on Miss Tullis's arm as the two began their journey to the school.

"Will you always be bothered with your injury?" Miss Tullis asked innocently.

Philomene nodded. "Dr. McIntyre says it's likely. Most of the time it's manageable."

"Except when you have to go running after a noodle-brained boy," Miriam said tersely.

Philomene shook her head. "Well, I might call Samuel Rosemund active, or energetic, or adventurous, but never noodle-brained." She stopped to massage the stitch in her side. "I surmise he takes after his father Edward."

"Indeed!" Miriam scoffed. "A Harvard professor with no common sense."

Miss Johnson grinned. "Now, Miss Tullis, don't go believing town gossip. The Rosemunds have done well with the Lund farm."

"Thanks to Mrs. Rosemund," Miss Tullis stated. "She's the one with land sense."

"Hmm," was Philomene's simple response. Silently she moved toward the school, her mind pulled back to past years and another woman who'd had "land sense"—a former student of hers, Alaina Lund. The young woman had been her father's trusted helper in the opulent groves of apple and pear trees, but since Samuel Lund's death, she and her husband, Mr. Nephi Erickson, were living hand-to-mouth in Salt Lake City. *If only Alaina and Nephi had been allowed to run the farm after Samuel died.* An angry growl escaped Philomene's throat.

"Are you all right, Miss Johnson?" Miriam Tullis asked.

"Yes, dear, fine. Just thinking how unfair the world can be."

"Yes, ma'am, that's a fact."

Miriam Tullis figured Miss Johnson was referring to her misfortune in Europe and the injuries sustained in the bombing, injuries which would forever compromise her health. In actuality, Philomene Johnson did her best to block lingering memories of those horrific days. When she did consider her summer in Belgium, she always tried to picture walking the sunlit cobble-stone streets with her dear Aunt Hannah, buying chocolates, and taking in the beauty of the Grand' Place. Philomene clenched her jaw, trying to keep out wrenching thoughts of the cruel circumstances her aunt now suffered in Brussels: her apartment taken over by the German occupiers, little or no food, loss of friends, and the constant threat of death and destruction. Hannah Finn was an exceptional woman, but she was aging, and such devastation was surely taking its toll. Philomene did not actually know her aunt's condition, as, over the years, letters had been few and censored. The only thing Philomene could do was pray for her aunt's safety and that the war would end—soon.

The school bell rang, and Miss Johnson focused her attention on academia and afternoon lessons. She also began formulating the discussion she would have at the end of the day with Samuel Rosemund's father.

* * *

"Well, I don't see what can be done after the fact, Miss Johnson. I am not dismissing your heroic act on my son's behalf, nor his culpability. I only mean to say I believe the lesson has been learned, has it not?"

Edward Rosemund sat beside his son in Miss Johnson's office looking calmly across the desk at the headmistress. His sandy red hair, beard, and mustache were all neatly trimmed, and with his wire-rimmed glasses he looked the very picture of the college professor he had been. His question was genuine and without any hint of rancor or superiority. Philomene Johnson was at a loss for words, a condition she rarely encountered.

Miss Tullis, on the other hand, standing to the side of Miss Johnson's desk, was motivated to respond. "Mr. Rosemund, as your son's teacher—"

"And an excellent educator from what Samuel tells us."

Miss Tullis blinked. "I . . . well, I . . . thank you, sir, but my point, *as an educator,* is that Samuel must be held accountable for his actions."

"Reprimanded?"

"Yes, sir."

"Whipped?"

Miss Tullis flushed. "Well, no, not necessarily whipped."

"Good, because I don't believe in corporeal punishment," Mr. Rosemund answered in the same measured tone.

Miss Tullis rallied. "There must be a consequence, Mr. Rosemund. Your son broke several school rules and could have sustained grave personal injury."

Edward Rosemund smiled. "I'm sure you meant to switch those two sentiments in order of importance, Miss Tullis."

Miriam Tullis stopped mid-thought, her mouth opened, her eyes wide.

Mr. Rosemund turned back to Miss Johnson. "Of course, Miss Johnson, I do understand that there must be consequences. First, I believe Samuel suffered a great scare." Samuel nodded. "Second, his toboggan is smashed at the bottom of the ravine. It will not be replaced." Samuel offered no protest. "Third, I'm sure his mother will have a few words for him." Samuel winced. "And last, since he broke school rules, he will be expected to compensate the school in some manner. What do you suggest?"

Philomene kept her face placid, though she wanted to smile. "Janitorial service to be performed for one hour every day after school for two weeks."

Mr. Rosemund looked at his son, who nodded. "Yes, sir."

"Don't tell me. The contract is with Miss Johnson."

Samuel looked Miss Johnson squarely in the face. "Yes, ma'am, and I'm sorry for breaking the rules, and I thank you for saving my life."

Miss Johnson smiled and stood. "Of course, Samuel, your life is precious to me."

Father and son stood immediately, and Mr. Rosemund reached out his hand. Philomene took it.

"Thank you, Miss Johnson. Miss Tullis," Edward Rosemund said, bowing slightly. He put his hand on his son's shoulder, and the two left the room without further comment.

"Well, he's an interesting man," Miss Tullis said, a bewildered expression on her face.

"Yes, he is. I like him," Miss Johnson replied. She reflected on the alert look in his eyes, which spoke of a brilliant and disciplined mind.

"Miss Johnson?"

Philomene brought her thoughts quickly back to the classroom. She looked down at her desk and began organizing papers. "Yes, Miss Tullis?"

"I said, is there anything else you need?"

"No, Miriam, thank you."

Miss Tullis turned to leave. "Perhaps I will make a list of jobs for our young Mr. Rosemund's employment."

Philomene smiled. "A very good idea, Miss Tullis. We would not want to disappoint his father's expectations."

5

Just outside the main square of the Grand' Place, a small group of onlookers stood in the winter cold watching in amazement as an old servant woman thrashed two young German soldiers with a long, freshly baked baguette. Pieces of the loaf were flying into the air as the soldiers laughed and held up their arms to protect their faces. The young Belgian girl the soldiers had been trying to molest had slipped from the loosened grip of her stocky attackers as soon as the first blow of bread descended. She was now several streets away and saying prayers for her deliverer.

Although older and gaunt, the tall servant woman seemed strong and carried an air of command and elegance. Some of the onlookers were surprised by her impeccable speech. A few began to smile at her courageous act, while others were sure the incident would end badly.

With each blow, the woman would upbraid the boys, switching from French to German with ease. She told them in their native tongue that their mothers would be shocked by their tawdry behavior, and then in French called them several unpleasant names. She pulled another baguette from her large basket and continued the beating. She hit the taller of the two men hard in the solar plexus and knocked the wind out of him. His laughter turned to an angry grunt, and his friend—his face now threatening, grabbed the bread from the old woman's hand, and raised his arm to strike her. The people in the crowd protested but were unsure how far to push their enmity. Pride and loyalty told them to protect one of their own, but fear and self-preservation held them in place. The rules of occupation were well established, as the Germans had been landlords in their Belgian homeland for more than three years; but from the looks on the native faces, it seemed this band of citizenry might be willing to defy authority.

The tall soldier pulled out his long blade knife and pointed it at the woman. "Fraülein, legen Sie den Korb nieder und kommen Sie mit uns!" he growled.

The woman stepped back. "He wants me to put my basket down and come with them," she said in French to the waiting crowd.

There was a rumble of dissent from the onlookers, and the soldier motioned them away with his knife. A few left quickly, but the more mulish stayed.

The soldier with the knife pulled the basket out of the old woman's hand, and his partner grabbed her wrist. Just then an imposing middle-aged gentleman with a well-kept beard and mustache stepped into the group. He addressed, in English, not the soldiers, but the woman.

"Janette, for heaven sake! We've been waiting for our bread all morning. Where have you been?"

"Treten Sie zuruck!" the tall German commanded, flicking his knife ominously at the man.

"Step back," the servant translated in a whisper.

"Now, listen here," the man answered with a cool bravado, "I am a very important person. Tell him, Janette."

The old servant translated, but the soldiers seemed unimpressed. The stocky soldier bristled. "Sie müssen zum Hauptquartier gehen."

The servant glared. "He says I have to go to headquarters."

"Now, *that* will be a report," the gentleman said unabashed. "Ask them, Janette, if they really want to tell that story to an officer?"

The woman translated, asking the young soldier if he really wanted to report being attacked by an older woman with a loaf of bread.

The stocky German looked nervously at his companion, who only scowled and shook his head.

"Oh, here!" The man reached swiftly into his coat pocket before the soldiers could react, and brought out a leather dossier case. "Here are my papers. Tell them Janette, that their commandant will be very angry if they abuse me or one of my servants."

Janette relayed the words.

The soldier let go of the woman's bony wrist and opened the case. He took out the papers and read for a moment, some of the color draining from his face. He glanced nervously at his companion. "Er ist ein Amerikaner der mit dem Fursorgeamt arbeitet. Er hat eine hohe Genehmigung."

Janette nodded. "He can see you are an American working with the Committee for Relief in Belgium, and you have very high clearance."

The soldier with the knife looked unsure, and the American smiled. "I think they're getting the picture," he said genially. He tipped his hat at the young men. "Janette, if you will, please tell them that I write important newspaper pieces about their impressive war machine."

She told them.

"And that I'm sure they don't want me to write a story about two young German soldiers being beaten with bread by an old Belgian woman."

Janette hesitated, and then translated the message.

The taller soldier looked murderous, but the American returned a cold stare. "Now . . . I would like my case, my servant, and my bread returned."

She told them, and slowly they complied. The tall soldier sheathed his knife and handed the servant her basket, as the other soldier did a little heel click and nod, holding out the papers.

"Herr Davis," he said with grudging politeness.

The American took the case and turned his back on the soldiers with such nonchalant disdain it made many of the still-present onlookers smile. The soldiers turned to leave, pushing a young couple out of their way. The husband pulled his wife to him and lifted his hat to the retreating men.

Mr. Davis bent down and picked up the larger pieces of scattered bread, replacing them in the woman's basket. She looked at him gratefully, her breath coming now in shallow rasps.

With the small knot of Belgian citizenry looking on with admiration, the man offered his servant his arm and the two strode regally from the square. As they turned the corner onto a deserted side street, the woman collapsed.

* * *

Richard Harding Davis pounded on the door of the servants' quarters. "Claudine! Claudine! Open up!"

A cold sleet began to fall, and Mr. Davis pounded again.

The old woman stood slumped against his side, her face chalky, her breathing ragged. "Richard," she said hoarsely, "be quiet. You'll alert the cranky upstairs landlords."

He looked at her as if he didn't care, and raised his fist to bash the door again.

The lock clicked and the door opened. A young woman in a shabby servant's costume stood staring at the sight. "Monsieur Davis!" she cried, stepping aside to let them pass. "I knew I should not have let her go out by herself. What has happened?"

Mr. Davis set the frail woman in the only upholstered chair in the small room. "Your mistress tried to take on some of the German army."

Claudine shut the door with a bang and spun around to look at him. "You are joking with me."

"No, I'm not," he said, picking up a baguette. "She attacked them with one of these."

Claudine looked shocked and went to kneel by her mistress. "Oh, Madame Finn," she said taking her hand and feeling her forehead. "Why? Why would you do such a thing?" The servant looked up at Mr. Davis. "Perhaps we should get her to her bed."

"I don't need to go to bed," came a response from the woman in the chair. She opened her eyes and smiled at the young woman. "Just some tea and a piece of bread—preferably the part that hit that one German ruffian in the ribs."

Richard Davis laughed loudly. "Hannah Finn! You are the Barnum and Bailey Circus in one woman."

"And you, Mr. Davis, are the biggest liar in Europe. Your servant, indeed! And Janette? Where did you come up with that name?"

Claudine was looking at the two conspirators with a wondering expression. "Who is Janette?"

"Mr. Davis's servant. Me." She chuckled.

Claudine looked puzzled.

Hannah Finn patted her hand. "Oh, he just made it up to get me out of trouble." She gave Mr. Davis a scathing look. "And just because my status in life has decreased over the last few years, don't think I'm going to start darning your socks. I have enough work just keeping my own rags together."

Claudine interrupted. "But what is the story with the Germans?'

Mrs. Finn waved her hand dismissively. "Oh, it was nothing."

"Hannah Finn, tell the truth," Mr. Davis encouraged, glad to see strength coming back into the statuesque woman's voice and manner.

She spoke with nonchalance. "Two German soldiers were playing cat and mouse with a young woman. I merely attempted to teach them some manners."

Mr. Davis laughed. "Teaching? You were beating the tar out of them."

Claudine's eyes flew open in amazement. "Oh, Madame! Such danger!"

The spunky woman ignored her servant's concern, replying instead to Mr. Davis's comment. "Yes, and I was doing a good job, wasn't I?"

Mr. Davis laughed, but Claudine frowned. "Madame, are you sure you should not go to bed?"

Hannah Finn patted the girl's hand. "No, my dear, no. I just need to sit here awhile and catch my breath."

"But—" Claudine began to protest.

"Now, Claudine," Mr. Davis broke in, "have you ever won an argument when your mistress's mind is made up?"

Claudine grinned. "No, monsieur."

"Well then, tea it is and I'll get the bread. Since I was an eyewitness, I know just the piece she wants."

Claudine shook her head and went to put on the kettle.

On her departure, Richard knelt quickly by his friend's side. "Now, the truth, my love, how are you feeling?"

"Better, Richard, thank you."

Mr. Davis noticed color coming back into her cheeks and nodded. "Should we call a doctor to make sure? An escapade like that would daunt any eighty-year-old."

"Richard Harding Davis," she bristled, "how unchivalrous to mention age."

He grinned. "I'll tell more of your secrets if you're not honest with me."

She smiled at him with great tenderness. "I truly am fine, Richard." She sat straighter in her chair and secured a few stray pieces of white hair back into the bun at the nape of her neck. "And I'll tell you, it did my heart good to give those Boche back a bit of their own."

"It did my heart good to watch it," Mr. Davis said with a wink, "but, it was very dangerous."

She scoffed. "You, my friend, are not one to lecture about people doing dangerous things. Now, bring over one of those uncomfortable chairs and we'll catch up on your escapades of the last few months." Before he could leave her side, she laid her hand on his. "Thank you, Richard, for rescuing me."

"Actually, it was a very self-centered act."

"Oh?"

"Yes. When the war ends, I don't want your niece tracking me down for not honoring my promise to keep you safe."

Hannah nodded. "Ah, I see. The fear of retribution."

"Exactly. Philomene Johnson is a formidable woman." Richard brought a chair over, sat down, and reached for the basket of bread. "How is she?"

Hannah sighed. "I haven't heard in months. I think most letters are confiscated."

Richard nodded. "The German hierarchy is desperate. They see spies around every corner." He tore off a chunk of bread and handed it to her.

Hannah took the offering, then narrowed her eyes at the giver. "And here you sit with the German Ministry of Transport right upstairs in my old apartments." She shook her head. "I don't know how you manage to keep running around the country delivering secret correspondence between the king and members of his defunct government."

"I am well thought of by our German occupiers. The German propaganda office wants to play nice with the American CRB. For all they know I might be the right-hand man to Herbert Hoover."

Hannah Finn became reflective. "That man saved the life of many Belgians." She gave Mr. Davis a scathing look. "CRB, indeed. You play a far more dangerous game, Richard."

Richard laughed. "You mean smuggling out my news pieces via underground sources?"

Hannah chuckled in spite of herself. "Underground sources. You certainly play the part of the brash American very well, Richard." She broke a piece of crust from her bread, then looked up at him, the light expression replaced by one of concern. "You will be careful, won't you? I lost dear Edith to this war . . . it would be devastation if I lost you also."

Richard nodded but didn't answer as Claudine came into the room with a tray of tea items. He noticed the mismatched and chipped cups and absence of sugar, finding a great refinement in the fact that Hannah Finn made no apology for her lowly state.

Hannah's husband, Mr. William Conner Finn, had been a wealthy American diplomat. He and Hannah had traveled the world and knew the royals and heads of state of many countries. Conner's last assignment had been as foreign attaché to King Albert of Belgium. He had purchased lavish apartments on the rue de la Montagne for him and his darling Hannah, and settled efficiently into his job. The two unpretentious Americans loved Brussels with its rich and varied history, the beautiful buildings, and the warm and talkative people, and often found themselves at the center of political and social activity. Conner's death saddened friends and dignitaries alike, and had covered his dear companion with a heavy grief. But Hannah Finn had come through the loss and sorrow with grace and resolve. Richard watched her now in her faded dress as she poured tea as if for a duke or visiting president.

"Where's Claudine?" Richard asked, finally noticing her absence.

"You were certainly off daydreaming," Hannah answered. "She left right after delivering the tea. She said the Germans wanted her upstairs to do some cleaning." She handed him a cup. "So, how goes the war, Richard?"

He winked at her. "It's turning. The Americans are starting to come in large numbers now with fresh supplies and armaments. The German army is played out. They are down to recruiting fourteen- and fifteen-year-olds. They've even pushed the upper age limit beyond forty-five." He set down his cup and took her hand, whispering in a conspiratorial fashion. "I think the ragtag group upstairs will be out on their fannies by September."

Hannah Finn held up her cup. "I'll drink to that."

6

"She won't eat muffins, Mrs. Todd, I'm tellin' ya." Kerri McKee held up her fingers and ticked off the breakfast items Mrs. Elizabeth Lund would not eat. "Muffins, toast, kippers, eggs, ham . . ." She stuck up her thumb on the opposite hand. "Oh, and oats."

Mrs. Todd sighed. "Well, she can't just have tea and corn bread every morning. If this week's ration wasn't sugar, I'd make her a little cake or something." The soft-spoken cook reluctantly cut a piece from the loaf of corn bread and placed it on the plate.

Miss McKee picked up the serving tray with a nod. "You're a good woman, Mable, to be worryin' about poor Mrs. Lund." Kerri pushed open the swinging door, stopping halfway out. "Maybe she'll have some of your delicious meat pie for noon meal."

Mrs. Todd looked up and nodded.

Kerri stepped out into the dim hallway, a lump of sadness in her throat. The weeks were bringing them closer to spring, and she was glad for it. She was tired of the dreariness of winter and the melancholy that sat on the house like dust. Her mistress, Mrs. Westfield, was incompetent when it came to more than flower arranging, social engagements, and noting breeches of decorum. She detested conflict and was certainly not equipped to deal with her sister's erratic emotional states. In the years since Mrs. Lund and her daughter Kathryn had been in residence, a gloom had settled onto the large Victorian house at 238 Beacon Street.

"Spring is comin'," Kerri mumbled. "Everyone will be feelin' better then." She tapped on Mrs. Lund's bedroom door with her foot. She didn't expect an answer, but the rules of service were always followed. Kerri hesitated, then placed the tray on one hip and opened the door. The room was dim, so she moved carefully toward the side table. She squinted, trying to see if Mrs. Lund was awake or still sleeping. It was always such a joy when she or Ina Bell found her asleep. As she drew near to the large bed, she realized Mrs. Lund was not in it. Kerri looked up quickly, causing the dishes to rattle on the tray.

"Who is it?" came a voice from the shadow.

Kerri's heart leapt. "It's . . . Miss McKee, ma'am. Come to bring your breakfast." She set the tray on the table.

"What day is it?" the silky, disembodied voice asked.

"Monday, ma'am."

"No, the date."

The dark outer curtain of the window was pushed back, revealing Elizabeth Lund. She stood staring out the wavy glass through the inner curtain of lace, her white skin illuminated by a pale sun. She had dressed herself haphazardly and had not pinned her hair—unkempt chestnut strands lay bunched on her shoulders. She ran her finger along the edge of the lace.

Kerri swallowed. "Ah, March sixteenth."

"I've missed my son's birthday." Kerri didn't answer, but set to straightening the bed. "He was born March eighth." She paused. "Do you know my son?"

"No, ma'am."

"No, of course not. He's never been here. Eleanor, Kathryn, and I came here when Samuel died."

"I've brought your breakfast, ma'am. Would you like to have it?"

"He was handsome . . . my son, tall and lanky with dark hair. I haven't seen him for three years."

Kerri turned on the lamp. "Your breakfast, ma'am. Corn bread and nice hot tea."

Mrs. Lund looked over. "Miss McKee, please turn off that light." Kerri complied, and Mrs. Lund's focus drifted back to the window. "And Eleanor?"

"Beggin' your pardon, ma'am?"

"My daughter, Eleanor? She's not here anymore, is she?"

Kerri hesitated. "No. She's livin' in Salt Lake City." Kerri debated, then took a chance. "She's studyin' to be a doctor." There was no response. "She's a bright one that Miss Eleanor."

"She is," Mrs. Lund answered in a clear voice.

Miss McKee stopped fussing with the bed linens to stare at the still figure by the window. She moved slowly toward her. "How are ya feelin' this mornin', Mrs. Lund?"

"Better, I think," the woman said, not turning to look at the approaching servant girl.

"I'm glad to hear it."

Mrs. Lund pushed back the lace undercurtain. "How can a woman be a doctor?"

Kerri stopped beside her. "Well now, it's a new century, isn't it? I think women are takin' on all sorts of new professions."

"When Ida and I were young, we would never have considered such a thing."

"Ah, yes ma'am, things were a lot different then."

"We thought only of marriage, and, of course, marriage to someone who fit into our social status."

Kerri grunted slightly before she could stop herself. Mrs. Lund looked over, her expression sad.

"Oh! I'm sorry, ma'am," Kerri stammered. "I . . . meant no disrespect."

Mrs. Lund's face became unreadable. "No, you're right. It was a condescending notion. The man I married was a farmer, and he was one of the earth's perfect men."

"Yes, ma'am, so I've heard."

"My sister Ida married well. Her husband Cedrick was from a wealthy banking family. He was a very good man, though, who never took advantage of his position."

Kerri smiled. "To be sure. He was always good to us."

Mrs. Lund smiled at her. "Is Kathryn awake?"

Kerri nodded. "Yes ma'am. She's in her room."

"Will her tutor come today?"

"Yes ma'am, in two hours."

"Hmm. Perhaps I will have my breakfast in with my daughter this morning."

Kerri was delighted by Mrs. Lund's lucidity and the lack of slur to her speech. "Yes, ma'am. I'll carry it over for ya."

"What do I have?"

"Ah . . . corn bread and tea."

"Is there any bacon?"

"Well, not on your tray, but I could get you some."

Mrs. Lund moved a step closer to the window. "That would be nice, thank you."

"I'll go and fetch it right away." Kerri curtsied and moved quickly to the door. As she moved out into the hallway she bumped into her co-worker.

"Ina Bell!" she said in an excited whisper.

"What?" Ina Bell gasped, nearly dropping the clean, folded linens she was carrying. "Kerri McKee, you scared the devil out of me!"

"What devil?" Kerri snorted. "You're so saintly the devil wouldn't dare come anywhere near ya."

Ina Bell started off down the hall.

Kerri sprinted after her. "Ina Bell Latham, stop. I'm needin' to tell ya somethin'."

"Well, be quick about it. I have work to do."

Kerri came close to her. "I don't think Mrs. Lund is takin' her medicine anymore."

Ina Bell stared at her friend. "But you can't just stop taking laudanum, Kerri."

"Well then, maybe she's cuttin' back. I don't know. All I do know is that when I took her breakfast in this mornin' she was up standin' by the window.

She was dressed and she had a right clear conversation with me . . . not angry or anythin'."

Ina Bell's pale blue eyes widened. "Really?"

Kerri crossed herself. "As I'm a true Catholic girl."

Ina Bell fastened a good-natured look of disbelief on her friend.

Kerri waved away her skepticism. "Well, never mind that. I'm tellin' ya, a clear conversation. She even talked about her son James and Miss Eleanor."

"Oh, that is such a good sign," Ina Bell said, emotion coming into her voice.

"Now don't start blubberin', Miss Latham, for we've work to do. Put those things away quick and come with me. We're going to make Mrs. Todd very happy."

"Mrs. Todd?" Ina Bell asked, running to the linen closet. "How shall we make her happy?"

Kerri grinned. "By tellin' her that Mrs. Lund has asked for bacon with her breakfast."

"Yook at Daddy's priddy buttons!" Katie said excitedly.

Nephi Erickson stood at the bedroom doorway in his marine uniform, looking official but uncomfortable.

Alaina rose slowly from the divan, releasing Katie off her lap. The little girl ran forward and threw her arms around her daddy's legs.

"My," Mother Erickson said, pulling a deep breath. "My, my, my. We've seen you in your uniform before, but I still can't get over it. It makes ya look brave, son." She smiled slightly. "Very brave." She hesitated, waiting for a word from her daughter-in-law that was not forthcoming. "Your letters from Camp Lewis were interesting, weren't they, Alaina?"

"Yes, ma'am," Alaina answered dully.

"Was Washington State as beautiful as people say?" Mother Erickson continued.

Nephi smiled. "Well, I didn't see much of it, you know. Just the camp, and that was about it."

"Of course," his mother responded. "Hard to believe you were gone almost two months." There was an awkward silence. "I'll . . . I'll start breakfast now that you're up and going. Are ya hungry?"

Nephi nodded. "I am Mother, thanks."

Nephi looked down at Katie, who was pulling on his sleeve. He picked her up. "So, what do you think of your daddy as a soldier?"

Katie smiled. "Bery nice." She rubbed her hands over his head. "But you hair is short and pokey."

Nephi smiled and looked over at Alaina, but she was staring at her shoes.

Mother Erickson came forward holding out her hands for Katie. "Here, give me that little pup so you two can talk."

Katie flung her head back, and Nephi had to lunge to keep her from falling. She started in with a caterwauling protest. "No! No! I stay wif Daddy. I stay wif Daddy!"

"Katie Eleanor Erickson!" Mother Erickson said sternly, taking her out of Nephi's arms. "You stop that now." Katie quieted, but real tears were running down her cheeks. Mother Erickson cuddled her and patted her back. "There now, you come with Grammy and we'll make Daddy a big breakfast before he goes."

Katie sniffled. "I would be yiking dat," she said in a sad little voice.

Alaina started crying, and Mother Erickson hurried into the kitchen, shutting the door behind her.

Nephi took his wife in his arms. They stood like that for a long while, neither speaking as they tried to hold off insisting circumstance.

"I will come home," he whispered.

Alaina stepped back, wiping her eyes and blowing her nose into her handkerchief. She looked into his face. "You can't know that." She stopped herself. "Of course, you'll come home. Of course you will." She had made a pledge to herself that she wouldn't tell him of the dream she'd had in the night—a dream of running, and huns with bayonet rifles, and thick smoke that stopped her breathing. She wrapped her arms tightly around him again.

"You have the address of Camp Upton in New York?" he asked, his voice husky with emotion.

"In my pocket. And you'll be there . . . ?"

"Two or three weeks before they ship us out," he finished her sentence.

"I see." Alaina stepped away again.

Nephi reached into his jacket pocket and pulled out some money. "Look, here's some money I've already saved for the jar . . . twenty-six dollars." He put it in her hand. She looked up at him and he smiled. "Most of the other men in my unit left training camp with hardly two dimes to rub together, what with drinking, and cigarettes, and gambling. So this is a good start, isn't it?"

She nodded and put the bills into her apron pocket. "I should help your mother with breakfast."

She turned toward the kitchen and Nephi caught her arm. "Please don't be angry with me. I can't stand the thought of going off today knowing that you're angry with me."

She took a deep breath and turned back. She spoke slowly, trying to keep the pain out of her voice. "I'm not angry with you. I'm sad and frightened." A lump came into her throat. "If anything should happen to you . . ."

He gathered her into his arms. Alaina was grateful he didn't speak—didn't try to reassure her with hollow words of comfort. After a time, a silent agreement seemed to pass between them that they would shoulder whatever hardships came, that they would honor each other by this commitment.

They heard the sound of the hardware truck pulling up in front of the house, which meant that Nephi's brother Elias had come to fetch him. They stepped apart and looked at each other. Nephi brushed a tear off her cheek. "You are dear to me."

Alaina nodded, pulling her hand out of his. "I don't want Elias to see me like this." She kissed him lightly at the corner of his mouth and headed for the kitchen.

The front door opened and Elias entered carrying his son Zachery. Behind him came his wife Sarah. Elias took one look at Nephi and his face lit up with admiration. He put little Zachery down and moved over to clap his brother on the back.

"Boy, oh boy, brother! You look tough as nails. What did they do to you at that training camp? Just give you a gun and a knife, and you'll scare those huns back to Germany just looking at ya."

Nephi shrugged his shoulders, embarrassed by his brother's exuberance. "The marines are a pretty tough lot, I guess."

"I would say so!" Elias said emphatically. "Man, am I jealous. How many times did you and I talk about going over there and teaching those huns a thing or two? How dare they keep me out over some little medical problem." Sarah moved closer to the two. "Hey, Sarah, doesn't he look good?" Elias asked, putting his arm around his wife's waist. "What a time! You'll be shipping out with thousands of others. I've read we're sending ten thousand men in every week now."

"Hello, Sarah," Nephi said quietly, wishing to change the subject.

"You do look handsome," Sarah said with a shy smile.

Elias laughed.

The kitchen door flew open with a bang, and Katie came running into the room. "Zacry! Zacry!" she yelled, running to the forgotten little boy.

Even though Zachery was seven months older than Katie, he was slighter of build and shy, his brown curly hair and brown eyes seeming to emphasize his retiring nature when paired with his more outgoing cousin.

Nephi turned his attention to his charging daughter. "Careful now, Katie, don't run him down."

She stopped before bumping into the little boy, taking his hand, and patting his head. "I not hurt him, Daddy. I love him."

"And that's a fact," Mother Erickson said with a laugh as she came into the room. "Hello, son. Hello, Sarah. Come on into the kitchen. Breakfast is ready."

"Scrimmy!" Katie yelled, pulling Zachery toward the temptation of eggs and scrapple.

"Scrimmy, indeed!" Mother Erickson said, smiling at her two grandchildren as they passed. She gave Sarah a kiss on the cheek and patted Elias's face. As Nephi moved to her, she took his arm and whispered in his ear. "And your sweet wife has burned a piece of toast for you son, just the way you like it."

Nephi smiled, but his heart filled with loss and loneliness. Burnt toast was a family joke and a simple secret tie between him and his wife. He shook his head. Maybe he wasn't doing the right thing. His number hadn't come up in the draft, so he wasn't compelled to go. Were his motives truly full of sacrifice on his family's behalf? Or did part of him long for the adventure and danger of the war front—a chance to prove himself? He sat in his chair at the kitchen table staring at the plate of eggs, and when his mother asked him to say the blessing, he quietly said he preferred not to.

Alaina took his hand under the table, and he gritted his teeth against the tenderness. He forced his mind to think of the marine rules of engagement and the many ways they'd shown him how to kill a man.

* * *

"I was drafted! There's nothing I can do about it!" Daniel Chart stood glaring at his mother who glared right back at him. She was a small woman with big opinions and fierce determination. Around strangers she was quiet, almost shy, but in her own home there was no doubt about her strength of character. Her second husband, Fredrick, was a solid bear of a man at six feet four. Yet he knew not to cross his wife when she set her mind, for she was his equal in force of opinion and his superior in intellect.

Daniel turned to his stepfather for support. "Father, please tell her if I don't go they'll throw me in jail."

"That's true, Edna, they will."

"There are other options," she stated flatly.

"What?" Daniel barked, throwing socks into his small suitcase. "You mean stand up as a coward? Be a conscientious objector?"

Edna Robinson flinched. "No, not that."

"What then, break my leg?"

"Daniel, please lower your voice," Mrs. Robinson said sadly. Her son had never spoken to her in such a disrespectful tone, and it broke her heart. She knew he was angry and upset about the stance she was taking, and that the difference of opinion set them at odds, but she couldn't help it. This was her firstborn son—handsome, and strong, and healthy. How could she send him off to a foreign place to be torn apart either physically or emotionally? She took a breath. "But you're needed here on the farm."

Daniel stood quiet with his hand on the edge of the suitcase.

"Now, Edna," Fredrick Robinson intervened, "that's not fair—"

"Why would you say that?" Daniel cut in, a controlled edge to his voice. "Why would you make me feel like I'm deserting you?"

Mrs. Robinson stood staring at her boy for a moment, then turned and left the room.

Daniel looked at his father. "Why is she doing this?"

Mr. Robinson handed his son a shirt off the bed. "You know the answer to that. She loves you, and she's afraid." He handed him his shaving kit. "I'm afraid, too, but I'm a man. I suppose we can see the other side of things when it comes to war. Mind you, I don't like it, but sometimes duty comes into it."

Daniel looked up at his father. "Exactly. I didn't enlist because I knew how she felt, but now that I've been drafted . . ." He tied the buckles on his suitcase.

"I have to go. I want to go. And it's not just duty or making the world safe for democracy like President Wilson said, it's because those people over there are havin' a rough time of it. Think how many French and British mothers are cryin' because their boys are never gonna come home. German mothers, too. Maybe us gettin' over there is gonna stop all that suffering."

Mr. Robinson's eyes filled with tears. "You're a good man, Daniel."

Daniel picked up his suitcase and walked out of his bedroom. His mother met him on the front porch. She was stoic, but her eyes were red-rimmed.

"I have a few things for you." She held out a small bag. "Don't open it until you're on the train."

Daniel took his little mother in his arms. "Thank you. I love you."

She patted his back and stepped away. "You have been taught how to behave," she said with a catch in her throat. "That doesn't change with place or circumstance, son."

Daniel nodded. "I know, Mother."

"Stay clean and true, and come home to us."

Daniel nodded again and turned quickly to the wagon. Mr. Robinson wiped his eyes on his jacket sleeve and picked up the reins. He waited to give the command until his son was settled. "Walk on!" he shouted to the two work horses. The wagon moved ahead, and Daniel turned to wave at his mother, but she was no longer on the porch. He opened the bag she'd given him. In it he found a big piece of her famous gingerbread, his baseball, and a man's handkerchief that she'd embroidered. He looked at it in disbelief.

"She knew all along I wasn't going to change my mind, didn't she?"

Mr. Robinson looked over at his son. "She did."

On the handkerchief were embroidered the first three lines of George Cohan's war song:

> *Over there, over there,*
> *Send the word, send the word over there*
> *That the Yanks are coming . . .*

* * *

Eleanor Lund stood alone on the front porch with her brother-in-law. A cold March wind was whipping down off the Wasatch Mountains, making the two hunch into their coats.

"Sorry I couldn't come for breakfast," Eleanor said, blowing warm breath onto her hands, "but Grandfather can't be left alone much anymore."

"I understand," Nephi answered. "I'm so glad he was well last night when I visited."

Eleanor smiled. "He loved that."

Nephi reached over and held her arm. "What a blessing you are to our family, Eleanor. You take such good care of him. Thank you."

"It's a blessing for me, and an honor," she answered, shaking her head. "To be able to be in the presence of one of the Saints who crossed the plains by wagon? . . . Such an honor."

They heard Katie's angry scream from inside the house.

Nephi sighed and looked straight into Eleanor's face. "I know you do it already, but watch over Alaina for me?"

Eleanor nodded. "Of course."

"Katie can be a handful, and . . ."

"I understand, Nephi. I'll step in. And . . . I won't let my sister dwell on melancholy things. I promise."

He nodded.

"Oh! I almost forgot!" she said hurriedly, digging in the pocket of her coat. "I bought you a present. It's a pocket-size journal." She handed it over. "I thought if you got sad or anything you could write it down and get it out of your head. You could draw pictures in there, too. I'd love to see one of the Statue of Liberty. You're such a good artist."

Nephi was about to thank her when the front door flew open and Katie came running out with Alaina right behind her.

"Katie Eleanor Erickson, you *will* put on your coat!"

Katie grabbed onto Nephi's legs. "No!"

"Well, Miss Katie," Eleanor said slowly, "I know several doctors at the hospital who would love to give you a great big shot when you get sick."

Katie spun around. "Auntie Eleanor!" She ran to her. "You was not here for breakfast."

Eleanor took the coat from Alaina and put it on Katie. "No, I was taking care of Grandfather Erickson."

"Where is him?"

"At his home."

"Is him alone?"

"No," Eleanor answered, buttoning the buttons. "Sarah and Zachery are with him."

Elias came out onto the porch followed by Mother Erickson. He held out a small rectangular box to Nephi. "Here, little brother . . . something to remember me by."

"Elias, you didn't have to . . ."

"Yeah, yeah, I know, but take it anyway."

Nephi opened the box. "A . . . wristwatch," he said slowly.

Elias laughed. "I know! What a kick! Remember when we called guys 'she-men' if they wore one of those things? Well, no more, buddy. The soldiers are wearing 'em in the trenches. Guess it won't do to be pulling out a pocket watch when the bullets are whizzing by."

There was a moment of awkward silence.

"Thanks, Elias." Nephi put his hand on his brother's shoulder. "Thanks."

"Well, I think it's time to get you to the train," Elias said abruptly. He patted Nephi on the back, then walked down to the truck, followed by Eleanor and his mother.

Nephi picked up Katie.

"Are you going to the war now, Daddy?"

Nephi swallowed. "Well, I'm going to France, little one."

She patted his face. "Den you'll be home for supper?"

"No, I . . ." He started crying, and Alaina came forward to wrap her arms around the two of them.

"Daddy? Daddy?" Katie asked desperately. "Why are you so sad?"

"I'm just going to miss you," Nephi said, "you and Mommy."

Katie started crying. "Don't miss us, Daddy. Don't miss us. Stay home with us."

Nephi kissed Alaina long and intensely. "I love you. I love you." He hugged them both tightly, picked up his duffel bag, and moved quickly to the truck.

As Elias threw his bag into the back and started up the truck, Nephi hugged Eleanor and his mother. He waved at Alaina and Katie and got into the truck. As the vehicle pulled away, Katie ran down the steps and out into the drive.

"Daddy! Come back! Come back!"

Mother Erickson and Eleanor both went to fetch her, and when they turned back to the house, they saw Alaina crumple onto the porch.

8

"How far along are you, Laina?" Eleanor asked gently. She sat at the edge of Alaina's bed, holding her hand and taking her pulse.

Alaina lay staring out the window, watching steel gray clouds move across the small square of her vision.

"Laina, answer me," Eleanor insisted.

"I don't know exactly . . . two or three months."

"And you've not been sick this time?"

"Not as bad as with Katie. I was able to hide it well."

"Why would you do that?"

Alaina turned to look at her sister, pushing herself higher on her pillow. "Why? Why would I tell him something that would only bring him grief? He'd already enlisted. He had to go." Eleanor saw her sister set her jaw against tears.

The bedroom door opened a few inches, and Katie peeked in. When she saw her mother sitting up, she brightened. "Mommy! Are you awight?" She ran to the bed and took her mother's offered hand. Eleanor lifted Katie onto her lap.

Mother Erickson came to the door, breathing hard from a quick dash. "Whew! Sorry . . . she got away from me. One minute she was there givin' hay to Miss Titus, and the next . . . gone."

"I ranned very fast," Katie said, all smiles.

"Yes you did, little rabbit," Mother Erickson said, coming into the room. "Here, give me your coat." As she helped Katie with the buttons, she studied her daughter-in-law's face. "You're feeling better?"

Alaina looked at her straight on. "I am." She drew her knees up against her chest. "I'm sorry I didn't tell you about the baby."

Mother Erickson smiled. "I knew about it."

Alaina's eyes widened. "You did? Why didn't you say anything?"

"I figured you were keeping it secret for your own good reason." Alaina nodded. "Are you going to tell him sometime?" Mother Erickson asked without the least hint of judgment.

"Sometime, but I don't know when."

Katie, with a frown on her face, had been looking back and forth between the women as they spoke. "Tell Daddy what?" she barked, breaking the momentary silence. "What baby?"

"Katie Eleanor Erickson!" Eleanor exclaimed. "You are too smart for your own good."

Katie giggled at the shocked expressions on all their faces. "I are not two smart. I are three smart. I had my burfday."

Alaina laughed and cried and held out her arms for her little girl. "Come here, you precious little thing."

Katie crawled off Eleanor's lap and into her mother's embrace.

Eleanor stood. "Alaina, can I get you anything before I go?"

"No Elly, thank you. You get back to Grandfather Erickson." Alaina wiped her eyes on her sleeve. "We're fine, aren't we, Katie?" Katie nodded as she snuggled against her mother.

Mother Erickson took off her coat. "And it's been hours since breakfast. I guess I'd better get some food prepared."

"Scrimmy!" Katie shouted, clapping her hands.

"I'll help," Alaina said, starting to get up.

"Ah! You settle in, little missy. I can take care of a simple meal. You and your daughter have things to talk about."

Eleanor laughed. "Can little one keep a secret? That's what I want to know."

"Secwet?" Katie asked. "What secwet?"

Mother Erickson and Eleanor moved to the bedroom door, and Eleanor paused. "I'll ask Dr. Lucien to come over in a day or two to check on you."

"Elly, that's really not necessary," Alaina countered. "I'm fine . . . really."

Eleanor smiled. "Well, I'll ask anyway." She and Mother Erickson walked out into the hall, shutting the bedroom door on Katie's inquiries about "secwets" and babies.

Patience Erickson moved through the kitchen to hang her and Katie's coats in the back porch, retrieving Eleanor's off the hook and bringing it to her.

"Are you all right?" Eleanor asked as she shrugged into her coat.

Mother Erickson looked surprised. "Me?"

"Yes, you," Eleanor confirmed, taking her hands. "You, who takes care of everyone else. Your son just left for war. That has to be hard."

A tear leaked out of the corner of Mother Erickson's eye. "You are a treasure, Eleanor Lund. The Lord surely knew what He was doing to bring you to us."

Eleanor smiled. "So, answer my question."

Mother Erickson sighed and more tears came. "I'm not doin' so good right now, but I'll be better tomorrow. My boy is just so tender hearted, always has been. Elias could go and stand up against all the ugliness, but Nephi . . ." she shook her head.

"I know," Eleanor nodded, handing her a handkerchief. "I know."

"I just have to have faith that the Lord will watch over him." She wiped her eyes. "No matter what happens." She tried to smile, but her lips trembled. "God loves him even more than I do, if you can imagine."

They heard the sound of a truck pulling up in front of the house, and Mother Erickson frowned. "What is Elias doing back here? He was supposed to be at the hardware store after dropping Nephi at the train."

The two women walked out onto the front porch and saw Alma Erickson coming across the yard.

"Oh Alma," Mother Erickson whispered, her voice ragged with emotion. She moved down the front steps to meet her husband, and without word or comment he took her in his arms to comfort her.

Eleanor backed into the house, her emotional control shattered by the poignant sight of a mother and father pushing aside edict and law to mourn together their departed boy.

* * *

"It's a good thing you'll not be going to war, Bib Randall. You'd never be able to hide in one of them trenches," Kerri McKee said teasingly as she punched down the bread dough in front of her.

Ina Bell Latham nodded her agreement. "Besides which, you do a lot for the war effort right here at home. You help the Home Service Committee hang those liberty bond posters, you gather used books for the soldiers—"

"And," Kerri broke in, "from what I understand, *you'll* be plantin' our victory garden."

Bib stopped polishing his boots to glare at them. "Women. You wouldn't understand."

"Oh, stop bein' so glum," Kerri said, folding the dough over and kneading it. She looked at the mass in front of her. "Do you figure they call our boys 'doughboys' because they're goin' over there not quite fully baked?"

"Don't be saying disparaging things about our soldiers," Bib directed with a frown.

Kerri raised her eyebrows. "Disparaging? Well now, isn't that a fancy four-star word? That's the kind of word our Eleanor Lund would be usin'." Mrs. Todd, the cook, came in from the pantry. "And how many rolls will we be doin' today, Mrs. Todd?" Kerri asked, suddenly intent on her work.

"Only ten dozen, Miss McKee. We'd do more, but we're low on flour."

"And I get to go with you to the train depot, right Mrs. Todd?" Ina Bell asked as she cleared the last of the breakfast dishes.

"Yes, Miss Latham, I believe it's your turn."

Ina Bell sighed. "I just love to see the soldiers' faces when we give them the bread."

Kerri McKee sighed too. "I just love to see the soldiers' faces."

The girls laughed and Bib grumbled. "Stupid flat feet."

Abruptly the laughter stopped as the girls noticed Mrs. Lund standing in the doorway of the kitchen. She wore her dressing gown, and her feet were bare. Her lips were pale and her eyes were dark smudges. She seemed unsure of where she was.

Bib stood up. "May we help you, ma'am?"

She looked at him vacantly.

He wiped his hands on a cloth and stepped toward her. "Mr. Palmer isn't here at the moment. Is there something I can do for you?"

"Has the post arrived?"

The servants noticed her slurred speech.

Bib answered calmly. "Not yet, ma'am, were you expecting a letter?"

"I . . ."

Kerri noticed the letter crushed in her hand. "Holy Saint Michael," she whispered. "She's got that letter from last week . . . that one from her son James."

Ina Bell stepped forward. "Mrs. Lund, would you like me to fix your hair for you? We could go to your room and I could brush it and put it up."

Elizabeth Lund's free hand went absently to her hair. She turned and glared at Ina Bell. "No! I don't want my hair done!"

Ina Bell looked down.

"I want the letter from my son! I want to know where he is." She shook her fist at them—the fist holding the letter. "Someone said he went to war, but he can't because he's just a little boy. He has chores and he has to go to school."

"You're not thinking straight," Mrs. Todd said gently. "Your son is a grown man and he's gone to war in France."

Mrs. Lund paced around the room. "No. He can't have gone to France. He didn't ask my permission." She shoved over a chair. "He has chores to do. Chores."

"Mrs. Lund!" shy Mrs. Todd said firmly, "look at the letter in your hand!"

The other servants stood stock still, stunned by the impossible scenario playing out in front of them. Obviously Mrs. Lund was stunned also by the cook's outburst, as she did not move or reply.

"There are lots of our young men going off to fight. We just have to face it." She moved to her and made her raise the letter to her face. "See there. That letter's from France . . . from your son, James. Now, look at it."

Mrs. Lund focused her eyes on the letter, choking down a pitiful whimper when she registered the writing.

Mrs. Todd's voice softened. "We don't like it, and it's not good, but there are bad leaders out there making kind young men suffer. Your son James is helping to stop it. So . . ." She moved over and tore a portion of dough from Kerri's lump, then she took Mrs. Lund by the arm and set her at the kitchen table. She took the letter out of her hand. "Now, we're making bread for the soldiers leaving on the transport trains. Why don't you help?"

Kerri's eyes widened as she watched Mrs. Lund's hands move slowly to the dough.

Mrs. Todd went quietly back to her work, and, after a moment's stunned silence, the other servants followed her example.

9

"There are so many more flags now, Mr. Greggs," Philomene Johnson remarked as she stood in the post office looking at the large war map of the European combatants. It was covered in small colored flags, most of which were arrayed along a wavy line that spread from the North Sea near Holland through Belgium and France, then to the border of Switzerland.

The tall, genial postmaster had kept track of the movements of the conflict since Germany's invasion of Belgium in the summer of 1914. Philomene marked how years of sunlight had faded the once-vibrant colors indicating separate countries. The areas were now nations without distinction.

Mr. Greggs pointed at Russia. "With that country's capitulation, I took all their flags off the eastern front and moved those German flags over to the western front. I think Ludendorff's mad with fright and fury, and he's gonna make his exhausted German troops fight till there's not one boy alive."

Philomene hung her head.

"Oh, sorry, Miss Johnson. I know you don't like to talk about the war."

Philomene took a breath. "I am an educator, Mr. Greggs. Whatever my personal abhorrence or distress, I must know the facts." She removed her glove and ran her fingers over the Belgian countryside, coming to a stop at Brussels.

Mr. Greggs shifted his weight. "I . . . I'm sorry I didn't have a letter for you today, Miss Johnson. Maybe when the mail truck comes in from Sacramento . . ."

"Not to worry, Mr. Greggs. To hear from my aunt at this point would be a miracle." She studied the map and pointed at the newly attached white flags covering the French landscape. "And I take it those represent our noble American soldiers?"

"Yes, ma'am. There's a heap of 'em over there now. Some units are sent to shore up the played-out British and French troops on the front, but General Pershing is mostly interested in seeing our boys fight as a group." He swept his hands along the front line. "I'm thinkin' pretty soon those white flags are gonna be pushin' those brown flags right off the map."

Philomene felt a shudder of apprehension run through her body as she thought of hands and legs and faces of precious young men, bodies caught in the uncaring grip of battle, disfigured and in pain. She knew of that anguish in the very sinews of her own flesh. Mr. Greggs was speaking to her, and she steadied herself on her cane and turned to focus on the words.

". . . don't know what those Bolsheviks are thinking to accomplish. They're gonna have a time of it organizing and feeding all those Russian people."

She nodded without comprehension. Just then a small truck pulled up in front of the office, and Mr. Greggs's entire demeanor changed.

"Well, look at that," he said brightly, "the postal truck from Sacramento! Let me go get the bag and see if there's anything in there for you." He grabbed an empty bag from behind the counter and hurried outside to the truck.

Philomene stood staring at the flags on the map, thinking that perhaps if she pulled out all the brown ones and put them back into Germany, the war would stop. The tired German boys would go home to bratwurst and school, to sports and marriage, to wholeness and life. She tapped her finger on one of the pins. She would love to have that kind of power. In her bleaker moments she wondered why God didn't exert His omnipotence—take out an evil leader with some mysterious disease, cause bombs and bullets to miss their marks, have reason and goodness be the highest ideals of nations. Her fingers reached again to Brussels, and an ache came into her throat. She was finding it harder to trust in a God who seemed so distant and uncaring. She had never envisioned Him as a floating mass of spirit, but if He had human attributes, then why wasn't He reaching down to stop the madness? Did He not have a heart that was breaking? How lonely it made her to read the scriptures and find no answers or comfort. Her faith had always been a wellspring for her—water in the desert, manna in the wilderness, but now . . .

"Miss Johnson, a miracle!" Mr. Greggs called happily.

She turned abruptly to see him standing in the doorway holding a letter high in the air.

* * *

She had come, as was her custom, to the graveside of her friend Samuel Lund. Just after his death in October 1913, Philomene had begun to visit his grave in the Methodist Church cemetery to read him her letters. Most of the correspondence was from his children, scattered now to many places. Samuel's children had been some of her most cherished pupils, and the man himself someone she admired for his goodness and common sense. She found it calming to sit on the squat stone wall next to his grave and share not only written sentiment, but her own personal fears and weaknesses that would never be spurned or judged.

She ran her hand over the headstone, noting the age and earthiness the granite now carried with its surface softened by lichen. The grave itself was blanketed by wild grass that would green in a month, and the massive oak which stood guard would leaf out and scatter the light into dappled patches.

"I have a letter!" she said triumphantly, holding out the envelope and smiling, "a letter from my aunt." She sat on the wall, propping her cane against the stones and gazing at the envelope. "So many months of not knowing." She slipped her finger carefully under the flap and opened it, drawing out three beautifully penned pieces of paper. The breath caught in her chest because she recognized the hand and knew her aunt was still alive. Then she noted the date—January 3, 1918. Her aunt's life could still be in jeopardy. Where had this letter been for nearly three months? Softly she began reading.

> *January 3, 1918*
>
> *My dear Philomene,*
>
> *Our dear friend Richard has promised to get this missive out by some clandestine method. It may take some time, and I do not know if it will reach you, but I must try. After many years of despair, a tremor of hope is running through the hearts of the people. Not just here in Brussels, but throughout the region. We hear that the German High Command is becoming desperate as American forces flock into France. I must confess I eavesdrop on conversations of the German office workers upstairs, and there is agitation and fear. I am glad I concealed the fact that I can speak fluent German.*

Philomene remembered the day of her escape from Brussels when their group had been confronted by two German soldiers on patrol, and Aunt Hannah had sorted everything out with her diplomacy and impeccable German. Hannah Finn was a remarkable woman and Philomene missed her terribly. She brought her thoughts back to the letter. She began again, reading aloud.

> *Russia has surrendered the eastern front and I'm sure Germany will transfer their fighters for one last push.*
>
> *Did your papers report what happened in Paris last July Fourth? There were 13,000 American soldiers parading through Paris, the streets filled with one million Parisians cheering so loudly they could probably be heard in Berlin. The parade ended at the tomb of Lafayette, and while General Pershing laid a wreath, his assistant, Colonel Stanton, called out in perfect French, "Nous voici, Lafayette!"*

"Lafayette, we are here," Philomene whispered. She took out her handkerchief and wiped her eyes. "I must tell my students this story." She rubbed her side. "What a strange world, Samuel. Once America and France fought together against Britain, and now the three fight together." She found her place in her aunt's letter and continued.

> *How long ago seems August 1914 when this nightmare began—*
> *when Kaiser Wilhelm told his departing troops that they would*
> *return home victorious before the leaves had fallen from the trees.*
> *The arrogance of men. Four years of devastation, and even though*
> *the death knell has sounded for Germany, they fight on like rabid*
> *dogs.*

Philomene noted the frailness in her aunt's penmanship and realized she must be tiring. Oh, how she longed to be in Brussels on the rue de la Montagne caring for her kinswoman. She read on.

> *I do believe the war is drawing to a close, dear niece, but I'm*
> *afraid our valiant American troops will yet see their share of*
> *bewildering death.*
>
> *Remember our joyous adventures to the Parc de Cinquantenaire*
> *or the Petit Sablon, in that peaceful June of 1914? It seems so long*
> *ago. At least Brussels has been spared destruction. The Grand'*
> *Place still shows its beauty, and Manneken Pis still shows his*
> *insouciance.*
>
> *Please don't worry about food. Claudine and I have enough, and, of*
> *course, our dear Richard brings us a surprise every now and then. It*
> *was bad in the beginning. The people of Belgium would have*
> *starved in those early months if it hadn't been for the American*
> *CRB and Mr. Hoover. That man fought all obstacles to bring in*
> *food.*
>
> *I'm rambling, dear one. I'm sorry. The hour is late and I can't*
> *seem to keep my thoughts in line. It's just that, as I sit here*
> *writing, these words tie me to you. I see you in your dear little*
> *cottage or teaching your students, and a rivulet of normalcy flows*
> *into my life.*

Philomene felt tears tighten her throat, and she found it difficult to continue.

Hold onto hope, dear niece. We do here at the battlefront. For a little strip of land, greedy men have decimated a generation and changed the structure of the world. Will this truly be the war to end all wars? We of faith will continue to pray for it with every breath.

I will see you on my threshold someday.

Love everlasting,
Aunt Hannah

Do not fret. God will make all things right.

Philomene wept.

"Nous voici, Lafayette. Nous voici, Lafayette," she whispered, her voice choked and broken.

She heard the snap of a twig and the sound of footfalls on the leaf-carpeted ground. She looked up expecting to see Pastor Wilton or his daughter Joanna, but instead she was presented with Edward Rosemund. She brushed away the tears and straightened her back. "Ah! Mr. Rosemund," she said in a falsely steady voice. "You gave me a start."

"Miss Johnson? I'm sorry. I should have called out, but I only just noticed you."

"Not to worry, Mr. Rosemund. My heart is regaining its normal speed."

He laughed and continued his approach to her. "Did I hear you speaking French, Miss Johnson?"

She put away her aunt's letter. "My, Mr. Rosemund, you have the ears of a fox, but yes, it was French."

"Est-ce que vous parlez beaucoup de Francais?" he asked.

"Do I speak much French?" she responded. "That is an unfair question, Mr. Rosemund. I speak enough to get me by in most situations."

He laughed again. "Getting by in most situations is a good thing, Miss Johnson, et votre accent est tres joli."

"Your accent is fine as well," she answered quickly. She hated anyone to see her emotional, and to know he'd seen her weeping was a humiliation. "Did you learn in France?" she asked to deflect her discomfort.

"Do you mind if I sit?" He took off his hat and absently ran his fingers through his hair.

"Sit? Why . . . of course. Please." At this close distance Philomene noticed how much gray he had at his temples.

"I am sad to say, Miss Johnson, that my French is only academic. I was always so busy teaching that I never found time to travel."

"Oh, that is unfortunate," Philomene said sincerely. "Travel is one of my . . . well, *was* once of my passions."

"Travel is fatal to prejudice, bigotry, and narrow-mindedness," he quoted.

"Mark Twain," she answered.

He nodded, impressed with her scholarship. "Yes, travel is grand, but now that I am a farmer, I doubt the opportunity will present itself." He looked out wistfully over the quiet cemetery. "Do you come here often, Miss Johnson?" he asked, turning to look at her.

Philomene hesitated, evaluating the sincerity of his question. "When I find a little extra time or have a letter to read. I visit my mother and father . . . their graves are there," she said pointing. "And I read letters to my friend, Mr. Samuel Lund."

"Ah," Mr. Rosemund said, leaning around to read the inscription on the gravestone. "The creator of our beautiful farm."

"And you, Mr. Rosemund?" Philomene asked. "What brings you here?"

"I come for the quiet," he said simply. "Whenever I'm in town by myself, I come for the quiet."

Philomene smiled.

"Don't get me wrong," he added. "I love my family dearly, but before taking on my dear brother's brood, and adding a few of my own, you must remember I was a stodgy, confirmed bachelor—a recluse, a man of letters."

Philomene laughed.

"Content with the boring, solitary life of academia."

"Would you like to go back?" she questioned.

"To academia?"

"To the quiet life?"

He smiled. "No. But I would like to return to Boston . . . if only for a visit. Eat on Boston's South Side, walk the Harvard Commons, and . . ." he hesitated, "of course see my parents and siblings again."

"Of course," Philomene nodded.

He sighed. "I am content here, truly." He twirled his hat in his hands. "Now, don't you have an aunt in Belgium, Miss Johnson?"

She had a distinct feeling he wanted to change the subject. "I do, Mr. Rosemund," she answered openly. "I just received a letter from her."

"And was it she to whom you were speaking French?"

Philomene gave him an uncertain smile. "Yes, in a way. She'd written of the American soldiers parading in Paris to the tomb of Lafayette."

Edward Rosemund smiled. "Ah, the now-famous words of C.E. Stanton, 'Nous voici, Lafayette!'"

"Yes," Philomene said nodding, "Nous voici, Lafayette.'"

"I wish I'd been there," Edward said enthusiastically. "I wish I'd been the one to say those words." They were silent for a time. "I guess we're about to pay our debt to Lafayette for his help in winning the Revolutionary War."

"What a costly payment," Philomene said quietly.

"Indeed," Edward responded.

A starling trilled in the oak tree, and they both looked up to find it. They sat quietly, listening to its song. Finally Philomene picked up her cane and stood. Mr. Rosemund stood, too.

"No, no, Mr. Rosemund," Philomene insisted. "Please, sit and enjoy the solitude. I must be off for home and test evaluations."

"May I escort you?" Edward asked.

Philomene was taken aback. She was so used to being independent that the offer seemed overly chivalrous. "I . . . I . . . that is most kind, Mr. Rosemund, but I will manage, thank you."

He tipped his hat to her and sat back down.

Philomene turned and smiled to herself. *How astute of him to not press the point,* she thought. *Quite a forward-thinking man . . . kind and forward-thinking.*

"Oh, Miss Johnson!" Mr. Rosemund's voice called after her. She turned back. "Is my boy Samuel behaving himself?"

Philomene nodded. "Quite the little gentleman."

She heard the Harvard professor laugh as she turned toward home.

10

Huge billowy clouds hovered over the horizon as the American transport ship slid its way into the harbor at Brest. Nephi Erickson stood at the railing with several other marines and watched the surroundings come into focus in the early morning light. The men around him were quiet, but he could sense their eagerness and anticipation. He himself felt larger than life.

Their convoy had crossed the Atlantic safely with only one U-boat sighting and no major storms. Nephi knew the smiles on the soldiers' faces meant the stress that they'd carried for the past twelve days was sliding away with each mile gained toward land.

"Hey, Erickson, thank heavens no more 'abandon ship' drills, huh?" a voice whispered beside him. Nephi smiled and nodded. "And I guess now they can mail those printed-up postcards."

Nephi looked over at Jimmy Gordon and laughed. "Yeah, I guess so."

Jimmy's brown eyes flashed as he stood by his companions. "What a kicker, hey, Erickson?" He pantomimed reading a postcard. "Dearest ___ fill in the blank ___ Mother ___ and now the printed part ___ the ship on which I sailed has arrived safely overseas." He shook his head. "Oh, and P.S., I'm writing this card as we sit in dock at Hoboken. They'll keep the card at the postal station until cabled that the ship has docked in some French port, having not been blown to smithereens, and then they'll mail it to you." He finished with a deep bow and was instantly shoved around by two of his marine buddies.

Nephi chuckled at the antics of Gordon, Duncan, and McLaughlin—amazed by the connection he had with these men after only three weeks. He found it especially interesting given they all had such disparate personalities. Jimmy Gordon from Syracuse, New York, was outgoing and bright, always ready with a joke or a cynical remark, while Cornell Duncan from Williamsburg, Virginia, was quietly analytical, and RJ McLaughlin from Emmert, Kentucky, was boyish and naive.

"Settle down," Cornell instructed, swatting Jimmy with his cap.

"Me?" Jimmy protested. "You guys started it."

Cornell Duncan gave his friend a knowing stare. "We do not want the Froggs to think we're an uncouth bunch of ruffians."

"Huh. I don't care what these Frenchmen think of me," Jimmy snorted, "as long as they give me something decent to eat. I swear, all that steamed food on ship was like eatin' a wet sponge."

RJ frowned at him. "I didn't think it were that bad."

"Well, of course not, RJ," Jimmy responded, "but, you're used to eatin' squirrel meat, now, aren't you?"

RJ looked at him as though waiting for a point, which made Jimmy bust out laughing. He slapped the big Kentuckian on the back. "Boy, oh boy, RJ, you stick close to me in this scuffle, now, will ya? And I'll see if I can keep you out of trouble."

Nephi turned back to the railing, looking out over the calm water of the harbor to the green hills rambling down to the water's edge. He thought of lessons he'd had at school about Europe and European villages—of the quaint low buildings of stone set along narrow winding paths and the little wooden boats tied along the shore. It made him a bit lightheaded to think that he was actually seeing these things with his own eyes.

He looked over to the huge metal transport ships tied at the dock. They were so out of place in this picturesque setting—the splotches of green and gray paint on their hulls forming grotesque patterns for camouflage. At sea the deception was remarkable and effective, but here in the quiet harbor the visage was unsightly and conspicuous.

The clouds had gathered and darkened during their voyage in harbor, and now and again a spatter of rain fell on the waiting soldiers. The general bell sounded and there was immediate movement as the soldiers pushed and jostled each other toward the access portals leading below deck. Now that the call for action had been sounded, the men seemed eager to secure their possessions for disembarking.

Jimmy Gordon clapped his hands and let out a whoop. "Here we go, RJ! You sure you got your dog tags?"

RJ searched for the strip of white cloth around his neck on which hung his identification tags. He smiled as he brought them out. "Yes, sir, right here."

As the two moved off, Jimmy continued to drill the affable Kentucky boy. "Rifle and ammunition belt?"

"Yep."

"Canteen, mess kit, pup tent?"

"Ah . . . yep."

"Wool blanket?"

"Yeah . . . but I still cain't fold it right."

Jimmy's voice faded into the general din. "We can't have that soldier. We'll have no sad sacks in this unit."

Nephi and Cornell shuffled along together, waiting their turn at the descent stairs, each preoccupied with thoughts of what the day would bring. Finally Cornell pushed out a breath of air. "Well, I guess there's no turning back now?"

Nephi noted the strangled expression on his friend's face. "It'd be an awful long swim," he responded with a chuckle.

A brief smile lifted the corner of Cornell's mouth. "You . . . I . . . I've seen you saying prayers sometimes, Erickson. You think God's going to get us out of this?"

Nephi shook his head. "I don't know."

"But, you believe there is a God?"

"I do, Duncan."

Cornell nodded. "Well, at least that's something. If He's really there, maybe He'll look out for us."

They reached the top of the steep stairway and had to concentrate as they went down. Nephi's body was pushed around by the crush of men moving down the steps, but his mind was fixed on Cornell's last question. *You believe there is a God?* Nephi looked around him. How many other men were going out to face battle and death with fear as a companion, or comforted only with the idea that death in a valiant cause was a pretty good way to square accounts with the world?

* * *

An hour later, as they moved down the gangplank to the checker station, it seemed to Nephi that the exuberance of the morning had faded and the men had lost their voices. The checker was having a hard time understanding the names and serial numbers the men were giving as they passed, even though the rolls had been arranged in the order of the march. Suddenly Jimmy Gordon's voice rang out loud and clear: "GORDON . . . JAMES . . . TWO MILLION EIGHT HUNDRED SEVEN TWO SEVENTY-FOUR . . . SIR!"

And immediately after, RJ's voice boomed out: "MCLAUGHLIN . . . ROBBIE JACK . . . TWO MILLION EIGHT HUNDRED SEVEN TWO SEVENTY-FIVE . . . SIR!"

The checker tilted back his chair, looked up at the men still on the ship, and shouted, "THANK HEAVEN! AMERICA IS SAVED! TWO LIVE SOLDIERS ARE GOING TO FRANCE!"

The soldiers all around let out with a big cheer, several thumping Jimmy and RJ on the back. There were hoots and laughter, and an overall lifting of feelings after that, and when Nephi reached the checker he saw that the man was still smiling.

As the soldiers formed into their marching lines, a scruffy group of little children from the village came among them—some asking for cigarettes or chocolate, but most just patting the men's hands and looking up into their faces.

The call to move out came, and as the army marched down the narrow streets to the train station, the children ran beside or followed. The columns passed women and older men, but the young men were conspicuously absent. A few of the ancient folks called out, "vive les Americains" or waved, but most just stood watching, staring intently at the smooth bright faces, the clean uniforms, and the jaunty swing of the soldiers' arms.

As they neared the railway yard one of the men next to Nephi pulled on the sleeve of his jacket. "Look at that now, will you?" he said in a whisper. "I'm thinking those are Germans."

Nephi looked over at the group of men sitting with their backs to the marchers. Their grayish green uniforms were stained with sweat and mud, and Nephi figured they must have just been captured and brought from the battle-front. Their French guards wore shabby blue field uniforms and expressions of disinterest. They seemed nonchalant about guarding the prisoners, but the German soldiers didn't seem much interested in escape.

A young German with a livid scar running from his hairline to his chin turned to stare at the passing Americans. His mien was one of defeated detachment, and Nephi felt a wave of sympathy wash over him. *Could I kill him? Even with all my training, could I kill him? He's God's son too. Can I kill one of my brothers?*

A train whistle blasted into his thoughts, and Nephi looked up to see a hospital train pulling to a stop. The uniforms said British soldiers, and every coach was filled with men suffering from wounds: heads bandaged, arms missing, torsos wrapped in tape. The sight struck him and the other Americans dumb, dampening whatever bravado they'd tried to muster.

Nephi shuddered. His mind was so full of new sights and experiences, he didn't know if he could endure an encounter so filled with pathos. The march formation had been dismissed, and Nephi looked over to see Jimmy, RJ, and Cornell moving to him through the crowd.

"Is that what we're headed for?" Cornell asked as he approached, never taking his eyes off the men in the train.

"Looks bad, don't it?" RJ stated.

"Well hey, you ladies, where'd you think you were going?" Jimmy asked with a snort. "Some sort of picnic?" He waved at a couple of soldiers who had their window open, then walked audaciously toward the train.

"Hey, Yank!" a soldier with one arm called out, seeing him approach. "Off to the front, are ya?"

Jimmy shouted. "Yes, sir! About time we got our carcasses over here, don't ya think?"

More Tommies were opening their windows.

"Indeed so." The one-armed soldier laughed. "Indeed so. Where ya from, Yank?"

"Syracuse, New York," Jimmy answered. "And you?"

"Stratford-upon-Avon."

"Ah, Shakespeare's stomping ground," Cornell said, coming to stand beside Jimmy. Nephi and RJ joined them.

"How long have you been at the front?" Nephi asked.

"Long enough to get broken up a bit," a different soldier called out.

"Long enough to lose me best chums," another yelled.

A soldier with a bandage draped across one eye slapped the side of the train. "Long enough to miss me mum's cookin', and she's dead awful at it."

All the soldiers hooted.

"You could eat at my house," RJ offered. "My mama's a real good cook."

"Yeah, if you like squirrel," Jimmy countered.

Several of the British soldiers laughed.

The train started up again, creeping its way toward the station some two hundred yards down the track.

The one-armed soldier called out to the Americans as they parted. "They need you where we came from, lads. Keep your wits about you. It's quite a game."

Someone on the train called out, "We're off to Blighty, boys!" and a cheer went up.

Nephi's group, like many others, stood staring after the train, trying to organize thoughts and feelings—trying to detach the image of injury and maiming from their own vibrant flesh.

"Blighty?" RJ asked.

"Must be their nickname for England," Cornell answered solemnly.

Nephi jumped when he felt someone shake his arm. He turned quickly to find a plump little woman putting a bottle of wine into his hand. He glanced around to see other women from the village offering soldiers bread, bags of hard candy, and tins of sardines. He stared down at the bottle, then into her kindly, eager face. He smiled. "Merci," he said.

She put her fingers to her lips, then reached out and placed them on his chest just over his heart. She turned and walked away.

"Hey, Erickson," Jimmy said, coming to stand beside him, "you look sad."

"What? Oh, no," Nephi answered. "She just reminded me a little of my mother."

"Oh," Jimmy said. "I thought you might be sad over your gift, seeing that you, as a Mormon boy, can't be drinking that." He tapped the wine bottle.

Nephi smiled. "So, have you come looking for a trade?"

Jimmy pulled a small round loaf of bread from behind his back.

"Done," Nephi said without hesitation.

Jimmy laughed as they traded. "You religious boys aren't so good at gambling or bartering, are you?"

"Ah," Nephi said with a nod. "But we are good at keeping our wits about us."

Another shrill whistle sounded, and the men picked up their gear and prepared for their final long trip to the front. Nephi packed his bread carefully in his duffel and turned to look back at the charming storybook town, catching a glint of blue from the harbor water. Months later, that gentle color would serve as his only connection to a world of goodness and beauty.

11

Doctor Thorndike entered the lecture hall in his usual somber mood. His students immediately stopped conversations midsentence, sat straighter, and cleared their minds of any thought other than human anatomy. The man laid his lecture notes exactly in the center of the lectern and hesitated.

Eleanor Lund looked sideways at Shawn Burbage, who shrugged his shoulders and shook his head.

"What is the USPHS?" Dr. Thorndike asked curtly.

The medical students in the classroom, usually a bright and competitive lot, sat in silence, a few turning their heads to see what their peers were making of this question.

"USPHS. Anyone?" he barked again.

Slowly, Mr. Cox raised his hand.

"Yes, Mr. Cox?

"The United States Public Health Service?"

"Yes."

Mr. Cox slumped back into his seat, relieved that he'd answered correctly.

Mr. Burbage leaned over to Eleanor. "What's going on?" he whispered. "Thorndike never asks questions outside his subject."

Eleanor didn't reply as Dr. Thorndike was looking directly at her.

"And the surgeon general of the USPHS?"

Mr. Burbage raised his hand to take the professor's scrutiny away from Eleanor.

"Yes, Mr. Burbage?"

"Dr. Rupert Blue."

"Yes." He turned back to the lectern. When he had positioned himself directly behind it, he paused again, and looked out over the forty students in attendance. "I would like a diagnostic evaluation."

Eleanor sat forward. This was definitely odd behavior from her anatomy instructor but extremely intriguing. She felt her mind snap to total attention.

"A young man, in strapping good health just hours prior, comes into a hospital so enfeebled he can hardly walk. He complains of aches in his muscles, back, joints, and head. He has a sore throat, pains in his eyes, and he feels dizzy. The doctor puts him into a bed for observation." Dr. Thorndike moved out in front of the podium, scanning the attendant faces of his students as he continued. "Several hours later the young man's fever is registered at 103 degrees and he is having bouts of delirium." Eleanor inched farther forward in her seat. "The next day there is no relief for him. His face now has a bluish cast, and he is bringing up blood-stained sputum."

"The next day?" a student interrupted, shocked incredulity in his voice.

"The next day," Dr. Thorndike confirmed. He continued without emotion. "In the evening, the patient is struggling to clear his airways of a blood-tinged froth that gushes from his nose and mouth."

Mr. Burbage made a sound of revulsion, but Eleanor's focus was so fixed on her professor that she hardly heard him.

Dr. Thorndike stood still at the front of the classroom. "A few hours later he dies of cyanosis. Simply put, he suffocates."

There was neither sound nor movement in the hall.

"The diagnosis?"

No one volunteered. Indeed it seemed that all the students had lost the ability to speak.

Dr. Thorndike looked again at Eleanor. "Miss Lund?"

She sat staring at him a moment, her brows furrowed. Finally, she took a deep breath. "I take it this case is not hypothetical."

"It is not," the doctor returned.

"And it is a recent occurrence?"

"Yes. A month ago."

Mid-March, Eleanor calculated. "Have there been others afflicted?"

"One hundred in one day. Five hundred in one week."

There were murmurs and sharp intakes of breath around the classroom.

"Do all perish?" she asked dispassionately.

"No. A percentage survive."

Eleanor's mind was racing. She looked steadily at Dr. Thorndike. "It is obviously not one of the recognized diseases that become prevalent from time to time."

Dr. Thorndike nodded. "Such as?"

Eleanor concentrated. "Bronchitis, laryngitis, pneumonia, coryza, or rhinitis."

"And your deduction, Miss Lund?"

She hesitated a moment. "The symptoms indicate a type of influenza, but certainly a type that we have never encountered."

"Thank you, Miss Lund, and you are exactly right. A strain of influenza that we have never encountered."

"Where did the outbreak occur, sir?" asked Shawn.

"An astute question, Mr. Burbage. Fort Riley, Kansas."

"All five hundred cases?"

"And more occurring in other military training camps around the country."

A sudden dread made Eleanor's stomach cramp. *Nephi was in a military camp in March.* She tried to bring her thoughts to a rational calm. They'd received a postcard that his ship had arrived safely in France, and a letter a week after that, and there was no mention made of any sickness in either correspondence.

She brought her thoughts back to the discussion. Mr. Cox had just made the suggestion that the Germans might be unleashing influenza germs on the American soldiers to keep them from fighting. Some of the students were guffawing and making disparaging comments, while others looked fearful of the possibility.

Eleanor raised her hand.

"Class, decorum please," Dr. Thorndike directed. "Yes, Miss Lund?"

"What's being done about the outbreak, sir?"

"Ah, there's the real question," Dr. Thorndike answered, clasping his hands behind his back. "The real question and the real concern. And the answer, Miss Lund, is . . . *debate.* Dr. Rupert Blue is a friend of mine, and we have spoken several times since the outbreak. He is maddened by the fact that the medical specialists are trying to define and minimize the disease so as not to alarm the citizenry. They have not reached a consensus on exactly what they are dealing with, and the public health officials are debating how to proceed."

"Sounds like mass confusion," Mr. Burbage stated.

"Sounds like they're hoping it will just go away," Eleanor added. "Hoping that the public is so focused on the war that the situation will disappear with few the wiser."

Dr. Thorndike nodded. "And what do you think, Miss Lund?"

"Five hundred cases in one week in a fixed area? It sounds like an epidemic to me." She dropped her head and her voice. "It seems to be a very virulent strain, and if the Public Health Service doesn't take action quickly, a lot of people are going to die."

The silence was total.

Finally, Dr. Thorndike walked back to gather his papers. "I will relay your thoughts to Dr. Blue the next time we speak." He walked out of the classroom.

The students rose and maneuvered their way out, all either avoiding proximity to Eleanor or staring at her back and whispering criticisms to their friends.

Mr. Burbage was the only one to stay near, and although he was silent as they moved out of the building, it was not out of jealousy, but respect.

"My word, Miss Lund," he said finally. "You surprise me at every corner. What a masterful diagnosis."

She felt herself flush. "Thank you, Mr. Burbage. And thank you for not casting me off as a misfit."

"You mean because you're a woman and smarter than the lot of us men put together?"

"Hmmm," she answered simply.

He laughed loudly and Eleanor smiled.

"That was for teasing me," she said with a chuckle. "I'm sure you're just as smart as I am."

"Not a chance," he answered, shaking his head. "But, that's all right . . . I'm better looking."

"To be sure," Eleanor said without rancor.

There was silence between them, and an unwelcome melancholy settled itself into their exchange.

Mr. Burbage looked at her straight on. "Do you really think things will go badly with this sickness . . . that it's more than just a few isolated cases?"

"Five hundred cases in one week is alarming," she answered without drama. "And you can be assured that, left unchecked, the movements of men and war shipments will spread the disease quickly. It may slack off over the summer months, but come September . . ."

There was a growl of thunder, and the two looked up at the brutish clouds gathering over the mountains. "Oh, my!" Eleanor exclaimed. "I'd better get home before the storm." She started off down the pathway. "I'll see you next class, Mr. Burbage."

"Miss Lund," he called, following after.

Eleanor stopped and turned to him.

"Would you like to attend the May art show with me? It's only a student art show, but I thought it . . ."

Eleanor smiled. "I'd love to, Mr. Burbage," she said without hesitation. "Thank you so much for asking me."

As she moved off for the trolley station, Mr. Burbage stood watching her in wonder. She was the most amazing woman he'd ever met: straightforward, honest, smart—and he was smitten. He knew if he took her home to meet his parents, his father would find her plain and his mother would question her common background, but he didn't care. He knew Eleanor Lund could captivate them and change their minds in two sentences.

He threw his hat into the air, caught it, and headed for his next class.

* * *

Eleanor sat in a comfy chair next to Grandfather Erickson's rocker and finished the story of Abraham Lincoln. She closed the book and looked over to see if the precious man had fallen asleep, but was delighted to find him awake and attentive.

"Vhat a fine story. Vhat a good man Lincoln vas," he said, nodding his approval. "Tank you for reading it to me. The author, he is fine writer."

"*She,* I'll have you know," Eleanor corrected. "And don't you remember what her name is?"

Grandfather shook his head. "I don't."

"*Eleanor* Gridley, so it has to be good."

"Oh, of course," the Danish man chuckled. "Anyone vit da name of Eleanor does everyting good."

Eleanor stood, laughing with him. "Hand me your water bottle and I'll heat it for your bed."

"Ya, good," he answered, bringing it out from behind his back. "Maybe you need one too after hard day at school."

"Maybe," she called from the kitchen. "It was a difficult class today." She came out to find the aged patriarch pushing himself out of his chair. "Grandfather," she said gently, "you're not suppose to get up without help."

"Ya, Ya. But, sometimes I like to try." He changed the subject as they walked toward his bedroom. "So, today your school vas difficult?"

"Yes, we—" Eleanor stopped. She did not want to tell him the subject matter of her class. He had enough to concern him with his own health problems and his grandson in the war—she did not need to add the sorrow of a possible epidemic. "We had an intense lecture about strong-willed pioneer men who still think they can do everything they did twenty years ago."

He grumbled as he shuffled along. "I vood be glad to do the same tings I did two years ago."

Eleanor took off his bathrobe and helped him sit on the edge of the bed, where she removed his slippers. She positioned the hot water bottle and helped him lie down and swing his legs onto the mattress. She covered him with the warm quilt and patted his face.

"You are an angel," he said.

"And you are a mountain," Eleanor replied.

He laughed. "Vell, I used to be a mountain, but now I tink I'm only a hill."

It was their familiar banter, and Eleanor loved it. She loved him. Tears pressed at the back of her eyes. She'd been caring for him three years now and had seen great physical diminishment over the past year. With her training and natural discernment, she recognized the symptoms of the small strokes he'd been having. Even at eighty-seven years old, his remarkable strength had helped him rally after each episode, but Eleanor knew it was only a matter of time.

He reached over and took her hand. "You are vorried tonight," he said softly.

She patted his hand. "The world is a little sad right now," she answered honestly.

"Ya, dat's true," he said, closing his eyes, "but, God is still in charge. Satan vill be overcome. Evil is never stronger than good, ya?"

"Yes, Grandfather," she whispered.

"Now, you sing a song. It vill make us both feel better."

Eleanor smiled and began singing a simple Danish song he'd taught her. As the sweet words and melody filled the room, sickness, sorrow, and war slipped out the open window and away into the star-filled night.

12

"Grampa Erickson, Katie is trying to stick a marble up her nose," Zachery said, pointing.

Grandfather Erickson sat in his rocker with the Chinese checkerboard on his lap. His great-grandchildren, Zachery and Katie, were busy pretending to play the game—moving the pretty, colored marbles haphazardly to different slots on the board.

"Katie Eleanor Erickson," Grandfather said with a slight grin, "are you doing that?"

Katie's face puckered into a frown, and she shoved her tiny fist at him. "Curbla!" she said gruffly, using one of her own words of defiance.

"Vell, you won't tink *curbla* if you get one of them stuck up there," he chuckled. "Now, find a good place to put it on the board."

Katie smiled, distracted immediately from her ill temper. She moved to the board and placed her marble in the tip of one of the star points.

"Ah," Grandfather said solemnly, "dat's a very good place."

Katie beamed and patted his hand. "Grampa, why is you fingers so broken?" she asked innocently.

"I've told you dis story before," Grandfather answered, looking thoughtful.

"About your sickness?" Zachery said, coming to stand beside the rocking chair.

"Na, not that old boring story." He winked. "Na, the one about riding a buffalo." The children stared at him wide-eyed. "You know vhat is buffalo?"

Katie nodded, and Zachery said, "It's a big brown furry cow."

Grandfather smiled at him. "Yep, big all right. In fact, the one I rode vas almost as big as dis room."

"Really?" Katie asked, bouncing up and down.

"Grampa, you're teasing us," Zachery said, narrowing his eyes at his grandfather. "You didn't ride a buffalo."

"Whose story is dis?" Grandfather asked in an affronted tone. "Now, do you vant to hear the story or not?"

"I do! I do!" Katie said loudly, bouncing up and down again.

Zachery nodded and plucked at the sleeve of Grandfather's shirt.

"Von day my Caroline and I vere riding in our vagon at the back of the vagon train . . ."

"Is that Grandma Erickson?" Zachery interrupted.

Grandfather Erickson smiled at his bright little grandson. "Ya, your great-grandma. Dat's her picture right over there," he said pointing, and Zachery went to retrieve it.

"And that's you," Katie said, pointing at the man in the photograph.

"Ya," Grandfather nodded, "but dat picture vas taken in Salt Lake City, when ve vere a bit older. Ve vere young when ve came across as pioneers. I vas only tventy-two, and I vas big and strong."

"So, what happened with the buffalo?" Katie asked, turning in a circle.

Grandfather smiled at her. "So, ve vere riding along, and all of a sudden the ground began to shake." Katie stopped turning. "It shook so much ve almost fell out of the vagon. I looked behind, and there vas a thousand buffalo coming our vay . . . maybe more." Zachery swallowed. "They vere coming fast, and I knew dat they vere going to smash up the whole vagon train." The children stood mesmerized. "Vhen that big old leader came up beside our vagon, I jumped on his back and grabbed on tight to his curly coat."

"Grampa!" Katie gasped.

"I turned him aside, knowing the rest of the buffalo vould follow their leader."

"So the wagon train didn't get smashed?" Zachery asked anxiously.

"No, the vagon train vas saved, but that big buffalo vouldn't stop running. After many hours, he flopped down in the grass and fell asleep. Ven I got back to the camp my fingers vere like this—" he held up his hands with their bent and crooked fingers "—from holding onto that buffalo's curly coat."

"And when they reached the Salt Lake Valley," Eleanor said from the kitchen door, "Brigham Young presented him with that little bronze buffalo statue as a thank-you for saving the wagon train."

Katie ran over to grab the statue off the bookshelf. "This one?"

"That very one." Eleanor said.

Zachery touched the statue reverently. "The prophet Brigham Young gave this to you, Grampa?"

"Vell, in fact he did," Grandfather Erickson said sincerely.

"If for a totally different reason," Eleanor whispered to the irrepressible storyteller. "Don't worry, I'll keep your secret." She smiled at him indulgently and looked over at Katie and Zachery. "Your Grandfather used to tell your fathers stories about two-headed dogs, fairy queens, and burying gold in his back pasture."

"Like the gold plates?" Zachery blurted out.

"Ah, now we've got them started," Eleanor said laughing. She walked over to the bookcase and brought out a brown book—the leather cover soft and worn with age and use. "When you're older and can read, you can read this," she said, holding the book out to them. "This is where Grandfather Erickson has written all his wonderful stories and adventures."

"You wrote a book, Grampa?" Zachery asked in awe, reaching up to touch it.

"A journal," Grandfather confirmed.

"Scrimmy!" Katie said, running around the rocker.

"But, first things first," Eleanor said, putting the book back on the shelf. "First, you have to learn your colors and your letters."

"I know my letters and colors," Zachery said simply.

"So, what's this color?" Eleanor asked, taking a marble from the Chinese checkerboard.

"White," Zachery said without hesitation.

"I want to say white," Katie fussed, stamping her foot.

"So, vhat color is dis one?" Grandfather asked, pointing to another marble. Zachery started to answer. "Now, Zachery, let Katie answer."

"Black!" Katie chirped.

"She always says black," Zachery said, rolling a marble on the wood floor. "She thinks every color is black."

"It is black," Katie insisted, a wounded tone to her voice.

"Vell, it's almost black," Grandfather Erickson said in a soothing voice. "It's blue."

Zachery came over to stand by the rocker. "That one is blue, and that's yellow, and that's green."

"My goodness, Mr. Zachery, I vas six or seven before I knew my colors."

"That's all right, Grampa," he said patting his hand. "You had to learn them in Danish."

The big man laughed. "Ya, dat's right . . . Danish, and Danish is much harder."

"Speak Danish to us Grampa," Katie said brightly.

"Hmm, let me tink . . . how about . . . Hvis vi havde høns, Kunne vi have æg til morgen mad."

"What does it mean? What does it mean?" the children chorused.

"If ve had chickens, ve could have eggs for breakfast."

The children laughed.

"We do got chickens!" Katie squealed.

"What's going on in here?" Sarah asked cheerfully, coming into the room.

Katie danced around. "If we had chickens we could have eggs for breakfast."

"But, we do have chickens," Sarah said flatly.

Zachery and Katie laughed, and Katie fell on the floor.

"Are they tiring you?" Sarah asked, moving to place her hand on Grandfather Erickson's shoulder.

Grandfather's rumbling laugh subsided. "No, no, not at all."

"Well, Alaina and I are almost finished with the cleaning, and now that Eleanor is back from class, we can take these two home for naps."

Katie started kicking her feet on the floor. "No nap! No nap! No nap!"

Little Zachery backed over behind Grandfather's chair, and Sarah made shushing noises that proved ineffectual.

Alaina appeared quickly at the door of the living room. "Katie Eleanor Erickson! Stop that!" She moved over, grabbed her screaming daughter around the waist, and lifted her to her feet.

"Alaina, be careful!" Sarah called out. "Your delicate condition."

"Oh, bother my delicate condition," Alaina snapped. "Do *you* want to take care of her?"

Sarah's face paled at Alaina's sharp words, and she stepped back. "I . . . I'm sorry, Alaina."

Eleanor's voice rose above the caterwauling. "I guess Katie doesn't want to hear the letter from her daddy."

Katie immediately stopped her tantrum. "What?"

"A letter from your daddy."

"I want to."

"Then stop being naughty and say you're sorry to everyone," Eleanor said.

"What?"

"Say you're sorry. Everyone had to hear your shrieking, so we should all hear you say you're sorry."

Katie glared up at her mother, who ignored her.

After several moments of silence, Eleanor walked to Grandfather Erickson and took the Chinese checkerboard off his lap. "Well, I guess she doesn't want to hear the letter."

"I do," Katie answered, her small voice trembling.

"Then?" Eleanor said calmly, putting the game in the cupboard.

Katie sniffed. "Sorry."

Alaina slid her arm around her daughter's shoulder. "Good girl. Thank you." She brought the letter out of her apron pocket. "You go sit on the divan with Auntie Eleanor, and we'll see what Daddy has to say."

Katie shuffled her way across the floor, not sure she wanted to be friends with her aunt.

"Come on, sweetheart," Eleanor said, sitting down. "You can sit on my lap, and Auntie Sarah and little Zachery can sit right next to us."

Katie climbed onto Eleanor's lap and laid her head back. Eleanor wrapped her arms around her and gave her a squeeze.

Alaina sat in the comfy chair next to Grandfather's rocker and took the letter out of the envelope.

"April twenty-second," she began. "My dearest Alaina, Katie"—Katie looked up at her aunt and smiled—"and family."

> *We are in France! Our boat dropped us off in a beautiful little seacoast town where they loaded us onto horse trains. Not trains pulled by horses, but train cars that could carry either eight horses or forty men. And from the smell, they'd obviously been used for both.*

Zachery giggled, and Katie frowned over at him, unsure what he found funny. Alaina continued reading.

> *I have made some friends, and we sure are a different mix of fellows. I haven't met any other Mormon boys, and I'll tell you, my platoon is full of a rough-tough gang. It seems that they're always spoiling for a fight. Some don't even speak English, being that they're Italian, Greek, or Russian immigrants. Some are just illiterate.*

"What's illiterate?" Katie broke in.

"It means they can't read," Alaina answered.

"Me and Zachery are illiterate."

The older family members chuckled.

"It's all right to not be able to read when you're little," Eleanor offered. "It's not a very good thing when you're older."

"I can almost read," Zachery said.

Katie glared at him. "Shhh I want to hear my daddy's letter."

Alaina found her place.

> *Some are just illiterate. A few say they don't care to learn, although the military is setting up programs on the base to teach them. The paymaster said they wouldn't get their pay if they couldn't read, write, and sign their name. That changed a lot of minds.*

Grandfather Erickson nodded.

> *We weren't sent right to the front because I guess they figured we needed a bit more training. We're at a camp now about twenty miles outside of Paris. Can you believe it? Paris, France! Our*

*training officers are British and French, and they can't get over
how healthy and strong we are. Their men have had a rough time
of it.*

*I'm learning a little French at the camp, mostly for commands
and fighting techniques, but I don't need to go into that.*

*I've drawn some pictures for you of the transport ship, a house in
France, and our new caps. We call them Dinky caps because
they're small compared to the hats we had when we first came
over. Us marines had hats that looked like a mailman's hat, and
the army fellows had broad-brimmed felt hats. In the old hats
those doughboys looked like a band of Boy Scouts. Here's a picture
of some soldiers in their Boy Scout hats.*

Alaina finished with the page and handed it to Eleanor so they could look
at the pictures.

*So, how are my darling girls doing at home? I think about you
every day and pray for you. Are you going to help Grammy plant
the garden this spring, Miss Katie? Be sure and plant peas for me.*

Katie sat up. "Can I do dat, Mommy?"
"I think that would be lovely," Alaina answered, trying to keep emotion
out of her voice.

*All I really want from you dear ones is to keep the home fires
burning, and it will not be long before we all come marching
home—our mission accomplished and happy to have suffered the
hardships of war.*

Alaina's voice grew husky.

*When you think of me in France, do not do so with a heavy
heart, but in a proud way.*

*One of the men in my unit has a camera. We're not suppose to
have one, but he keeps it hidden. I'll see if he'll take some pictures
of us in our uniforms and send you one.*

My dear Alaina . . .

She stopped, then read the last part of the letter silently.

"What does him say, Mommy?" Katie asked, crawling down off Eleanor's lap.

Alaina took a deep breath and put a light tone into her voice. "Just that we're to be happy, and you're to be a good girl."

Katie hugged her mother's arm. "I will, Mommy."

Alaina folded the letter and put it into her pocket. "So, time for a nap?"

Katie let go of her mother's arm and frowned, but Grandfather Erickson interceded. "I say ve move my rocker onto the porch, and Katie and Zachery can lie down out dere on some quilts."

Katie's face brightened.

"Is it warm enough?" Alaina asked.

"Ve have plenty of quilts," Grandfather said, smiling.

"Scrimmy!" Katie yelped, taking Zachery by the hand and dancing about.

* * *

An hour later, Sarah and Alaina sat on the cool front porch in wicker chairs, watching Katie, Zachery, and Grandfather Erickson as they slept. Eleanor stood by one of the carved posts supporting the porch roof, running her fingers over beautifully crafted daffodils, hyacinths, corn flowers, and forest animals.

"Did you know he carved a replica of Caroline's face?" Eleanor asked, moving to the post at the far end of the porch.

"I didn't," Alaina said, rising. She walked quietly past Zachery and Katie, snuggled in their quilt nests, and looked where Eleanor was pointing. "Oh, how beautiful," Alaina whispered, wrapping her shawl about her and reaching out to touch the exquisitely carved image. "It's a younger Caroline."

Eleanor nodded. "Carved from loving memory."

Alaina looked over at Katie. "I feel so fortunate to have the last piece of furniture he carved."

"Katie's cradle," Eleanor said, nodding.

"Well . . . soon to be the newest Erickson's cradle," Sarah said softly.

Alaina smiled and moved back to sit by her sister-in-law. "Sarah," she said, taking her hand. "I'm sorry I spoke harshly to you earlier. My frustration over Katie's behavior does not give me the right to be short with people I love."

A tear of release rolled down Sarah's face. "I . . . I'm sure . . ."

"No," Alaina said smiling, "you mustn't make an excuse for my cranky behavior, you kind soul. Just accept my apology."

Sarah gave Alaina's hand a squeeze and nodded.

Alaina released her hand and sat back. "Good. Now I can go to work on one of my many other faults."

Sarah looked shocked, but Eleanor chuckled.

"Yes, how about the one of keeping secrets from your husband?" Eleanor pressed.

Alaina sobered. "I know. I've been praying about when to tell him, but so far it's only been a stupor of thought."

Grandfather's quilt began slipping from his lap, and Eleanor went to put it back in place, tucking it gently around his hips. "Dear man," she whispered.

Alaina looked over at the sleeping patriarch. "Just think of all the things he's seen in his life."

"And done," Sarah added. "You know he did a lot of the decorative carving in the Salt Lake Temple?"

Eleanor nodded.

"Mother Erickson told me," Alaina said, sitting forward in her chair. "It sounds beautiful."

"The temple is exquisitely beautiful," Sarah affirmed. "It's like being lifted off this world into heaven."

Eleanor looked out to the Oquirrah Mountains, watching a line of gray clouds forming. She pressed her lips together and took a deep breath. She had just been about to remark on how much she wanted to go inside that sacred building, how much she wanted to continue with her progression, but she knew such a comment would make Alaina feel uncomfortable, so she held her tongue. For some reason, her sister wasn't ready to move forward in her spiritual commitment, and Eleanor knew she had sorrowful feelings about that. With the many other hardships that sat at Alaina's door, Eleanor was not about to add to the burden. Besides, she couldn't go to the temple until she was married anyway, and that might not be for a long time, if at all. Of course . . . she *was* going to the art show with Shawn Burbage.

"What are you grinning about?" Alaina asked in her sisterly voice.

Eleanor checked her expression. "Grinning? Was I?"

Alaina's smile broadened. "Yes, and it must have been a pleasant prospect. So?"

Eleanor lifted her chin. "You don't need to know all my secrets, Miss Nosey."

"Oh, yes I do," Alaina insisted. "How else can I tease my little sister?"

"Exactly," Eleanor said.

"I tink our Eleanor has a boyfriend," Grandfather Erickson said, his eyes still closed.

The three women turned to look at him. They burst out laughing as a grin spread across his face.

13

The violent thunder of the storm made the men of the ambulance team jump. The British corporal called them to order and they complied, but the horses, tethered to the triage wagon, were squealing with fear and pulling frantically at their harnesses. The wheels of the wagon began sliding with a gush of mud into a ditch, dragging the bucking animals backward. Without orders, an inexperienced lad lost his head and rushed into the melee, grabbing hold of the reins and trying to get the horses under control. The lead horse reared, knocking the soldier sideways underneath one of the sliding wheels. The young man's scream was drowned out in another crack of thunder.

The commander swore and called out. "Lund!" But James had already jumped forward, speaking to the frantic animals in a soothing but firm tone to be heard above the wind and shelling. He grabbed the harness.

"Here now. Here now, calm down." He ran his hand down the neck of the huge Belgian draft horse, pulling him forward with commanding strength. "Come on. Come on, now. Let's get you out of this mess." The horse tossed its great head and squealed but slowly followed James's insistent pull.

As James led the team to a position farther behind the second line of defense, Clune and a few other men from the unit rushed forward to retrieve the mauled soldier. An artillery shell landed twenty feet from the road where the rest of the company was hunkered down, blowing the nearest men back against a stone-and-wood fence. The living retreated a hundred yards farther back, positioning themselves momentarily behind a deserted farmhouse.

The thunder and shells continued to pound, and the rain came in relentless waves. James secured the horses and rejoined his buddies as they dove into the damaged structure.

"Stinking Boche!" Clune hissed as he slid down against the wall, trying to wipe the mud and water off his face. "I think they got Middlebrook and Sheppard."

James crashed into the side of the big Englishman as another shell hit close. "Seems like they've changed their range," he yelled as he seated himself on the broken tiles of the floor.

They heard the whine and strike of three more shells, and the house shuddered.

Clune swore. "You'd think they'd be polite enough to stop for supper."

James smiled at his friend. He heard muttering and turned to look at the man across from him. It was a young recruit just arrived from the training camp. Hatless, his short, curly hair was plastered to his head by rain and mud. His eyes kept darting back and forth as each shell hit.

"Stop!" he screamed. "Stop! Make them stop!"

James was at his side, a viselike grip around the lad's wrist to keep him from bolting. "Just come up, did ya? That's right, I thought I saw you come up with one of the supply wagons."

Clune moved to the boy's other side, bumping a seasoned British comrade out of the way. "American, aren't ya now?" he asked, trying to distract the soldier from the sound of more shells exploding close.

"It won't stop," the young man rasped, gritting his teeth and clenching his fists. "It won't stop."

"Yeah, sure it will," James assured. "It always stops."

The soldier put his head on his knees. "It won't! It won't, I tell you!" he snapped angrily. "It's been going on for two days!"

"So, what's yer name, friend?" Clune asked as though he were at a social. "I'm Wheaten Clune from Shrewsbury, and this is Mr. James Lund of California."

The man looked over at him in shocked silence.

"What state are you from?" James questioned with a smile.

The man's head swung around to look at the other cordial lunatic. "Huh?"

"What's your home state?" James asked again, as if expecting an answer.

"Utah," the man said weakly.

"No kiddin'?" James exclaimed. "My sisters live in Utah. One of them married a Mormon. Are you a Mormon?"

The man nodded.

"What's your name?" Clune asked quickly, as he heard the whistle of a fast-approaching shell.

The two men took hold of the recruit under the arms and scrambled with him to the other side of the room just as the bomb exploded, tearing off the corner of the house where they'd been sitting. Stone and wood flew in every direction. The recruit screamed and scrambled on all fours toward the gaping hole.

Clune and Lund grabbed him, dragging him back to the opposite corner.

"Ah, can't be goin' out there now, lad. There's a big hole in the roof and it's raining. You'll catch yer death," Clune said in a matter-of-fact tone.

The soldier crumpled against the wall, and James and Wheaten positioned themselves on either side.

"You're mad," the boy said into his hands.

"Who me?" Clune asked. "Me?" He shrugged. "Well, I dare say I am a bit. What do ya think, Lund, am I a wee bit mad?"

"Oh, you're much more than a wee bit mad, my friend."

Clune laughed. "Only way to keep your sanity in a place like this."

The recruit stared at him. "Have you been here a long time?"

Clune patted him on the back. "Three years, laddie, and the Boche haven't even nicked me."

"Three years?" The soldier's voice was a strangled whisper.

"So, what's your name?" James persisted.

The young man answered without taking his eyes off Clune's face. "Marcus Hill."

"My sister married an Erickson. Know any Ericksons in Utah?" James chatted on affably.

Marcus shook his head. "I'm sorry, I don't." He looked down at his hands. They were shaking uncontrollably.

James and Wheaten could hear the slowing of the barrage but knew Private Hill was a long way from fortitude. Wheaten gave James a look that indicated he should keep the boy talking.

"Yeah, my father actually joined your church," James said.

"He did?" Hill said flatly, still looking down.

"Yeah. He read that Book of Mormon."

Hill looked over, a flicker of life in his eyes. "Really? In California?"

"Yeah, we read in California," James said, grinning.

Private Hill managed a slight smile. "I . . . I didn't mean that. It's just that the Church doesn't have many members in California. Who introduced you to the Church?"

"Whoa, not me!" James said, putting up his hands defensively. "I'm a heathen from way back."

Clune laughed.

"No," James continued. "Our farmhand was a Mormon fellow from Utah, and . . . a . . . he gave my father the book. His name was Nephi . . . Nephi Erickson. That's who my sister married."

The shelling stopped, and Clune winked at James. "Heavenly days, Lund. That question certainly got you flustered," Clune said, grinning at his friend.

James laughed.

Clune stood up. "See there now, Hill, you've survived your first Boche barrage."

The soldier looked around him, noticing that other men in the unit were getting to their feet, noticing also that the shelling had stopped. His eyes filled with tears. "Thanks."

"Don't mention it," James said, reaching down to help him up. "We're in this mess together." He repositioned his field helmet.

Hill stood. "It is a mess, isn't it?"

"Aye, that's why me and Lund are here to clean it up. Care to join us, Private Hill?" Clune barked, slapping him on the back.

Hill nodded and winced. "Ow. My head hurts," he blurted out.

"Oh, it's just a bit of concussion from the shelling. You'll get over it pretty quickly," James assured him. He could hear their commander barking orders outside. "Come on, you two, we have work to do. You all right, Hill?"

Private Hill stood trembling. "I . . . I don't know, sir."

"Oh, he's no sir, laddie," Clune said. "Just call him Lund like the rest of us do." Clune laid his hand on Hill's shoulder and guided him out of the ruined house.

The sight that greeted them was starkly beautiful. The rain had diminished, and a strip of red light glowed on the western horizon, where the clouds were breaking and the sun was setting. The closest dark clouds were smudged crimson in places where ammunition dumps were on fire—the flames leaping into the air, while back behind them several village houses were burning bright.

"Lund! Clune!" the corporal called as soon as he saw them. "Get over to the pit and see what you can find. We've lost our chaplain, so . . . you . . ." He looked squarely at Hill. "What's your name?"

"Private Marcus Hill, sir."

"You accompany them and retrieve the name tags."

"Yes, sir."

They could hear the short-range artillery and rifle fire coming from the front line, and James saw Private Hill flinch.

"Come on, Hill!" James said abruptly as he and Clune picked up empty sandbags from the supply wagon and laid them on the stretcher. "Watch out on the duckboards, they're slippery when there's been this much rain."

The men moved cautiously forward on the slippery wooden planks until they reached the blasted road. Here they had to maneuver around dead horses and mules, shattered supply wagons, and a toppled cookstove still steaming.

Clune swore as they passed by. "There goes my supper," he growled.

"I keep getting stuck in the mud!" Hill called, trying to keep up.

"Oh yes, you'll have legs like a rhino by the end of the war," Clune laughed.

They came first to the stone wall and found three of their own from the ambulance unit flung over the rocks and log rails like rag dolls.

"But . . . but they don't have any major injuries," Hill said as they laid the bodies out on a patch of grass. He was bending over them with his knife and slicing off the bottom length of cotton tape, which held one of the two identification tags.

"Concussion can kill you if you're too close," James explained.

Private Hill suddenly stopped and sat on his haunches, staring at the bodies.

"Hill?" James questioned as he laid straight the legs of the last soldier.

"I . . . I've never seen anybody dead before."

James and Clune shared a look.

"They went quick," Clune said gently. "That's a blessin' now, isn't it?"

Hill swallowed. "I guess so."

"Your religion might come a little harder out here," James said, surprised at how hard and cynical his voice was. He looked over at Hill and wanted to take back the words.

Tears rolled down the new recruit's cheeks and he nodded. "What do I do with these?" he asked softly, holding up the aluminum tags he'd removed.

"When we get back to the triage area, you'll mark the names and numbers in a book, then turn the tags over to the Graves Registration Department."

Several small explosions sounded at a distance, and the men crouched. "Come on!" Clune yelled. "Sounds like the fight is heating up."

Hunched low, the three soldiers moved forward through the mud as fast as they could to the edge of the shell crater. A pale shaft of light shimmered across the blasted wasteland, casting an eerie glow onto the lip of the newly formed pit. Hill looked down in horror. There at the bottom in the freshly turned earth were five bodies. The violence of the explosion had pushed them deep into the dirt. Three of the bodies were terribly mangled but still intact. The fourth was crushed into the side of the pit—stuffed in like a bloody rag. The soldier's arm stuck straight out of the clay, the hand smooth and undamaged, a silver ring encircling a finger. The fifth body was in pieces. Hill turned from the pit and vomited.

"Hill!" James called, sliding down into the pit. "You're going to have to help us lift these men out."

"I . . . can't," Hill moaned.

"Yes, you can!" James yelled. "These men deserve our respect!"

Hill's body straightened and he wiped his mouth. "Yes, sir," he answered, mustering courage and moving to the edge of the pit.

James handed up the bloody dog tag from the soldier in pieces as Clune reverently collected the parts and put them into the empty sandbag.

Hill set his face as he reached down to help collect the soldier.

Clune heard the boy praying, and moved to James. "I think he'll be all right."

James nodded.

Over the next several hours the soldiers on the front line fought, and their comrades of the ambulance corps collected bodies and salvaged the wounded. Private Marcus Hill worked with determination, keeping pace with Lund and Clune, and even venturing out to the edge of the safe zone to drag in a broken soldier.

"Hill!" Clune hissed. "Get back here. You're much too far out this time!"

Hill was on his stomach, wriggling forward like a salamander. He was headed to the frontline trench. In front of that were rows of barbed wire, and beyond—the blasted waste of no-man's-land.

"Hill, you're too close to death out there!" Clune warned.

Hill kept moving. "I hear someone calling!"

Suddenly James was there, crawling forward into the depression where Clune was hiding.

Zzst . . . zzst . . . zzst.

"Hear that, Private?" Clune called harshly. "Those are bullets." He turned to James. "I think a sniper has him in his sights."

"What's he trying to prove?" James snapped. "One day in the war and he's gonna get himself killed."

A volley of rifle fire sounded from the Allied line, and the shots from the German marksman were silenced.

"That Hill is one lucky soldier," James said, crawling forward on his belly.

Clune growled but moved also.

They met up with Hill at the edge of another shell crater—this one only ten to twelve feet deep but half full of slimy gray water. James had heard frightened sobs and pitiful wails as he'd advanced through the dark, and as he looked over into the pit he realized the source. Barely discernable in the small amount of moonlight was a nightmarish scene of devastation. A dead body floated in the water, and two wounded soldiers were grasping at the sides of the pit—hurt and exhausted, they were sliding toward death.

"They're going to drown!" Hill choked, moving as if to slide over the edge. Clune grabbed him. "Wait! It's too slick. There's no way to get them."

"You're crazy, you're crazy!" Hill screamed, kicking. "Don't you see, they're drowning!"

"Marcus!" James said, grabbing his jacket, "you don't have the strength left. You'd drown with them."

Hysterical pleas gurgled from one of the soldiers. Hill kicked Clune hard in the chest and slid over into the water. The putrid sludge was swallowing the nearest soldier, the thick water pouring into his open mouth. Hill grabbed him and shoved him up—shoved him high enough for James to grab his hair and Clune the back of his jacket. He went for the soldier at the other side of the pit. One of the man's arms looked to be in shreds, but with the other arm he kept grasping at the slippery mud, crying out for God to help him. His field helmet had been blown off and a constant stream of blood poured across his forehead.

Hill grabbed him, and the man screamed—sure that a new terror had come to murder him. Hysterical with fear, the wounded soldier tried to writhe out of Hill's grasp, sending Hill sprawling back against the dead body in the pool. The putrid water sucked the young recruit under.

"Hill!" James screamed. "I can't see him!" he called to Clune as he crawled frantically around the edge of the pit. "I can't see him!"

"Look!" Clune yelled, his face a disbelieving stare. He pointed at the wounded soldier. "His body's comin' up the side of the pit!"

Suddenly Hill's head broke the surface of the water, and they could see him pushing up against the man's backside.

"How's he doin' that?" Clune asked in wonder as he reached down to grab the soldier's jacket. James helped him pull the man away from death. They moved immediately to retrieve Hill, Clune holding onto James's legs as Hill grasped his coat sleeves. They pulled him out of the pit.

Brackish water poured out of Hill's nose and mouth, but he waved off assistance. "Go help them," he choked.

Clune and Lund went to check the wounded.

"This one's alive, but barely," Clune said, examining the first soldier they'd pulled out. "How about yours?" He didn't get an answer. "James?" He looked over to see James staring down at the unconscious man on the ground.

Hill crawled over. "I didn't get to him in time, did I?" he moaned, wiping slime out of his eyes and looking desperately at the wounded soldier. "He didn't make it."

James was leaning close over the body and wiping blood and mud gently off the face. "I know this man," he said with a sob. "He's . . . a friend from home." He took the soldier's hand. "Hold on, Daniel. Hold on. We'll get you to a doctor." James looked over at Hill in awe. "You saved him. You saved my friend."

14

"I'm afraid Dr. Robbins has no word for you on your friend's condition," the field assistant said frankly. "As you know, we've had a large number of casualties to deal with this morning."

James nodded. "Yes, of course . . . I was only hoping to . . . to see if he survived."

"I'm sorry, I can't say." With that the orderly moved back into the tent, leaving James alone.

He walked away from the stench of the infirmary; it was an odd mixture of boric acid, charred flesh, and blood that mingled to make his stomach turn. He was tired beyond measure, and he calculated he hadn't eaten in forty-eight hours.

Dr. Robbins is a brilliant surgeon, James told himself. *He'll see Daniel through.* His thoughts drifted back to 1913 and the Fourth of July picnic in Sutter Creek. It was the year Nephi Erickson came to work on their farm. Daniel and Nephi had been the star players in the Fourth of July baseball game. How young and carefree they'd all been.

The strength went out of James's legs, and he slumped to the ground by the side of the road.

"Hey, soldier, you all right?" the driver of an ammunition wagon called out to him.

"Just tired," James said flatly.

"Yeah, war is a hard business," the driver answered as the rig moved past.

James put his head in his hands. *A hard business.* Yes, that's what it was to the leaders in their offices—business and numbers. Just keep sending out men, a never-ending stream of bodies to be chewed up in war's meat grinder.

He was back on the farm in Sutter Creek. The apple trees were in blossom, and the green meadow was thick with lupine and buttercup. Lois Drakerman was riding her big plough horse on the top of the hill. She waved and was gone over the crest. Someone was whistling. He looked to the ridge of pines and saw his father walking toward him—the dark hair and green eyes and the easy motion of his lanky body.

"Private? Private Lund?"

James opened his eyes and blinked. *Where was he?* He focused on a patch of small blue cornflowers, and then on a pair of black boots. His head pounded as he sat up, groaning.

"Are you injured, Private Lund?"

He shook his head. "No, tired."

"Exhausted, I would say."

James looked up into the kindly, bearded face of Dr. Robbins.

"What are you doing here?" James asked slowly.

"Well," Dr. Robbins replied, "my orderly was worried when he couldn't wake you."

James silently chided himself. "I'm sorry, sir. You're far too busy to be playing nursemaid to me." He tried to stand but flopped back.

"Here, let me help you," Dr. Robbins said kindly as he placed a strong arm around James's waist and lifted.

James felt like a little boy, being lifted so easily, and he wondered if it were merely because Dr. Robbins was so strong or because he'd lost so much weight over the past months.

Dr. Robbins watched him carefully. "Now, do you want to go to the cook station for some food or to see your friend?"

James focused his attention. "He's alive?"

"He is," Dr. Robbins said without smiling.

"But?" James asked warily, a feeling of dread settling in his chest.

Dr. Robbins began walking to the holding tent. "He has multiple injuries." James followed silently. "The Germans wanted to soften the line, so they sent a barrage over. His unit was caught out in front of the first trench. Somehow one of the German flame throwers got through to them." James's stomach churned. "He has a bad burn on his neck and the side of his face. We're not sure if we can save his ear."

James nodded, trying to keep the bile out of his mouth.

"We removed a piece of shrapnel from his head and stitched the wound. He should have no trouble with that, but . . ." He stopped walking. "I think he took the full brunt of the shell blast in his left arm. I believe he raised it instinctively to protect his face."

James's gut twisted. "Did he lose his arm?"

Dr. Robbins put his hand on James's shoulder. "No. I was able to save it, for now. The breaks will mend, but there's extensive ligament and tendon damage. And of course infection is always a dire problem. Gas gangrene— infection from the filth—nasty business. We'll watch it carefully until we ship him off to the main hospital in Arras." He started walking again. "You all right, then?"

James swallowed. "Yes, sir."

"I normally don't give out that much information, James, but I figure you've seen a lot in your time here. I wanted you to know so you could help your friend."

James nodded. "Yes, sir."

"I think he's going to have a rough time of it."

"I understand." They reached the hospital tent. "Thank you for saving his life, sir."

Dr. Robbins lowered his head, and then looked up at James with a gentle expression. "It's not me, James. God is over all."

James stepped back. "God is . . ."—his voice broke—"over all? Surely you can't believe that after all you've seen."

The big man nodded. "Especially after all I've seen." He looked at James kindly. "Miracles, James . . . miracles of young men living where there shouldn't have been a hope . . . miracles of young men dying and calling out to loved ones that have died before."

James shook his head. "But, that's just shock or the morphine."

"Is it? I'm a doctor, yet you'll never convince me of that. You've seen it too, James, even men who die frightened and in pain. Once death takes them, there's a peace surrounding the men."

James pulled his mind to those who'd died in his arms, and he knew exactly what Dr. Robbins was talking about. Death was more than just the stopping of their moans or screams; it was a quiet, reverent moment.

"God is over all," Dr. Robbins said again.

James nodded, still not convinced, but comforted.

Dr. Robbins patted him on the back. "Now, let's go see your friend."

* * *

Dr. Robbins left James at Daniel's cot and moved off to check on other patients. Daniel was a mass of bandages—head, face, arm. Blood was oozing through the wrappings in a couple of places, and James found himself looking down at his boots. A British Red Cross nurse brought him a stool, and he sat down. He was grateful, for his legs were shaking. She returned a few minutes later with a cup of water and a slice of dark bread.

"Dr. Robbins said you might be 'ungry."

James smiled at her. "Thanks." Before she left, he asked, "Do you think he'll be awake soon?"

"It's 'ard to say," she said softly. " 'E's been in and out a couple a times." She patted James's shoulder and left.

James ate the bread. It had a wonderful flavor, but he found it hard to swallow. Something was constricting his throat. He forced down a bite as he looked around at the rows of cots. He, Clune, and Hill had brought in a lot of these men. He watched as the nurse pulled the sheet over the face of one of the soldiers—he looked away quickly to find that Daniel had his eyes open. He leaned forward.

"Daniel?"

Daniel Chart looked at him without recognition.

"Daniel, it's me, James Lund from Sutter Creek."

"Sutter . . ." The word came out a harsh whisper. Daniel groaned and his right arm flailed about. He started yelling.

James called out, "Nurse! Nurse, something's wrong!"

She came over quickly and took Daniel's arm, holding it firmly against the bed. "It's all right, sir," she said to James, "He's just comin' out of the morphine. I expect he'll be needin' more." She nodded to an orderly, who brought over a syringe. The nurse administered the drug, and James watched as the taut fear that had clamped itself onto Daniel's features began to ease.

She leaned close to Daniel's ear. "Would you like a little water?" she asked softly.

Daniel nodded.

"He can have mine," James said, holding the cup out to her.

"Well, that's right nice of ya," the nurse said, smiling. "Why don't you give it to 'im yourself? I'll bring more when I get a minute."

James nodded. "How do I . . . ?"

"Just put your 'and carefully behind 'is 'ead and lift 'im up a bit. Not too much, just a bit." She gave him a nod and left.

James followed her instructions and gave his friend a drink of water.

Daniel opened his eyes halfway and stared.

"Hey friend, it's me—James. James Lund."

Daniel frowned slightly. "Sutter Creek?" he whispered. James nodded as Daniel struggled to speak. "How . . . how did . . . get here?"

"Me? On a boat, same as you," James said, trying to lessen the tightness in his chest.

Daniel was finding it difficult to process the information—his brown eyes tried to find focus.

James took his hand. "Why don't you just rest, and I'll sit here with you awhile."

Daniel's eyes closed. "Am I shot?"

"Let's not talk about that right now. You just rest and I'll tell you stories about Eleanor and Alaina."

Daniel's eyes opened a slit. "Eleanor . . . here?"

James patted his hand. "No, she's living in Salt Lake City now, remember?"

Daniel mumbled something, but James couldn't make it out.

"She's going to medical school, if you can believe that."

"Sunshine," Daniel said softly.

"Sunshine?" James asked, leaning closer.

"Eleanor . . . sunshine," Daniel murmured.

James watched as he drifted away into a deep sleep.

The nurse was at his side with more water. "Did 'e recognize you?" she asked, handing him the cup.

James drank the water down. "I don't know. He seemed to know my sister's name."

"Well, sleep's the best thing for 'im. I expect 'e'll come more to 'imself later on."

"I like your accent," James said.

"Whot? Cockney?" she asked in a shocked voice. "I'll 'ave you know it's the grand standard speech of England. Talk about accents, blimey! American's about as strange as it gets."

James laughed, and a couple of the soldiers in the beds nearby laughed, too.

"Ah . . . now we've gone and done it," she said, looking around her. "They'll be up singin' and dancin' next."

The soldiers smiled.

James stood. "Well, I'd better get back to my unit. I'll come again tomorrow if I can." He held out his hand to the nurse. "Thank you for all you do, Miss . . ."

She took his hand. "Vieites. Miss Anita Vieites."

"Miss Vieites." He looked again at Daniel then turned and left the tent. As he walked the mile back to his unit, the gentle evening breezes of spring ruffled his hair. He found it odd that five miles behind this sad and blasted piece of earth there were quaint French villages still peopled with bakers, pharmacists, and café owners; marriages were taking place and babies were being born. There were farms where alfalfa, corn, and barley were being planted. Because of the war, everyone knew that life was tenuous—that they might have to leave place and possessions in an instant, yet they carried on with determination and even some gaiety.

The storm had momentarily cleaned the air of the stench of death, and James breathed deeply. Spring was coming on, and for the moment, gunfire and shell blasts were in the distance. James yearned for a time when they'd never start up again.

The lavender sky turned azure at the horizon, and the first pale stars appeared. He thought about writing a letter to Daniel's parents to let them know about their son's condition. He saw Daniel lying in the bleak field hospital with a gruesome burn on his handsome face and his arm shredded. James shook his head. He would wait. He would wait until there was something secure to tell them.

15

"Well, it's a good thing the Boche seem to want a slack afternoon," Jimmy Gordon announced to his buddies in the trench, "because I've certainly gotta take care of a little personal hygiene." He pulled his shirt from his pants and began scratching around the waistband. "Miserable little devils." He secured one of the lice and squeezed it efficiently between his fingernails. "Huh! Take that, Mata Hari."

Cornell Duncan laughed. "Another Mata Hari? You killed about twelve of her yesterday."

Jimmy killed another. "Kaiser Wilhelm then."

Cornell shook his head. "You've killed him off, too."

"General Ludendorff!" Jimmy said triumphantly.

"Most likely you're killing off Mata Hari's children and grandchildren."

"And good riddance to 'em."

Cornell laughed. "We get our two days off tomorrow. You can go over to the delousing station."

"Yeah, and the minute I get back into the trench they'll be on me again. If that fellow at the recruiting station had told me about these little critters, I would have thought twice about signing up."

RJ McLaughlin looked up from his food. "What I can't stand is them rats. Some are the siz'a little dogs. And they ain't got no fear. I woke up the other night and one was gettin' into the pocket of my jacket lookin' fer food, and my jacket was on me!" He shoved a spoonful of tinned meat into his mouth.

Jimmy shuddered. "RJ, how can you eat that monkey meat?"

RJ looked over at him. "This? It ain't half bad."

"No, it's *all* bad," Jimmy argued. "You might as well be eating rat stew."

"Hey, that's an idea!" RJ said, laughing. "Next time I shoot a couple, we'll take 'em back to the cook station and have 'em cooked up."

The men laughed.

"Better us eating them, than them eating us," Nephi said, looking up from his letter writing.

"That's a fact," Jimmy said with disgust. "Did you notice after the last barrage how they cleared out of the trenches? Yeah, they were all out in the new shell craters looking for supper."

It was obvious Cornell had had enough rat talk. "So, Erickson, are you writing to your wife?"

Nephi smiled. "Done that already. This one's to my brother Elias."

"You are one good letter writer," RJ said with admiration. "My mama gets a letter maybe once a month."

Jimmy mimed writing a letter. "Dear Elias, having a wonderful time with the rats, and lice, and dysentery, and mud, and stench. Wish you were here."

Nephi laughed at his buddy's antics, but his stomach churned. He did tell his brother about many aspects of the war that he couldn't tell Alaina. He tapped his pencil on the paper, thinking back to all the times he and Elias had talked about joining together, about the test of combat and the glory of victory. It was nothing like that. It was . . .

"So," Cornell's voice interrupted his mental wanderings, "what are you writing about, if you don't mind my asking?"

Nephi looked over at him. "Not a bit. I was just telling him about those tanks we saw the other night."

"Man, they were something!" Jimmy broke in. "If I were a German and saw one of those things coming at me, I'd run my tail back to Berlin crying 'Mama' all the way."

"I like them big metal track things they have 'stead of wheels," RJ said, nodding.

"Caterpillars. Yeah!" Jimmy answered with enthusiasm. "Those things will roll over anything—craters, barbed wire, German soldiers." He and RJ laughed.

"I sure don't know why they call 'em tanks, though," RJ said. "I'd call 'em somethin' like metal monsters."

"Espionage," Cornell said.

RJ looked at him. "Huh?"

"It means spy stuff," Jimmy clarified.

RJ shrugged, still not understanding.

"The Brits wanted to keep their manufacture top secret," Cornell explained, "even from the factory workers."

RJ scoffed. "Now how'd they do that?"

"They told them they were making moving water carriers—water tanks— for the part of the war going on in the Turkish desert. Well, the workers started calling them tanks, and the name stuck."

RJ guffawed. "Ah heck, Cornell Duncan, you and yer big brain jest made that up!"

Cornell looked offended. "I did not."

"Yes, you did," RJ persisted. "How ya gonna know about somethin' like that lessen you made it up?"

"I spoke to one of the tank mechanics as they were passing through."

RJ looked at him with a frown. "You did not. When?"

Nephi and Jimmy were getting a kick out of this exchange.

"The night they passed through. Remember when I was back at the dressing station getting medicine? The British corporal was in getting salt tablets or something for his men."

"I'll bet," Jimmy broke in. "Those metal boxes must be hot as Hades inside."

"Anyway," Cornell continued, "I started talking to this mechanic, asking questions about the tanks, and he told me."

RJ narrowed his eyes. "You sure yer not jest pullin' my leg, Cornell?"

Cornell crossed his heart. "I am telling you the absolute truth."

RJ's face broke into a wide grin and he chuckled. "That's a good one, Cornell. Water tanks. I'm gonna have to write my mama about that one."

Nephi stood, shoving the unfinished letter into his pocket. "I hear aeroplanes . . . coming from the German side."

Seconds later the command came down for all to be "at the ready," and the soldiers scurried into the small niches carved into the side of the trench. The buzz of aircraft engines increased overhead, as well as the rumble of guns from behind as anti-aircraft artillery started firing. A strafing of bullets slammed into the opposite side of the trench, showering the Americans with dirt and bits of wood.

"I'd like to get my hands on the guy who figured out how to get machine guns to work on aeroplanes!" Gordon yelled.

Another strafing of bullets came through. Nephi knew that the main focus of the German pilots were the artillery gunners—to keep them pinned down and scrambling, unable to shoot down the reconnaissance planes. The soldiers hated the reconnaissance planes, as once they got back to their German comrades with sightings and positions, the big guns would lock in and start pounding—pounding and pounding.

Nephi's hands clenched and unclenched on his rifle as he mumbled to himself in a harsh whisper, "Please God, please have our aircraft come quickly. Please." He hated the shelling. To die from a bullet seemed nothing—part of the person remained intact—but to be dismembered or blasted into pulp . . . When the barrage started you never knew . . . you just never knew when a big 9.2 shell would slam in on top of you, smashing you to jelly. What good were identification tags then? Nephi started to laugh bitterly, then checked himself. *Enough of that. Get ahold of yourself, Erickson. You have a job to do. You don't see Jimmy, or RJ, or Cornell coming apart at the seams.* "Dear Lord, please don't let me get blown up."

The few weeks they'd been in the trenches seemed like forever. Forever in a dark nightmare. One night he and his three buddies were returning to their front positions after a day break. They'd taken a wrong turn in the miles of complicated trench lines and ended up in a British unit's area. One side of the Tommies' trench had been blown out by a shell, the earth churned up, exposing a previously buried soldier's arm. The Tommies had hung several of their gas masks on the stiff appendage. Nephi shuddered at the memory and pressed himself against the back of the niche. He knew they'd done it just as a way to survive the grisly horror that surrounded them. Just like Jimmy and RJ talking about the rats. *Think of something else—anything else.* Suddenly a picture of Alaina jumped unbidden into his mind. Alaina standing in the moonlight in the back pasture, wearing his work coat and telling him that she loved him. He groaned. *Not that . . . Don't think of that.*

"Erickson!" Cornell called out. "You okay? Are you hit?"

"No, no." Nephi shot back, annoyed at himself. "I've . . . just got a cramp in my leg."

Gordon hooted. "A cramp? Come on Erickson, buck up. You're a soldier, not a ballerina."

"Shut up, Gordon!" Nephi said with a laugh.

"Or what?"

"Or I'll come over there and give *you* a cramp."

"Yeah? You and what German army?"

"Wait! Hear that?" Nephi yelled suddenly.

"What?" Cornell questioned, his voice fearful.

"Our planes have engaged. It's a dog fight!" He looked up to see a German Fokker looping low and sideways to avoid the gunfire of a French Spad.

"Yahoo!" Gordon yelled. "Look at 'em go! Hey! What d'ya think? Maybe it's Rickenbacker . . . greatest American pilot ever. I'm gonna name my first son after him."

The men laughed, and Nephi felt his mind calm and the trembling in his hands retreat. He'd get through this . . . he had to. He had a wife and daughter waiting at home. He had to get through.

* * *

They waited hours for the heavy barrage that never came. There was shelling up and down the line, but Nephi was becoming aware that such a sound never ceased. It was odd the things he listened for now. Not people's voices in the kitchen, but the direction and distance of machine-gun fire; not Miss Titus's whinny in the back pasture, but the siren sound that warned of poison gas coming over; not his daughter's giggles, but the whine of different caliber shells just before they smashed into the ground.

Nephi looked down the line and noticed men extricating themselves from their shallow dirt cupboards and stretching out their backs, legs, and arms as much as possible. He followed suit. He took a drink from his canteen and looked over at the lowering May sun. White clouds with pale pink underbellies hung on the horizon in front of a glorious blue sky. Nephi quickly took out his pocket journal and stubby pencil, sketching the transient scene with deftness and longing. *I'll give it color when I get home.*

"Hey, Erickson!" Jimmy called to him. "If you're not too busy, the lieutenant would like a minute of your time."

Nephi looked over to see a cluster of men standing around their commanding officer, and he quickly moved to join them, saluting the officer as he approached. Lieutenant Edwards was in his mid-thirties but had the eyes of a hardened veteran. The hair under his helmet was black and cropped short, and he always had a rough stubble of beard as though no razor could subdue it.

"Grub and munitions are coming up on the light rails," he barked without preamble. "You ten will bring it up." He nodded to the group. "Tonight, pack your belts with ammunition and grenades. Check and clean your rifles. At dawn tomorrow we're going over the top."

Nephi glanced over to see Cornell's face, but he was at the back of the pack, and his face was hidden.

"Many of you are as green as they come. Nothing wrong with that if you'll keep your heads and follow orders. You'll be feeling like you want to jump out of your skin, but that's normal. Every soldier feels that way before going over, and if they say they don't—they're liars."

The men chuckled at this and the tension dissipated.

"Now, our artillery boys will soften things up to begin with, then we'll bring on the tanks."

"Tanks?" Jimmy blurted out excitedly.

"Yes, Gordon, tanks, and if you're not more quiet about it, I'll shoot you for giving secrets away to the enemy," the lieutenant growled.

Jimmy lowered his head, grinning sheepishly. "Sorry, sir."

"You are to follow the tanks as they plow forward. It will be slow going, but trust me, let the tanks take the brunt of it. No glory runs. Got it?"

The men nodded.

"Our objective, sir?" It was Cornell's voice.

The lieutenant looked over. "Duncan, isn't it?'

"Yes, sir."

"Well, Duncan, a thousand yards in that direction," Edwards pointed across no-man's-land to the German line, "is a bombed-out little village called Cantigny. The Germans have it, and we marines are gonna take it back."

The men all smiled and stood straighter.

Lieutenant Edwards gave them a stern look. "Once the push begins you're gonna feel bigger than life . . . like nothing can get you. You gotta keep that under control, or you'll end up doing something stupid that'll most likely get you—or worse, one of us—killed."

The men nodded, then looked at each other with commitment.

"Now, are there any other questions?"

"Will we get breakfast, sir?"

It was RJ.

The lieutenant grinned as he looked over at RJ's boyish face and large physique. "Well son, I think you'd better have two breakfasts."

RJ smiled and Jimmy thumped him on the chest.

The lieutenant became grim as he looked around at the group. "Seriously, you will have to eat something even if you don't feel like it. And make sure your canteens are full . . . with water, not that cheap red wine you guys somehow get your hands on. You drink that and go into battle, it's gonna sour in your stomach, then you'll be out there puking instead of fighting. Got it?" They all nodded. He saluted, and they saluted back. "I have every confidence in you, men. Now, go get that stuff."

* * *

"Erickson?"

It was Cornell Duncan's voice in a harsh whisper.

"Yeah?" Nephi answered, turning to look at his friend. He was kneeling on the parapet at the front of the trench, peering carefully through a cranny at the top of the pile of sandbags as Cornell approached.

Cornell joined him. "Can you actually see anything from there?" he asked in a strained tone.

Nephi turned and sat down. "I thought if the light came early, or maybe if flares went up, I could get a little better idea of the lay of the land."

Cornell nodded. "I couldn't sleep either." There was a pause. "So . . . have you ever killed anyone?"

Nephi started. "Are you joking?" He had to force his voice to a whisper.

"I guess I should have said *anything*. Have you ever killed anything?"

Nephi took a breath. "Yeah . . . mice, rats, that sort of thing. Elias and I took Grandfather's rifle and shot rabbits once."

Cornell nodded. "I went pheasant hunting with my father. I don't suppose this is going to be anything like pheasant hunting."

Nephi shook his head.

"You're married, right?" Cornell asked suddenly.

Nephi took a breath. "I am."

"Her name's Elaine?"

"Alaina," Nephi corrected.

"Oh, that's right. Pretty name. And you have a daughter?"

"Katie," Nephi said, smiling. "She's three. Had her birthday just before I left. Quite a handful."

"And a brother, right?" Cornell asked.

Nephi nodded. "Elias. And you have two brothers?"

"Three brothers and two sisters," Cornell offered, talking to keep himself from thinking. "Me and my brothers are named after universities. My oldest brother is Yale, then me, then Cam . . . that's short for Cambridge, and my little brother, Stanford."

Nephi smiled at his friend. "Good thing there's not an Oxford."

Cornell smiled too. "Yeah, we'd call him Ox for short. And my sisters are named after flowers . . . Daisy and Violet."

"Quite a family," Nephi said. "I'd like to meet them."

Cornell dug in his pocket and pulled out a picture showing a crowd of smiling, good-looking folks. "Here they are," Cornell said proudly, shoving the photograph at Nephi. He pointed out each person and told a story about them as he did so.

They heard shell blasts in the distance and stopped talking. They were silent for several minutes, then Cornell said. "I wonder what time it is?"

"I'd tell ya," Nephi answered, "but, I can't see my wristwatch."

"That's a nice one, by the way," Cornell said.

"My brother gave it to me."

"Nice. Much more practical than a pocket watch."

Nephi nodded. "Much."

Cornell held out his hand. "Good luck today, Erickson."

Nephi took it. "You too, Duncan."

Cornell sighed. "I hope the four of us can stick together. I feel better when I'm around you guys."

"Me too," Nephi admitted.

Cornell cleared his throat. "And I suppose you've said your prayers this morning?"

Nephi nodded. "I think I've been praying nonstop since the lieutenant gave us the news."

"Well, that's good, but . . ." He hesitated.

"What?" Nephi asked.

"I suppose the Germans are praying, too. So, who's God going to answer?"

"Hmm." Nephi nodded. "Well, I'm not praying that they die. I'm just praying for peace and a way out of this mess. Praying that not too many get killed today."

"That's nice of you." Cornell swallowed. "And the ones that do?"

"That they won't suffer much and they'll go straight home to God." Nephi looked over at Cornell. "Sounds naive, I know."

Cornell shook his head. "It doesn't. It really doesn't."

A huge blast shattered the morning as the Allied barrage began. RJ and Jimmy came scrambling out of the bunker as Cornell and Nephi secured their helmets and threw on their ammunition belts.

"Man, oh man!" Jimmy yelled. "Listen to that, will ya? We're letting them have it full force!"

The shells were going overhead in a screeching yowl that didn't stop. The sound was deafening, and the ground boiled and heaved with the explosions. Nephi gritted his teeth and tried not to think of the poor German boys on the receiving end of the fire.

The four friends sat in the bottom of their trench trying to choke down bread and dried apples, waiting for the call to go over the top. When they heard the rumbling advance of the tanks, they knew the moment was inevitable.

"Hey, RJ!" Jimmy yelled to be heard above the noise. "You stick close to me!"

"Yes, sir," RJ answered with a smile. "Don't worry, I'll be there to save your sorry skin."

Jimmy hooted.

The four friends looked at each other, then stood as one to await the command. It came quickly up and down the line, and hundreds of men poured screaming out of the trenches. The rolling barrage in front of the tanks was blasting everything into bits—trees, stones, timber, equipment, and bodies all smashed up and whirling around with the dirt and smoke.

Nephi couldn't see anything much beyond ten feet in front of the tank. His heart was hammering in his chest, and he kept looking over at the crushing metal tracks of the tanks. How would it be to have one of those roll over you? Your arms and legs would snap like twigs and your head would smash like a melon. *Stop! Keep your mind on what you're doing.* He looked over at Cornell, whose eyes were fixed ahead as he held his rifle exactly how they'd been instructed at training camp. All the soldiers in the line were advancing thus, and it seemed that none were going down, breaking ranks, or running. Nephi felt a surge of confidence. *One thousand yards,* Lieutenant Edwards had said. *Only one thousand yards.* How far had they covered? The smoke was clearing as the barrage slowed, and Nephi saw gray shapes running toward their line. He raised his rifle and saw Cornell do the same, but the order was called not to fire. As the bodies neared, Nephi could see that they were indeed German soldiers, arms raised high in the air, running to surrender. As they passed through the Allied line to be taken by the military police, Nephi saw terror and exhaustion etched on their faces.

The tanks moved on—climbing in and out of shell craters, grinding over fallen trees, and chewing through barbed wire—and the green American soldiers followed along unflinchingly with their fellows. Shortly the bombardment stopped and the smoke cleared. Nephi saw that they were at the edge of the village, and there was no resistance, not even sniper fire. The ruined town was deserted. Had they routed the enemy? Had they taken Cantigny with only a few Allied casualties?

A cheer went up and Lieutenant Edwards barked at his unit to stand firm. "We've not won it yet, boys. You can bet the Boche are gonna give us some of our own back. Now, let's get into that town and secure it."

Jimmy and RJ joined up with Cornell and Nephi as they followed their commanding officer into Cantigny.

"Boy, our lieutenant's one hard man to please," Jimmy said with a snort. "Hand him Ludendorff on a platter and he'd say, 'Fine, but where's the kaiser?'"

The friends laughed quietly so as not to draw attention to themselves, but Nephi could tell that they all felt heartened, having made it through their first battle safely. He knew the war was far from over and that there'd be much more to face, but the rapid win and lack of carnage did much to bolster his nerve.

Cornell dropped back to walk with him. "Hey, Erickson," he said, patting him on the back. "Seems like your prayer for this battle was answered. How about praying for the kaiser to kick the bucket, and the Germans to just give up and go home?"

Nephi smiled over at him as they hefted their rifles and moved in to secure the village.

16

"Peach-pit Saturday!" Mother Erickson called as she came in from feeding the chickens.

Alaina smiled at her exuberance, putting away the last of the morning mending and standing to take off her apron.

Mother Erickson entered from the back porch. She gave Alaina a warm smile and moved to the sink to wash her hands. "What a lovely May morning, and your Miss Titus certainly has become a beauty. Such a spunky personality."

Thoughts of Miss Titus took Alaina back to the California farm on that cold November day when her friend, Joanna Wilton, had presented her with the treasured filly. It was Joanna's parting gift just prior to Alaina and Nephi's departure to Salt Lake City. She had not seen her childhood friend since and wondered how she was doing.

Alaina ran her hand over her protruding abdomen. Here she was five months along on her second baby, and Joanna was married to Jim Peterson. How was that possible? Wasn't it yesterday that she and Joanna were whispering secrets to each other behind their teacher's back, or trying to sit quiet in church as Joanna's father preached? And she was sure it was just a day or two ago that she and her sister Eleanor were running up to the small waterfall—that they privately called Niagara Falls—to share secrets and stories.

Mother Erickson turned from the sink, fixing her daughter-in-law with an astute look. She often caught Alaina daydreaming, especially now with Nephi off to war and their baby due in four months. Sometimes Alaina's face showed worry or distress, but today the look was reflective.

"Alaina?" Mother Erickson said softly. "Are you all right?"

Alaina looked over and smiled. "Yes, ma'am. Just thinking about Joanna Wilton."

"From what you've told me, she sounds like a dandy girl. I hope to meet her someday."

Alaina folded her apron and put it into the drawer. "I'd love for you to meet her, and Philomene Johnson, and Fredrick and Edna Robinson and their son Daniel."

Mother Erickson nodded. "Daniel Chart?"

"Yes, ma'am."

"Isn't he another one of our boys in the war?"

Alaina put the mending basket away. "He is. He sent that letter a month or two ago from the training camp. He should be in France by now."

Mother Erickson headed for the pantry. "So many good young men offering so much . . ." She disappeared into the depths of the cupboard, calling out from inside. "What do you say we go and do our part?" She emerged from the pantry dragging two fifteen-pound gunnysacks of peach pits, and Alaina moved to help her.

"Ah! No such thing," Mother Erickson warned, "you will not be lugging around peach pits in your condition. Do you think I want my grandchild coming into the world with muscles?"

Alaina laughed.

"No. We'll leave these for Elias to tote when he comes to pick us up." She set the sacks by the pantry door. "That's all we have left from last year's harvest. Guess we'll have to start gatherin' again."

I really hope we *don't* have to gather anymore," Alaina said, an edge to her voice. "I don't want the government to have to make more gas masks."

Mother Erickson nodded. "Well, you certainly do have a point there, little muffin. No more need for such dreadful equipment would be a blessing." She kicked the bag of peach pits. "Never understood how they made gas masks out of these things anyway."

Alaina shook her head. "I've never understood much about science of any kind. Now, I bet we could ask Eleanor, and she'd know all about it."

Mother Erickson headed for her bedroom. "Isn't that the truth? That sister of yours is as bright as they come. I'm just gonna get my hat and coat so I'll be ready when Elias and Sarah get here."

At that very moment they heard the hardware truck pull up in front of the house.

"Oh, my!" Mother Erickson said, hurrying toward the bedroom. "Tell 'em I'll be out in a minute."

Alaina put on her light coat and moved to the front door. Just as she put her hand on the doorknob, the door opened and Sarah came bursting into the room. "Oh! Alaina, sorry! Did I bump you?"

Alaina shook her head. "No. No, I'm fine. Mother Erickson will be ready in a minute. Elias can come get the sacks. They're back in the kitchen."

Sarah grinned openly, and Alaina stared at her for a moment. An open grin was not a usual expression for her sister-in-law. Sarah was retiring and normally covered any smile with her hand.

"What are you grinning about?" Alaina asked suspiciously.

Sarah brushed strands of mousey brown hair away from her face. "Elias can't get the sacks because he's not with me."

Alaina blinked. "But, I heard the hardware truck."

Sarah grinned again. "I know. I'm driving." Alaina was so surprised her mouth dropped open, and Sarah laughed.

"You're—you're driving?" Alaina stammered.

"I am," Sarah answered brightly, a note of pride in her voice. "Elias had to help Father Erickson unload a big shipment at the hardware store, so he said I should drive us to the meeting."

"Can you drive?" Alaina questioned.

"I can," Sarah said assuredly. "I love to drive."

"I've never seen you," Alaina countered, still unable to accept this occurrence, which seemed so unlikely considering Sarah's personality.

"No one knows except Elias," Sarah said. "He taught me, and I just drive around our property."

Alaina shook her head in disbelief. "And today?"

"Well, he couldn't get out of work, so he said I could take over." Sarah beamed. "Elias says I'm a very good driver."

"And driving downtown with other automobiles?" Alaina pressed.

Mother Erickson came into the room and smiled at Sarah. "Where's Elias?"

"Not here," Sarah announced.

"Not here?" Mother Erickson asked.

"Sarah's driving us," Alaina reported, waiting for her mother-in-law's reaction.

"Sarah?" Mother Erickson looked at the normally shy young woman with an unreadable expression. "Dandy!" she said with a chuckle, giving Sarah a one-armed hug. "Let's load up!"

Sarah and Mother Erickson took the gunnysacks and hefted them into the back of the truck.

"Oh, my goodness!" Mother Erickson chirped just as Sarah was ready to put the truck into gear. "Wait a minute!" She jumped out of the vehicle, moving quickly toward the house.

"What? Did you change your mind about my driving?" Sarah called after her good-naturedly.

"No. I forgot the dress I finished for Emmaline Wells. She'll be at the meeting and I want to give it to her."

The two young women chuckled lovingly at Mother Erickson's fast-paced waddle.

"She is the dearest person," Alaina said, watching her mother-in-law disappear into the house.

"She is," Sarah agreed. "Too bad she's the second wife. I often get the feeling that Father Erickson would rather be with Patience instead of Eunice."

"Sarah!" Alaina was shocked by Sarah's candid words. "You . . . you are making my head spin today. First driving, and now . . . blunt honesty?"

Sarah smiled over at her. "Oh, it's only my own puny observation. I may be wrong," Sarah said dismissively.

But Alaina could tell by her expression that she didn't think herself wrong. Alaina had never seen Sarah like this. What had happened to make her so much more assured and open?

Mother Erickson returned, put the box into the back of the truck, and climbed in. "Off we go, Miss Sarah."

Sarah put the truck into gear and drove smoothly out of the driveway.

Mother Erickson rolled down the window and waved at Mrs. Stewart as they passed. "Hello, Myrtle! My daughter-in-law Sarah is driving. Whatd'ya think of that?"

* * *

The meeting of Relief Society sisters was heralded a success as one thousand pounds of peach pits were collected for the war effort, and a report was made on the continued increase in the wheat amounts being stored by the General Relief Society for emergency relief. Alaina and Sarah helped other sisters in quilting coverlets for wounded soldiers recovering at Holy Cross, LDS, and St. Mark's hospitals, while Patience Erickson visited with Emmaline Wells.

Sister Hudson, a woman Alaina had met once at church, was critically scrutinizing every stitch that she and Sarah made, and Alaina's irritation began to boil at the sister's superior attitude. *How dare she look down her nose at our charitable efforts*, Alaina thought hotly. *We're trying to give our best effort for our fighting men, and that certainly should be good enough for the old hen.* Her temper flared as she thought about her precious husband fighting in France.

"And where is your little one today?" Sister Hudson asked Sarah in an accusing tone.

Alaina's attention snapped back to the quilt, and she looked down at the sharp needle in her hand.

"With his Aunt Eleanor," Sarah said simply.

The woman's look was disapproving. "Oh, yes. Isn't that the young woman who's studying?"

"Yes," Sarah answered quickly, cutting off Alaina's angry response. "Yes. One of the few women accepted into medical school. Eleanor is absolutely amazing."

Mrs. Hudson pursed her lips. "Well, if you ask me, it's a waste of time for women to study, unless of course there's no prospect of marriage for them."

Alaina stood up. Sarah put a hand on her arm but knew the gesture of appeasement was futile.

"You don't know what you're talking about," Alaina said in a biting whisper.

Mrs. Hudson blinked at her in shock.

"How . . ." Alaina's voice now had volume. "How dare you sit there smugly passing judgment on a person and situation you know nothing about?"

Mother Erickson was by Alaina's side in an instant. "Hello, Sister Hudson. What a beautiful quilt you're doing."

Alaina had a head of steam going and would not be deterred. "It's my sister you're talking about, by the way, and she could be a doctor, take care of a family, and run circles around you ten times over . . . you . . . you mean-spirited old cow."

Mother Erickson put an arm around Alaina's waist and moved her away from the quilt frame. "Well, ladies, keep up the good work. We're just going out for a bit of air."

The women in the room watched the retreating pair with varied reactions ranging from amusement to offense.

Out on the sidewalk of East Temple, Alaina broke away from Mother Erickson. "Ooh! The old cow!" She paced up and down, her hands clenching and unclenching. "The narrow-minded, judgmental old cow!"

People on the street turned to look at her.

"Alaina," Mother Erickson said softly, "let's walk over to the temple grounds. I need a little stroll."

Alaina abruptly stopped pacing. "Are you all right?"

Mother Erickson grinned. "Hmm . . . just a little stiff. You don't mind walking with me, do you?"

Alaina took her arm. "Of course not."

The two women crossed the street and walked into the stillness of Temple Square, where they were greeted by serenity and a profusion of flowers. Alaina took a deep breath, and Mother Erickson watched as the angry expression on her face slid away. They walked for a long time in silence, enjoying each other's company and the peaceful surroundings. Finally Alaina stopped and looked up at the temple.

"I don't know what gets into me sometimes," she said with remorse. "I seem to get so emotional every time I'm going to have a baby."

"It's not uncommon," Mother Erickson said, patting her hand.

Alaina shuffled her feet. "I know, but it's no excuse for bad manners."

Patience Erickson nodded. "Well, that's plain truth. Although Martha Hudson's sharp tongue can try the patience of any saint."

"I just don't see why there are people like that in the Church," Alaina said harshly.

Mother Erickson looked at her straight on. "You might as well be wondering why there are people like that in the *world*. Havin' a testimony of the Savior, or the Prophet Joseph Smith, or the Book of Mormon isn't enough in itself to change somebody's ornery nature."

"Like mine," Alaina said, dropping her eyes.

"You are a sweetheart," Mother Erickson corrected.

"Who just yelled at a sister in the middle of a Relief Society gathering," Alaina countered.

Mother Erickson chuckled. "Well, that was just temporary bad nature."

Alaina shook her head. "Temporary? I don't know about that. I've always been stubborn and quick to temper. I fight against my faith, and tithing, and going to church." Her voice grew thick with emotion. "I make excuses for all my weaknesses."

Mother Erickson patted her back. "You have much to worry about right now."

Alaina sat down on a stone bench and started crying. Mother Erickson sat down beside her.

"I miss him so much," Alaina sobbed, trying to get her voice under control.

Mother Erickson handed her a handkerchief. "Oh, you dear little muffin," she whispered, her voice husky.

"And I was distant and cold when he left because I was so afraid . . . and I was angry because he was leaving me alone when I was carrying our baby." She put her head in her hands. "And what if he never comes back? What if . . . ?"

"Can't go thinkin' down that path," Mother Erickson cautioned gently. "We just have to have faith that God is in charge."

Alaina took in a sharp breath. "I don't have faith." She stood. "I don't, Mother Erickson. I think God's there, but I don't know if He actually takes care of things."

Mother Erickson was quiet for a long time. Finally, Alaina looked over at her and found her looking up at the temple.

Patience Erickson sighed and smiled kindly at her daughter-in-law. "You have to find out, little muffin. You have to put some effort into finding your Savior and what He means to you. You won't know peace until you do that."

Alaina put her head into her hands and wept again. She loved Mother Erickson and was aware that compassion and concern wrapped itself around every word of the admonition. *Peace.* Oh, how she longed for that. *Dear Lord,* she prayed silently, *help me to fight my pride and stubbornness and to find my way to You. I am so afraid.* She felt fear and loneliness like a knife-point in her heart, and she wanted it to stop. "I just need him to come home to us."

Mother Erickson patted her back. "Maybe it's time to write him about the baby. Maybe you've been carrying around the burden of that secret for too long."

Alaina looked up at the temple again and nodded.

17

"I like it," Shawn Burbage said with conviction as he stood looking intently at a painting in the student art exhibit. "At least I think I do. What's it called?"

Eleanor grinned and looked down at the gallery brochure. "Evening on the Lake."

"And the style the student was trying to copy?"

"Impressionism."

"Ah," Shawn said, rocking back on his heels. "Of course, Impressionism."

Eleanor laughed at his antics and was promptly shushed by one of the docents.

"Oops," she whispered. "I guess I'm disturbing the paintings."

They moved into another room filled with portraits that demonstrated varying degrees of artistic competence. They admired the skill of several of the student artists and wondered at the work of one poor fellow who seemed to have little, if any, talent. They debated the merits of the piece—Eleanor suggesting that perhaps they were just too uneducated to make a judgment. But when Shawn referred to it as "Childism," Eleanor had to hide behind a window drapery to stifle her laughter. When she emerged, Shawn apologized profusely, taking her hand and leading her into the next room, which contained beautiful landscapes.

"My brother-in-law is a wonderful artist," Eleanor said as they stood looking at a painting of Silver Lake.

"Really?" Shawn responded, turning to her. "Has he ever sold anything?"

"Oh no," Eleanor answered. "He does it mostly as a pastime. But he can do portraits, landscapes, miniatures, anything really. My sister wears a locket he gave her with two precious pictures he drew." She paused, and Shawn waited silently for her to continue. "One is a wonderful likeness of our father, and the other is an apple tree." Her voice grew husky. "One of the apple trees on our farm."

"It must be a beautiful place," Shawn said softly, "your farm."

"So beautiful." She moved to the next painting. "I miss it, but from what my brother writes us, the family who bought it is tending it well."

"Is it a lot of work growing apples?"

"Oh, my goodness," Eleanor said with a chuckle, "you've no idea. During harvest we'd work twelve to fourteen hours a day. Well, my father and sister did most of the work in the groves, and then of course Nephi, when he came to us."

Shawn put his hand on her elbow as they moved to the next picture. "I would like to have met your father. He must have been a man to admire."

Eleanor nodded. "Yes, he was. Hard working, funny, and so kind. And, oh could he sing."

Shawn took note of the brightness of her expression. "How long has he been gone?"

Eleanor ran her finger along the edge of one of the picture frames. "Five years in October. It doesn't seem possible."

"And your mother is in San Francisco?"

Eleanor walked to the next painting. "Yes, still in San Francisco with my youngest sister Kathryn. And my brother James is in the war. Somewhere near Arras."

Shawn noted how subtly Eleanor had moved the conversation away from her mother, and although he was curious, he decided not to pursue the topic. "Have you heard from your brother recently?"

Eleanor shook her head. "Not for almost a month." She smiled. "He's not very good about writing." She moved to the next wall of pictures. "Oh! I love this one!" she said, stopping to gaze at a picture of a rugged mountain covered in pines and golden aspen trees.

"I've been to that place," Shawn announced as he joined her. "It's up Big Cottonwood Canyon. I can take you there if you'd like, and on up to Silver Lake."

"Really?" Eleanor said, turning to him with a look of wonder on her face.

He smiled. "Of course, but we'll have to wait until summer when the road's not a mud pit."

"Will we still be seeing each other in the summer?" Eleanor asked sincerely. She looked at him straight on without the least hint of flirtation.

Shawn took a step closer to her. "I hope so, Miss Lund, because I admire you very much."

Eleanor stared at him and swallowed. No man had ever spoken to her in such a deep, serious tone. She felt her heartbeat quicken. "Posterior ventricular branch," she said, stepping back.

Shawn started laughing. "What did you say?"

Eleanor laughed with him. "Posterior ventricular branch. I . . . I was thinking about my heart because it was beating faster, and I . . ." She snorted and they both laughed louder. "So . . . so my silly brain went right to seeing its anatomical parts."

The docent who had previously reprimanded Eleanor came into the room. "Do you mind?" she said sternly.

"Mind what?" Shawn asked in a cheeky tone, and Eleanor gasped with delight.

"Sorry. Sorry," Eleanor said backing toward the next room. "We were . . ." She was trying hard to control her laughter. "We'll just . . . Sorry."

Shawn moved close and took her by the arm. They moved into the next room, and, thankfully, the docent didn't follow. Eleanor went behind another drapery, attempting to regain a modicum of control, and Shawn followed her.

"Good thing not many people are in the gallery today," Shawn said, sniggering. "Your behavior, Miss Lund, is deplorable."

"*My* behavior?" she whispered haughtily. "You started it."

"Me? Ah no, Miss Lund. I definitely think posterior ventricular branch started it."

Eleanor started giggling. "Stop. Please, stop. Don't get me started again."

Shawn slid his arm around her waist, and she stopped giggling immediately. "So, your heart was beating faster?" he asked in that same rumbling tone. "And why was that, Miss Lund?"

"Shawn?"

From the opposite side of the drapery, a man's deep bass voice had interrupted whatever Eleanor was going to say, and for a few moments all was silent. Then, with as much dignity as he could muster, Shawn stepped out to face the tall, austere man and the well-tailored woman at his side.

"Father," Shawn said regally. He stepped forward and kissed the woman's cheek. "Mother. How good to see you. I didn't know you were going to be at the gallery today."

"That's quite obvious," Mr. Burbage answered.

Shawn's mother raised her eyebrows. "When you told us you were bringing your new friend to the gallery, we thought we might come to meet her and take you both out to dinner. Is that possible?"

"What? Dinner?" Shawn asked, a boyish grin spreading across his face.

His mother shook her head and indicated the drapery. "No, foolish boy . . . to meet her."

Eleanor stepped from behind the drapery, smoothing back her hair and standing as straight as possible. She extended her hand. "How do you do?" she said in a steady voice. "I'm Eleanor Lund."

Shawn smiled at her—impressed with the fact that she didn't apologize or try to explain away their outlandish behavior.

Mrs. Burbage was clearly not impressed, either with Eleanor's features or lack of proper manners; nevertheless, she took the offered hand and shook it once. "How do you do."

"I'm sorry," Shawn said, stepping up beside Eleanor. "Where are my manners? Mother, Father, this is my friend, Miss Eleanor Lund—most assuredly the brightest student at the university." Eleanor coughed. "Eleanor, my father, Mr. Howard Burbage, and my mother, Mrs. Mary Smyth Burbage—that's Smyth with a y."

Eleanor nodded at both of them, then turned with an inquisitive look at Shawn's mother. "Smyth? Isn't he the one who wrote the hymn 'Joseph Smith's—'"

"—First Prayer," Mrs. Burbage broke in. "Yes. AC Smyth."

"Are you related?" Eleanor asked with obvious excitement.

"Yes," Mrs. Burbage said in an aloof tone. "He is my great uncle."

"Oh my," Eleanor exclaimed, looking over at Shawn. "I keep forgetting about all the people here with pioneer heritage. It's very exciting."

"Why were you two behind that curtain?" Mr. Burbage asked abruptly.

Shawn groaned. He was hoping his father's mind had been distracted from that incident by the subsequent conversation, but he should have known better. His father was a lawyer, and nothing escaped his scrutiny.

"Ah—well—we—" Shawn stammered.

Mr. Burbage turned his eyes to Eleanor. "Is it common practice with you, Miss Lund, to hide behind draperies?"

"Only when I'm being pursued by an overzealous docent," she replied, smiling.

Mr. Burbage narrowed his eyes, Mrs. Burbage blinked, and Shawn burst out laughing.

"Eleanor, you are a gem!" Shawn said, giving her a quick hug.

Eleanor looked at Mrs. Burbage's face and figured the woman was probably seeing her more as a lump of coal than a gem. Eleanor remembered back to her auntie's elite circle of friends in San Francisco and how critical they'd been of her country upbringing and uncultured ways. But even at fifteen she'd eventually won over Mrs. Fitzpatrick with her grasp of current events and enthusiasm for civic causes. Eleanor smiled to herself. *If I can win over a woman as formidable as Mrs. Fitzpatrick, I can certainly take on the grand niece of AC Smyth.* It interested her that she wanted to win over Shawn's parents. *It's not as if we're more than just classmates and friends*, she told herself. But then she thought of how her stomach felt when he'd put his arm around her waist, or when he'd said he admired her. Eleanor felt color come into her cheeks, and she quickly moderated her expression before looking up at Mr. Burbage. She'd been wise to do so, for he was observing her closely.

"So, is it dinner then?" he asked in a businesslike tone.

Shawn looked at Eleanor, and she smiled at him and nodded.

He smiled back. "Are you sure Grandfather Erickson will be all right without you?"

Eleanor nodded again. "Mother Erickson is with him today."

"Oh good," Shawn said, offering his arm. "Then we'll keep you as long as we can."

"Is it Lars Erickson?" Mr. Burbage asked with interest.

"Yes, sir," Eleanor answered.

"Lars Erickson is your grandfather?"

"By marriage only," Eleanor explained. "My sister Alaina married his grandson Nephi."

"Interesting," Mr. Burbage said, taking his wife's arm and walking toward the exit. "Lars Erickson is one of the great men of this valley. A great builder of this city."

Eleanor smiled. "You should see his enchanting little cottage. He's carved all the front-porch posts with flowers and woodland creatures."

"How delightful," Mr. Burbage said warmly. "Have you seen his carvings in the Salt Lake Temple?"

"Well, of course not, dear," Mrs. Burbage said, a shocked edge to her voice. "She's never been inside the temple."

Shawn leaned over to Eleanor and whispered in her ear. "That's not to say she couldn't be going inside sometime soon."

Eleanor looked over quickly to see if Shawn's parents had heard, but they'd moved on ahead, oblivious of their son's very forward words. Eleanor walked numbly at Shawn's side—her mind a muddle. How in the world was she going to eat a bite of anything with so many emotions swirling around in her stomach? *Soup, Eleanor. Order soup.*

18

"The ghost is walkin' around upstairs," Kerri whispered into the dark.

"I know," Ina Bell whispered back. "I've been awake ten minutes."

Kerri listened to the erratic walking. Mrs. Lund seemed to be roaming the house, going back and forth from the main floor to the upstairs bedrooms.

"Should we go up to quiet her?"

Ina Bell moaned. "I'm tired. Let Mr. Palmer go up."

Just then there was a crash, and the two servants bolted from their beds. They grabbed their robes and headed for the back stairs. They passed Mrs. Todd's door and heard loud snoring.

Kerri scoffed. "A blessing to be half deaf, I suppose."

As they reached the end of the hallway, Mr. Palmer came out of his room. The girls stopped with a gasp, Ina Bell clutching her chest as if her heart was going to jump into her hands.

"And where are you two going?" Mr. Palmer questioned.

"Up to Mrs. Lund," Kerri panted, trying to calm her breathing. "You scared the devil out of us, Mr. Palmer."

"If only that were possible," he answered with a droll grin. He retied the sash on his dressing robe and pulled out his pocket watch. In the dim light emanating from his room, he checked the time. "Two fifteen," he said, snapping it shut. "Well, she's sleeping a bit longer, even with the lower dose."

Kerri and Ina Bell exchanged a look. "D'ya think it's wise for us to be cuttin' down her doses without the doctor knowin' about it?" Kerri asked in as innocent a voice as she could conjure.

"The doctor is an ignorant buffoon," Mr. Palmer snapped, "and the only thing I want to tell him is to take the laudanum himself and see how his life falls apart."

Ina Bell shivered. "My father used to put it on my gums when I was teething."

"They didn't know as much about opium then," Mr. Palmer answered. "They do now, and they know the consequences."

Another crash, and moments later the bell on the call-board sounded.

"Wonderful, now she's woken Mrs. Westfield. You two go up and see what you can do for Mrs. Lund, and I'll answer Mrs. Westfield."

Kerri and Ina Bell immediately ascended the stairs to the main level, then on up to the second floor, hearing muttering and weeping as they reached the landing. The muttering was coming from Elizabeth Lund, but the weeping came from her daughter Kathryn. Mrs. Lund had a viselike grip around her wrist and was dragging her down the hallway.

Kathryn turned when she heard the girls approaching from behind. "Oh, come help me, please!" she called. "She won't let me go!"

The thirteen-year-old was frightened and angry, and both emotions showed in her voice.

Ina Bell moved forward and, just as Mrs. Lund stepped into her room, caught hold of Kathryn's hand. Mrs. Lund turned to glower at whatever caused her to stop, momentarily loosening her grip on her daughter's wrist. Kathryn pulled her arm back and retreated behind Miss Latham.

"I can't sleep," Mrs. Lund spit at them. "I can't sleep. I need my medicine. Don't you understand?" She rubbed ceaselessly at her lower back. "My body hurts." She moved into her bedroom, and the servants followed. "My body hurts, but this part of me is numb. I can't feel it." She crawled across her bed. "I'm so tired, but I can't sleep. Don't you understand? I can't sleep. I need my medicine."

Mr. Palmer appeared at the doorway. He had hurriedly changed into his black trousers and white shirt but did not have on his vest, tie, or black jacket. "Miss Kathryn, please return to your room," he said with authority. "We will take care of your mother."

"Gladly," Kathryn said, rubbing her wrist. "I don't want to be anywhere near her." She turned without a second glance at her mother. "Why don't you just give her the medicine? She was much more quiet when you did." She disappeared into her room.

Mr. Palmer took a deep breath and assessed that Miss McKee and Miss Latham had things calming down. "I will see to Mrs. Westfield."

"Who is that?" Elizabeth Lund called in a harsh voice. "Is that the doctor? Are you the doctor?"

"No ma'am, it's Mr. Palmer."

Mrs. Lund tried to get off the bed to go to him, but she was too feeble. Besides, Kerri and Ina Bell had ahold of her nightdress.

"Mr. Palmer!" Mrs. Lund called out. "Come here. Come here. Are you the doctor's assistant?"

"No, ma'am. I work for your sister, Mrs. Westfield."

This response seemed to confuse the struggling woman even more. "My sister?" She rubbed at her back and whimpered. "I can't sleep, Mr. Palmer. I need my laudanum. Do you have it?"

"I do not, madam," he lied kindly. "Perhaps the doctor will bring some in the morning."

"In the morning? Isn't it morning now?" she said, scowling.

"Ah, no ma'am, 'tis the middle of the night," Kerri interjected, maneuvering herself in front of Mrs. Lund so Mr. Palmer could leave unnoticed. "Ina Bell and I are here to keep you company till ya fall asleep. Come on, now . . . lie back on these nice, soft pillows." Kerri and Ina Bell gently tugged Mrs. Lund back.

"I can't sleep," she hissed at them. She looked over at Ina Bell. "Get me some medicine."

"I can't do that, ma'am. I'm not a doctor."

Mrs. Lund tried to kick her. "You don't understand. I want to strangle myself. I want to strangle myself . . . but, I don't. I don't because I might get more laudanum to drink . . . I might if I stay alive."

"Hush that now," Kerri said firmly. "We'll have none of that. We're right here with you. We'll stay with you every minute, won't we Miss Latham?"

"Yes ma'am, every minute."

Mrs. Lund lay sideways on the pillows, vainly rubbing at her back.

"Here, I'll do that for you," Ina Bell said, climbing up onto the bed and moving the woman's hands aside.

"I don't know what to do with myself," Elizabeth Lund said. "I'm so tired, but I can't sleep."

"Shall I tell ya a story?" Kerri McKee asked, sitting down on her other side. "A story?"

"Of course. Me da used to sit by my bed at night when I was fretful and tell me wonderful stories sure to take my mind off my troubles."

"I'd like a story," Mrs. Lund whimpered, and Ina Bell had to bite her lip to keep from crying at the sight of a grown woman reduced to childlike dependence. "Will I get better, do you think?" the suffering woman whispered. Her voice was filled with loss and fear, and Ina Bell patted her reassuringly while she struggled for words.

"You will," Kerri said with surety. "You will. And we're all trying to help— me, and Ina Bell, and Mr. Palmer. 'Tis a very hard time right now, ma'am, to be sure, but you will get better. Trust in the good Lord, ma'am. As me da used to say, 'His strength shines brightest in the dark night.'"

There was a long pause, then Mrs. Lund's body relaxed. "I need my story," she said.

"Yes ma'am," Kerri answered in a soothing tone. Me da called this one 'The Enchantress of the Blue Lake.'"

19

"RJ, what are you doing?" Jimmy scolded. RJ only grunted at him. "Are you actually eating these rations the Froggs left behind when they retreated?"

RJ turned his back on his friend. "I'm hungry," he grumbled, "and our supply wagons haven't showed up."

"Probably won't for a while," Cornell said with an edge to his voice. He was digging into the earth with his bayonet, dirt and sweat caking his face. "The lieutenant said to dig shallow trenches, RJ, so get to it."

RJ flung the empty tin aside. He searched in his backpack and came up with a field shovel.

"Where'd you get that?" Nephi asked in amazement. "I've been using my hands for the last twenty minutes, and you've had a shovel?"

"Sorry," RJ said sincerely. "I forgot. I took it off a dead German."

Jimmy laughed. "After you're finished digging there, RJ, you can come finish my section."

"And ours," Cornell added.

"Where are we anyway?" RJ asked, tossing a shovelful of dirt. "And what were they thinkin', transporting us through last night on roads all choked up with wagons and trucks?"

"Obviously they needed us someplace fast," Nephi supplied.

"You're not complaining, are you, RJ?" Jimmy asked.

"No, I ain't complainin'. I'm just wonderin' where I am."

"You're in the military, RJ . . . in France . . . waiting to be told what to do after we get through digging these trenches." Jimmy threw down the cup he'd been using to scoop out dirt and cussed. "I just wonder when proper supplies are going to catch up with us."

"You ain't complainin', are you, Gordon?" RJ said, smiling.

Jimmy threw a dirt clod at him.

"And what about them soldiers who drove us here?" RJ continued. "Where was they from?"

"French Indochina," Cornell answered.

"Chinese men?" RJ asked, his eyes wide with wonder. "What are they doin' way over here?"

Cornell shrugged. "Helping France in the war effort, I'd imagine."

RJ shook his head. "Well, it's a mixed-up world, and that's a fact. I ain't never seen the like."

"I'd imagine not," Cornell said smiling. "My, oh my, RJ, what stories you'll have to tell back in Emmert."

"Heck, nobody'd believe me," RJ said, shaking his head. "Wished I had one of them cameras. I could take me a picture or two." He looked out across the wheat field. "Hey, nobody's told me where we're at."

"What's it matter?" Jimmy asked. "You gonna write it in your diary?"

"No," RJ said, casting Jimmy a dirty look. "I might be writin' my mama, and I want to know the name of the place."

"We're near the town of Belleau," Cornell said. "See the forest area on that rise?" He pointed across the wheat field. RJ nodded. "That is Belleau Wood, and I have a feeling it's crawling with Germans, and I have a feeling that's where we're going."

* * *

"James Lund!" Daniel said, smiling and trying to sit a bit higher in the hospital bed.

James approached his friend with a mixture of relief and sadness. He was glad to see that Daniel recognized him and was well enough to sit up, but he also noticed the siphoning tubes coming from the bandages on his arm, and the raw and peeling skin on his neck and the side of his face. James supposed that the doctors here in Arras had subjected Daniel's face to the painful process of debridement—scraping off the dead and injured skin, then scrubbing the area with an astringent solvent.

"Hey, farm boy from Sutter Creek!" James said, rallying himself and coming to the side of the bed and taking Daniel's outstretched hand. "What are you doing in this crazy place?"

"Trying to get myself blown up, I guess," Daniel answered, his voice a bit too cavalier. "And what are you doing so far from your post, mister?"

James smiled. "I have leave for the day. I borrowed a horse and rode on up here when I heard you'd been transferred."

"I'm touched," Daniel said. "You mean I won out over the YMCA or some cute Red Cross nurse?"

James looked over at a beautiful nurse just passing by with a tray of medical instruments. "Seems like you have your share of lovely women here."

"Ah, you leave that one alone," Daniel threatened. "As soon as I learn French, I'm asking her out on a date." His voice caught, although he tried to pass it off. "That is if she'll have a busted-up American soldier. Hey! Sit down," he said, motioning to a chair. James took off his wide-brimmed hat and sat. "So, isn't this something? How in the world did we bump into each other? I mean, I'm sure glad we did, or I'd be playing my harp by now." His voice quieted. "You guys saved my life."

"Actually, it was Private Marcus Hill who pushed you out of the crater. Clune and I only helped," James said softly.

Daniel shook his head. "Amazing that you would be there . . . right at that time." Pain knifed through his arm, and he clenched his jaw. "Hmm . . . two boys from Sutter Creek." His breathing was heavy as he fought to get hold of the pain.

They were silent for several minutes as Daniel tried to find a more comfortable position, and James looked over to find the French nurse.

"So," Daniel said finally, "tell me what you're doing. You've been over here a long time."

"Almost a year," James answered. "But who's counting?"

"Man . . . I didn't even make it a couple of months," Daniel said. "Lotta good I did the war effort."

James felt his stomach clench. He had seen the bodies of too many young men—gassed, broken, twisted, blasted beyond recognition. It was hard for him to see the "war effort" in the same way he had those first weeks of being out. "You did great, Daniel," James said, refocusing his mind on his injured friend. "Just the massive number of Americans coming over is scaring the devil out of the Germans—more and more surrender every day."

"So, you think it will be over soon?"

James looked straight at him. "Yeah. Couple of months maybe."

Daniel nodded. "Sure wish I could have stayed to the end."

James noted the forced bravado in Daniel's voice. "I'm just glad you're alive," James said bluntly.

Daniel's face drained of color, and James knew he was fighting another wave of pain. "We were stringing wire," Daniel said, his voice strangled and distant. He blew out a breath of air and gritted his teeth. "We were out . . . out about thirty yards in front of our first line." He attempted a smile as the pain released. "Remember how good I was at digging and pounding fence posts at home? Well, I guess that's why I got picked for wire duty . . ." He laid his injured arm across his chest. "What a crock. Us taller guys had to do the pounding. We had these stakes and we'd drive 'em into the ground with a mallet—a mallet covered with a gunnysack . . . I guess to drown out the sound of the blows."

James sat listening, knowing that the desperate flow of words was helping his friend scour his mind of the scars and sickness of battle.

"So anyway, we were out there one night pounding stakes and wrapping the wire around. We didn't have gloves, so we were trying not to get our hands torn up on the barbs. We sure cussed the Germans when that happened." He tried to smile, but it came out a grimace. His gaze turned hard, and he pressed his lips together. "We heard the shells coming over, and we dropped our tools and started running. The bombs were falling all around us. I . . . I was running next to Enright, and a shell hit on his side. His arm was blown off. I saw it. I saw it happen just before I was knocked over by the blast. I . . . I couldn't get my bearings after that. I think Enright was killed." Daniel's face was a wash of pain.

"Oh . . . I hope he was killed right away. I was crawling around like a madman trying to get my bearings. I was crawling toward the enemy line once and I saw them coming over . . . hundreds of them . . . little electric lights on their chests. Is that what I saw? I don't know. I thought maybe some of my brains had been knocked out." Daniel's breathing came hard, and James looked over to see the soldier in the next bed cover his head with his pillow. Daniel kept talking, looking down at his injured arm. "We were boxed in . . . artillery pounding in front of us . . . and then a flare went up and all I could see behind us were Boche in their coal-scuttle helmets . . . all I could see."

Then he started crying. "And I didn't have anything to defend myself. I'd put my rifle down to do my work . . . and . . . and then the sky lit up with flames . . . a couple of Boche were coming at me with . . ." His voice was filled with panic at the memory. "Fire . . . these flame throwers were going to roast me! Roast me! And I could see their faces . . . they seemed pleased about it."

Daniel sobbed and the soldier in the next bed yelled at him to shut up. James saw heads turn, and a nurse pointed toward Daniel's bed, but Daniel kept talking. "I rolled to the side, but not soon enough . . . I could feel my skin bubbling and I knew the next flame would take me. I was praying . . . praying that I would go quick, and then there were a couple of shots, and my killers went down." He looked at James, and James took his hand. "I jumped up and ran. I don't know how, but I did. All of us were running . . . and everybody was getting blown up or chopped up by machine guns. I knew I was going to die, James, and all I could think about was my mama at home . . . worrying about me and praying for me." James flinched.

"Something hit my helmet and knocked it off. After that I couldn't see very well . . . Then . . ." Daniel bit his lip and groaned. "Then I don't know . . . there was a sound, and . . ." He took the bed sheet and wiped distractedly at his face—blood and skin coming away on the white fabric. "I was down and crawling again . . . someplace to hide . . . anyplace. Three of us slid into the crater . . . we didn't know . . . didn't know about the water." Daniel's eyes held terror at the memory. "Lieutenant Berg was there . . . he was hit bad, and . . . he drowned . . . drowned in that slime." James moved closer, and Daniel put his head on his shoulder. "If you hadn't come . . . I would have gone like that . . . drowned in that . . . in that . . ."

James felt helpless. He wanted to hold his friend—to comfort him, but Daniel had so many injuries.

A French doctor was at James's side, his hand on his shoulder. The healer stood quietly for a moment, then spoke to Daniel in broken English. "Private Chart, the nurse will give you medicine. It will help you to . . . ah . . . rest." He turned and moved off to other patients.

Daniel nodded slowly and sat back. His breathing was ragged and punctuated by sobs. James could see now the pretty French nurse standing on the opposite side of the bed holding a syringe. She deftly administered the medicine, laying aside the syringe and helping Daniel to lie back. She adjusted his bed sheets, folding away the bloodied area. She stood for a moment, then ran her fingers lightly over the undamaged skin of Daniel's face. "Quel beau et corageux soldat Americain vous etes!" she said with such a tender look that it made James's heart ache. She turned and walked away.

Daniel looked over at James. "I wish I knew French," he said slowly.

James nodded. "I don't know much, but I think she said something about brave, handsome American."

Daniel was silent, and James knew he was questioning both those sentiments. He watched as the tightness in Daniel's jaw relaxed. James had a strong feeling that his friend would survive but wondered how he would manage life with the limitations of his injuries. He forced his mind to topics of hope and consolation.

"You know what you should do on your trip back to California?"

"What?" Daniel asked, smiling weakly at James's obvious attempt to lighten the mood.

"You should stop in Salt Lake City and see Alaina and Eleanor."

Daniel stared at his friend—a quizzical look on his face. "Really? They wouldn't consider it an intrusion?"

James laughed. "Not at all! They would love to see someone from home, and you know Eleanor's studying to be a doctor, so you'd be a great specimen for her to practice on."

The two laughed together, though the sound was full of pathos.

"A doctor." Daniel shook his head. "I knew she was smart, but, oh my. And Alaina with a baby . . ."

"Well, Katie's not really a baby anymore," James corrected. "She turned three in March."

Daniel shook his head. He carefully repositioned his arm. "I *would* like to see them again. Alaina was always a good friend, and Eleanor was a little piece of sunshine."

James noted that this was Daniel's second reference to Eleanor as sunshine, and he smiled inwardly at the implication. "So, do it!" James encouraged.

"I don't know when I'll be getting out of here," Daniel said with an understandable degree of frustration. "But, I'll ask the doctor if a little side trip would be possible."

"Great!" James said enthusiastically.

"And you're sure there will be a place for me to stay?"

"I'm sure," James answered immediately. "Nephi has family all over Salt Lake City."

Daniel smiled. "It will be good to see Nephi again, too. I always admired him."

James sobered. "You probably won't get that chance."

"Why not?" Daniel asked, yawning.

"He's over here with us."

Daniel frowned. "Really? I thought with a family he'd . . . was he drafted?"

James shook his head. "Enlisted . . . as a marine."

Daniel yawned again. "Hmmm . . . that doesn't seem like him." He lay farther down on his pillows. "I mean fighting, yes, but leaving his family . . ." His eyelids drooped as the sedative began to take effect.

James laid his hand on Daniel's arm. "I'd better be getting back to my unit."

Daniel forced his eyes open. "Where will you be, James? I want to keep track of you."

"I'm not sure. We're about fifteen miles south of here right now, but there's talk of sending us up into Belgium . . . Ypres or someplace like that. I think the generals are getting ready for a big push all along the front."

Daniel nodded, a look of sadness in his eyes.

"Your service made a difference, Daniel. You're one of us Yanks who's making the kaiser turn tail and run." James put on his hat and saluted.

Daniel extended his hand, and James took it. "Come home safe, James."

"I'll do my best."

Daniel's eyes filled with tears. "Thank you for coming to see me, James, and thank you for saving my life." James started to protest, but Daniel cut him off. "You, and Hill, and Clune. Tell them for me."

James nodded and changed the subject. "I'll write to Alaina and Eleanor and tell them you may be stopping for a visit."

Daniel wiped the tears off his face and tried a slight smile. "Something to look forward to." His fingers grabbed a piece of James's sleeve. "Can I ask for one more favor?"

"Of course, Daniel, anything."

"Would you write a letter for me?"

James hesitated. "Well, my penmanship is awful, but I'd be glad to. A love note to your beautiful nurse?"

Daniel smiled. "No. Would you write to my mother and father and let them know I'm alive?"

20

"We've got to push back this bulge," Lieutenant Edwards informed the men around him. The men of the marine platoon were crouched low in a drainage depression as they passed around the roughly drawn map that indicated their position and objective.

"The Marine 6th has the order to take hill 142 in this area of Belleau Wood," Edwards said, poking his finger at the map. "We've heard word that some hotshot German officer has put a couple hundred machine guns in those woods—all the nests protecting each other. If we're gonna take that hill we need to get around behind those nests and take 'em out."

No one commented on the absurdity of the prospect, but the lieutenant read it in their faces. "Listen, men, with this bulge the Boche are forty-five miles from Paris. We've heard that people are pouring out of the city in a panic. It's us standing between the invader and those innocent people." A few heads nodded. "And I'm telling you, it's more than just a patch of forest at stake. We've got to crack the Germans now . . . break 'em up physically and mentally."

"Yeah!" Jimmy Gordon responded.

Lieutenant Edwards nodded at him. "All along this part of the front it's us Americans—the U.S. 2nd Division. We're fighting as a unit now, just like General Pershing wanted, and we need to show our Allied brothers the stuff we're made of!"

Half the unit cheered their commitment.

"The enemy's been bombarding us for the last couple of days now, thinking they can just sweep away the inexperienced Yanks. Well, we've stood up to them, and now we're gonna go over there and teach 'em some English!"

Nephi looked over at Cornell, who wasn't cheering with the majority of the unit, but instead was looking soberly at the map.

Lieutenant Edwards took off his helmet and rubbed his hand back and forth over his short, cropped hair. "At dawn tomorrow morning we'll move out in four lines . . . seventy-five meters between lines . . . riflemen and grenadiers in each line. Our artillery will be laying down a barrage in front of us, so don't move out too fast or you'll be caught in it . . . and stick with your platoon. Any questions?" There was silence. "Duncan? You normally have a question or two."

Cornell looked up and shook his head. He handed the lieutenant the map. "No sir, seems pretty straightforward to me."

When the lieutenant left to inform more units of the next day's operation, Nephi met up with RJ, Jimmy, and Cornell. Jimmy looked nervous and excited.

"I don't think this is gonna be anything like the taking of Cantigny," he said, doing a little shadow boxing at RJ. "What do you think, Cornell, no walk in the park this time?"

Cornell had pulled his duffel bag out of the bunker and was searching for something. He looked at Jimmy and smiled. "No, Gordon, no walk in the park."

RJ shook his head. "I don't get what we're gonna do, just tromp through that green wheat out there? I mean, ain't that some farmer's field?"

Gordon stopped boxing, and the three men stared at RJ with various looks of bewilderment, pity, and envy. Finally Jimmy thumped him on the back.

"Come on, RJ, let's go fill our canteens and see if we can find some supper." He turned to his other friends. "You two coming?"

Nephi shook his head. "No thanks, Jimmy. I'm not hungry."

"And I have to organize my duffel," Cornell said in a mock British accent.

RJ looked confused, but Jimmy hooted. "Cornell, you are one odd duck."

"Would you mind filling our canteens while you're at it?" Cornell asked, holding his out. Nephi followed suit.

"Sure, why not?" Jimmy said, taking them and turning to leave. "Hey, Cornell, while we're gone, see if you can put your big brain to work on figuring out how to get us all through this."

Cornell looked up from his duffel to watch them walk away. "Well, the war has done one thing for me," he said wistfully.

"What's that?" Nephi asked, taking out his pocket journal and pencil.

"Opened up my circle of acquaintances."

Nephi laughed.

"No, I mean it," Cornell said. "You think I would have bumped into those two on the university campus, or at the country club? It's been a privilege for me." He looked at Nephi. "Three finer men I couldn't imagine."

Nephi nodded, feeling exactly the same.

"I've even come to understand and appreciate the odd Mormon boy," Cornell said, smiling. He pulled a letter out of his bag and sat quietly looking at it.

Nephi began sketching him, leaving him to his solitude.

"I wonder if you might do me a favor?" Cornell said after a while.

"Sure," Nephi answered.

Cornell held out the envelope. "This is a letter to my family. If I don't survive, will you make sure it gets to them?"

Nephi stared at it. "Come on, Cornell, you're going to—"

Cornell cut him off. "I haven't had a premonition or anything . . . I'm just being reasonable. I have a spare in my duffel."

Nephi nodded and reached to take the envelope. His hand was shaking, so he put it and the letter quickly into his pocket. *Get ahold of yourself,* he berated. *What's wrong with you?*

There were trees surrounding their hiding place, and Nephi stood up and moved over to lean against one. He gazed out over the field and saw the red poppies scattered like drops of blood in the green wheat. His throat tightened and he could hardly breathe. *What if I don't make it? What if I never see Alaina and Katie again?* Anguish knotted his stomach. *We're not sealed in the temple, so I . . . I could lose them forever.* He bit his hand to keep from crying out. *What am I doing here? Oh, dear Lord, what am I doing here? What's tomorrow? June 5th? June 6th? Will I be alive at the end of tomorrow?* His body shook, and he pushed himself closer to the tree, feeling the rough bark against the side of his face. *I could run.* He dug his nails into the bark. *But I can't leave Cornell . . . can't leave my friends.* He shut his eyes against the sunlight. *Please . . . Oh, please God, help me out of this . . . please.*

"Erickson?" It was Cornell's voice from far away. "Nephi?" Cornell's hand was on his shoulder. Nephi jumped. "You okay?"

Nephi shook his head. "No . . . no, I'm not feeling well."

"Yeah, you don't look well. Maybe you ought to go back to the dressing station, see if they can give you something." Nephi nodded. "Maybe you just need something to eat," Cornell encouraged. Nephi's stomach clenched. "I haven't seen you eat anything in a while."

Nephi stood straighter—keeping one hand on the tree to steady himself. "Yeah, maybe that's it. Maybe I'll just go back to the cook station." He turned away from Cornell so his friend wouldn't see his hands shaking. "I'll just go see if I can find some bread or something." He walked away.

Cornell watched him with great empathy. "Dear God, somehow get us all through this," he prayed.

* * *

Men were falling in the green field of wheat. Dawn had come and with it Lieutenant Edward's order to move out of their shallow trenches.

"Come on men! Do you want to live forever?" he yelled as he pushed out into the open.

His men followed him obediently. With the appearance of the first line as the men stepped from the trees, the woods opposite began to crackle with machine-gun fire. The marine lines pressed forward in orderly fashion. Nephi ran with his squad fifty feet and dropped. He flattened himself against the earth. He listened to the bullets zing overhead and shuddered when several thumped into the ground near his face.

"Erickson? You all right?" Cornell yelled.

"Yeah," Nephi grunted. He had shut his mind down. All he felt was the dirt beneath him and the hard wood of his rifle butt. He smelled the sweet green wheat and gritted his teeth against its illusion of life.

A second squad moved past them—the grenadiers tossing their little bombs, and the infantry firing. The artillery shells screamed overhead, and Nephi moaned. He was seeing evil, and it assaulted his spirit. It wasn't the German soldiers, for they were men just like him—men and boys frightened and longing not to be ripped to shreds. No, the evil was war itself—Satan's hideous tool of despair and destruction. He heard the lieutenant's call to move forward, and he jumped up and obeyed. Six men around him were cut down, and he and Cornell raced forward to a small ravine and dove in.

"Was it the lieutenant? Did you see the lieutenant go down?" Cornell gasped.

"I didn't see," Nephi answered, a strange detachment in his voice.

A man next to him put his head up and was shot through the eye.

Nephi looked away.

"How about some ax throwing?" Cornell said, ripping a potato-masher grenade from his ammunition belt.

Nephi did the same, and they threw the bombs together. Bullets slammed into the ground behind them, and they pressed themselves low, listening for the explosion of their grenades. Within seconds of the report, Lieutenant Edwards and several other marines jumped into the ravine and lay panting in a heap.

"You two saved our butts," the lieutenant said, crawling on his knees to them. "We've got three machine-gun nests about forty yards apart. I think you got the nearest on the west side. Let's move to the end of this ravine and see if we can get in behind 'em. We're at the edge of the trees now, and the hill rises, so watch it." He turned to Cornell. "Duncan, you and Erickson stay in the ravine and sharp shoot."

"Where's the rest of the unit?" Cornell asked.

"There's only about half of us left," the lieutenant said as he moved. "Let's go blow some birds outta their nests . . . and look out for these wood piles . . . I think there's a machine gun behind each one."

They moved to the end of the ravine, and the lieutenant and five of his men went over. Machine-gun fire opened up, splintering trees around the soldiers until Cornell and Nephi pinned down the Boche with rapid-fire shooting.

They heard a long loud yell, and searched frantically for the source.

"Where's that coming from?" Nephi shouted, his grip tightening on his rifle. He imagined a huge storm trooper jumping into the ravine behind him and shoving a bayonet in his back.

"Look!" Cornell yelled, pointing. "It's RJ."

RJ was running toward the machine-gun nest from a position farther back and to the left of where the lieutenant and his men were trapped. He was yelling and running at full speed, jumping bushes and fallen logs as though he were squirrel hunting in Kentucky. He was firing his rifle on the run and his field knife was in his teeth. Before the Germans could turn the Maxim gun to face him, he leapt into the pit, stabbing the nearest soldier with his bayonet and slashing the throat of the second with his knife. The third gunner kicked out with his legs, knocking RJ back. With a mad growl the German fired his field pistol.

Cornell and Nephi jumped from the ravine, screaming.

RJ slumped forward, jabbing the gunner in the stomach.

Another scream was heard above the gunfire and the shelling. It was Jimmy racing through the wood on the same line RJ had taken. "No RJ! No!" he cried as he jumped into the pit, grabbing his big friend around the shoulders and pulling him back. "No!"

Nephi pulled one of the dead Germans out of the nest, shoving him aside and scrambling into his place. Cornell hunkered down behind the wood pile and threw several grenades toward the next pocket of machine guns. As the *chat-chat* of their deadly fire died away, Cornell crawled on his belly to the edge of the pit.

"Gordon, how is he?" Cornell barked.

Jimmy looked up, his face a mixture of fierceness and desolation. "Dead," he growled. "He's dead." He patted his friend's face as a dark stain spread across the front of RJ's jacket. Jimmy started crying. "Why didn't you stay with me, RJ? Why didn't you stay?" An animal scream rose up from his gut. He snatched RJ's gun, and went to jump out of the pit. Nephi grabbed him around the waist.

"Don't do it, Gordon! Wait for the lieutenant!"

Suddenly the trees behind them exploded as Allied shells ripped into the woods. A flying branch slammed into Jimmy's helmet, throwing him back against the side of the pit, the thinner branches whipping Nephi across the face. The pain forced him down onto his hands and knees.

"Get out of there and move back!" he heard Lieutenant Edwards yell. He stood to obey, but everything was a blur. He ran his hand across his face and felt a sticky wetness.

"Fall back! Fall back!" the lieutenant was yelling. "Our guys are bringing in another barrage!"

Nephi felt hands grab him and drag him out of the pit. He stumbled after the retreating shapes, slinging his rifle over his shoulder and wondering if he'd lost one of his eyes. Someone shoved him forward.

"Where's Gordon?" he yelled. "Did somebody get Jimmy?"

"I got him!" Cornell rasped. "Now shut up and keep moving!"

They fell into the green wheat just as another score of shells slammed into the trees behind them.

* * *

Alaina joined Grandfather Erickson on his front porch. She sat down, poured herself a glass of lemonade, and took the straw hat off her head. "Whew! It's a beautiful spring day, but warm already, and it's not even ten o'clock."

"You have been vorking too hard pulling veeds," Grandfather said, giving her a stern look. "And I vas going to yell at you, little sparrow, if you tried to climb dat ladder into de apple tree."

Alaina giggled. "I may be headstrong, but I'm not foolish."

"You are not headstrong, you are determined," he answered, patting her hand.

Alaina nearly spit out her mouthful of lemonade. "Determined? That's very kind of you, Grandfather, but some people would call it stubborn or prideful."

Grandfather shook his head. "No. I vatch you, little sparrow. Dis last month dere's been a softness come into your heart."

"I'm trying," she said after a pause, "trying to be better."

He took her hand in his gnarled fingers. "Ya, me too."

Alaina chuckled. The precious man was earnest in his statement, and totally unaware of the greatness of his humility. A surge of gratitude filled her heart as she thought about this family and her dear husband. *Come home, Nephi. Come home to us.*

She and Grandfather sat together in the shade of the porch, enjoying the peace and each other's quiet company.

21

Dear Elias,

I will write another letter to you and Sarah, but this one I needed to write to you alone. As my brother, I know you'll understand. We have won the battle of Belleau Woods, and I can tell you our commanders are happy—especially the French general. We hear tell that he's going to have the name of the place changed to Bois de la Brigade de Marine which means something like the Forest of the Marine Brigade.

There's enough of our blood out there in those trees to justify the name change. They don't have a final count yet, but I've heard we marines had about 5,000 casualties. That's about half of us. On the first day of battle alone—back 20 days ago—we lost over 1,000 marines. A thousand in one day! My friend RJ McLaughlin died that day. He was a good man. Actually, he was more like a boy—always looking for something to eat. So innocent.

Somehow Jimmy, Cornell, and I made it through. I got some welts on my face from some blown-apart tree limbs. Thought I might have lost my eye, but I didn't. Jimmy Gordon got hit on the head with a log, and a few days later was shot in the arm, but he just had the field-station guys patch him up and send him back. I don't know whether he's brave or just plain crazy. He's a fighter, that's for sure.

I'll tell you, all us marines fought hard. Some of the German prisoners said we were savages, and others called us Teufel Hunden, which means DEVIL DOGS. Most times I feel like hell is all around me. The woods and wheat field are covered with dead bodies, both marines and Germans, and there hasn't been a chance to bury them, so the smell is terrible. When men of the 26th Division came in to take over our sector, a lot of them were sick from the smell.

I've seen horrible things, brother, and my spirit is . . . I don't know. I try to block it out, but it's not possible. Well, enough of that. Please don't tell the girls any of this, especially Mother and Alaina. I know their tender hearts wouldn't be able to stand it. When I was first out, Mother sent me the April 1917 general conference talk by President Smith. I've read it over and over. I have it here in front of me, a thin piece of paper, very worn and fragile. Many of the words are rubbed off, but I have them in my head—always in my head. The part where he tells us Mormon men who enlist that we're soldiers of the cross as well as soldiers of our country—that we should not go with destruction in our hearts—that we must be virtuous. Entrusted with protecting the nation's honor, the soldiers who go out from Utah have a righteous mission to perform and they must not have the thought of murder in their hearts, or even hate.

Oh, Elias—how do I do that? How? You haven't seen what I've seen. They killed my friend RJ—just a boy from Kentucky. An innocent boy whose mama will mourn him the rest of her life. Right now my body is shaking at the memory of what I've seen, and what I've done—and shaking because of what's ahead. How many German mothers will be mourning for the sons I killed?

I used to cry when I killed someone. Cry after a battle and ask God to forgive me. I'd pray for Him to take the souls of all the dead home to Him. I can't pray anymore. My heart feels like a stone in my chest. War is evil. Maybe that's what Satan wants— for the evil to just twist our hearts and spirits into lifeless rocks so that we can't feel happy anymore—can't see anything beautiful— so that we stop having faith.

Please Elias, if this letter somehow slips past the censors, promise that you won't tell Alaina any of this. I just had to get this out of my head. I knew I could tell you, but I can't tell my sweet wife. I'll try to make it through, but so many of us are dying. Sorry for the bad penmanship. It's late and I'm tired. I don't know where they're sending us next. It doesn't really matter.

Your brother,
Nephi

* * *

June 27, 1918

My dear Nephi,

I have news that I hope will bring some joy into your life. You and I are going to be parents for a second time. I know this will be a shock for you and you'll wonder how it's possible. You see, I was nearly three months along when you left for the war.

Please forgive me, dear husband, for not telling you, but I thought it would only bring you grief and make our parting that much more difficult. I remember how protective you were of me when we were awaiting Katie.

Please don't worry, Nephi. I'm healthy and strong and not nearly as sick as I was with Katie. Mother Erickson makes sure I eat well and keeps me busy. So, everything is as it should be, except that you're not home with us.

The baby is due the end of September. Maybe you'll be home with us by then.

The garden is planted and already your sugar peas are to the top of the line and producing wonderfully. And, under Grammy's instruction, Katie is becoming quite the little gardener. You should see her with dirt, head to toe.

As you know, last spring was wet and cold, but this spring has been a delight. We've already been into the canyon for a picnic, and next month Eleanor's new "friend," Shawn Burbage, may take us all the way up to Silver Lake for a day's outing.

I know what you're thinking, and I promise not to overtire myself. I also promise that I'm not riding Miss Titus, but oh, how I miss it. She is such a magnificent creature.

Last month Sarah thought she might also be having a baby, but she's not. Has Elias already told you? Did you know that Sarah can drive? She's amazing. You may have to teach me to drive when you get home. You may think that strange, but women are doing many things that we never used to, aren't we? And remember, we now have a woman in Congress. Eleanor says the vote for all of us is right around the corner.

Grandfather Erickson is doing as well as can be expected, and Eleanor is taking good care of him. He actually plunked out a few notes on the piano the other day, and we sang.

I'm trying to go to church more often—even though Katie is a handful—and I'm trying not to be so stubborn. You'll be glad about that, won't you?

Mother Erickson and I saw your father in the city the other day and he actually came over to talk to us and to find out how you were doing. We had a more recent letter, so we brought him up to date. He seems much more friendly.

So, there is a report on all of us at home. We always keep the home fires burning for you dear soldiers. Oh! I almost forgot! We received a letter from James just yesterday, and he says Daniel Chart's been injured in the war and is coming home! He saw him in the hospital. He also informs us that Daniel may stop in Salt Lake City for a visit. Wouldn't that be grand?

Of course, the grandest thing would be to have you in my arms again.

I hope you are glad for the news about the baby and will find it in you heart to forgive your little wife for not telling you sooner.

Katie loved the pictures you drew of the French countryside. It did my heart good to think you have something beautiful to look at.

I will love you forever,
Alaina

22

"And these are called?"

"Foxglove," Philomene replied, running her fingers along the soft pink petals. "The Latin name is *Digitalis*. And these happy little fellows are *Centaurea yanus* or bachelor's buttons."

Edward Rosemund wrote the names in his notebook along with descriptions. "I can't tell you how much I appreciate this, Miss Johnson." He looked up from his scribbling to take in the glory of the educator's garden. "It is impressive and soul soothing," he mused. "I very much suspect it would resemble an English garden."

"Ah," Philomene smiled, "not near so grand or expansive." She looked around. "I do love all the colors though." She stepped over to remove dead flower heads from a stand of roses. "Now, are there any others you think Mrs. Rosemund would like?"

"I don't know . . . well, I mean, of course she would love them all. Is there any way we could just pick up your entire garden and move it to the front of our house?"

Philomene laughed. "But then you wouldn't have the joy of planting and tending for yourself."

Mr. Rosemund gave her a wry look. "Is that truly a joy?"

Philomene continued laughing. "For some it is."

Edward took off his hat and fanned his face. "Maybe I've bitten off more than I can chew with this surprise. It's just that Victoria keeps talking about flowers at the front of the house, but she never has time. And of course, it won't be this year as we're busy with the orchard already."

"Of course," Philomene agreed. "Apples wait for no man."

"Or woman," he said, smiling. "I just thought I'd come see what everything looked like for planting next spring."

Philomene nodded. "Very wise of you, Mr. Rosemund." She moved over to a lovely tangle of vines and flowers covering the sides of her arbor. "Most of my plants, like this honeysuckle, are perennials, which means you can plant them in the fall and they'll come up next spring, and just keep on from year to year."

"Well, how intelligent of them," Edward said, writing *perennials* down in his book. "Honeysuckle?"

Philomene nodded. *"Lonicera caprifolium.* Their symbolic meaning is 'bonds of love.'"

Edward leaned close to the small flowers and breathed deeply. "My, those smell good. I definitely want those in the garden. And you have seeds for everything?"

"Seeds or starts. You just let me know when you want them. I would be glad to come out and help."

Edward closed his book. "That would be very kind of you, Miss Johnson." He grinned. "As you may have heard, I'm not the smart one when it comes to growing things." They laughed together. "I just do what Victoria tells me to do, and it all works out."

"She is an astute farm woman," Philomene said sincerely.

Edward smiled openly. "She is, isn't she?"

Philomene took note of the look of pride on his face.

"I just wonder why she tolerates my bumbling attempts at horticulture." He put the notebook in his pocket. "Maybe it's because I'm such a good cook."

"Are you?" Philomene asked, more surprise in her voice than intended.

"Yes, but that's our secret," he threatened. "Please don't go spreading it around town. The men think I'm odd enough as it is."

Philomene chuckled.

"Actually, my neighbor Mrs. Robinson and I have been exchanging recipes."

Philomene laughed loudly.

"I'm trying out her chicken stew tomorrow night."

"Stop! Stop!" Philomene scolded with little conviction, trying to catch her breath. "It is unseemly for a woman of my age to be laughing like a school-girl."

Edward took her by the arm. "Well then, for heaven's sake, woman, sit down on this bench and get ahold of yourself." She took a deep breath, and he flipped a page in his notebook. "I'd really be grateful for a blue ribbon piecrust recipe, though."

Philomene started laughing again. "You, Mr. Rosemund, are a scoundrel." She pressed her fingers against the stitch in her side. "And you wonder where your boy Samuel gets his irreverence."

Edward sobered slightly. "I'm sorry, Miss Johnson. Are you all right?"

"Yes, yes, I'm fine . . . just a laugh ache. Really . . . I should be grateful . . . there hasn't been much to laugh about recently. Indeed . . . not much joy in the world." She paused reflectively, looking at the flowers. "We should all surround ourselves with lily of the valley—it means 'return of happiness.' We could all use some of that."

Edward sat down as well. "Well, here's a bit of happiness. You have heard the news about the Robinson's boy, Daniel, coming home from the war?"

Philomene continued to rub her side. "Yes, I have."

"He was injured, but he's on his way home, and I understand he's been awarded both the Croix de Guerre and the Silver Star."

"So I hear," Philomene replied flatly.

Edward evaluated her response. "Medals are not much consolation for what he's suffered, are they?"

"I do not discount them, Mr. Rosemund, for surely they pay homage to the man's bravery and sacrifice . . . It's just that I . . ." She hesitated, thinking of the nightmares and terror she experienced when memories came of the bombings in Antwerp—the shrapnel ripping into her body—the emotional and physical scars that had woven themselves into the fabric of her existence. Scars that pulled and twisted even on beautiful summer days sweetened with laughter and the vision of flowers.

"Miss Johnson?" Edward's voice was low and soft. "Did I say something wrong?"

Philomene forced her mind to the moment. "No, Mr. Rosemund. It's just that I have empathy with the trials Daniel will face . . . empathy for all the young men in the war. Their lives will be forever altered."

Edward nodded. "Indeed."

She reached over and pulled off a stalk of purple snapdragon. "I hope it ends soon." Absentmindedly, she pulled a floweret off the stalk, gently pinching the sides of the bloom so that the petals opened like a mouth.

"Ah!" Edward said delightedly. "I know that. It's called snapdragon because of the resemblance."

Philomene smiled at him. "Yes. *Antirrhinum majus*. You know, Mr. Rosemund, we may make a horticulturist out of you yet."

Edward stood, chuckling. "Well, Miss Johnson, I reluctantly must be on my way. I was sent to town for supplies, and I can only feign so much ignorance of screws and three-penny nails." He reached out his hand to help her stand. When she was on her feet, he said, "Look around, Miss Johnson. The world is still full of beautiful things . . . beautiful things that you have planted and tended." She gave him a slight smile. "Despite the gloom, we humans seem to find a way back to peace and beauty. I believe we will again when this blight has ended."

She fought to control her emotion. "Thank you, Mr. Rosemund."

He nodded and changed the subject. "I hope you have a wonderful summer. Do you have any plans for outings or adventures?"

"No, not this year," she said calmly. "Perhaps next summer I will go up to Placerville to visit my friend, or I may venture as far as Lake Tahoe. I've heard from one of my former students that it is a spectacular place."

Edward smiled. "I'll keep it in mind. Of course, my family would have to go in the winter, which may prove a problem."

"Unless you don't mind tromping sixty miles on snowshoes," Philomene responded.

"Hmmm," Edward replied, making a face. "Perhaps not."

They walked down the path to the front gate in affable silence. Philomene opened the gate, and Edward passed through, putting on his hat and moving to his automobile. He paused before getting in. "Thank you again, my friend."

Philomene waved and felt a lifting to her heart. It was good to have Edward Rosemund as a friend.

23

"This man is burning up and delirious!" the nurse snapped. "What cold-hearted idiot would put him on a hospital ship when his wounds aren't even half healed? And look at that arm."

The second nurse pulled back the sheet to expose the unwrapped appendage, her eyes narrowing with disgust. "That arm's going to have to come off. I'll get the doctor." She turned and moved quickly out of the ward.

The remaining nurse placed a cold cloth on the soldier's head. "Poor fellow." She looked at his papers. "Poor Daniel. I hope you have something to hang onto. Something to help you fight."

But Daniel was lost in chaos and fearsome images: faces of soldiers and flashes of light, fence posts and horses screaming, his mother's embroidered handkerchief and fire. Sometimes he would call out after Eleanor, and sometimes she would come—floating into his mind like a spirit. She would push away the terror, and his breathing would slow.

"Eleanor . . ."

"That's right, Daniel," the nurse said, placing a cool cloth on his head. "That's right. Just keep whispering her name and maybe we can get you through this."

* * *

The afternoon breeze fluttered the aspen leaves and sent Katie's hat tumbling to the edge of the lake.

"My hat!" Katie squealed, running after it.

"Stop!" Alaina commanded. "Don't go near that water!"

"I'll get her," Shawn Burbage said as he moved in long, easy strides after child and hat.

Katie's toe caught in a gopher hole, and she fell flat on her stomach. Shawn scooped her up before she had time to think about crying and raced with her to the edge of the lake. The little white hat plopped into the water and began floating away.

"Yook, Mr. Man, my hat is a boat," Katie giggled.

"Then you'll just have to be the captain and sail it home," Shawn answered seriously.

Katie leaned back against him. "I can't go in the wadder."

"No, of course not," he assured. "You'll just fly in like an aeroplane."

He held her securely around the waist and dipped her down to the water's edge. Katie stretched out her little fingers until they grasped the brim of her hat.

"Me got it!" she grunted.

Shawn brought her back and set her on her feet. "Nicely done, Miss Erickson."

Katie giggled, shook the water off her hat, and pushed it forcefully onto her head.

"It would stay much better if you put on the chin strap," Shawn counseled.

Katie frowned at him. "I don' yike the strap." She turned and marched back to her mother and auntie—Shawn following.

"Thank you, Mr. Burbage," Alaina said as they neared.

"My pleasure," he answered. "She certainly has a mind of her own."

"Hmmm," Alaina said, raising her eyebrows. "I think she gets that from me."

Eleanor laughed good-naturedly at her sister's comment. "Really? I always thought you were rather even-tempered growing up."

Alaina laughed as she followed Katie on their continuing walk around Silver Lake. "Oh yes," she said in a teasing tone. "I always did exactly what Mother wanted me to do."

Katie stopped on the narrow path, turning to frown at her mother. "Is your mother Grammy?"

Alaina's smile faded. "No Katie, Grammy is your daddy's mother."

"Then who is you mommy?"

"I've shown you the picture. Remember the lady standing next to the bronze statue?"

Katie looked perplexed.

"The picture of the lady with the big hat?" Alaina added.

Katie squinted as she concentrated. "The hat wif flowers?"

"Yes. That's Grandmother Lund. My mother and Auntie Eleanor's mother."

"I don' know her," Katie said simply.

Alaina's heart twisted. "No. She lives in San Francisco."

Katie picked some yellow flowers. "Can she come see me?"

Alaina looked out across the lake. "She . . . she could . . . but . . ."

"San Francisco is very far away, dear one," Eleanor said brightly. "A very long trip."

Katie opened her mouth to ask another question, but Alaina stopped her. "Enough questions for the moment, Miss Curiosity. Off you go now. You're blocking the path and we're all hungry. Is anyone else ready for a picnic lunch?"

"I certainly am," Shawn said.

"I'm famished," Eleanor added.

Katie giggled at them and turned to run down the path.

"Slow down," Alaina cautioned, "or you'll fall!"

The adults followed at a slower pace, taking in the beauty of granite cliffs against a vivid blue sky and the swatches of green foliage covered in Queen Ann's lace and pale yellow columbine.

Alaina took a deep breath. "Thank you, Mr. Burbage, for letting Katie and me tag along."

"Not tagging along at all," he immediately responded. "You have not only been a charming guest, but have been our necessary chaperone, Mrs. Erickson."

"Oh, really?" Alaina laughed. "In that case you must call me Alaina." She laid her hand on her abdomen. "I feel matronly enough as it is without being called *Mrs.*"

Mr. Burbage chuckled. "Very well then, Christian names all around. Are we all in agreement?"

"Yes," Alaina said firmly.

"Agreed," Eleanor answered, a sparkle in her eyes.

"Good," Shawn said. "Though this does make us all very forward-thinking, you know."

They reached a wider part of the trail where they could walk side by side.

"Actually, since you made me your chaperone," Alaina said, "I'm going to be very old fashioned, Mr. uh . . . Shawn, and ask you some questions."

"Oh, dear," Eleanor sighed. "We shouldn't have given her a title."

Shawn smiled. "Ask away, Alaina. Hopefully I have nothing to hide."

Eleanor raised her eyebrows. "Hopefully?"

Alaina ignored her sister. "Do you have siblings, Shawn?"

"Yes, ma'am. Five brothers and one sister."

"And you are where in line?" Alaina continued.

"Second oldest. My older brother is a lawyer like my father and is in my father's office. Thank heavens."

"Why 'thank heavens'?"

"It means there's not as much pressure on me to be a lawyer."

"Not what you want?"

"No." He looked over at Eleanor. "I've chosen what I want." He looked quickly to Alaina. "Ah . . . medical work . . . to be a doctor."

"Of course." Alaina smiled. "It's Eleanor's passion as well."

"I know," Shawn said, nodding. "And she's absolutely brilliant. But, of course, you know that."

"I do," Alaina answered.

"That's more than enough flattery," Eleanor said firmly.

Shawn stopped walking. "Plain truth is never flattery," he countered.

Eleanor laughed. "How can you possibly say that with a straight face?"

Shawn laughed with her and reached over to take her arm.

Alaina watched their playful interchange with interest and a bit of envy. Her heart ached as she thought about Nephi so far away. He could be dead this very minute, and she wouldn't know. She wrenched her mind away from such miserable thoughts and looked back over the lake toward Brighton Lodge.

"Have you ever stayed there, Shawn?"

Shawn pulled his gaze away from Eleanor's face to answer Alaina's question. "At the lodge? No, I haven't, but my parents have been guests several times."

Alaina seemed far away. "Maybe Nephi and I can go there when he gets home."

"I'm sure he'd love the peace and quiet," Shawn said distractedly as he tucked a piece of Eleanor's hair behind her ear.

Alaina felt a small coil of anger snake its way into her head. "And why didn't you go to war, Mr. Burbage?"

"Alaina!" Eleanor reprimanded.

Alaina focused. "Oh, I'm sorry, Mr. Burbage. That was uncalled for, and none of my business."

"Please, call me Shawn . . . and there's nothing for you to be sorry about. I can't even imagine how difficult it is for you." He looked down at the ground. "I would have gone, but . . ."

Alaina interrupted. "Really, Shawn, you don't owe me an explanation."

"It's all right, Alaina. I'd like you both to know." He looked at Eleanor. "You see, three of my younger brothers enlisted, and my mother was distraught over the thought of four of her boys serving, so my father encouraged me to stay and concentrate on my studies. He said there was going to be a great need for doctors."

Alaina was stunned. "Three of your brothers are in the war?"

"Yes, ma'am. One in the Navy assigned to convoys, and the other two are someplace along the front."

Alaina felt sick. "I'm sorry, Shawn. I need to learn to bridle my tongue."

He reached out and took her arm. "It's all right, Alaina, really. You had no way of knowing."

"Your mother must be sick with worry," Eleanor said, "yet neither she nor your father said anything about it when we dined together."

"They're pretty private about personal matters," he said with a wry smile. "Unless, of course, they are the personal matters of other people."

Alaina sat down on a log by the side of the path.

"Are you all right, Laina?" Eleanor asked.

"No, Elly, I'm not," Alaina growled, her voice thick with tears. "I feel awful about what I said."

Shawn came over and knelt down beside her. "Please, Alaina, don't be upset over it. We all have heartaches to suffer because of this war. You have a husband who's fighting, and . . . " He looked up at Eleanor. "And a brother. Your mother must be heartsick, too."

Alaina scoffed. "Our mother? I doubt it."

Shawn was taken aback and looked to Eleanor for explanation.

Eleanor debated how much she wanted to tell him. She'd always prided herself on being truthful and straightforward, but she also needed to be compassionate. "Our mother has always suffered with melancholia, Shawn. That, along with her austere upbringing, made her a bit distant to . . . well, everyone except our little sister Kathryn and our father. When Father died . . . she . . . well, she never truly recovered. A doctor in San Francisco started giving her laudanum, and . . . "

"And now she's addicted," Shawn finished.

Alaina put her head into her hands.

"Oh, you dear things," Shawn said in a whisper. "You've had your share of trials and then some."

Eleanor turned to look out across the lake.

A scream from Katie shocked them all from their serious thoughts.

"Katie!" Alaina called, standing and moving quickly toward the picnic area. "Katie, what is it?"

Eleanor and Shawn ran ahead and met Katie racing down the path to them. "Come on! Come on!" she screamed. "It's in the basket!" She waved frantically to her mother who had slowed her pace when she'd seen that Katie was unharmed. "Come on, Mommy!"

As they all drew near to the secluded spot where they'd left the picnic things, they saw the rump end of a raccoon sticking out of the picnic basket. Katie squealed with excitement, and the raccoon pulled its head up quickly, a bunch of grapes in his mouth.

"Him's got our grapes!" Katie screeched. And before anyone could stop her, she was running toward it.

"Katie, stop! Don't chase it!" Alaina called feebly. She was laughing so hard she had to stop and lean against a tree.

Eleanor and Shawn nearly smashed into each other as one went after Katie and one went after the zigzagging raccoon. Katie squealed and ran around in circles enjoying the mirth and chaos. Eleanor finally stopped, putting her hands on her knees and gasping for breath while Shawn picked up Katie and brought her back to the clearing on his shoulders.

"Well, I'm afraid to say," he announced, "that the bandit got clean away with the goods."

Eleanor looked up into his handsome, exuberant face and had to catch her breath all over again. "Oh, dear."

"And another thing," he boomed as he reached her side.

"What?" Katie asked, patting his cheeks.

"I haven't had this much fun at a picnic since I was six!"

"Scrimmy!" Katie chirped.

Alaina looked over at the three revelers as Shawn took Katie off his shoulders and hugged the two girls. She blinked at the glory on Eleanor's face. *Where has the sadness gone?* The prior unhappy memories and feelings had faded like wisps of gray smoke.

Alaina smiled. When she was a little girl she'd watched in wonder as a magician materialized a white dove from under a silk handkerchief. She remembered her heart lifting in delight as the bird flew into the air. For a moment, on this beautiful summer's day, her heart felt the same.

24

Kathryn Lund stood at the doorway into the servants' quarters scowling at her mother. "You do not have to sit there at the kitchen table, Mother, and wait for the post. The servants will bring it up."

Elizabeth Lund raised her eyes from her darning. "I like sitting here."

Kathryn's eyes darted from Kerri McKee to Mrs. Todd, then back to her mother. "Well, it's a lovely summer's day, and I thought you might like to go with Aunt Ida and me to the Cliff House for luncheon."

Mrs. Lund shook her head. "No thank you, dear. We are having creamed tuna on toast. You could join us."

Mrs. Todd nodded.

"How disgusting," Kathryn said before thinking.

Mrs. Todd stopped chopping vegetables and looked up at the peevish thirteen-year-old.

"I . . . I didn't mean your cooking, Mrs. Todd," Kathryn stammered, "I just meant . . ." She stamped her foot. "Well really, Mother . . . you would rather stay here with the servants and have creamed tuna on toast than to come with us?"

"I would."

"But . . . there will be cracked crab, and avocado salad, and French pastries," she whined.

"Mmm," Mrs. Lund said softly. "I'm sure you'll enjoy that."

"Mother," Kathryn's voice rose in pitch, "I do not like all the time you're spending with the servants!"

Kerri McKee rose from her seat as Mr. Palmer entered the room.

"And is there something wrong with us, Miss Kathryn?" Mr. Palmer said in his most controlled voice.

Kathryn jumped. "I . . . no . . . I mean, it's just that she's . . . a . . . she's . . ."

"Might the word yer searchin' for be, *better?*" Kerri asked, her voice on the edge of anger. "She's *better* than us?"

Kathryn glared at her. "She *is* Mrs. Westfield's sister, Miss McKee, and that certainly puts her above you."

"That's enough, Kathryn," Mrs. Lund said firmly. "Now, please leave and go to your luncheon with Aunt Ida." Her voice softened. "And wear your new blue frock. You look lovely in that."

Kathryn opened her mouth to speak but closed it again as Bib Randall and Ina Bell came into the room. There was a silent tension in the air until Kathryn gave a frustrated growl and turned from the gathering of servants.

Bib looked around at the varied expressions in the room, surmising the gist of the conversation. He smiled as Kerri brushed her hands together in a dismissive gesture, and Mrs. Todd went back to chopping. Ina Bell shrugged and went to put her polishing basket away, and Mr. Palmer picked up the accounts book.

Mrs. Lund went back to her darning. "I'm afraid I spoiled her," she said. No one responded. "I just didn't want to spend much time with her, so I gave her things, and didn't discipline her." The sock she was working on would not be wearable, but none of the servants censured her effort. "Of course, I didn't want to spend time with any of my children. With my . . . sickness it was too difficult." She stopped darning. "I ruined them, I'm afraid."

Bib sat down next to her at the table. "May I speak freely, ma'am?"

Mrs. Lund nodded.

"You know, my father was a preacher, a Bible-thumping, perdition-threatening preacher."

Mrs. Lund nodded again, trying not to smile.

"Heaven's sake, he named me Bible New Testament Randall! Now what kind of name is that?"

Kerri and Ina Bell laughed.

"And he dragged me and my mother from one length of California to the other before settling in San Francisco. He chewed tobacco, refused to have his hair cut but twice a year, and wasn't real fond of people. But he never drank, never hit me or my mother, and he taught me how to swim."

Mrs. Lund gave Bib a curious look.

"My point is," Bib said, smiling, "is that we are not our parents . . . good or bad. We are not what our parents did or didn't do for us. I've known folks who've had hard upbringings that turned out fine, and some who seem to have everything that made a mess of their chances. There comes a point where a child chooses what kind of a person they're gonna be. When we grow into ourselves, we look around at the world and say, 'There's the path for me,' and whether good or bad, we choose it." Everyone was staring at him. "Now, my father was odd, no doubt about it, but I didn't grow up odd."

"Well, some would dispute that, Mr. Randall," Mr. Palmer said, not looking up from his book.

"Leave him be, now, Mr. Palmer," Mrs. Todd said. "He's making a good point."

Mr. Palmer smiled. "Which is?"

"That he's not odd," Kerri said promptly.

"And that he swims like a fish," Ina Bell added.

Bib groaned, and Mrs. Lund laid her hand on his.

"It's all right, Mr. Randall. I understand, and I'd like to believe you, but . . ."

Ina Bell plucked up her courage. "Just look at James, and Eleanor, and Alaina. They're fine folks."

"I believe that's in spite of me, or because of the strength Samuel gave them," Mrs. Lund answered.

The three younger servants grew quiet.

"Pshaw!" Mrs. Todd scoffed, moving to throw the vegetables into a pot of simmering stock. "You take too much on yourself, Elizabeth, and I believe that's only going to add to your sadness."

Kerri and Ina Bell looked at each other, shocked that Mrs. Todd would call Mrs. Lund by her given name.

"Mabel's right, *Elizabeth*," Mr. Palmer followed on. "You're a brave woman to come through what you've come through. You need to concentrate on that and be proud of yourself."

Mrs. Lund looked into each face and shook her head. "It's thanks to all of you," she said finally.

The postal bell at the back door rang, and Mr. Palmer stood.

Kerri and Ina Bell crossed their fingers under the table, wishing for a letter for Mrs. Lund. She came down every day, waiting for another letter from James, and every day left empty-handed.

Mr. Palmer opened the door, catching Miss Justus as she moved up the back steps.

"Good day, Miss Justus," Mr. Palmer said politely.

"Good day, Mr. Palmer." She pointed at the letterbox. "Special letter there today, I'm thinking."

"Thank you," he said, giving her a salute and retrieving the letters from the box. Miss Justus continued on with her route, and Mr. Palmer turned back into the house and shut the door. "I think it's grand we have female letter carriers while the men are away at war," he said.

"My word," Bib responded, "there are women working everywhere. I even saw a woman policeman . . . or should I say police woman?"

Mr. Palmer nodded. "And I think they may want to go on with those jobs when the men return."

Kerri snorted. "Aye, so you're just figurin' out that we women can do most everythin', are ya?"

"We have our Congresswoman now," Ina Bell said proudly. "Jeannette Rankin from Montana."

Mr. Palmer was surprised by the uncharacteristic gleam in her eyes.

"Yep, and soon *all* the women will be wanting to vote," Bib teased.

"As it should be, Mr. Randall," Kerri said with conviction.

Elizabeth Lund was not paying attention to the idle banter. She had her eyes fixed expectantly on the envelopes in Mr. Palmer's hand.

He pulled one carefully from the group and handed it to her. "A letter from France, ma'am."

She took the letter reverently and stared at it. "All the way from France," she whispered. She pressed it against her chest, then handed it toward Kerri. "Would you please read it out loud to us, Miss McKee?"

Kerri stopped polishing the silver and took the letter. "I'd be pleased to, ma'am, but don't ya want to read it first . . . see if there's anything personal?"

"I have no secrets from any of you," Mrs. Lund said earnestly, urging the letter forward.

Kerri smiled, took the letter, and opened it. She stood and cleared her throat.

Bib rolled his eyes. "What a preparation! You'd think she was reciting on the stage."

Kerri gave him a withering look. "Would the groundlings please settle down? This is an important letter."

"So begin! Begin!" Bib said, pretending to tip his hat to her.

Kerri sniffed and began reading.

July 2, 1918

Dear Mother,

I am well, and even though some of the battles have been bad, I am a fortunate fellow to have received no wounds. Not even a scratch. I am still with the British and their ambulance unit. We have 6 ambulance wagons now, and I have 18 horses and 8 mules to tend. The poor animals have a rough time of it when the shelling comes near. Some of my faithful chaps get used for artillery portage. They load some of the bigger horses with 200 pounds of ammunition and send them out to the big guns. It breaks my heart to see how brave they are.

Kerri stopped reading and took a deep breath. "Oh, my. Your son's got a right tender soul now, doesn't he, Mrs. Lund?"

Elizabeth Lund nodded and Kerri continued reading.

I think they're going to move us soon, but I can't tell you where. It may be north of where we're at now. There are several Americans that have come into our unit, and boy am I glad to see them. Most

*of the AEF are fighting together farther south from our area, and I
hear they're doing a crack job. You won't believe who I met up with.
Daniel Chart! He's on his way home because he got into quite a
mess, but the docs have patched him up and he's on his way. He
said he might stop by in Salt Lake City to see Alaina and Eleanor.
That would be something.*

*I'm sorry I can't give you names of places we're at, but the censors
here are very tough, and it would just be marked out anyway.*

*I got several of your letters all at once, Mother, and I'll tell you the
later ones are so much better than the earlier ones. Remind me to
bring my field pistol home with me to shoot that doctor who kept
giving you laudanum.*

*Seriously, I must come to San Francisco and shake hands with
Mr. Palmer and thank him . . .*

Kerri's voice grew husky.

. . . thank him for getting you out of that nightmare.

Kerri stared at the next words, her eyes blurring with tears.

*I have to tell you, dear one, that I'm proud of you for fighting
through. You're a brave little soldier to fight such a battle, and I
am so glad you had your band of comrades around to watch out
for you, just like we do out here.*

Mrs. Lund put her head in her hands and wept. Bib Randall patted her
shoulder as the women all grabbed for their handkerchiefs.

*I see things differently since I've been out here, Mother. More like a
man, I guess. I used to think mainly of myself, but since being out
here I realize there are a lot of things that are more important than
me . . . a lot of sorrow in the world that I should pay attention to.*

*I also know it's normal to miss everyone . . . to be homesick for
Sutter Creek. I think about the Regosi ranch, and Emilio and Rosa,
but do you want to know the silly things I miss most? The smell of
your fresh-baked pies, the chatter of Alaina and Eleanor's voices,
and all of us sitting out on the front porch on a spring evening.*

Kerri choked back tears. "I don't think I can finish, Mr. Palmer."

"I'll do it," Mrs. Lund said, reaching for the letter. She wiped her eyes and read.

> *I realize the paradise I lived in since being out here, and I pray that I can get back to it. Sorry I've gone on so long. I think this is the longest letter I've ever written. If the mail carrier comes tomorrow, I can get this sent before they move us. Don't be worried if you don't get a letter for a while. Hold onto hope. I think the war will be over soon.*
>
> *Your son,*
> *James*

No one spoke or moved for the longest time. Finally, Mrs. Todd stood to turn on the flame under the cream sauce. The call-board rang and Bib rose to put on his jacket.

Mr. Palmer stood also. "The automobile to the front, Mr. Randall."

"Yes, sir."

"I will see Mrs. Westfield and Kathryn to the transport." He paused in the doorway looking at Mrs. Lund. "Last chance to join them."

Elizabeth Lund looked up from her letter. "No thank you, Mr. Palmer, I have darning to finish. Besides, I'm looking forward to creamed tuna on toast."

25

Eleanor Lund stood on the station platform watching for the train from Denver. She was the self-appointed lookout, having insisted that Alaina stay in the somewhat cooler confines of the station house. It was August, and it was hot—not the kind of weather for a woman eight months pregnant to endure. Alaina consented to the confinement only after Eleanor promised to retrieve her from the building at first sight of the train.

Eleanor thought back to her own arrival in Salt Lake City nearly four years earlier: the crush of disembarking passengers, Alaina's joyful face, and the tentative hug from her brother-in-law. She remembered being scared and tired, yet relieved to be at journey's end. Would Daniel be relieved to be back among friends after his ordeal overseas?

Eleanor looked down the tracks but saw only buildings, trees, and sky. She fanned herself and wondered how Daniel must be feeling. He'd sent a letter from Calais, France, a week before his departure, and a telegram from Kansas City telling of his train schedule, but about his injuries he'd been silent. They had received a brief letter from James telling of the daring rescue by a Private Marcus Hill, and about the visit he'd had with Daniel in the hospital, but James had also been vague about the seriousness of Daniel's condition. He'd alluded to a burned face and a shrapnel wound to Daniel's head and arm, but he did not elaborate.

She took a deep breath and fanned her face again. *Well,* she told herself, *the doctors surely would not let him travel if he were gravely ill.*

"Nothing yet?" Alaina asked, sliding in beside her and speaking in an agitated tone.

Eleanor jumped. "Goodness, Alaina! You scared the dickens out of me."

"Sorry, but you didn't come to fetch me."

"That's because the train isn't arriving."

"Well, where is it? It's half an hour late."

Eleanor gave her an indulgent look. "It should be here shortly. More and more people are showing up on the platform."

"Hmm," was all Alaina said. She took out her fan and began fanning her face in earnest. "Whew! It must be over a hundred degrees." They stood in silence for a moment, and then Alaina said softly, "I'm nervous to see him."

"Nervous?" Eleanor questioned.

"Well, I haven't seen him since my wedding, and . . . we've never had a chance to talk since . . . well, since he turned down my marriage proposal." She tried to make light of it, but Eleanor could see that the memory was painful.

Eleanor took her sister's hand. "Oh, Laina, I'm sorry. I'd forgotten. That was a horrible time for you . . . a desperate time trying to save the farm."

"It's all right, Elly,"Alaina said, squeezing her hand. "It worked out the way it was supposed to. I ended up marrying the man who loved me, remember?"

Eleanor nodded. "And Daniel is still your friend."

"I always thought it was brave of him to be honest with me," Alaina stated, thinking back to that day when she and Daniel had gone on the carriage ride to Miller's Bend back in 1913. There had been a skiff of snow. *1913. Could it possibly be that many years ago?* "What do you think he'll be like?' she blurted out. "I mean, we haven't seen him for what . . . four years?"

"Almost five," Eleanor said. "I was fifteen."

"Remember how handsome he was?"

"Alaina!" Eleanor said in a shocked tone. She didn't know why, but her sister's comment bothered her. Daniel *was* handsome, to be sure, but he was also witty, genuine, and self-effacing. She thought about how much fun she'd had verbally sparring with him, and he always seemed pleased to see the two Lund sisters, though they were plain creatures compared with Joanna Wilton or Maddie Cross.

"What are you smiling about?" Alaina asked.

Eleanor looked over. "I'm remembering times together on the farm."

The sound of a distant train whistle brought their attention to the tracks as a press of people moved in around them. People leaned out to see the steam billowing, while others wanted to be first to see the number on the front of the train. The pushing became more intense.

Alaina struggled away from the crowd. "I think I'll wait back here. I'm feeling a bit dizzy."

"I should have brought you a drink of water," Eleanor chided herself.

"Don't be silly, Elly. I'll be fine," Alaina answered. "Oh, look! Here it comes!"

The dark engine seemed to take forever to crawl past them, dragging its burden of boxcars and passenger coaches. As these latter cars came into view, people's voices became more animated, and some folks waved. Eleanor felt a thrill of anticipation as the brakes hissed and the train stopped. Porters and loaders moved forward efficiently, and almost immediately people began disembarking. Periodically a soldier would step out of the narrow opening to be met by calls of their names, sobs, and fierce embraces. Each time a uniform appeared at the top of the step, Eleanor and Alaina would squint to see the face and press a bit nearer to the train.

Suddenly there was a hush in the crowd as two porters carried a soldier in a wheelchair down the metal steps. The crowd moved back in deference to the wounded hero, and Alaina gasped.

"Elly, that's Daniel. That's Daniel, but . . ." Her words strangled in her throat. "He's missing an arm."

Daniel had his head lowered slightly, but there was no mistaking the line of his face. He looked up tentatively, searching the near faces for the sign of his friends. Eleanor pushed forward through the crowd, unaware that Alaina was not following. Several soldiers, fit and not visibly blemished, were approaching Daniel with reverence, shaking his hand and patting him on the back. One mother, who had brought a gift for her returning boy, shoved the small box into Daniel's hand, and kissed his undamaged cheek.

Eleanor was in front of him, her face radiant with fierce pride and friendship. Inside, her stomach churned, but she used her medical training to detach from tears. The side of Daniel's face was badly burned, his left arm was missing, and his skin had a waxy yellow color. She concentrated on his handsome brown eyes.

"Daniel. Oh, Daniel," Eleanor said brightly. "How good to see you."

Daniel pushed himself onto his feet—a large sturdy man helping. Daniel turned to him. "Thank you, sir."

The man, overcome with emotion, nodded and stepped back.

Daniel turned to Eleanor, a look of wonder on his face. "Can this possibly be little Eleanor Lund?" he asked teasingly. "The scrawny little thing that used to be such a tomboy?"

Eleanor laughed and hugged him, favoring his right side so he could hug her back. "You forgot *bookworm* tomboy," she said playfully.

Daniel smiled, grateful for the old banter. "Well, we certainly can't say tomboy anymore, can we?" In his hand he held a bouquet of flowers. "These are for you, Miss Lund. Isn't it your birthday shortly?"

Eleanor beamed at him. "Tomorrow! How did you remember?" He smiled at her, but her attention was drawn to the weariness in his eyes rather than the smile. He was putting on a brave show, but Eleanor could tell he was at the end of his tether. She touched his hand. "Thank you, Daniel."

The curious crowd was failing in the attempt to be inconspicuous regarding the poignant exchange; the women cast furtive glances, and the men spoke in lifted voices. One small boy peeked out from behind his mother's skirt and pointed. "He doesn't have an arm."

Daniel focused his gaze on Eleanor. "Did you come alone?" he asked, his body swaying slightly against hers.

"No, I . . ." Eleanor turned, noticing for the first time that Alaina wasn't beside her. "Ah, no . . . Alaina was . . . oh, there she is!" She lifted her hand into the air and called. "Alaina, we're over here!"

Alaina looked startled, but began walking toward them.

"It takes her awhile to get anywhere these days," Eleanor offered as an excuse. "She may be a bit shy about you seeing her in such a motherly condition."

As she approached, Alaina folded her fan and held out her hand to Daniel. "Hello . . . Daniel. We're so glad you came to see us." Daniel took her hand, and she burst into tears. "I'm sorry . . . sorry. It's just that . . ."

Daniel hung his head as several people turned to look at the sad picture.

Eleanor stood straighter. "Oh, for heaven's sake, Alaina Erickson, get ahold of yourself!"

Alaina gasped and stepped back. She wiped the tears away with a gloved hand, and steadied her resolve.

"You'll have to forgive her, Daniel," Eleanor said lightly. "Pregnant women are so emotional."

Alaina and Daniel were stunned into silence—one, because of Eleanor's commanding attitude, and two, because she'd used the word *pregnant* in mixed company. Daniel stared at his friend, then began laughing, and much to Eleanor's relief, Alaina joined him.

"It's true," Alaina said. "I just don't have any control of my silliness." She took his hand between hers. "It is wonderful to see you, Daniel."

He drew his hand away slowly, then reached into his pocket and brought out a small silver rattle. "Actually, James told me about the upcoming event . . . proud uncle and all." He presented the gift to Alaina. "For the baby." Before Alaina took the precious offering, the rattle tinkled with silver mirth as Daniel's hand trembled and a shudder ran through his body.

Eleanor was alerted to the fact that pain had settled into some part of his flesh. "All right," she said brightly, "let's be on our way. Alaina, go find a porter and have him bring Daniel's things to the front of the depot."

"Are you going to play bossy younger sister?" Alaina asked, smiling.

"I am," Eleanor responded, "so on your way."

Alaina left to fulfill the order, grateful for the chance to temper her emotions.

"And you," Eleanor said, giving Daniel a firm but kindly look, "are to sit down in this chair before you fall down."

Daniel hesitated briefly, then sat down. "Thank you, Eleanor."

His voice held such misery and sweetness that Eleanor swallowed hard to maintain her control. She pushed him away from the compassionate stares, and began talking of practical matters.

"My brother-in-law, Elias, will pick us up in his father's car."

"Pick us up?" Daniel questioned. "How did you two get to the depot?"

"We walked."

"You walked?"

Eleanor laughed. "No, of course not. Elias dropped us off and then went to run an errand. He should be back by now." She maneuvered the wheelchair efficiently into the station house. "The car's big enough to fit us and your luggage."

"Luggage?" Daniel answered. "I only have one small suitcase and a duffel." His body stiffened in pain.

Eleanor knelt beside him. "Where's your pain medicine?"

"Pocket," he managed. "Cup . . . water."

She rummaged in his pockets until she found a small tin cup and the packet of powder.

"How many ounces?" she asked.

"One," he said through gritted teeth.

Eleanor ran to the public water closet to fill the cup and mix the powder. She returned quickly and administered the medicine, helping him to hold the cup until he finished.

Daniel closed his eyes. "Oh, Eleanor," he moaned, his voice husky with pain, "this is a bad business."

She knelt down beside him, suddenly realizing she was on his damaged side. She laid a hand on his shoulder. "It is a bad business, Daniel, it is . . . but you'll get through it." She patted him. "I have very capable associates."

Tears leaked out of the corners of his eyes, and Eleanor brushed them away with her white-gloved finger. "Now, let's get you to Mother Erickson's," she said, standing. "She has the screened porch all ready for you." She moved him toward the front doorway.

"I shouldn't have come," Daniel said in a mumble. "I'm going to be a burden."

Eleanor stopped. "Well, I can put you back on the train," she said. "But then, of course, you'd miss Mother Erickson's delicious home cooking, clean sheets, and a feather pillow, and," she put her hand on his shoulder, "a friend who can stand up to your teasing."

Daniel was silent for a long while. "I'll stay," he said finally.

"Good," Eleanor answered, pushing the chair forward again and out into the bright August sunshine.

26

Daniel slept most of the time for three days. Dr. Lucien came each afternoon to refine his instructions to Eleanor and to administer treatment and relief. Under the pair's efficient ministrations, Daniel's health improved at a steady pace. Of course, Mother Erickson's happy countenance and homemade soups cheered him immensely.

Alaina avoided the room, always making excuses of household duties or a desire to keep Katie occupied so she wouldn't be a pest, but Eleanor knew the real reason, and it had nothing to do with current duties or past embarrassments. It galled her that Alaina would be put off by Daniel's appearance, and she meant to question her sister about such lack of compassion at first opportunity.

She found Alaina one morning out in the small back pasture giving oats to Miss Titus. It was one of those rare times that the two were alone and away from the chance of others hearing.

Alaina saw her sister approaching across the pasture, and waved. "Good morning, Elly!" she called.

"Morning, Laina," Eleanor answered. She came to her sister's side, reaching out to the chestnut mare and running her hand down its neck. "This is such a beautiful animal."

Alaina beamed. "She is, isn't she?" She set down the bucket of oats and picked up the curry comb. "I can't wait to get back to riding."

Miss Titus whinnied and bobbed her head as though she shared the sentiment.

"And smart, too," Eleanor chuckled. "Too bad if anything should happen to her."

Alaina looked around abruptly. "What do you mean?"

"Well, I was just thinking about what James wrote about those horses being killed and maimed in the war . . . those magnificent brave creatures."

Alaina looked back at Miss Titus. "Well, she'll never be going over there."

"Good thing," Eleanor replied tersely, "because who knows what reception you'd give her if she came home injured."

Alaina started brushing Miss Titus in earnest. "Stop it, Elly. I know what you're trying to say, and I don't want to talk about it."

Eleanor persisted. "Alaina, why are you treating Daniel so badly?"

"I'm not treating him badly."

"You're not? You never go in to visit with him, or care for him. You won't even take in food. Do you think he doesn't feel your aversion?"

Alaina lowered her head. "It's not that. It's not."

"Laina, please tell me what's grieving you."

Alaina turned to her sister with such a fierce look on her face that Eleanor stepped back. "What's grieving me? How can you even ask me that question? You wonder why I don't go in to visit our childhood friend?"

She threw the curry comb hard against the side of the small shed. The crack made Eleanor jump and Miss Titus squeal. "You wonder why I don't go into that room and give him sips of water and dress his wounds? Because . . . because . . ." she snarled, "because that's the war in there, the gruesome war that mangles young men into nothing! That mangles Nephi into nothing. He brought the war into that room, Elly . . . into my life. It's not what Nephi writes me . . . it's not!" Anger and tears were constricting her throat. "It's evil that grinds everything to dust . . . grinds James and Nephi to dust!"

"Laina, stop! Stop! I'm sorry. I'm sorry." Eleanor was crying. "I was stupid . . . stupid to ask you. I should have realized." Alaina slumped to the ground and Eleanor held her. "Stop, stop now. All this upset isn't good for the baby. I'm sorry."

The back porch door opened and Mother Erickson was there helping Daniel down the steps. "Look who felt like a walk out of doors!" she called happily over her shoulder, not seeing the scene in the pasture.

Eleanor looked up and caught Daniel's eye. Even at this distance she could see his look of registered concern, and she watched as he said something to Mother Erickson. The little woman turned.

"Oh, my goodness!" She helped Daniel to the bottom of the steps, then moved quickly to the girls.

Eleanor brushed at Alaina's tears. "Mother Erickson is coming, Laina."

Alaina nodded. "I don't want her to know." She took a deep breath. "I don't want her to worry."

Patience Erickson came up in a fluster. "What's wrong? What's wrong, little muffin?" she puffed as she took Alaina's offered hand. "Are you in pain?"

"No, Mother, it's nothing. I'm fine. Well, actually, I just got a little wobbly on my feet. I thought it was cool enough this morning to do a few extra chores, but . . ."

Eleanor stood and helped her sister to stand. "She just felt faint."

Mother Erickson looked into the young women's faces. "Are you sure?" They both nodded. "But, you've been crying."

Alaina hesitated. "Well, don't I do that every day?" she answered, making a show of brushing off her skirt.

"And I just . . . thought I'd join her," Eleanor added lamely.

Alaina gave her mother-in-law a hug. "I'm fine, really."

Mother Erickson reached up and put her hands on Alaina's face. "I don't know if I believe you."

Daniel arrived in the group, standing next to Mother Erickson and frowning at Alaina. "Are you all right?" He held out his hand to her, and she ignored it.

"Yes, yes, I'm fine," she answered, not looking at him.

Daniel withdrew his hand.

"She just felt faint," Eleanor broke in. "It's not uncommon."

"Well, common or not," Mother Erickson said, putting her arm around Alaina's waist, "she's going to go in for some lemonade and a little lie down."

Katie came running from the house. "Mr. Soldier Man!" she yelled.

"Oh dear," Mother Erickson groaned. "I thought I had her busy with her sewing cards."

Katie rushed to Daniel and took his hand. "You are walking outside!" she said excitedly.

Daniel chuckled. "I am."

"I will walk with you," she announced.

"Well, I think we're all going back in now," he said.

"No! No, don't be silly," Alaina snapped, glancing at him with a forced smile. "You enjoy the morning. I'll just take a little rest."

"Scrimmy!" Katie said, dancing about in a circle.

"Oh! I need to put Miss Titus away," Alaina said, turning back.

"I'll take care of her," Daniel answered, a note of life in his voice.

"Oh no, that's not necessary. I can . . ."

"I'm still capable of doing a few things, Mrs. Erickson," Daniel said flatly.

Alaina felt her face flush with a sick embarrassment. "Oh Daniel, I didn't mean . . ."

Daniel moved away from her apology to untie Miss Titus's lead from the hitching post.

"Come on," Mother Erickson said. "I hear lemonade calling us. Eleanor?"

"No, I actually feel like a walk this morning."

Daniel looked over at her and smiled.

"And you behave," Mother Erickson called back to Katie. "Do what your Auntie Eleanor tells you."

"I will," Katie promised.

Eleanor looked at her niece with raised eyebrows. "So . . . stand on your head."

"What?" Katie yelped.

"Stand on your head. You promised Grammy you'd do everything I told you to do, so . . . stand on your head."

Katie stared at her a moment, then started giggling. "Auntie Eleanor, you are teasing me."

Daniel came back from securing Miss Titus in the stable to find Eleanor and her little niece playing a game of tag.

"Join us!" Eleanor called.

"I don't know if I'm that steady on my feet yet."

Eleanor stopped, catching her breath and smiling at him with openness. "Then a good strength-building walk it will be," she said, taking his arm.

Katie went to take his hand. "Oops, you hand is not here." Unabashedly she scrunched up the empty sleeve of his shirt, and held it in her tiny fist. "I weddy now," she said.

Daniel looked down at her in wonder, taking a moment to regain his composure. "All right then, off we go."

"How lucky are you, Mr. Chart?" Eleanor said teasingly, "to have a charming girl on each arm?"

Daniel swallowed. "Very lucky."

They walked along carefully with Katie singing a little tune of her own making. A recurring breeze blew away any bothersome heat, and a profusion of wild sunflowers set them an inviting pathway to wander. When Katie ran ahead to chase a groundhog, Daniel turned to look at Eleanor's profile. "I want to thank you for helping me through this time."

"Daniel, I . . ."

"No Eleanor, there were times on the train . . . coming across the country, when . . . when I didn't know if I would survive. I didn't know if I wanted to survive. I thought everybody was going to treat me like the people at the train station, or they'd see me like . . . like Alaina sees me . . . disgusted by my . . ."

Eleanor stopped walking and looked at him. "Daniel, that's not how Alaina feels about you."

"It isn't?" he asked with an edge to his voice.

"No, it isn't. I thought that too . . . but, I've talked with her. May I tell you plainly why she can't look at you, or be around you?"

"Please," Daniel said stiffly.

"Because you shatter her illusion of what the war is. Nephi's been writing her about the charming French countryside and French people . . . funny stories about the men in his unit, of the food and YMCA entertainments. Oh, of course, he mentions some fighting going on, but it is always at a distance, he's always away from the danger. She's not stupid . . . she realizes its worse than what he writes, but until she saw you, she had no idea. She can no longer hide from the reality." Daniel groaned, but Eleanor went on. "The reality that her husband and our brother are still over there . . . still fighting . . ."

Daniel bent over, placing his hand on his knee. "Of course. What was I thinking? What was I thinking coming here?" His voice was ragged. "It was so selfish of me."

Eleanor touched his shoulder. "No. Not selfish at all. We're glad you came. I'm glad you came. You are my dear friend." He straightened up to face her as she continued. "When I look at you I don't see the war, I see Pine Grove and Sutter Creek. I see you driving your wagon up the track, and our beautiful apple farm. I see all of us at the Fourth of July picnic, a time when we were carefree, and . . ." She stopped speaking as a strong emotion caught in her chest.

Daniel stared at her. "Eleanor, you are such a good person." He stepped toward her, and she stepped back.

She was unbalanced by the emotion on his face. "I . . . I . . . oh, my goodness. What a goose. Listen to me just going on and on. You'd think I had more sense."

"You are amazing."

"Amazing? Really? What happened to scrawny, bookworm tomboy?"

He took her arm. "Oh, she's still in there somewhere . . . somewhere under brilliant friend and soon-to-be doctor."

"Well," she blushed, "I do have a few more years of study."

They started walking. "Medical school," Daniel mused, shaking his head. "I always knew that you'd take on some unique endeavor, Miss Lund."

"Unique as in odd?" Eleanor questioned.

"Unique as in amazing. Your father was very proud of your brilliance, you know? I remember him saying that he hoped the world wouldn't hold you back. That you would be able to accomplish whatever the good Lord had for you to accomplish."

Eleanor swallowed hard. "He wanted that for all his children." She looked up to the mountains. "I think of him often when I'm having a difficult time at school."

"You? I can't imagine you having a difficult time."

Eleanor smiled. "Well, not with the course work, but with my peers. They seem to think that the medical field should be the exclusive domain of men."

Eleanor didn't see how this bit of information put a grin on Daniel's face. "So, they're all perfectly horrid to you?"

"For the most part, but there is one student, Mr. Burbage, who is my friend."

The grin faded. "Mr. Burbage?"

Eleanor went on with her usual openness. "Shawn Burbage. He's a very adept student."

"Studious?"

Eleanor nodded. "Yes."

"Intelligent?"

Eleanor looked over at Daniel, her eyes narrowing with suspicion. "Yes."

"Unattractive?"

She laughed. "Unattractive? No, actually, he's very handsome. Not as handsome as you, of course," she teased.

Daniel laughed with her. "Well, that's good to know. And I'm certainly grateful that you could take time from Mr. Burbage to look after me."

Eleanor found this bit of conversation odd and a bit unsettling. She wasn't sure whether there was double meaning in Daniel's words and voice. "Well, it's worked out perfectly," she said brightly. "I had the time off from classes, and Sarah's been watching Grandfather." She stopped and turned to him with excitement. "Oh, Daniel, now that you're up and about, you can go and meet Grandfather Erickson!"

"I've been eager to meet him after all I've heard."

Eleanor beamed. "And so you shall, right away! And I know he will love you." She gave him such a fond look that his heart twisted with longing.

"Come on, you!" Katie yelled to them. She held up what looked like a rope. "I catched a snake!"

"Oh, mercy!" Eleanor gasped, running forward to take Katie in hand.

Daniel stood and watched his friend run down the path toward her impish niece, and suddenly in his mind she was running in a different place and time. Her clothes were simple, and her hair was done in girlish braids. *Queen of the County Fair,* he reflected wistfully, and as Eleanor moved away from him, he wondered if his heart's desire was forever out of reach.

27

Waves of British, French, and Belgian soldiers marched through the once-beautiful city of Ypres, ingesting the ruin like rotten meat. Though the Germans had hammered the Belgian city for four years, it had never fallen into their hands, but the devastation was total. The men stood in the rubble of stone and shattered stained glass that had once been the cathedral, smelled the charred wood of the cloth merchant's exchange, and watched ragged children playing skittle in a graveyard. The troops moved on through the city, grim faced and cursing, and on to the small town of Hooge. Here in the muggy afternoon gloaming, James Lund and Marcus Hill stood with a small group of Belgian and British soldiers watching Wheaten Clune throw rocks and muddy dirt clods at a damaged building. The group was understanding of the rage that prompted the action. For the brief space of time the Germans had struggled forward and held the town of Hooge, they'd meant to have their presence felt and their propaganda remembered. Painted in precise, large block letters across the side of the bookseller's shop were written the words, *"Gott strafe England!"*

"Does it mean 'God suffers England'?" Private Hill asked as he applauded a well-placed hit by his burly friend.

A Belgian soldier leaned over, speaking to the two Americans in clear English with a beautiful French accent. "It says 'God punishes England.'"

"Ah," Marcus said, nodding, "no wonder he's a bit angry."

The Belgian soldier laughed and held out his hand. "I am Jean de Broqueville," he said, "from Brussels."

Marcus took his hand and shook it enthusiastically. "I'm Marcus Hill from Utah, and this is my friend James Lund from California."

Jean smiled and extended his hand to James. "California. Yes, I know of California, but Utah? I'm sorry, I'm not so sure."

James patted Marcus on the back. "It's a state—east of Nevada and west of Colorado."

"Oh, cowboys!" the Belgian said, brightening.

James laughed. "And a few Mormons thrown in for good measure."

Monsieur de Broqueville looked perplexed, and Marcus was about to clear things up when a loud crack and a cheer brought their attention back to the wall.

Wheaten had just heaved a big rock at the writing, effectively pulverizing most of the word "strafe." He came back to the group smiling and dusting off his hands. "That's more like it," he said. "God and England. I like that."

"Mr. de Broke . . . de Broka . . ." Marcus stumbled with the name.

"De Broqueville," Jean offered blithely.

"Mr. de Broqueville, this is our friend Wheaten Clune from England."

Jean smiled. "Yes, I could tell by the uniform. And please, call me Jean."

Wheaten shook his hand. "De Broqueville?" he asked, looking intently at the young soldier's face. "Isn't there a de Broqueville who's a mite close to the Belgian King?"

Jean nodded. "He is my father."

"Well, I'll be," Clune said, stepping back and looking the young man over. "Ya look like a regular soldier to me."

"That is a very high compliment," Jean said, grinning.

Clune turned to James and Marcus. "You two Yanks mind your manners now. His father is the head of the Belgian government, and a baron besides. You just happen to be in the presence of royalty."

"Really?" Marcus said, his eyes widening.

"No, Monsieur Hill," Jean answered humbly, "today I am a soldier just like you. How can I be anything else when my king is also a soldier and fights beside me?"

The men who had been watching Clune demolish the writing were moving off to find a meal or a drink, and Jean looked around for some of his comrades.

"We're just headed over to the canteen for a bite to eat," James said. "Care to join us?"

"I would be honored," Jean answered.

Marcus looked surprised, but fell into step with the other men.

"So, you are with the medical teams brought up from Arras?" Jean asked casually.

"We are," James answered.

"The number of infantry and artillery units grows daily," Jean said, nodding. "The final push is coming."

"That's what we're thinkin'," Clune said solemnly. "And this time we won't allow the defeat we suffered at Passchendaele."

"No," Jean said, shaking his head. "This time we will push the Germans out of my beautiful country." He looked intently at Clune. "I cannot tell you the depth of feeling we have for you and your brave countrymen. So much sacrifice you have made here."

Clune nodded.

"And now with the Americans joining, there is hope that this madness will end."

James felt uncomfortable with the praise. "It would have been nice if we'd signed on a little sooner," he muttered.

"Well, your President Wilson is a cautious man," Jean replied diplomatically.

James scoffed. "That's one way of putting it."

"Of course," Jean continued, "and he is not ruthless. When we have beaten them, the Germans will most assuredly want to deal with your President Wilson rather than Premier Clemenceau of France."

"Or Prime Minister Lloyd George," Clune added.

Marcus Hill's attention had been wandering with all the political talk, but with Jean's comment on beating the Germans, he joined in. "So, you think this war is gonna be over soon, Mr. de Broqueville?"

"I do, my cowboy friend," Jean answered affably. "We hear of many riots in German cities, and mutinies in their military. A good people can swallow only so much of their leader's propaganda."

Marcus Hill didn't understand much of what the polished Belgian aristocrat was saying. He was only interested in the fact that the man thought the war would be over soon. Marcus swallowed hard against emotion. He was homesick. He'd never let his buddies know, but he missed his family and the simple patterns of his life in Salt Lake City.

"Hey! Look at that," he said suddenly, stopping in his progression and pointing to a group of black soldiers in flamboyant uniforms of bloomer-like red pants, blue capes, and red fezes. "Where are they from?"

Monsieur de Broqueville turned to join him. "They are Senegalese, from Africa. They come to fight with their French brothers."

"Aren't they dressed awful fancy for combat?" Marcus asked with naive candor.

Jean shook his head. "Ah, don't let their uniforms fool you, Monsieur Hill. They are fierce warriors."

Hill shook his head. "So many people mixed up in this war," he said sadly.

"Indeed, you are right," Jean answered. "We are one little pinpoint in this big war, but here on this precious piece of dirt we will fight together: Belgians, French, British, American, Irish, Scots, and many others."

Wheaten and James came to join them.

A bagpipe began playing in the distance, and they all turned toward the sound. "Ah, oui!" Jean said with great fervor. "Speaking of the Scots, there is something the Highlanders are doing that I think you would like to see. May we postpone eating for a little while?"

"Of course," the men agreed, following quickly behind Jean as he raced toward the outskirts of the town. They passed several outlying farmhouses and barns, coming at last to a large open pasture. There, at the far end of the field was a line of Scottish soldiers in tan field jackets, blue plaid kilts, and white spats over their boots. They held their rifles firmly in their right hands. Their left arms were extended beside them—their hands grasping an imagined object in space.

"That's the Black Watch infantry!" Wheaten Clune boomed out.

"It is!" Jean chorused his enthusiasm.

"What are they doing?" Marcus asked.

"They are pledging their honor to the upcoming battle," Jean said with reverence. A bugle sounded. "Watch now! They reenact the famous charge their ancestors made a hundred years ago at the battle of Waterloo."

On the third blast of the bugle, the soldiers yelled loudly and ran forward, gaining momentum with each stride.

"See their left hand? Each man pretends to grab the stirrup of a cavalryman of the Scots Greys," Jean explained.

James's heart was pounding as the soldiers neared. "The men ran beside the horses?"

"They did!" Jean replied, his voice lifting to match the increasing din. James noted the look of fierce resolve on his face.

Marcus was amazed at the power and grace of the soldiers as they passed. "Look at how fast they're running!" he yelled.

"The two regiments rushed with terrific momentum against the enemy! Here they are saying, 'Nothing will stand against us! Nothing will turn us back!'" Jean shouted.

James and Wheaten cheered, becoming aware that their voices were joined by a hundred others who had come to watch the demonstration of commitment and bravery.

The onlookers stood transfixed for a long while after the soldiers had passed, each heart filling with a renewed spirit of possibility. The months and, for some, years of madness and grief would not turn them from their duty. They would see the horrific conflict through to its end; they would force evil to retreat and bring again hope to the world.

"Thank you, Mr. de Broqueville," Marcus said finally. "I'm glad we didn't miss that."

Jean de Broqueville nodded. "We will need that strength when the battle begins, my friends." He turned to them with a smile. "And now, should we eat?"

28

"The Germans had this gun the Brits called Big Bertha. It shot shells fifty miles into Paris. Fifty miles! Some say it could do eighty." Daniel shook his head. "You just can't imagine the weaponry, Elias . . . aeroplanes, millions of rounds of artillery, grenades, machine guns, phosgene gas, tanks . . . men can't stand up against that." He took a step back into the shade of the cottonwood tree. "Wars will never again be wars of valor."

Elias looked at him with a skeptical expression.

"Oh, don't get me wrong, there will be brave acts, even heroic acts, but we will never again be gentleman warriors. The modern weapons make the killing too distant . . . too impersonal."

Elias leaned back against the hardware truck. "I just wish the Germans would admit they're done for."

"Stubborn," Daniel answered. "Oh, they know it's over, and so do the Austrians and the Turks, but they're stubborn. Ludendorff just keeps slaughtering his country-men in the hopes of gaining a stronger position in the treaty negotiations."

Elias scoffed. "And they keep petitioning President Wilson to intercede on their behalf."

Daniel shrugged. "Well, they see him as the weak link, with his fourteen points and everything."

"A league of nations—" Elias said, fanning his face with his hat, "think that will ever work?"

Daniel shook his head. "No. I mean, I wish it would. It's a Utopian idea, but you've got to have honest, fair-minded gentlemen to play the game and make it work."

Elias kicked at a stone. "Well, that's not likely, is it?"

Daniel shook his head. "I'm afraid not. There will always be power-hungry madmen in the world."

"It is the nature and disposition of almost all men, as soon as they get a little authority, as they suppose, they will immediately begin to exercise unrighteous dominion," Elias quoted.

"Is that from Lincoln?" Daniel asked.

Elias smiled. "No. From one of Joseph Smith's revelations."

"Interesting," Daniel returned with a good-natured grin. "I wish I'd had more time to investigate the Church while here, but the women have kept me busy with getting well."

"And they've done a good job of it," Elias chuckled. "Tell you what, I'll send you a Book of Mormon when you get home."

Now it was Daniel's turn to chuckle. "That won't be necessary, Elias. Grandfather Erickson has already given me one."

"Well, of course. I should have known," Elias answered as he moved over into the shade. "Isn't he an amazing man?"

Daniel nodded. "I liked him from the start. You can just see the goodness in him."

"And the humor," Elias added.

Daniel smiled. "He is quite a character. And what a story. There's not much chance anymore to meet someone who came across the country in a wagon train."

The front door opened and Alaina, Eleanor, and Mother Erickson came out onto the porch.

Elias called to them. "About time you three made an appearance. We're melting in this heat."

Mother Erickson came down the steps waving her hand dismissively at her complaining son. "Oh, just hush now. We had important things to do. Besides, you could have come up to the cool of the porch."

"She has an answer for everything," Elias said aside to Daniel.

"I heard that," Mother Erickson warned as she walked toward the two men.

"And ears like a fox." Elias turned to the approaching women. "What were you doing in there anyway?"

"Preparing going-away gifts, if it's any of your business," Mother Erickson answered, winking at her son.

"And we know you two," Eleanor added. "You were probably glad for the time to talk politics."

Mother Erickson moved to Daniel and gave him a hug. "These two weeks have gone much too fast. I was just gettin' used to you."

"Thank you for everything," he replied, trying to keep his voice steady. "You made me feel so welcome."

Mother Erickson patted his arm.

"And your baked goods," Daniel added. "Oh, my! I think I've found someone who can rival my mother when it comes to chocolate cake."

Mother Erickson beamed. "I'm just glad we could put some meat on your bones." She handed him a package. "Here now, I've made you a shirt so you can have something fresh and new to put on when you meet your parents."

Daniel looked down at the brown wrapping. "How kind. How very, very kind," he said softly.

Alaina stepped forward and handed him a beautiful wedding-ring quilt. "For your mother and father." She blushed at the look of wonder on his face. "We . . . we all quilted it." Her voice caught. "Please, tell them hello from me, and that . . . that they are precious to me."

Daniel looked at her tenderly. "I know it's not proper," he said after a moment, "but, may I hug you? You're my dear friend and I care about you."

The tears coursed down Alaina's face as she moved to him.

He held her in the embrace of the quilt and whispered so only she could hear. "Be brave, Alaina. I have a feeling Nephi will make it through."

She sobbed, and Mother Erickson came to console her.

Daniel looked over at Eleanor, whose face was full of tenderness and light. She hid her present behind her back. "Oh, no. You'll get my present at the train station."

Daniel brightened. "If you're coming to the station, that's present enough for me."

"You wouldn't say that if you knew what this is."

"Well then, off we go!" he said, holding the vehicle door open for her.

"Wait! Wait, Mr. Man!" came a small, frantic voice.

The company turned to look as Katie raced around the side of the house carrying a bunch of wild sunflowers.

"I am wanting to give these to you!"

"Oh, my goodness." Grandmother Erickson smiled. "I wondered where she'd run off to. Didn't want to be left out of the gift giving, I guess."

Katie came up breathless and sweaty. She shoved the bouquet at Daniel, and everyone tried not to laugh at the fact that most of the flowers had been yanked up by the roots.

Daniel handed the quilt and package to Eleanor and took the flowers gallantly, surreptitiously shaking off the majority of the dirt clods still clinging to the roots. He knelt down to her eye level. "Thank you, Miss Katie. What a thoughtful gift. It will remind me of the day we took the walk together."

Katie smiled and kissed his forehead. "You is a nice man. Come back tomorrow to see me."

Daniel stood, struggling to control his emotions. "Thank you all. I'm very glad I came."

"We are too, Daniel," Mother Erickson said in a motherly tone. "We are too."

"On we go, then," Eleanor said, touching his arm, "or you're going to miss your train." She slid into the seat and Daniel followed. Elias pulled the truck away from the house, and Daniel waved out the open window.

Alaina dried the last of her tears. "Good-bye, Daniel. Good-bye!" she called.

* * *

"I'll get these things to the loading dock," Elias said, hefting Daniel's over stuffed duffel bag and suitcase.

"Thanks, Elias," Daniel answered, very grateful that he would have time alone with Eleanor. He found her standing by a noisy crowd of people near the train. She turned to him when he touched her elbow, and the sparkle in her eyes made his heart pound.

"Well, that was fast," she said.

"Actually, Elias took the bags."

"Oh good," she said simply. "They'll probably be loading anytime."

They stood for a moment in silence, then Daniel took her arm and whispered in her ear. "May I speak to you a moment?" he asked, pulling her gently away from the crowd.

"Of course," she said.

They moved to the edge of the platform where the branches and leaves of several large trees shaded them from the bright sun.

Eleanor felt a rush of anxiety as she looked into Daniel's unguarded expression. "We're . . . we're so glad you came to see us, Daniel . . . Alaina, and . . . me."

He was momentarily offset by her statement, but then his heart took over again, and as he looked at her face, sweet memories of their youth flooded back to give him courage. He smiled. "Do you remember when you and Alaina used to race each other?"

Eleanor relaxed and smiled. "Of course, and I was always the winner."

"Queen of the County Fair!" he said, grinning at her.

"That's right! How did you remember that?"

"I remember a lot about our times together, Eleanor, and even though I was a few years older . . ."

"Nearly seven," she offered.

"Nearly seven . . ." He stepped closer to her and continued, "I was always captivated by your brightness and joy of life."

Eleanor swallowed and stepped back. Her heart was pounding and she felt a bit lightheaded. This was Daniel . . . her childhood chum . . . at one time Alaina's beau. He was the one who always teased her about being a tomboy . . . about being scrawny and . . . why was he speaking to her like this? She looked questioningly into his brown eyes. This was the most handsome man she'd ever known . . . the most handsome next to Shawn Burbage. She stepped back again, checking her erratic emotions. During the weeks that Daniel had been visiting, she'd only mentioned Shawn in passing, and she'd never indicated that he was a suitor. *A suitor? Is that what Shawn is? And is that what Daniel desires?* Eleanor felt dizzy. She had no experience with this type of encounter. What was wrong with these silly men? Couldn't they be content with friendship?

"What a goose," she said out loud as she swayed against Daniel's side.

"Are you speaking of me or you?" Daniel asked with trepidation.

Eleanor steadied herself. "Me, of course."

"I don't think you're a goose, Eleanor Lund."

"Scrawny tomboy?" she said, trying to deflect his sincere tone.

"No. You amaze me with your brilliance, and you've grown into a beautiful young woman."

She laughed at that. "Daniel, we've been friends for a long time, and you know I am not beautiful. I am a standard-looking girl."

He smiled at her honesty. "To me you are beautiful." Eleanor gave him such an intense look that he lost his courage. "Of . . . of course, you may not find me . . . I may be reaching way beyond . . . considering my injuries . . . my drawbacks."

"Oh fiddle," Eleanor said bluntly. "You certainly know me well enough to know I don't care a fig about your wounds. They are a mark of honor to your bravery and character."

He moved toward her and she held up her hand.

"Now, just stop for a moment, Mr. Chart," she said innocently. "Are you telling me you have feelings for me?"

He gave her his disarming crooked smile. "Miss Lund, I have had feelings for you for the past five years." He lowered his head. "It's one of the reasons I couldn't say yes when Alaina asked me to marry her. How could I marry one Lund sister when I loved the other?"

"Love?" Eleanor's eyes widened. "You loved me . . . even then?"

Daniel nodded. "I did. Of course, I knew I'd have to wait until you grew up a bit." He looked briefly at the ground, then up into her face. "And now I see I may have waited a bit too long."

"What do you mean?"

"Well . . . I think that Mr. Shawn Burbage may have stronger feelings for you than friendship, Miss Eleanor."

Eleanor looked at him straight on. "I don't know what to say to that, Daniel. Shawn and I are very fond of each other, but we are both so busy with our studies that there's never been time for a discussion on the matter."

Daniel laughed, and much of the tension of the past few minutes was swept away. "'Time for a discussion on the matter?' Eleanor Lund, you are the sun in the sky!"

"Are you making fun of me?"

"Absolutely not."

The train whistle blew and they both jumped.

"Oh dear," Eleanor said grabbing Daniel's shirtsleeve and dragging him back toward the train. "This is a strange situation."

Daniel laughed and drew her back. "Not strange at all. I'm not asking for a promise, Miss Eleanor. I just want to know if you have any feelings for me."

She took a deep breath. "Feelings?"

"Yes."

Eleanor's forehead furrowed in concentration. "Man-woman kind of feelings?"

Daniel chuckled. "Yes."

She looked into his face, now flushed with health and anticipation, and felt a quiet remembrance settle into her heart. Her features softened. "Yes, Daniel, I have feelings for you."

He grinned at her and brushed his hand gently across her cheek.

Eleanor's face blushed as she realized that several people on the platform were watching them.

The train whistle blew again.

"Oh, my goodness!" Eleanor said with an agitated growl. "How are we going to sort this out?"

"Write to me."

"What?"

"Write to me and we'll 'discuss the matter.'"

"Now you *are* making fun of me."

Daniel took her hand. "Eleanor, you can't figure this out with your brain, no matter how brilliant it is. We'll just have to see what happens. Besides, I have just as much right to court you as Mr. Burbage does."

Eleanor opened her mouth to refute Daniel's assumption that she was being courted by anyone, when Elias rushed up to them. "Hey, where have you been? Didn't you hear the whistle?"

Daniel was beaming. "Sorry Elias, I didn't. I was only listening for one word."

"Well, you're about to miss the train!"

Daniel grabbed Eleanor's hand and ran. "I guess my parents would have a hard time understanding if I didn't come home."

"Without question." Eleanor affirmed. Daniel stopped abruptly, and she bumped into him. "Really, Daniel, staying is not an option."

He laughed. "No, it's that I forgot to give you this." He reached into his pocket and brought out a small box.

"Oh! Me too!" Eleanor gasped, reaching into her purse and handing him a small package. It's just some silly thing I found from our younger days."

He saluted her with the package. "Back before the flood, you mean?"

"Very funny." She turned him around and pushed him toward the train. "Now, get on that train before it leaves without you."

He shook Elias's hand. "Bye, Elias, thank you for everything." He bent down and shyly kissed Eleanor's cheek. "Bye, Eleanor. I'll write." Without waiting for any such assurance from her, he turned and stepped onto the train.

* * *

As Eleanor sat in the truck heading back to Grandfather Erickson's, she unwrapped an exquisite Art Nouveau enamel pin. It had been made in France, and Eleanor felt a tug of emotion as she considered the miles and perils it had come through to be resting now in the palm of her hand. She held the treasure against her heart and sighed heavily, trying to discipline her mind as it stumbled over the images and emotions of the last hour. She was not a girl for all this fervor and sentiment. She knew her heart was tied to Daniel because of shared adventures and youthful attachment. Indeed, her sense of honesty made her admit that Daniel was important to her, but her practicality kept showing her pictures of Grandfather Erickson, anatomy charts, and Dr. Thorndike's class. She also thought of the young man who sat next to her in those anatomy classes. Eleanor sighed again and put the pin back into its velvet bag. *Daniel's my friend and we'll write to each other,* she though placidly. *Just letters between friends.* She rolled down the truck's window and let her hair blow in the breeze.

* * *

Daniel gazed out the train's window as Salt Lake City slid away into a hot hazy afternoon. He was glad he'd come, and even though he was unsure of his chances of winning Eleanor's affections, he was peaceful about telling her his feelings—feelings he'd carried for a very long time. He thought about Mr. Burbage and knew that his rival was nearer to Eleanor in age, place, and interests, but that would not deter him from being a worthy rival.

He looked down at the present in his hand and removed the wrapping. It was a drawing of Eleanor as a young girl at Sutter Creek's Fourth of July picnic. Her hair was loose about her face. She had on a white summer dress, and was running barefoot through a patch of yellow dandelions. He read the note through his tears:

Dear friend,

I found this silly picture of me in some of Nephi's drawings. He must have drawn it from memory, because he forgot the fact that the Lund girls were wearing black that Fourth of July in reverence for my Uncle Cedrick's death.

Even though it's not quite right, I thought you might like it.

Eleanor

Daniel closed his eyes and took a deep breath. *Not quite right?* It was perfect. *And like it?* The image went straight into his heart.

Jimmy Gordon burst into the YMCA patio rest area carrying the newspaper and smiling from ear to ear. "Wait till you guys see this!" He guffawed, slapping the folded paper on his hand.

"Hush up, Gordon!" Cornell said sharply, "Erickson's trying to sleep."

"Sorry," Jimmy said, plopping down next to Cornell on the wooden bench and unfolding the small war-front gazette. "I'm going to be laughing about this one for a long time. Look at that!" He pointed to a picture of a chaplain standing up on a small hillock blessing a group of soldiers as they marched by him.

Cornell put aside his boot-polishing things and leaned forward. "Hey, that's Chaplan Duffy."

"Yep," Jimmy nodded, "and that's our unit marching by singing at the top of our lungs."

Cornell nodded. "I remember that day. So what's so funny?"

Jimmy chuckled. "Look at what the caption says under the picture."

Cornell took the paper from him and read. "Chaplan Duffy blesses troops as they march by singing 'Onward Christian Soldiers.'"

Cornell laughed loudly and Jimmy rolled on the ground hooting.

"'Onward Christian Soldiers'! Can you beat that?" Jimmy howled, crawling forward on his hands and knees to take another look at the picture, erupting with laughter as soon as he saw it.

Nephi sat up on the makeshift cot, rubbing his hands over his face.

Cornell tried to quiet his laughter, but with little success. "Oh . . . sorry, Erickson . . . it's just that . . . well, there's this picture . . ."

Jimmy handed the paper over to him. Nephi yawned and tried to focus on the picture. "That's Chaplan Duffy."

Jimmy nodded, holding back his mirth. "Read . . . read the caption."

Nephi read silently, and then said, "'Onward Christian Soldiers'?"

Jimmy and Cornell burst out laughing again.

Nephi looked at them, a slight smile at the corner of his mouth. "You guys weren't singing that."

Jimmy wiped the tears from his eyes and took the paper from him. "No, we weren't. If I remember correctly, at that moment we were singing some bawdy little song about French tarts and how they lifted their . . ."

"Jimmy, that's enough," Cornell said, kicking at him playfully. "Go show that to BC and Parkinson. I think they're inside. They won't stop laughing for a week."

Jimmy stood. "Yeah, they sing those songs louder than anybody." He moved off chuckling. "Maybe I'll look for Chaplan Duffy, too."

Cornell looked at Nephi's disappointed expression.

Nephi saw him watching and looked away. "Thanks for making Jimmy shut up."

"Don't mention it," Cornell answered.

Nephi poured water from his canteen and splashed it onto his face.

"You never sing those songs, do you?" Cornell asked, watching Nephi intently.

Nephi wiped away the water with the sleeve of his shirt. "No."

"And when we start talking dirty about women you walk away if you can."

Nephi looked at him straight on. "It offends me," he said quietly. "I think about my sweet wife and my brilliant sister-in-law . . ." His eyes filled with tears. "Would I want anyone saying those nasty things about them? Women are precious creatures—"

Cornell cut in. "Well, not all. Some are—"

"No," Nephi said emphatically, "they're all precious. If some of them have fallen, we men have to take the responsibility. We're the ones who've twisted up lust and love. We're the ones who put them in those demeaning roles because we can't control our passions."

Cornell sat staring at Nephi, a powerful feeling of affirmation coursing through his body.

Nephi paused, watching Cornell's face and discerning the look. "You know what I'm saying is true, don't you?"

Cornell nodded. "How did you . . . ?"

"That's the Holy Spirit, Cornell," Nephi said reverently, "the Holy Spirit confirming the things I've told you."

Cornell nodded again. "So . . . is that what every Mormon man believes? I mean is that what your church teaches?"

Nephi smiled and wiped the tears off his face. "Oh, my friend, if you only knew what the Church teaches about the magnificence of women, the power, glory, and magnificence of women." He shook his head. "But no, not every man in the Church treats women with the respect they deserve."

"I think I'd find your religion a fascinating study, Erickson, if it wasn't so restrictive."

"I suppose I can understand that," Nephi said, "but I've never felt like I was missing anything. I figure it's a small price to pay for a clearer look into heaven."

"Different from other churches?"

Nephi smiled. "A bit."

A high-pitched whistle sounded and the two men stood, their contemplative expressions replaced by eager anticipation.

"Mail call!" they chorused.

All the other men at the center had also risen at the sound and were moving to the place where the French mail carrier stood with his little box of letters. It was clear he liked his job. The mail carriers, along with the cooks, were the most loved men of the war. As the American soldiers moved toward him, his smile broadened, and he readied himself to hand out their precious connections to home.

* * *

Cornell laughed. "My brother Stanford was bitten by a dog!"

"No kidding?" Jimmy said, looking up from his own letter. "Is it serious?"

"Only when he wants to sit down."

Jimmy laughed. "My dad's thinking of selling the bakery, but, boy, oh boy, he'd better not. I want to run that place when I get back."

"My, that *would* make you a doughboy then, wouldn't it, Gordon?" Cornell said, saluting him.

"I'm a marine and proud of it," Jimmy answered, puffing out his chest.

Cornell looked over at Nephi. "Hey, Erickson, you're awful quiet. Everything all right at home?"

"My wife . . . she wrote this almost two months ago."

"Messed-up mail system," Jimmy complained.

Nephi stared blankly at the paper in his hand. "She's pregnant."

Cornell and Jimmy looked at each other, trying hard not to jump to any conclusions.

"She was almost three months along when I left, and she didn't tell me. She figured it would make my leaving too difficult if she . . ." He stood abruptly and started pacing. "She's . . . she's got to be eight months along now . . . and she's never said anything."

Cornell stood and held out his hand. "Congratulations, Nephi! Good news!"

Nephi stopped pacing and stared at Cornell's encouraging smile. He took his hand, shaking it slowly at first, then with more and more enthusiasm.

Suddenly Jimmy was beside him, slapping him on the back. "Good work, Erickson! This calls for a drink!" He moved off toward the supply tent.

"Remember, I don't drink, Gordon," Nephi called after him.

"But I do!" Jimmy returned. "I'll bring you some milk."

Nephi laughed. He looked over at Cornell. "It is good news, isn't it?"

"It is, Erickson. And . . . Alaina, that's your wife's name, right? She's doing well?"

Nephi sobered. "That's what she says, but . . ."

"But, what?" Cornell asked, putting on a clean pair of socks.

Nephi stared down at the letter. "I should be there. I should be with her."

"You have family nearby, right?"

Nephi nodded. "Yeah . . . she's living with my mother, and her sister's there . . . but it's not the same, Cornell."

Cornell put on his boot and began lacing it up. "Of course it's not the same, but at least you know she'll be taken care of."

Nephi silently reread the letter. "What am I doing halfway around the world?"

"Ah," was all Cornell said as he started lacing his other boot.

Nephi began pacing again. "What am I doing over here getting myself killed when I have a wife, and daughter, and baby at home?"

"You're not going to get killed, Nephi."

"Maybe not today, but the odds are pretty much against me, aren't they?"

"You must have thought it was the right thing to do when you enlisted," Cornell said without judgment.

Nephi stopped pacing. "I did. I felt it was the right thing to do."

"Well then," Cornell added, "whatever happens . . . happens."

Nephi looked over to a stand of trees alive with their summer-green leaves. *Where is my faith?* he asked himself. *Do I put my life and the life of my family in the hands of a loving God, or don't I?*

Cornell was beside him with his hand on his shoulder. "It is good news, Erickson . . . a little brother or sister to keep your daughter busy. Didn't you say she was a handful?"

Nephi nodded as tears ran down his cheeks. He brushed them away with his shirtsleeve. "Yeah, little Katie . . . she's a handful."

"All right then. We'll get these Germans taken care of in short order and have you on a boat for home."

Nephi nodded and began carefully folding the letter.

"Oh, no," Cornell said.

"What?" Nephi asked, looking up.

"It's Lieutenant Edwards," Cornell said, nodding his head toward the approaching figure.

Nephi turned. "Maybe he's just coming for a little relaxation."

"Lieutenant Edwards never relaxes," Cornell countered. "I bet he's just received new orders and we're off for more fighting."

Jimmy was at the side of his friends with three tin cups. "Is that Edwards coming down the road?" he asked, handing around the drinks.

"Big as life," Cornell answered.

Jimmy cussed. "You'd think they'd give us more than a couple hours rest." He looked down at the cup of liquor and brightened. "Well, anyway, here's to Nephi and his wife . . ."

"Alaina," Cornell prompted.

Jimmy smiled. "Alaina, and their new baby!"

"Cheers!" Cornell said.

They all raised their glasses and drank.

Jimmy raised his cup again. "And may the kaiser be plagued with never-ending dysentery."

"Not very cheerful, Gordon," Cornell said, lifting his cup. "Appropriate, but not very cheerful."

Lieutenant Edwards stopped near them. "Finish up there men, then gather at the building. We've got new orders." He turned to look at Nephi. "Finally caved into temptation, did ya, Erickson?"

Jimmy laid his hand over his heart. "Alas, it's only water, sir. Me and Cornell have been trying to corrupt this boy the whole war, but he won't budge." Edwards laughed. "Even now, he's drinking the news of his new baby with water."

Lieutenant Edwards slapped Nephi on the back. "Congratulations, soldier. Boy or girl?"

"I . . . don't know, sir," Nephi stammered, "the baby won't be born for a month."

The lieutenant gave him an odd look.

"It's a long story, sir," Cornell broke in. "We'll tell you when there's more time."

"That may not be for a while, men. We're into the thick of it. General Pershing is sending us to push back the Hun at the Saint-Mihiel salient, and after we've mopped up there we're joining in the last big push along the front. We have 'em on the run, boys!" He turned to gather other members of the company. "I say we get this war over with!" he shouted.

"I'm with you, sir!" Jimmy yelled, shoving his fist into the air. "Here's one for my friend RJ!"

"RJ!" Cornell and Nephi yelled.

"And mothers and children at home!" Cornell added loudly.

"And for my sweetheart in Memphis!" another soldier called out.

Soon the air was punctuated with more pledges of valor and dedication as the men of the Marine 6th gathered for orders.

30

The laboratory door opened without warning, and Eleanor Lund looked up quickly from the microscope—her mind simultaneously formulating an explanation and inventing a false permission. If it were a member of the janitorial staff it would be easy to circumvent the rules, for they thought all medical students were a bit odd and they avoided any excess of contact. Eleanor waited nervously for the person to present himself, and gave an audible groan when Dr. Thorndike entered the lab and switched on all the lights.

"Miss Lund?" he questioned, the look on his face a mixture of censure and astonishment. "Have you permission to be in the lab this early?"

"No, sir."

"And did anyone authorize the use of that equipment?"

"No, sir . . . but I . . ."

"But you felt you had some compelling reason to break the rules?"

She hesitated as she evaluated Dr. Thorndike's unwavering expression. "Yes, sir. I've been thinking about the patients admitted to the ward with the influenza."

"We're not calling it that, Miss Lund."

She gave an exasperated grunt. "Yes, I know . . . for the sensibilities of the other patients, but we know what it is. It gave us warning last spring, and now that it's September and the weather is turning cold, it's back . . . and I believe with a vengeance as the season progresses."

Dr. Thorndike moved to sit on the lab stool next to hers, giving her a side-long look and a frown. "How long have you been here, Miss Lund? You look . . . exhausted."

Eleanor evaluated Dr. Thorndike's crisp appearance and quickly attempted to smooth her wrinkled skirt and pin up strands of her tousled hair. "Sorry, sir . . . I snuck in when they first opened the building at five." Eleanor thought she caught a slight grin at the corner of the professor's mouth.

"So, what is it, exactly, that you're doing, Miss Lund?"

Eleanor took a deep breath. "Well, several things, actually. I've taken blood and sputum from the patients, and I've made cultures. I'm checking the blood for antibodies."

Dr. Thorndike's eyebrows rose. "The Wassermann test?"

"Yes, sir. And I'm checking the sputum for *Bacillus influenzae.*" Dr. Thorndike started to say something, but in her excitement for the subject matter, Eleanor talked right on without pause. "Now, Pfeiffer's tests in the 1890s declared *Bacillus influenzae* the influenza agent, but tests since have discredited his findings, and I tend to agree with them."

"Oh, you do?"

Eleanor stood up and started pacing. "Yes, sir. The bacillus shows up in too few cases. So, building on Pasteur and Koch's clear and proven theories—"

"Bacterial agents as the cause of disease?"

She turned to him. "Yes, sir. I thought . . ." She knew she was speaking too quickly, and took another deep breath to calm herself. "I thought . . . what if the infectious microbes were smaller than germs . . . than bacteria . . . Perhaps it's a filter-passing virus."

Dr. Thorndike was stunned. He looked intently into his student's exhausted and exuberant face, and found he could not speak.

Eleanor felt the need to defend her line of thinking. She paced again. "We know that Pasteur developed a vaccine for the rabies virus, and we know it's a living organism that's beyond the range of microscopic vision."

Dr. Thorndike cleared his throat, and Eleanor stopped talking. After a pause, the learned man looked at her straight on. "This is very advanced thinking, Miss Lund." He tapped his fingers together. "So, you think our influenza is viral?"

"Yes, that's why we can only treat the symptoms and not the disease itself. And . . ." She hesitated.

Dr. Thorndike smiled at her. "Yes, Miss Lund? There is more you've been contemplating?"

She nodded and sat down next to him. "Yes, sir. I was thinking that perhaps if it is a virus, that there may be a symbiosis between the virus and the secondary bacterial infections. That's what makes it so deadly. We can treat the secondary infection, but we have nothing to combat the virus."

Dr. Thorndike stared at her again.

There was a chuckle behind them, and they both turned to see Shawn Burbage at the door. "And we won't let them vote, can you imagine that?" He moved over to the lab table and set down a picnic basket. "Good morning, Dr. Thorndike."

"Good morning, Mr. Burbage. Are you assisting Miss Lund in her experiments?"

Shawn laughed. "Me? Oh no, sir. She is way beyond my puny brain."

Eleanor blushed.

"I just come to bring her food and unchain her once in a while from the microscope."

Dr. Thorndike laughed. "Well, don't get her too distracted." He stood. "I must say, I'm fascinated by the work she's doing." He looked at her with deference. "Have you thought about the work of Paul Erhlich and the immune system?" he questioned.

Eleanor brightened. "Yes . . . I have. That's why I was investigating Wasserman's theories on antibodies. What if you could make a serum from the blood of the convalescent patients? A serum of antibodies that could be used to boost the immune system?" The men were silent. "It's—it's only a thought," she stammered.

The professor's head nodded several times. "Keep thinking, Miss Lund." He smiled at her. "By all means, keep thinking. And, in the meantime, I'm going to check with my friend Dr. Blue at the PHS and find out the newest research being done. He may find several of your ideas interesting. Now, if you two will excuse me, I need to get my implements for our next class. Don't be late."

"We won't, sir," Shawn promised.

Dr. Thorndike turned to the storeroom, leaving his students alone with their picnic and sense of amazement.

Shawn plopped down on the stool vacated by their professor. "Dr. Thorndike was talking to you like you were a real person."

Eleanor stared at the door. "I know. That was very odd, wasn't it?"

"Well, actually, no. You obviously overwhelmed him with your intellect."

Eleanor rubbed her tired eyes. "My work, you mean. He was interested in my far-fetched ideas."

Shawn gave her a crooked smile and began unpacking the picnic basket. "Far-fetched ideas . . . of course, that was it," he scoffed. "He was looking at you as if you might be Pasteur himself."

"Don't be silly."

"Well, *Miss* Pasteur, then. And stop rubbing your eyes."

"They're just so tired," she moaned.

"Well, I've heard a little sleep does wonders for that. How many hours do you get a night, anyway?" He handed her a hard-boiled egg.

"I don't know," she hedged.

"Eleanor."

"Five or six."

"Eleanor."

"Four. I'm sorry, I just can't sleep. I'm worried about this influenza season. I think it's going to be worse than anyone imagines. What's this?" she asked, focusing on the egg.

"Egg," Shawn offered. "E-G-G. Egg." She stared at him. "If you didn't want me mothering you, Miss Lund, you shouldn't have told me about the secret extra hours in the lab."

She smiled at him and cracked the egg. "Thank you, how very thoughtful. I'm starving."

He smiled at her disarming frankness. "And there are peanut-butter sandwiches, apples, cinnamon puffs, a promise ring, raisins, honey cakes . . ."

Eleanor looked down at the assortment of things he'd set out on the table. There among the food items was a simple silver ring sitting in a petri dish.

"I thought I'd better put it in that," Shawn said, "or you might not have noticed it."

"A promise ring?"

"Yes. In your tired state, don't eat it."

She reached to take the ring. "What does it mean?"

"It . . . well, it . . ." He hadn't anticipated this question.

She looked over at him, her face pallid from lack of sleep, her hair messy, and he felt a longing to take her in his arms. Instead, he laid his forehead on the table and laughed.

"I'm sorry," she said with chagrin. "This was supposed to be a tender moment, and I ruined it."

"No," Shawn answered, sitting up and taking her hand, "I should have picked a better time . . . and better food."

Eleanor giggled, then yawned. "Oh, my goodness. I must look like something out of a monster book."

Shawn took the ring from her and put it on the end of his index finger. "This, Miss Lund, is a promise ring. It means that I will promise to continue to honor and admire you—which will not be difficult—promise to make you laugh, and promise to be your friend. In return, you will promise to go on outings with me—when you have time—promise to let me help you when things get difficult, and promise to continue to be my friend . . . until the time comes for us to talk about being more than friends."

Eleanor felt her heart pounding, and she concentrated on not blurting out anything stupid as she was prone to do when her emotions overwhelmed her. The moments passed, then slowly she reached over, took the ring, and slipped it on the ring finger of her right hand.

Shawn leaned over and twined a piece of her hair around his finger. "Miss Lund, your friendship is . . ."

The class bell rang.

Eleanor stood with a yelp, shoved a cinnamon puff into her mouth, and began cleaning. "We're going to be late!" she mumbled through the puff.

Shawn laughed and began helping.

"Don't laugh at me," Eleanor scolded after swallowing her food.

"I would never laugh at you," Shawn vowed, laying his hand on his heart. "It's just that I think it's funny that you're worried about being late. With what Dr. Thorndike witnessed of your work, he probably wouldn't mind if you missed half the class."

"Well, I'd mind," Eleanor returned, "so, hurry." She handed him the microscope to put away. "Hurry, but be careful."

Shawn walked with an exaggerated step until Eleanor growled at him. Within five minutes they had everything in order and were sprinting hand-in-hand to Dr. Thorndike's class.

* * *

Rain, cold and heavy, hammered on the rooftops and pelted the head of any Sutter Creek citizen unlucky enough to have an errand that sent them out of doors. Philomene Johnson had walked in the blustery rainless morning to the café for a meeting with the Cultural Society, and now found herself trapped by the sudden downpour.

The women had been busy for several hours with breakfast and talk: The agenda included discussions about the selling of war bonds and the sewing of clothing for the soldiers. They'd also talked about the canceled speaking engagement of Professor James E. Talmage from the Mormon Church. When the notice had first arrived about the learned man's nationwide speaking tour and his stop in Sacramento, Philomene was intensely curious about the subject matter. Professor Talmage was the Church's official spokesman, and his lecture would concern the stance of the Church concerning the Great War in Europe and America's involvement. Philomene was also hoping Professor Talmage would make reference to his book *Jesus the Christ,* which had been published only a few years earlier. She had made up her mind to attend the event, even if it meant venturing away from the safety of her home. But now the lecture was canceled, and she well understood the reasoning. Since the circulation of the notice, there had been several reported cases of a virulent influenza in San Francisco and Sacramento, and Philomene supposed the Church did not want to risk the health of one of its members.

"I don't think it's going to let up anytime soon," Frank Bigler, the café proprietor, said.

"I know," Philomene sighed, bringing her thoughts to the present. "I should have left with all the others."

"Do you want another cup of tea?"

"No, thank you, Mr. Bigler, three is my limit." She sat drumming her fingers on the windowsill. "I shall just sit here and wait for a break in the storm." She was at the point where she would brave even a slight slackening.

She looked up and squinted. Although the incessant rain obscured detail, she was sure she saw young William Trenton dismounting a horse on the opposite side of the street. He hurriedly tied the reins to the post and dashed to the office door of Dr. McIntyre. He tried the handle and found it locked. He pounded on the door and even kicked it.

Philomene stood. "Oh my," she whispered. "Mr. Bigler, have you any notion of Dr. McIntyre's whereabouts?"

The proprietor looked up from a stack of bills. "He may be down to Pastor Wilton's. I hear tell his wife's not well."

Philomene threw on her coat and grabbed her cane. She moved as quickly as she could to the door.

"You can't go out in that!" Frank called to her as she stepped out onto the rain-splattered walkway.

The walkways were sheltered by an overhang, but the wind was blowing the torrent of rain at such an angle that such offered no protection. Within moments Miss Johnson was drenched.

William Trenton was attempting to remount his horse as she crossed the street. "Mr. Trenton!" she yelled, waving to get his attention.

The slight sixteen-year-old rushed to her and took her arm. "Heaven's sake, Miss Johnson, what are ya doin' out in this?" He led her to the covered walkway in front of Dr. McIntyre's office.

Philomene steadied herself on her cane. "Are you looking for the doctor?"

"I am, ma'am, yes. Mr. and Mrs. Regosi are very ill." Urgency and fright were stamped on William's face.

"Try Pastor Wilton's."

"Thank you, ma'am." He turned to go, then turned back. "Let me get you home, Miss Johnson."

"I'll be fine, Mr. Trenton," she said firmly. "Go fetch the doctor."

"Yes, ma'am." He threw himself into the saddle and quickly turned the Appaloosa toward the pastor's home.

Philomene watched until the rain swallowed him in a blur of gray. A shudder ran through her, either from cold or apprehension. *Both Rosa and Emilio ill?* She had never known either of them to suffer with more than slight colds; besides, hadn't she talked with Emilio just the other day? The spry horseman had been excited about a buyer from San Francisco—Pastor Wilton's wealthy brother who'd come to the ranch to look at breeding stock. The man had ended up purchasing two mares and a stallion.

Philomene's stomach twisted as she considered the grim possibilities, and her mind jumped to a recent letter from Eleanor Lund. It warned of a harsher-than-normal flu season and suggested she keep a close watch on her students.

A stiff wind rattled the overhang, bringing Philomene's attention to her sodden clothing. As she did, she straightened her spine, grasped the cane with frozen fingers, and moved off toward her cottage. She gritted her teeth against the storm and a feeling of dread.

31

The sun was setting against the cloudy horizon in sheets of gold—brilliant, honeyed flecks fanning out to orange and ginger over the craggy hillsides and woods of the Argonne forest.

Nephi looked away from the splendor to his tin plate of biscuits and hash. He wanted to look at the sunset, but he found it painful to look at something so beautiful, for it spoke of hope and future, and those things did not exist for him. He lifted the forkful of food to his mouth, half of it splattering back onto his plate from the shaking of his hand. He glanced around to see if anyone had noticed. There were a few men walking toward the village, a few asleep in the small farmhouse, and Jimmy and Cornell were playing a game of blackjack. They were sitting quite close to him, yet their voices seemed far away.

He looked down at the gray muck on his plate. Lieutenant Edwards said the battle for St. Mihiel had been a victory for the mostly untried American troops. *A victory?* Nephi's stomach clenched as images of the battle assaulted his memory. The German soldiers were at the end of their strength and were surrendering by the thousands. Lieutenant Edwards said American troops had taken over ten thousand prisoners in the four days of the battle. Thousands had been taken on September 13 . . . General Pershing's birthday . . . Edwards said it was a great birthday gift. September 13? He felt madness tap at the edge of his mind. When was that?

"Gordon," Nephi called, his voice sounding ragged.

"Yeah?" Jimmy answered.

"What day is it?"

"You mean like day of the week?"

"No," Nephi said, pushing the spoon around on his plate. "No, the date."

"Oh. September twentieth."

"And the battle started?"

"On the twelfth. But, it only lasted four days." Jimmy threw down his cards and came over to sit beside his friend. "What are ya thinking about that for, Erickson? Let it go. That battle's over and we're all still here."

Nephi dropped his plate to the ground. "Yeah. Yeah, you're right. Hey! How about Lieutenant Edwards coming up with all those prisoners and his pistol was empty? He'd fired all his shots, and he led off a couple hundred prisoners with an empty pistol. That's some story, isn't it?"

Jimmy gave Cornell a worried look. "Yeah, some story."

Cornell came over and put a blanket around Nephi's shoulders.

"What's this for?" Nephi asked.

"You're shivering. I thought you might be cold."

"Oh," Nephi said, tucking his hands into his armpits. "Yeah, I guess I am."

"So, why don't you go in and try and get some sleep?" Jimmy suggested, keeping his tone casual as he nodded toward the farmhouse.

"No," Nephi said immediately. "No . . . I . . . why can't we just sit here and talk?" His vivid blue eyes were filled with fear.

Cornell sat down on the rickety bench on the other side of him and rested his back against the wall of the house. "Sure, Erickson, let's talk. But not about the battle or the war."

"Sure, sure . . . not about the war," Nephi returned, stomping his feet several times to get the circulation going.

"I received a letter from my sister Violet the other day," Cornell said immediately. "Seems she and Daisy have volunteered with the Red Cross—making up the lost numbers for some of the medical personnel over here with us."

"Yeah, that Spanish Influenza is starting to creep in all over the place, from what I hear," Jimmy blurted out. "So, no sneezing you two, do ya hear me?"

Cornell cast him a warning look, but Jimmy didn't catch on.

"It's really taking hold in the military training camps back home," Nephi mumbled.

"Ah, they'll get it under control," Cornell said, his voice actually sounding confident. "So, Jimmy, what baseball team do you like?"

Jimmy gave him an odd look. "You know the answer to that, Cornell. We talk about it all the . . ."

Cornell did a little head nod toward Nephi. "Humor me, will ya? I forgot."

"Oh yeah, well," Jimmy said, catching on, "New York Yankees, of course—the greatest team ever. Of course, I like that Ty Cobb guy from the Detroit Tigers. Around my neighborhood they call me the Ty Cobb of Cooper Street."

"How about you, Erickson?" Cornell asked. "You play baseball back in Salt Lake City?"

Nephi nodded and looked up at him. "I did. My brother Elias and I were on the Union team."

"What position did you play?"

"First base."

"Were you any good?"

Nephi grinned. "I guess so."

Cornell nodded. "I'll bet you were, and probably a pretty good hitter, too."

Jimmy laughed. "Probably not much cussing or chewing goin' on in those Mormon teams, I'd imagine."

Nephi stiffened, but smiled over at his friend. "No, but the coach made sure we had milk and cookies at the end of the game."

Jimmy hooted. "And how about you, Duncan? They let you play sports in that fancy college of yours?"

"Well, I was a member of the rowing club."

Jimmy hooted again. "Oh, boy! I bet the girls went wild over that."

Cornell smiled. "Actually, they did."

"Hey! Speaking of girls—"

Cornell sobered immediately. "Not now, Gordon."

"No, no. You got me wrong. I wasn't gonna say anything bad. I was just thinking of Nephi's girl . . . ya know, his wife." Cornell groaned. "No, I mean, it's nearing the end of September, and isn't that when your baby was supposed to be born?"

Nephi stared at him as though he'd just been punched in the stomach.

Cornell swore.

"What?" Jimmy said, trying to redeem himself. "That's a good topic, isn't it? I mean we're all excited about the new baby."

"Gordon, shut up," Cornell said softly.

"Sorry, Erickson," Jimmy said.

Jimmy and Cornell were speaking to him, but their voices were far away. His mind was sliding sideways. He could feel the tearing of thoughts . . . images shredding and regrouping in pictures and words that didn't make sense . . . Alaina pitching for the Union team . . . Cornell rowing a boat across a black lake . . . Jimmy making bread . . . Alaina sneezing into a German flag . . . his mother holding a crying baby. He pressed his hands against the sides of his head and rocked back and forth. *Stop. Stop. Think of something real. Open your eyes and look at the beautiful sunset.* He opened his eyes and stared down blankly at the mess of food on the ground. He groaned as his gaze flickered to his muddy boots, and suddenly his mind fell away.

He was running—running and looking for cover as 100,000 artillery shells screamed overhead and a million bullets cut across his body like slivers of glass. Rockets and flares in all directions. Running forward fifty yards and falling— falling into a machine-gun nest—killing two soldiers—the third soldier shrieking at him—shrieking and running off in a mad fit. *They were probably his friends . . . I've killed the German boy's friends.* His soul was coming out of his mouth! He bit the back of his hand to keep it in. *Please, Father, please don't let me lose my soul.* He was screaming and someone was shaking him.

"Erickson! Erickson, listen to me! You're not out there! You're not in the battle!"

Something hit him hard across the face, and his mind focused on the cold night air. He choked. "The sun's gone down. The sun's gone down, Cornell."

Cornell held him tightly. "Yes, the sun's gone down, but we're together . . . you, me, and Jimmy."

Nephi clutched Cornell's coat and laid his head on his friend's chest. "I'm sorry, Cornell. I'm no good to you guys. I don't know what's happening to me. I've gone yellow."

Cornell pushed him up. "No, you haven't, and you haven't let me or Gordon down yet, has he Jimmy?"

Jimmy swallowed, unsure how to answer. "No, Erickson, you've never let us down."

"You're just tired, Erickson. I don't see you sleeping much," Cornell stated.

"That's true, Erickson," Jimmy confirmed, "not enough sleep—and that can make your mind do funny things."

Nephi latched on to this idea as redemption. "You think that's it? Not enough sleep?" He clenched and unclenched his hands to make them stop shaking.

"Sure," Cornell said firmly, watching his friend with a wary eye. "You're just worn out."

Nephi stood slowly, picking up the blanket and looking over to the darkening horizon. "Maybe I'll try to get a few hours."

"Take a few days," Cornell said. "Lieutenant Edwards said we're not going anywhere for a while, so pretend you're a bear and hibernate."

Nephi smiled gratefully over at him. "Thanks Cornell . . . Jimmy." He moved to the open farmhouse doorway.

"Oh, and say your prayers," Cornell instructed. "I haven't seen you saying your prayers lately."

Nephi hung his head, then nodded.

After he'd gone in, Cornell and Jimmy stood in silence several moments, each searching their loyalties and misgivings.

"Let's go down to the village," Jimmy said suddenly.

"To get a drink?" Cornell said, smiling.

"No, there's a church down there."

"A church?" Cornell questioned, giving Jimmy a sideways look.

"Yeah, a church!" Jimmy said defensively, then his voice softened. "I feel like sitting in a church for a while. You have a problem with that?"

Cornell smiled. "Not at all."

32

"I want Eleanor here!" Alaina yelled. "I want my sister!"

"She's on her way," Dr. Lucien assured. "Now stop yelling at me, young woman."

Alaina gathered her senses and breathed deeply. After a minute she offered, through gritted teeth, "Sorry. Sorry, Dr. Lucien. I just need her here." A tear slid out of the corner of her eye.

"I understand," the competent healer said, taking her pulse. "Relax. Now I'm sure—" The front door opened. "Ah . . . there, you see? You just needed to trust me."

The bedroom door opened and Eleanor came bustling into the room, shedding her coat and scarf and smiling from ear to ear. "Hi, Laina!"

"Oh, Elly. I'm so glad you're here."

"Good evening, Dr. Lucien," Eleanor said, tossing her outerwear behind her onto the living room floor.

"Elly!"

"Oh, I'll pick them up later. There are more important things to take care of right now."

Dr. Lucien smiled. "Indeed."

"How's she doing, doctor?"

"Excellent. We should have a baby shortly."

"Should I put on the kettle?" Eleanor asked, smiling down at her sister.

"Let me do that," Dr. Lucien answered. "You stay here and monitor her pulse and contractions."

Eleanor smiled over at him. "Yes, sir."

"I'm placing you in very competent hands, Mrs. Erickson. Try not to yell at her now, all right?"

"Yes, doctor," Alaina answered contritely.

Dr. Lucien chuckled and left the room.

"What was that all about?" Eleanor questioned.

"Oh, I was just a little upset because you weren't here with me right away," Alaina confessed.

Eleanor smiled. "So you yelled at poor Dr. Lucien?"

"I did."

"Heavens, Alaina, what with all the family having telephone boxes now, I thought I got here pretty fast." She placed a cool cloth on Alaina's head. "Mother Erickson called the doctor, then me, and then Sarah."

Alaina groaned.

"Are you having a contraction?"

"No," Alaina said. "Do you know if Agnes McGinnis was the operator on duty?"

"I'm not sure. Is she the one who tries to sound like a sultry actress?"

"That's her."

"Yep. She was on."

"Wonderful," Alaina said resignedly, "by now half of Salt Lake City knows I'm having the baby. Well, the half with telephone boxes anyway."

Eleanor laughed. "Well, I guess every modern invention has its draw-backs."

"You mean like Katie and the telephone."

"Oh, she hasn't?" Eleanor said flatly, trying to keep the giggle out of her voice.

"Oh yes, she has. She drags her little step stool over to the box, cranks the bell, gets the operator on the line, and has a nice little chat."

Eleanor covered her mouth, but her body shook with laughter.

"I'm tempted to use that little stepstool for firewood," Alaina threatened in good humor.

They were both laughing when Dr. Lucien came back into the room.

"Well, this is more like it," he said approvingly. "A baby should come into a world filled with warm blankets and laughter."

At that moment the look on Alaina's face changed from mirth to pain, and Eleanor went immediately to get another cool cloth. "I'm right here, Alaina . . . right here with you."

"Miss Lund," Dr. Lucien said after checking to make sure that everything was progressing normally, "how would you feel about delivering this baby?"

"Me?"

"Yes. Without question you are qualified. You have performed deliveries in your studies?"

"Several," Eleanor responded. "It seems to be the one area of medicine where men defer to women."

"Well, then?"

Eleanor turned excitedly to Alaina. "It's up to you, Laina—if you'd rather I not . . ."

"Oh, don't be a goose, Elly. I'd love you to bring this baby into the world."

"And I'll be here to assist if you should need me," Dr. Lucien said with a smile.

"Thank you, doctor."

As Eleanor went to scrub her hands, Alaina took the opportunity to tease Dr. Lucien. "I'd practice putting those cold towels on my head," she instructed. "With Eleanor in charge, I'm afraid you won't have much else to do."

Dr. Lucien laughed.

* * *

Two hours later, Eleanor placed a squalling little boy in her sister's arms. "Queen of the County Fair for the second time," she announced. They were alone, as Dr. Lucien had been called away on an emergency.

Alaina wept as she looked at her son, wept with relief that he was well and healthy, with joy at the new life in her arms, and with loneliness that Nephi was not beside her.

"Oh, Eleanor, you were wonderful!" Alaina said. "You're going to be the best doctor in the history of the world."

Eleanor finished drying her hands and took a deep breath. She turned away from the window where she'd been gazing out at the starry night and saying a prayer. "Thank you, Laina. I do love it." She came over and knelt by the side of the bed. "Have you decided on a name?"

"I'm not sure," Alaina answered. "I'd like to share something with you, and see what you think."

Eleanor nodded. "Of course."

"Get into the top drawer of the dresser, and bring me the first letter in the pile, please."

The baby was calm now, and Eleanor moved quietly to the dresser and brought back the letter. "This one?"

Alaina looked it over and nodded. "Read it to me."

Eleanor knelt back down by the bed. "Are you sure?"

"Yes."

Eleanor took the letter quietly from the envelope and began reading.

My dear Alaina,

For some reason the mail was delayed, and I have just received your letter. I am writing this quickly so it can go out today with the letter carrier. They are sending us someplace else, and I don't know when I may get the chance to write again. Anyway, enough of that. I'm not angry with you, and I'm excited about the baby. I just wish with all my heart that I could be there with you. If I could somehow run away from this war and back to you, I'd do

*it in a second. Let Mother and Eleanor take care of you. You are
my precious girl.*

*Love,
Nephi*

If it's a boy, maybe Samuel would be a good name.

Tears welled up in Eleanor's eyes. "Oh, how kind of him."

Alaina took the letter. "I know, and I've thought about it, but it seems to be better to name him after his father."

"Alma?" Eleanor questioned, looking perplexed.

Alaina smiled. "No, the baby's father. Nephi," she said with conviction. "Nephi Samuel Erickson. What do you think of that name?"

Eleanor looked at the baby. "Perfect," she said. "The perfect name for a perfect little boy."

33

"Tout le monde a la bataille!"

The battle cry of Field Marshall Foch was repeated a thousand times along the front as communications officers received the word via field telephones and telegraphs, and then filtered it down to the company commanders and platoon leaders. "Everybody to battle!"

Nephi sat in the cold misty night with the group of men that he had come to think of as brothers. He had found a place in his madness that hardened his resolve—it was submission to fate. It didn't matter what happened, because there was no meaning to any of it anyway—no grand purpose as he'd always supposed. A godly plan only made sense to a man walking to work down a sunlit street . . . a man wearing a suit, cloth hat, and soft leather shoes. It could only make sense to a woman taking a roast and potatoes out of the oven to feed her family. Here, in the cold mud and drizzling rain, the master was Fate, and he was a dispassionate companion.

"Erickson! Pay attention!" Lieutenant Edwards snapped.

Nephi swung his head slowly in the lieutenant's direction. "Yes, sir. Sorry, sir," he answered.

Jimmy Gordon and Cornell Duncan shared a look.

Lieutenant Edwards continued with instructions. "General Pershing himself chose this section of ground for us to take because he thinks that the British and French troops don't have enough fighting spirit left for the task."

One of the men swore. "Is it any wonder, Lieutenant? The poor sods have been hanging on for four years."

"I agree with you, Private. So let's get in there and do our part. During the last couple of weeks we've brought out about 200,000 Allied soldiers and replaced them with about 600,000 of us."

"Wall-to-wall Americans!" Jimmy called out.

Edwards smiled. "Yeah, wall-to-wall Americans." His voice gained in strength. "So, let's not let the general down!"

Some of the men murmured assent, some growled deep in their throats, while others just gripped their rifles more tightly.

"We're going into that forest, aren't we, Lieutenant?" Jimmy asked fearlessly.

Lieutenant Edwards nodded. "But it's not just a forest, Gordon." He looked at the men straight on. "Reconnaissance flights and our good, French mapmakers show us that the Meuse-Argonne region is a tangle of ravines, woods, and rocky cliffs. It's a perfect area for defense, and the Germans have held it for four years. You can pretty much bet that they've improved on those natural defenses during that time: machine-gun nests, barbed wire, spikes, cement bunkers and pillboxes . . ."

Some of the men looked sick.

It doesn't matter, Nephi thought calmly. *Kill or be killed.* That was war. That was the necessity.

Edwards poked at the map. "We're moving to take out these railway systems near Sedan. We can divide the German armies here, forcing a collapse of the German position on the front."

Nephi watched as several soldiers set their jaws in acceptance.

The lieutenant continued. "But we've got to break the Hindenburg line first—it's mess of fortifications the Germans don't think we can bust through." He looked at their defiant faces. "I'm gonna be honest with you men, it's gonna be a tough fight, and once the push starts we just keep on pushing."

Nephi smiled. He wished RJ was here to ask a question about food, or if they were going to push the Boche clear back into Germany. *RJ . . . good ol' RJ.* Well, at least his friend from Kentucky no longer had to suffer the sound and stench of the battlefield, or the fear of being gutted or gassed. Nephi shook his head and looked over to Lieutenant Edwards.

"General Pershing wants certain objectives met by certain dates, and we're going to try to accommodate him."

Jimmy, along with several other men, smiled.

"You will go into action carrying only your gas mask, two hundred rounds of ammo, two ammo bandoleers, rifle, iron rations, and water." Edwards paused and ran his hand over his short hair. "There will be no blankets, no overcoats, no raincoats."

Cornell looked over at Nephi, who sat staring at the lieutenant with an unreadable expression.

"No extra weight to hold back the attack. Understood?" The men nodded. "And don't expect to receive any supplies for forty-eight hours—those units will be moving a lot slower than us."

Nephi smiled to himself. At this point RJ would have been complaining about no hot breakfasts.

"All of you have been in battle at this point," Edwards continued, "so you know what's expected and how to behave. Look out for your buddies, because they'll be looking out for you." Edwards stood and folded the resin-covered map. "It's been a great honor to serve with you, men. I'm proud of the job you've done." His voice became hard and intense. "Now, let's go get this war over with so we can get back to American home cooking."

"Yeah!" Jimmy yelled, and several other soldiers cheered.

Burnt toast. Nephi felt his mind slip, and he yelled out, "Let's kick the kaiser over to Kentucky! We'll let RJ's family take care of him!"

There was dead silence for a moment as everyone stared at him, then several soldiers shouted approval while others laughed.

Jimmy thumped Nephi on the back. "Well said, Erickson! Well said!"

As the men drifted off to their various preparations for the upcoming battle, Cornell came over and sat down next to Nephi, who was pretending to inspect his gas mask.

"Are you going to make it through this?" Cornell finally asked.

Nephi didn't look at him. "What do you mean?"

"You know what I mean, Erickson. Are you going to be able to keep it together? Because Gordon and I were thinking you might want to go over to the hospital and have a talk with one of the doctors."

"You think I'm yellow?" Nephi snapped.

"No," Cornell answered sadly, "I think you're one of the finest men I know, and I think that even though you're suffering in ways I can't imagine, you're going to stick with the rest of us through this nightmare."

Nephi nodded. "That is exactly what I'm going to do, Duncan. I'm not gonna let you guys go out there without me."

Cornell took out his pocket watch. "And what about your wife and daughter?"

Nephi gave an anguished cry. "Don't! Don't talk about them!"

Cornell laid his hand on Nephi's shoulder. "This last push is going to take everything we've got, Erickson. You better be able to pull strength from somewhere."

Nephi looked straight at his friend, his vivid blue eyes holding a savage determination. "The only way to the other side, Duncan, is through."

Cornell stared at him for a long moment, then patted him on the back. "Then through it is."

* * *

The battle began in misty rain and heavy fog. The woods smelled of pine and rotted leaves as the American troops pushed forward into the Argonne sector. Jimmy, Cornell, and Nephi moved together into the mutilated terrain, keeping low and listening hard for the shrill whistles that conveyed commands. Nephi's hand went to the satchel that carried his gas mask. He wanted it available immediately at the first sign of yellow smoke. Of course, the AEF artillery gunners were periodically sending over camouflage smoke shells with the rest of the missiles, and that, coupled with the fog, made it nearly impossible to see anything.

"Erickson!" Jimmy yelled, grabbing his arm and yanking him sideways. "Look where you're going."

Nephi stared down at the carcass of a headless horse he'd been about to fall over. "Thanks, Gordon!" he yelled. He forced his mind to push forward into a dark world with pinnacles and ridges of frozen mud, deep shell chasms half filled with rusted tangles of wire, bare, splintered trees, thickets of gorse, and dead soldiers. Some bodies seemed newly dead or dying, while it was obvious some had lain on the unconsecrated ground for days.

Through the din of shells, Nephi heard rifle fire shortly ahead and to his left. He thought he heard Lieutenant Edward's voice calling to take cover. The whistle blew the gas warning, and Nephi scrambled into a muddy shell hole and threw on his mask. Suddenly the sky shone with a bluish-white light as the Germans sent up a myriad of star flares, then fanlike flares mounted the heavens like flames from a hundred smelters, and signal rockets burst in green, red, and white flashes.

A soldier slammed in beside him as the German counterattack began, and Nephi involuntarily shoved the man aside.

"Hey, Erickson, it's me!" Cornell shouted, resettling his gas mask.

"Sorry, Duncan!" Nephi yelled back. "Didn't recognize you."

Cornell nodded. "We're trying to make it up to that ridge."

"What ridge? I can't see a thing," Nephi growled.

"The lieutenant said to just follow the whistle blast."

At that moment the sound came, distant and to their left.

"Come on!" Cornell said, crawling over the side of the pit. "We don't want to get separated!"

Nephi followed, finding it difficult to keep his friend in sight. A team of stretcher-bearers emerged from the fog carrying an infantry man with a chest wound.

The wounded are already coming back? Nephi wondered. *How long have we been out here?* He jerked his head around, and Cornell was gone. Panic began to settle in his chest. *Keep moving . . . just keep moving.* The whistle blew again and Nephi corrected his course to follow it. More rifle fire sounded, and he slouched behind a tree. The sky was growing lighter, the fog lifting slightly, allowing him to see about twenty feet around him. At the edge of the fog he could make out the blurred form of a marine kneeling on the ground. *Is that Duncan?* Nephi rushed heedlessly forward. A few stray bullets flew past his head, and he fell flat on his stomach and crawled. *It is Cornell! It is! Is he shot?* Cornell had his mask off and was speaking broken bits of German.

Nephi screamed. "No!"

He thought Cornell had taken off his mask too soon and was now dying and delirious.

Cornell turned toward Nephi's approach and yelled at him. "Stay back! Stay back, Erickson!"

Nephi ignored him, yelling back. "Put on your mask, you idiot!"

"They sounded the clear!" Cornell barked, pushing Nephi away from him. "I told you to stay away."

"Are you hurt?" Nephi gasped, stripping off his mask. "Are you hit?"

"No!" Cornell said fiercely, swinging his focus back to the scene in front of him.

Nephi suddenly realized that the danger might be what Cornell was focusing on. He scrambled onto his knees and aimed his rifle in the direction of Cornell's gaze.

"No!" Cornell screamed. "They've already been hit!"

Down the slope about ten feet from Nephi and Cornell's position were two young German lads. The one looked to be about thirteen or fourteen years old. He'd been hit in the gut with shrapnel, and he was jabbering nonstop. The other boy seemed only a few years older, and a piece of shrapnel had pierced his lung. The younger boy held a heavy nickel pocket watch in a hand covered with blood. Broken wheels and pieces of brass fell out of the watch through a jagged hole. A bullet had gone clean through it.

Nephi could not understand how the boy was keeping up such a fluid conversation with so serious a wound. "What's he saying?" Nephi asked in a strangled voice.

Cornell looked sick, and dirty tear tracks stained his face. "He says the other boy is his brother and that his name is Rudolph. They've been in the war . . ." Cornell's voice broke, "a month. He . . . he wants to know if they can surrender."

With a strangled gurgle, Rudolph died. His younger brother was so lost in shock from his injury that the tragic moment passed without realization. The boy kept on talking.

"He wants to know if the French can fix his watch. His mother gave it to him just before he came out and . . . he doesn't want her to think he's been . . ." Cornell searched for the word, "careless." Cornell swallowed hard, speaking to the boy. "Don't worry. The French are good with watches." Cornell lowered his head. "Ja, ja mein junger Freund. Mach Dir keine Sorgen. Don't worry."

The boy smiled and slowly lay back against the soft bank of the hill. His arm slid over and rested against his brother's face.

The whistle sounded shrill and faint, and Nephi and Cornell jumped to their feet and ran, not seeing the pocket watch as it tumbled through the veil of mist into the forest undergrowth.

* * *

"It's the machine-gun nests," Cornell reported bluntly. "They're ripping us to shreds."

Sixteen men were hunkered down around Lieutenant Edwards in an unblasted stand of trees.

"Yeah," Jimmy pitched in, "it seems those gunners have made some sort of suicide pledge for their Fatherland."

Lieutenant Edwards took a drink from his canteen and surveyed his beleaguered men. They had been shoving forward for five days with little rest and food against an enemy offering more resistance than expected. The fiercely held heights of Montfaucon had finally been taken, with a devastating loss of life. Edwards felt the water hit his empty stomach, and he gritted his teeth against the anguish he felt for his men. He looked out at the gray day.

"The supply units should catch up with us tonight," he said in his officer's voice, not knowing if it were true. "Today we make it to the top of this rise, taking out the machine guns as we go. We have to keep up with our flanking platoons, so keep moving."

"I spotted a concrete pillbox with the field glasses," Cornell informed him, "about two hundred yards up that slope. Looks like it's been shelled, but it would offer some cover."

"Good job, Duncan," Edwards said. "That's our next objective, men. And Erickson," he snapped, "find a helmet."

Nephi looked up, surprised to hear his name. "Yes, sir." He hadn't been aware that his helmet was missing. *Helmet. Helmet. I have to go up that hill and find a hat.* He smirked. *What difference will it make? I've seen lots of helmets with bullet holes in them, or ripped apart by shrapnel.*

"Erickson." Jimmy and Cornell were by his side. "What happened to your helmet?" Jimmy asked. "I thought RJ was the only one who lost anything."

"I've taken his place, I guess," Nephi answered. "And I don't know where my helmet is. I fell down a couple of times as we were coming off that last hill." The shelling had been intense, and he'd actually been moving too fast to keep his legs under him. "Now, if I'd known, I would have grabbed a hat off that pile back by where the grave detail was working. With all our dead soldiers, there were a couple hundred to choose from."

Cornell flinched; just then the word was passed along to move out. "Size seven and a quarter," Nephi murmured to a couple of the men passing by him, "just in case you see anything." Then he shouldered his ammo bandoleer and picked up his rifle.

The unit started up the slope, finding whatever cover they could. Jimmy had become especially expert at "playing the wily rabbit" as he called it. He could find the slightest depression under a log and disappear completely. He was crouched low in an abandoned machine-gun nest when Nephi jumped in beside him.

"Look! I found a helmet already!" Nephi yelled to be heard above the scream of artillery.

"That's a coal-scuttle helmet!" Jimmy yelled back.

"I know, and they're good and thick, let me tell you."

"You can't wear that, Erickson! You stick your head up with that on, you're gonna get shot by one of us." He took the helmet off Nephi's head and threw it down the slope.

A shell hit thirty yards away, showering them with mud and wood debris. The two jumped from the hole and started running toward the concrete bunker.

"Hey! Look at that!" Jimmy yelled, charging sideways to another machine-gun nest. This one was not completely abandoned. A German gunner lay sprawled over his weapon, a field pistol in his hand, and two dead Americans in front of him.

Jimmy and Nephi carefully checked the American soldiers, taking their rifles and extra ammo. They grabbed the machine gun and headed again up the hill, their progress slowed by the extra weight.

"We've got these huns on the run now," Jimmy grunted as he hefted the gun over an escarpment of rock. "Erickson! You forgot to grab a helmet off one of those soldiers."

"Well, I'm not going back now," Nephi yelled. "Hey! There's the lieutenant at the corner of that pillbox."

Several men stood around the perimeter of the structure, their backs pressed against the concrete, and all avoiding the dark doorway. The lieutenant saw Nephi and Jimmy's approach and motioned them to the side.

"What's wrong?" Jimmy asked as they met up with Cornell on the back side of the building.

"Apparently there's a live German soldier trapped in there," Cornell answered. "The lieutenant took a quick look in and figures some of the roof came down on his leg."

Just then they heard the soldier yelling something from inside.

"What's he saying?" Jimmy asked.

"He's yelling for help," Cornell answered. He moved quickly to the side of the lieutenant, and Jimmy and Nephi followed. "Sir, I think he wants to surrender. He's calling for help."

Edwards frowned over at him. "You sure? I think he may have a rifle."

The voice inside called again. Cornell listened carefully. "He keeps saying, 'Hilfe!' and that means *help*. I'll go in, sir."

Edwards shook his head. "We'll go together . . . you right behind me. And keep telling him we're coming to help."

"Yes sir," Cornell answered, calling out the information loudly as Lieutenant Edwards stepped to the opening. The German fell silent. Edwards took a step inside and was shot in the chest. The force of the bullet propelled him back, blood splattering the doorframe, his body crashing into Cornell. They both fell. The other men in the unit stood stunned, unable to comprehend the scene that had just played out in front of them. Suddenly Jimmy gave an angry scream, threw down the machine gun, and jumped in through the doorway, firing his pistol. There was no responding fire.

Nephi and several other men ran to the lieutenant. Cornell was sitting up, cradling Edwards in his arms. "That German was calling for help," Cornell muttered desperately. "I know he was calling for help."

Jimmy joined the others. "Well, he won't be telling any more lies, that's for sure," he said through clenched teeth. He knelt down beside the lieutenant and put his hand on the blood-soaked chest. "He went right away. I'm sure of it."

Cornell looked up at his friend, his face a mask of grief and self-recrimination. "It's my fault. We shouldn't have come to this bunker."

"Enough of that!" Jimmy barked. He gently pulled the lieutenant's body out of Cornell's embrace and laid it carefully by the cement wall.

One of the other men in the unit picked up Edwards' helmet and held it out to Nephi, "Wear it well, Erickson."

Nephi took the proffered hat and put it on his head without comment.

"What are we gonna do now?" Jimmy asked, helping Cornell to his feet. "I'm sure the lieutenant would have wanted you to take charge."

The other men nodded.

"Not me!" Cornell answered fiercely.

"Yes you!" Jimmy countered. "You're the smartest one here."

"Yeah, and look where that got us," Cornell returned angrily.

Any response was drowned out in an explosion on the downside of their position, and the men hit the ground.

Jimmy swore. "Duncan, get us out of this!"

Cornell gritted his teeth and growled "All right! We'll continue on an angle to our left to the top of the hill. Hopefully we'll meet up with another platoon with an officer."

Jimmy thumped his friend on the back. "Right. Let's go, men."

The men of his platoon gave Lieutenant Edwards a final salute of respect and headed off in the fading light toward their unknown objective.

Nephi paused at the door of the bunker to look at the dead German. A few shafts of light danced on the man's face, and Nephi wondered at the fact that he felt neither anger nor remorse.

34

Kerri McKee lifted her head off her pillow, listening with compassion to the muffled sobs coming from the bed across from her. She slid out from under the warmth of her covers and crept over to the weeping girl. "Ina Bell," she whispered.

Ina Bell jumped. "What?" She sat up. "Oh, I'm sorry, Kerri. I woke you, didn't I? I'm so sorry."

"Enough of that," Kerri said, sitting on the bed with her. "You can cry all you want. I just feel sad for ya."

"I try not to think about it," Ina Bell choked, "and when I'm busy during the day, I do all right, but, at night it's . . . what if he dies and . . ." A sob cut off her words.

Kerri took her hand. "There, there now. Nobody's gonna be dying. Bib's a strong lad."

"But lots of strong lads are dying, and Mr. Palmer won't let me go down to the hospital to see him."

"And rightly so. 'Tis no place for you to be goin' and gettin' sick yerself."

Ina Bell gave Kerri's hand a squeeze. "Why didn't I ever tell him how I felt?"

Kerri slipped her feet under the covers. "Because you're a shy thing and yer tongue would sooner be fallin' out of yer mouth then tellin' such secrets."

Ina Bell brought out a handkerchief from under her pillow and blew her nose. "Well, no more. If he lives I'm telling him straightaway."

Kerri was surprised by her friend's declaration. "Good for you," she encouraged. "Who knows what life will bring?"

"Exactly, and even if he doesn't love me back," Ina Bell sniffed, "at . . . at least I won't be carrying around this heartache."

"You're a brave woman, Ina Bell Latham."

Ina Bell blew her nose again. "No, I'm not. I'm a goose. All my prayers over the years for Bib to love me, and me doing nothing about it? I'm a goose."

"Ah, but you're a dear goose," Kerri answered tenderly.

"And now it may be too late," Ina Bell said, shivering.

Kerri sobered. "Enough of that, now." She brightened. "I know . . . let's say a prayer for our Mr. Bib Randall."

Ina Bell started crying again. "Not me . . . I don't know what to ask for anymore. I think maybe God has deserted me . . . deserted all of us." She sat up, bringing her knees to her chest. Kerri leaned toward her, patting her back. "Everything is so terrible right now, Kerri . . . the war and this horrible sickness. Is God punishing us for something . . . or is He even there?"

Kerri shut her eyes and stilled her breathing. It was hard to listen to Ina Bell talk like this. Her friend had always been the assured, reverent soul on whom she could rely. Kerri thought about her da and how he used to say that there were some prayers that sank like lead to the bottom of the ocean, some prayers that swirled around like dry leaves in a winter wind, and some prayers that tickled the ears of God and made Him smile. Those were the prayers of Ina Bell Latham, and it made Kerri sick at heart and a bit afraid to find that her friend's faith was wavering. Kerri had always trusted in God because Ina Bell's eyes shone with conviction. Now she had to ask herself what she believed. Where was her faith? As a little girl she'd been awed by the exquisite statues of the saints in the cathedral and entranced by the singing of the nuns in a language she couldn't understand, but those things weren't faith—they were only objects that led one to search and ponder. Kerri felt empty and alone like she had in 1906 when her parents had both died in the earthquake.

Ina Bell took her friend's hand. "Are you all right?"

Kerri shook her head. "No. No, I'm not. I'm thinkin' I don't know God all that well." Ina Bell patted her hand as Kerri continued. "I know that we pray to Him as 'our Father who art in heaven . . .' our Father. And I know me own da would never desert me." Ina Bell lay still, listening intently for consolation. "Sometimes he let me learn things . . . even hard things . . . for my own good. I don't know. Maybe God is lettin' the world learn somethin' . . . hoping we'll learn somethin'."

Ina Bell leaned her head against Kerri's shoulder. "Maybe to reach out for Him. To reach out and see if He's really there."

Kerri felt her fear retreat a few steps.

Ina Bell choked back her tears. "Dear Lord, Thy will be done."

* * *

Edward Rosemund sat by the side of the hospital bed holding the hand of his young wife. He stared at her intently, as though mental power could heal her—push air into her lungs, and bring down her fever. Finally he blinked and straightened his back. He glanced around at the temporary medical unit, vaguely registering the rows of occupied cots, or that everyone was wearing a gauze mask exactly like the one he had on. One of the patients had his mask lifted as he retched into a pan at the side of his bed. Edward looked quickly back to his wife's face and found no comfort there—her eyes held a look of fear, and under the mask he knew her lips were pale blue.

"Children?" she wheezed.

"They're with Miss Johnson . . . You know, Philomene Johnson, the head-mistress at Samuel's school."

Victoria gave a slight nod. "Yes, I . . . know her."

Edward did not have the heart to tell her that only June, Samuel, and baby Elizabeth were with Miss Johnson, as their two older boys, William and Jacob, were sick with the flu in the room adjacent.

Edward steadied his voice. "I finished bottling the cider. Fredrick Robinson came over to help me. The hay is in the barn, and June and Mrs. Robinson finished up the last of the canning."

"How good of them," Victoria whispered. "Thank them." Edward nodded. "You've done well for a man of books." She offered him a look of tenderness.

Edward swallowed hard. "*We* did very well this year, you brilliant farm woman. Eight thousand pounds of apples at six cents a pound. With the war, we're getting top dollar for everything."

She nodded and closed her eyes.

Edward chided himself. "Here I am going on and on when you're tired."

"No," she said immediately, "I like it." He leaned forward to be able to hear her. "I like your voice . . . talking . . . farm." A tear slid out of the corner of her eye. "I like . . . harvest." Her breathing was shallow, and she had to pull at every word.

"Don't talk now, honey," Edward said, rubbing her hand. "Let me do that." He tried to lighten his voice. "Let the ex-lecturing professor do the talking."

"Thank you . . . gave up . . . Harvard for me," she strained.

"Shh, now," he said softly, brushing the hair back from her forehead. "You've given me the world. To be lucky enough to raise my brother's children and to have a couple of our own . . . well, Harvard can't hold a candle to that." He kept talking so he didn't have to hear the rattling in her chest. "I think next spring we should consider painting the barn . . . maybe red like the Robinsons'. I certainly like the look of their barn. And William and Jacob can help me."

Victoria struggled to open her eyes. "So . . . boys . . . all right?"

Edward lied. "Yes . . . yes, fine. Dr. McIntyre said they only have slight colds."

Her eyes closed. "But, I thought . . ."

Edward rubbed her arm. "No, we were wrong . . . not the flu, so you just rest easy."

He noted the clammy pallor to her skin and could see life draining out of her. He went back to talking. "Yes, I think we will paint the barn, and Samuel may even be big enough next summer to help. We'll just make it through this winter and we'll see. And I think you should follow through on planting those flowers in the front of the house. I know the meadow is beautiful with its scattered array of wildflowers, but flowers close to the house would be lovely. We could plant bachelor buttons, and lily of the valley . . ."

Victoria gasped for breath, and her hand went slack in his. He stared at her blankly for several minutes, then reached up, closed her eyes, and took the gauze mask off her face.

"I . . . I think perhaps we'll plant honeysuckle. Miss Johnson says their name means 'bonds of love.' And I think . . . we should plant beans and more carrots in the garden." Tears coursed down his face. "That way I could make you a beef and vegetable pie. I have the recipe from Mrs. Robinson. It's . . . it's suppose to be the envy of every woman in Amador County."

A half hour later, when Dr. McIntyre made his rounds, he found Edward Rosemund tenderly holding his wife's cold hand and talking about the harvest of Bartlett pears and the hope for another good crop the following year.

* * *

The next day Edward Rosemund's two sons died. The word spread quickly through the town of Sutter Creek, and every heart grieved for the learned man who had given up his life in the East to take on farming and his brother's family.

What would he do now? the town wondered. For everyone knew it was his wife who'd had the "land sense," his wife who directed the planting and the harvest. What would Edward Rosemund do now? What could *they* do to help him?

Philomene Johnson gave him a hot cup of tea and time alone with his remaining children. As they sat crying in her kitchen, she went out into her dormant garden, sitting on the stone bench and trying unsuccessfully to sort out the vagaries of life. Her mind seemed to want to focus on the evening five days earlier when Edward Rosemund had shown up on her doorstep with three of his children.

"Miss Johnson, I've taken Victoria and the two boys to the hospital. They have the influenza. These three do not. Please, may I intrude on your generosity to keep them for me?" His face was stricken. "I don't know where else to take them."

Philomene had brought the children into her home at once, and Mr. Rosemund had gone immediately to the hospital. June and Samuel she'd put to work on tasks, but she, having never dealt with non-school-age children, was flummoxed by Elizabeth. The four-year-old was fractious and whined continually for a special blanket that her father had understandably forgotten in his haste and distress. When the little one began crying in earnest, Philomene tried walking with her, offering her apple slices, even taking her outside in the cold night air to look at the moon. Nothing worked. Finally, June took her little sister into the spare bedroom and sang her to sleep.

Over the next five days the foursome fell into a companionable if guarded existence. Since the school had been shut down due to the flu pandemic, Philomene was able to spend every waking minute with her charges.

June, at sixteen, was a young woman and not distracted by play, so Philomene put her to work at the sewing machine making a yellow gingham tunic dress for Elizabeth. She also helped with the cooking and cleaning, and was given permission to read any of the books in Philomene's library. Samuel cleaned out the dead vegetation from the garden, roamed the town, climbed every tree in Miss Johnson's yard, and built a variety of items from bits of this and that he'd scavenged from the neighbors. And, much to Miss Johnson's amazement, even little Elizabeth accepted a new blanket from the storage trunk and played happily with some Hopi Indian dolls Philomene had brought back from her travels to the Grand Canyon.

"Miss Johnson?"

Philomene looked up into the tired face of Edward Rosemund. She stood. "Yes, Mr. Rosemund?"

"You must be freezing out here. Please, come back into your house."

"I'm fine, Mr. Rosemund," Philomene said stoically. "I wanted to give you and the children privacy and whatever time you needed."

He looked at her straight on. "How can I ever thank you for what you've done?"

"Mr. Rosemund, I only . . ."

"You saved the life of my children. They were sure to be infected if they'd been exposed much longer. You gave them a safe place."

"I . . ." She saw the gratitude in his eyes. "I was glad to help. Honored that you would think of me. They are wonderful children."

Edward nodded. He removed his glasses and wiped his eyes.

"I'm sorry for your loss, Edward." She put her hand on his arm. "Please let me continue to be of assistance." She looked over to see Samuel stumble out of her house. He ran to stand beside his father, taking his hand, and looking up at Miss Johnson. She could tell he had been crying.

"My mother is dead, Miss Johnson."

"I know, Samuel."

"And my two brothers."

Mr. Rosemund bit his lip and looked away.

"Yes, Samuel," Miss Johnson said softly. She put her arm around his shoulder. "I'm very sad for your loss."

Samuel hung his head. "Maybe I was bad, and that's why God took them away."

Both his father and Philomene protested this sentiment.

Edward knelt down in front of his now-weeping boy, and took him in his arms. "Oh, little champ, what did your mother teach you about God? That He loves you and that He's watching over you. Isn't that what she taught you?" He looked into his son's face.

Samuel nodded. "Yes, sir."

"Your mother and brothers got sick, Samuel. That's all there is to it. Somehow, from somebody else here in town, they got sick. It was nothing you did. I love you, and Miss Johnson loves you. You are a good boy."

Samuel looked up again at Miss Johnson, and she nodded. "Believe your father, Samuel. He's telling you the truth."

Mr. Rosemund stood slowly, putting his hand gently on Samuel's head. "We'll be on our way now, Miss Johnson." He took her hand. "Thank you, dear friend."

Philomene watched as Edward Rosemund bundled up his children and placed them into his automobile. There was an ache in her chest and a sudden loneliness as the vehicle pulled away into the night, Samuel waving from the back.

She pulled her coat around her and walked back into her little home, feeling for the first time that it was too quiet. She picked up one of the stick figures Samuel had made for his little sister. It was lashed together with twine and fitted with yarn hair and a yellow gingham dress. It looked like a very simple version of Elizabeth, and Philomene pressed it to her heart and cried.

35

"Move those blasted sledges!" the British major yelled, glaring in frustration at the row of wounded men waiting to be transported off the battlefield.

James smacked the withers of the huge draft horse, and it labored forward against the mud. The rain pounded down and James took a quick look back at the two wounded soldiers on the sledge. The one had either passed out or died, but the second was howling with pain.

Clune moved beside James, yanking his own horse forward by the harness. "Come on, Lund!" he called. "I'll race you to the field station!"

"A mile?" James yelled over at him. "You'd better pace yourself."

James's horse gained a more solid footing and lunged ahead with such momentum that James had to run to keep up. Several times he slipped and ended up facedown in the muck. A portion of his mind went back to a rainy afternoon on the apple farm in California. He was a little boy of four, riding on his father's shoulders. They were walking through the rows of blossoming apple trees, and a spring rain was dancing in a shaft of sunlight. His father was singing . . . something . . . What was it? He couldn't remember the words of the hymn, but the feeling of that moment was vivid even after twenty years.

Marcus Hill brought up his charge, stopping to help James to his feet. "Pretty strange, Lund, to be smiling about a kisser full of mud."

James smirked at his younger companion and spat out a mouthful of grit.

"Disgusting," Marcus said as he moved on. "You'd better get a big tetanus shot when we get to the station, or you might die from some unknown mud germ."

James stopped smiling. "There's enough out here to kill us already, Hill. You don't need to be adding any new maladies."

Marcus laughed as he slogged away in the rain, and James shook his head at Hill's stamina. They'd been at the job for eight hours, and the boy looked like he'd just had a nap.

Just as James got the big horse moving again, a column of German prisoners appeared through the murky curtain of rain looking dazed and broken.

They saw the line of sledges carrying the wounded away from the battle, and silently joined their ranks. It was an odd procession, and James wondered why they were without military escort.

A homely German youth in a tattered coat came over to take hold of the horse's harness and lay his head on the animal's neck. He spoke to the giant roan in words of throaty pleasure—weeping, James figured, sentiments of gratitude for being able to leave the madness of the battlefield. James could just see the boy's head over the horse's shoulder, and every time the wounded Brit on the sledge would cry out in pain, the German would bite his lip, and a look of remorse would wash over his face.

When they reached the camp, the prisoners huddled together, watching furtively as the casualties were tagged and transferred to the field hospital or ambulances.

James finished with his drop and turned the horse in the direction of the fighting. As he passed near the group of prisoners, the German lad reached out to run his hand along the horse's neck. James stopped for a moment, noticing a tag hanging from one of the boy's coat buttons. He indicated to the soldier his desire to look at the tag, and the young man shrugged.

James flipped over the card and was pleased to find it written in English, as he knew only a word or two of German. He read silently.

> *Be lenient with this prisoner. He was found in a shell crater*
> *giving water to a wounded Allied soldier.*

James studied the German boy's rough features and vacant eyes. He wondered about his family and the town or city where he lived, trying to imagine him in civilian clothes, his mouth not so rigidly set, but laughing with a group of his friends. Maybe he lived on a farm and cared for the horses, or managed the plowing. And where did his strength of character originate . . . strength of character that would allow for acts of compassion even to his enemies?

Suddenly the boy was yanked to the side by a member of the Allied military police, and just before he disappeared into the crowd of prisoners, James called out, "Read his tag!"

"Feeling all right?" Wheaten asked as he and Marcus came up beside him, their horses snorting and stamping.

James nodded and started walking toward the battlefront. He glanced back once to see if he could spot the German prisoners, but they were gone.

They had trudged through the mud about a quarter of a mile when a runner caught up to them. "Excuse me, sirs?" the private said, his voice ragged from running.

"Yes?" James answered, pulling his horse to a stop.

"The corporal wants you back at the main camp area, sirs."

Clune frowned. "Do you know why?"

"No, sir," the soldier answered. "He just wants you back immediately."

Clune bristled. "But, we have wounded men out there, Private, who are depending on us." His large frame was intimidating, and the messenger stepped back.

James turned his horse. "Come on, Clune. He couldn't change the command, even if he wanted to."

Wheaten growled and followed Marcus and James back to the camp.

* * *

"How are we gonna see in the dark?" Marcus whispered as he stood with his two friends at the artillery depot, watching as the munitions detail loaded canvas blankets with shells for the big guns.

"I think there's a full moon tonight," Clune teased, "behind all those rain clouds. And, who knows . . . maybe the Germans will accommodate us with a few flares to light our way."

Marcus gave him a skeptical look.

"Actually, the darker the better," James said bluntly as he helped one of the munitions officers adjust the blanket on his horse's back. As the weight of the final shell was loaded in its pocket, the big Belgian draft horse snorted and stepped sideways. "I don't think he's too fond of it," James stated, rubbing his hand along the horse's chest and checking the powerful legs. "They've already suffered a lot of misery today."

"No help for it," the officer said. "We can't find passable roads out to the frontline positions. Even caissons won't make it through that muck. In Flanders at the end of October, you're not going to get sunny skies and dry roads."

Marcus's horse squealed and tried to buck. Marcus calmed him as well as he could with soothing words, but the animal's ears were flicking back and forth, showing fear and anger.

"Wish there was some other way," the officer stated, "but the engineers said they won't have the road ready to go till midmorning tomorrow. The gunners need this ordnance for an early-morning barrage. This will hopefully tide them over."

James nodded. "Yes, sir. We understand."

Clune patted the neck of his iron gray Ardenne. "We don't quite understand, do we Champion? We're ready for food and sleep."

The munitions officer looked compassionately at the exhausted men. "When you get done with this assignment, you get a two-day leave."

"*If* we get done with this assignment," Wheaten quipped.

A sturdy young soldier of the munitions detail stepped forward pulling a flat wagon and looking grim and apologetic. "We need each of you to carry extra bandoleers of ammo," he said flatly.

James looked at his two companions and nodded.

When they were loaded, they moved out into the unwelcoming night. A flash of lightning lit the eastern darkness, and all three horses pulled against their leads.

"Come on, Magic," James encouraged, keeping a firm tension on the rope.

"I wish I hadn't let on I knew so much about horses when I joined up," Marcus called to his friends. "Maybe I would have been put in a different unit."

"Oh yeah," Clune called back, "maybe camouflage-sniper detail, or machine-gun detail . . ."

"Or wire-laying detail," James chimed in, "or ambulance driver, or tank commander."

Marcus was silent.

"Sorry, Hill," Clune said finally. "We were only kidding."

"You're right, though," Marcus said. "There really aren't any safe jobs in a war."

A cold sleet began to hiss down around them, and the men stopped talking as they trudged on through the mud. It was only three miles to the big gun's position, but it seemed like ten. James's back and shoulders felt like they were cracking under the weight of the bandoleers, and his arms felt the strain of the constant pull on the lead rope as he tried to keep the sensitive horse moving toward the sound of artillery fire and the stench of death.

There were only periodic shells coming over now, but James knew he and his friends would soon be moving into dangerous areas. He clenched the lead rope with determination and fought on through the mud that was attempting to pull the boots from his feet. The cold night air seared his lungs, and he strained to see potholes and shell craters that appeared suddenly a foot in front of him. Several times he came upon a dead body, the skin of the face and hands a pearly white. Magic would squeal in fear and step carefully. James was in awe of how the horse was always careful not to step on any part of the dead body. He knew Clune and Hill were having similar experiences, as periodically he would hear Clune swear when he came upon one of the causalities.

The men pressed on, each struggling to hold onto sanity—to find a way through the ghoulish scenes and physical pain, each reaching deep within himself for previously unknown reserves of strength.

Suddenly a flare lit the ribbons of sleet in an orange glow. The men pressed their bodies against the warm bellies of their horses and hid their faces from the light. The sleet ran chill down the backs of their necks, and their breathing came in ragged gasps.

When the light faded, Marcus came up beside James. "Do you think we were tagged?" he asked, a slight quaver in his voice.

"I don't know," James answered. "Let's keep moving. We can't be far from the gun now. We've come a couple of miles."

The three companions urged their horses forward.

In the darkness, and encased in its camouflage netting, the big artillery gun was nearly invisible. Wheaten spotted it only because he caught the movement of a few of the gunners.

"Righto!" the commander whispered enthusiastically as they passed the sentries and entered the staging area. "We're certainly glad to see you blokes, aren't we then, Smith?"

The junior officer offered his hand to the arriving soldiers. "We certainly are, sir. Yes, indeed. We certainly are."

"Yanks, are you?" the commander asked of James and Marcus. His tone was jovial and his expression bright.

James smiled. "Yes, sir." He saluted. "Private James Lund, sir. And this is Private Marcus Hill."

"Fascinating," the major said, looking the two over. "Well, well, well. Yanks. All mixed up in the soup with the rest of us, eh?"

"Yes, sir," James answered. "Private Hill and I are on special assignment to the British units . . . I suppose because we know a little about horses."

"Begging your pardon, sir," Clune said, saluting the British gunnery officer. "Wheaten Clune here, and I think you should be informed that these two know more than a little about horses."

The commander laughed as men from his unit came to relieve the new arrivals of their burdens. James stretched and rubbed the muscles of his lower back. He saw Clune and Hill doing the same.

"Well then," the commander said after finishing instructions to his junior officer, "let's arrange for some strong coffee and a good breakfast for you three brave men, eh?"

James felt his stomach growl at the mention of food, and he chuckled at the look on Marcus Hill's face. You would have thought someone had just offered him a hundred bucks.

* * *

When the shell hit, James had been feeling a modicum of peace and contentment. They had left the artillery unit warmed from food, coffee, and friendly conversation. They were heading back to the prospect of a two-day leave, and the rain and sleet had stopped. The scream of the incoming shell had come unexpectedly, and now James was not sure where he was. He was vaguely aware of a great weight on his chest and the feeling of being suffocated. His body sank back a little into the mud, relieving some of the pressure on his body. *Was he hit? Had he fallen into a shell crater?*

He opened his eyes and a wave of pain coursed into his head. He tried to scream, but there was no air in his lungs. *No air!* He couldn't breathe. Was he in water and drowning? He closed his eyes. *Dear God, please help me! Tell me what to do!*

Calm flooded his body, and he pressed back into the mud. Cold air flowed into his lungs, and he wept weakly with relief. The pain came again, but this time he didn't panic. He guessed he must have been unconscious, but for how long? He figured it couldn't have been too long because it was still dark.

"So, James, you gonna try and tame that cinnamon stallion? I think he gonna be a match even for you."

He smiled at Mr. Regosi's roundabout compliment and challenge. "I think I'll just give it a try and see what happens."

Mr. Regosi slapped him good-naturedly on the back and handed him the lead rope. "Yeah, James, you give it a try," he chuckled. "You give it a try, but I gonna stay outside the corral so I don't get trampled."

James smelled the strong musk of a horse, and the memory of what happened hit hard with another wave of pain. A shell had exploded close, and the belly of the exquisite Belgian draft horse had been ripped open by shrapnel. James groaned and tried to block the memory of the gentle animal screaming in pain—screaming and falling sideways onto him. James clenched his jaw against terror. He was being crushed to death by the magnificent creature. The animal had at first saved his life by unwittingly taking the brunt of the blast . . . but now . . .

James turned his head slightly, and a knife of pain sliced into his shoulders. He didn't care, he wanted to see Magic's elegant head. He wanted to run his hands over the gentle giant's coat and tell him it was all right . . . it wasn't his fault, but his arms were pinned at odd angles, and he couldn't feel his fingers.

The clouds were breaking, and a pale yellow sky shone beyond the ragged gray covering. Sunrise was coming on. Sunrise. Was this to be the last sunrise he would ever see? Would he ever hear his sisters' voices? James heard bees. *It's winter,* he told himself, trying to keep his mind from insanity. *Winter. There are no bees in winter.* He looked again at the light pouring into the morning canopy and saw a hundred aeroplanes flying combat formation over his piece of sacred ground. The weight of his giant friend pressed against his fragile human frame, and James thought he heard his back crack. He looked up at the beauty and lightness of the planes as they looped and swirled through the parting clouds. Then he closed his eyes and was gone.

* * *

"Get those ropes taut!" Wheaten Clune yelled as he braced his feet against the spine of the horse and began pushing. The muscles in his powerful legs trembled as he used every ounce of strength to move the 1,800-pound horse. "Pull!" he growled at the rope handlers.

The dead horse moved enough to expose the body pressed into the shallow, boggy creek bed. It looked like a discarded marionette, with legs and arms bent at odd angles.

Wheaten crawled to his friend, pouring out a stream of pleas and promises. When he reached James's side and saw the condition of the body, he howled in rage and sorrow. "Ah, no! No! Dear God, please! Not another tender soul! You took Private Hill home to ya. You don't need to be taking this one, too." He pulled out his field pistol, and the three soldiers of the ambulance team hit the ground. "Where's the kaiser?" Wheaten yelled. "Where is he? I'll kill him myself. I'll kill him myself. I'll go to Berlin and shoot him right between the eyes!"

"Sir!"

One of the medics had crawled forward to inspect the body during Wheaten's rampage. "Sir!" he called more loudly. "This man is breathing!"

Wheaten stopped, his face a mask of bewilderment and disbelief. "What?"

"He's breathing, sir."

Wheaten stowed his gun and wiped the tears from his face. "Well, bring on the stretcher!" he bellowed, "and let's get this soldier to the hospital!"

36

Jimmy Gordon was dead. Shot through the neck during a rough engagement of hand-to-hand combat. Cornell and Nephi searched for him after the battle and found his body facedown in the cold mud. *The man from Syracuse—the bread maker . . .*

Cornell went through Jimmy's pockets looking for the packet of letters he'd instructed be sent back to his family in case he didn't make it. Now Cornell and Nephi sat in a half-destroyed barn sorting the letters and trying to keep warm as a chill November wind rattled the bones of the wooden structure.

"We can wrap the ones his family wrote and send them back all together," Cornell said.

Nephi nodded. "And should we give these over to the mail carrier?" he asked, holding up two newly penned letters.

Cornell stared at the envelopes, then closed his eyes and spoke slowly. "Yeah, maybe I'll write a little note on the back about how bravely he died, and . . . how much we liked him."

Nephi noted the emotion in Cornell's voice and wondered why his buddy hadn't found, as he had, the way to detach from pain and loss.

"He carried this one around for a while," Cornell said, looking down at the ragged envelope in his hand. He flipped it from front to back several times, then lifted the flap and took out the letter.

"What are you doing?" Nephi questioned.

"I'm curious," Cornell answered, unfolding the well-worn paper. "You want to hear?"

"No," Nephi answered, standing and moving to get his canteen.

Cornell shifted the letter into a shaft of light, and started reading silently.

My dear boy,

Your father says to tell you that he will give his son to his country, but that he will "blanky-blank" (never mind what!) if he will

*give all his new suspenders. He says you pinched three pairs from
the top drawer of his dresser. He adds that he "is onto your
curves."*

*Nora says you were very wise to take them, and she would give
you all of hers, if she had any. Betty says to tell you that she hears
Jack Ellis sails next week—I know just how his mother will feel
for those ten days while he is crossing. But she wouldn't have him
stay home any more than I would have had you. All the same, she
won't have a good night's sleep until she hears he's landed. I keep
thinking what a different world it will be to mothers when you
all come marching home again!*

*And when you do come marching home, old fellow, bring me
back the same boy I gave my country—true, and clean, and
gentle, and brave. You must do this for your father and me and
Betty and Nora—and most of all for the daughter-in-law you
will give me one of these days!*

*Dear, I don't know if you have even met her yet—but never mind
that! Live for her, or if God wills, die for her, but do either with
courage—"with honor and clean mirth!" But I know you will
come back to me.*

Mother

Cornell sobbed—all the fear and anger gushing out of him like poison.
Nephi came over and picked Jimmy's letter off the ground, brushing away the
bits of straw and dirt.

"Don't read it! Don't read it!" Cornell screamed at his friend.

"I won't," Nephi said dispassionately, folding the letter and putting it back
into the envelope.

Cornell stood and pressed his hands against the rough walls of the barn,
trying to stop the convulsions that shook his body. He screamed again, and
again, and again—his mind searching frantically for a way to make sense of
the carnage and sorrow.

Nephi held out the canteen to him. "You're never going to figure it out,
Duncan. Never. Our minds and our spirits won't ever understand this."

Cornell shuddered and looked over at his friend. Though devastating, that
thought was his salvation. He sucked in several deep breaths of air, and wiped
his face with his shirtsleeve. He took the canteen, and Nephi turned away,
placing Jimmy's letter in his pocket with the others.

The splintered barn door was shoved open, and a flustered private stuck his head inside. "Come on, you lugs!" he yelled. "The whistle's blown. We're making our last push to Sedan and the Meuse River."

He turned abruptly, and they heard his footsteps pounding off down the path. It was only then that they became aware of the rumble of tanks, the explosion of artillery shells, and the shouts of men.

Cornell stood straight. "There's only one way out of this, and that's through," he said.

"Yep," Nephi answered mechanically, picking up his canteen and rifle. "Yea, though I walk through the valley of the shadow of death . . ."

"You say something?" Cornell asked, pushing open the heavy wooden door.

Nephi shook his head. "No. Nothing,"

The two soldiers stepped out of the barn into the cold day.

Mr. Regosi held out his hand and James took it, feeling the strength and rough-
ness from years of hard work.

"I'm very proud of you, James," he said, his Italian accent heavy and soothing.
"Come home now and manage the ranch."

"I can't Mr. Regosi. I want to come home, but I can't. I went to war, and I'm
not in very good shape."

"Come home, James. Come home to us."

James tried to sit up, but it was no use. A hoot owl cried out, and he
stopped struggling. The bird called again and again. James slowly opened his
eyes. *What is that noise?* He heard it again. Focusing on the walls and windows
of the hospital ward in Lille, his head began to clear. There seemed to be a lot of
activity in a place where calm and quiet were mandatory. He heard the hooting
again and realized it was a man singing and a bagpipe playing. He turned his
head slowly and saw a man in a hospital gown and kilt dancing a jig, while
nurses and other patients stood around clapping. *Has the world gone mad?*

"James?"

He knew that voice. He moved his eyes toward the foot of his bed and saw
the bushy brown beard and warm smile. "Dr. Robbins? What are you doing
here?"

"I've come to heal you, my boy," the man said, laughing. He pulled a stool
near to the bed and sat down.

James stared at him and noted the look of merriment that colored his
entire demeanor. A roar went up from the group of revelers, and James
frowned. "What's going on?" he questioned, turning his head with difficulty
to watch the kilted man dancing with one of the nurses.

Dr. Robbins leaned forward, a look of pure joy on his face. "The war has
ended, James!" he said fiercely. "It's over!"

"The Germans surrendered?" James asked.

Dr. Robbins shook his head. "They signed an armistice. They've stopped
fighting."

James was too distracted by the noise and excitement to concentrate long on the distinction. *The war was over!* His heart was beating fast, and he wanted to shout, but his broken body restricted him. A tear leaked out the corner of his eye.

"When . . . when did you come up?"

"Last night." A whoop erupted from the group, and Dr. Robbins turned to them and called, "Gentlemen and ladies, a bit of decorum, please."

They smiled over at the doctor and quieted.

"And the war ended today?"

Dr. Robbins nodded. "This morning at eleven."

James felt like he was suffocating again. He wanted to dance and sing like the others. He wanted to run, but the traction fixture kept his injured body immobile. "May I sit up a little?" he asked tentatively.

Dr. Robbins smiled and checked his chart. "I don't see why not. Just a little, though. We don't want to put too much weight on that pelvic bone."

Besides the cracked pelvis, James had a broken femur and wrist, a crushed ankle, a cracked rib, a broken clavicle, six broken fingers, and a dislocated shoulder. Miraculously, his spine had not been injured. He had casts, splints, and wrapping on almost every part of his body.

Dr. Robbins enlisted the help of two strong orderlies, and after having readjusted the tension of the traction lines, the three gently maneuvered James into a slightly elevated position. When they were alone again, James pressed for information about the transfer that brought this gentle and capable man back into his life.

"So, did they send you here to run this section?" James asked, feebly reaching for a glass of water from his table.

Dr. Robbins held the glass for him. "Actually, I'm to run the entire hospital . . . along with my Belgian counterparts, of course. We've so many Brits here that General Haig figured it would expedite things."

James stopped drinking. "General Haig? General Haig himself put you here?"

Dr. Robbins nodded.

"My goodness, I had no idea you were so important," James teased.

The healer shook his head and set down the glass. "Well, I don't know about that, James. I think it's more because I've been here so long."

The kilted patient and several others came over to congratulate James on his progress. They stayed for a few minutes, then meandered away to other more jovial diversions.

"Well, my boy," Dr. Robbins said, standing and stretching his back, "I must return to my duties."

"Of course," James answered lightly. "We wouldn't want General Haig to find fault."

"No indeed." The kind man picked up James's hand. "I'll do my best for you, James. We'll take it slow and steady until we get you back on your feet."

James gave a slight nod. For the first time in weeks, he felt a tremble of hope.

A nurse came to the bedside. "Excuse me, doctor," she said in a jaunty voice. "Here's a bit of post we've been holding for this soldier. Do ya think he's well enough for a little catch-up?"

Dr. Robbins laughed. "By the look on his face I would say yes. You may have to read it to him though, Nurse Hawkins, if he doesn't mind."

"Not at all," James said immediately.

Dr. Robbins chuckled and left his patient in the nurse's optimistic care.

"I've put the letters in chronological order," she said efficiently, sitting down and picking up the first envelope.

James smiled.

"It's great news about the war endin', isn't it?" she said, a look of wonder washing over her face. "And we've made it through . . . we've made it through." She sobered. "A couple of my friends who came out with me didn't make it."

"Mine too," James said softly.

Nurse Hawkins took a deep breath, the sparkle returning to her eyes. "I guess the good Lord will sort it all out."

"I guess," James answered, finding himself wishing he could share her child-like trust.

"Shall we get on with it, then?" she asked, opening the flap on the first letter. "We'll begin reading at the furthest back." She read Eleanor's letter of Daniel's visit and of her concerns for the upcoming flu season. The letters from his mother showed that she was making continual progress, and Alaina's letter announced that he was an uncle for a second time. Then came Eleanor's letter of the influenza outbreak reaching Salt Lake City, and a letter from Miss Johnson telling of Joanna Wilton's mother being stricken with that terrible sickness, along with Emilio and Rosa Regosi.

"Are you all right, sir?" the nurse asked as she noted the grayish cast to his skin. "We've been goin' on for quite a while . . . Shall we give you a rest?"

"Yes," James said through his discomfort.

She checked the few remaining letters as she stood. "There is an official-looking one here," she announced. "Should I glance at that one for ya?"

James nodded, not really interested in an impersonal piece of paper that probably had something to do with his injury.

Nurse Hawkins took out the document and glanced over it. "Oh my," she said at last, looking down at James. "You . . . you may want to wait for this one, sir."

"No, what is it?" James said as he tried to find a comfortable position for his head.

The young woman looked on the verge of tears. "Are you sure, sir?"

"Yes!" James answered, a note of irritation in his voice. "Sorry. Sorry, Nurse Hawkins. Whatever it is, I want to know."

"Well . . ." she said, trying to soften her voice, "well, it seems your friend Mr. Regosi and his wife have passed away."

James had expected this news after Miss Johnson's letter, but now he had to steel himself against the actuality of loss and pain. "And it says that in a legal document?"

Nurse Hawkins shook her head. "Not directly sir, no, but it's indicated. You see . . . it seems your friends have left you their ranch."

* * *

Wheaten Clune stood in the frozen and blasted field with his arms lifted to heaven.

Thirty yards away a contingent of German soldiers stood staring at the big man, smiling and elbowing each other in amusement.

Wheaten opened his eyes and frowned in disbelief. Slowly his hand went to his field pistol, and the smiles dropped from the German faces. One of the older soldiers stepped forward.

"Nein, Kamerad," he called, raising his arms in surrender. "Nein, nein mein Kamerad. Es ist vorbei." He raised his hands higher. "Is done."

Wheaten tried to slow his breathing. *Of course, it is done.* He'd heard the word himself from the field communications officer not ten minutes before. And now the shelling had ended, and it was eerily quiet. The war was over— he understood that. What he could not understand was why these Germans were out in the field—a field that held so much of his countrymen's blood.

Wheaten saw movement from the side and turned to look at a couple of Allied soldiers making their way to where the Germans stood. He was shocked as he watched them shake hands and attempt to communicate.

The older German soldier eyed him warily for a moment, then turned to join the celebration. Wheaten backed away in disgust. More than four years of blood and sacrifice had hardened him against the enemy. He knew the blame did not lie with the individual soldier, but their bullets and bombs had killed or maimed his friends, and taken away his innocence. The world would never again be a fair and glorious place. He turned back to find the men of his unit. With these men he would celebrate the escape from purgatory. With these men he would drink, and dance, and sing.

* * *

Cornell and Nephi stood on a hill overlooking the Meuse River, listening to the village church bell ringing, and its citizens cheering. Neither of the men spoke, nor moved, nor even breathed too deeply.

Through. They had made it through.

* * *

Hannah Finn and Claudine walked with their arms around each other's waist to the Grand' Place. There they would join thousands of Belgian citizens dancing, cheering, and singing together. As they neared the edge of the square, Hannah reached into the pocket of her ragged coat and drew out a small box.

"I had a premonition to purchase these yesterday," she said, a twinkle in her eyes. She opened the box to reveal two beautiful chocolates.

Claudine gasped. "Oh, madame! How wonderful . . . tres magnifique! But, where did you get the money?"

"It doesn't matter, my sweet girl," Mrs. Finn answered. "Perhaps I kept some secret money for chocolate hidden in my shoe."

Claudine laughed.

"Now, take one," Hannah Finn said, smiling. "Today is a good day."

Claudine nodded. "Together," she insisted. "For this joy to be always!" Claudine shouted, raising her hand triumphantly.

"For this joy to circle the earth and touch my dear Philomene!" Hannah Finn cheered, following the example of her exuberant servant. "May she know that we have survived!"

The two women joyfully popped the delicacies into their mouths. Claudine kissed a nearby gentleman, and then danced around her mistress like a child.

Mrs. William Conner Finn clapped her hands and laughed, seeing manifest in front of her the feelings of her soul.

* * *

"Grandfather? Grandfather," Eleanor whispered respectfully. She nudged the aged patriarch gently on the shoulder, not wishing to startle him from his sound sleep, but she knew he would want to be told—want to share in the joy and relief. "Grandfather."

Grandfather Erickson snorted and came awake. "Ya? Vhat?" His hand came over to grasp her arm. "Vhat Caroline? Vhat is it?"

"Grandfather, it's Eleanor," she said softly. She helped him as he tried to sit up against his pillow. "I'm sorry, I didn't want to startle you."

"Ya, ya, it's all right. Are you vell?" He rubbed his hand across his face. "Vhat time is it?"

"Two o'clock."

"Two o'clock . . . in the morning?"

"Yes," Eleanor answered, a bright ring to her voice.

Grandfather focused on her beaming face. "But, you are not sad."

"No. It's wonderful news and I knew you'd want to know." She knelt by the side of the bed and took his hand. "The war is over! It's over."

A deep intake of air swelled Grandfather's chest, and he began crying. "Over? It's over?"

"Yes." She cried with him.

"How . . . how do you know?"

"Your son Alma came by with the news. They found out in the city about an hour ago, and he said everyone is ignoring the influenza curfew and taking to the streets. Bells are ringing and automobiles are dashing along the roads with tin cans and other noise-making things tied to their bumpers." The two were laughing now. "The Armistice was announced yesterday, November eleventh, and the fighting stopped at 11:00 AM." She gulped down a sob. "The fighting has stopped." She laid her head on the bed, and Grandfather stroked her hair.

"Ya, little angel, now your brother James comes home . . . and Nephi." Tears rolled down his cheeks. "Now my Nephi comes home."

* * *

Patience and Alma Erickson stood on the front porch with their daughter-in-law Alaina; they were beating pots with wooden spoons and cheering. Their granddaughter Katie, in her nightgown, red coat, and boots, was running in circles and ringing a bell. The entire neighborhood was awake and engaged in some similar form of riot.

The hardware truck pulled up in the driveway with Sarah driving and Elias holding little Zachery. Sarah stopped the truck abruptly, shoved on the brakes, and jumped from the vehicle. She raced toward Alaina, her arms outstretched, and Alaina dropped her pot and ran down to her. They met in a joyous embrace.

"He's coming home! He's coming home!" Sarah yelled.

Little Zachery squirmed out of his father's arms and ran for Katie. He was carrying a little American flag.

Katie squealed with delight. "My daddy is coming home, Zacry!"

"Scrimmy!" the little boy yelled, taking his cousin's hand and waving his flag.

The adults laughed and cried as each heart felt a burden of darkness lifting.

* * *

Kerri and Ina Bell found Mrs. Lund standing outside on the cold walkway in her nightgown—her feet bare, and her unkempt chestnut hair blowing about her face in a chilling breeze.

"Oh dear," Ina Bell said weakly.

"We've found her, Mr. Palmer!" Kerri called back into the house before descending the steps.

The servant girls shared a look of sadness before reaching the side of the poor unfortunate woman.

Mrs. Lund was crying, and Ina Bell's heart wrenched at the sight.

"Mrs. Lund," Kerri said, putting the dressing gown around the woman's shoulders. "It's five o'clock in the morning. What are you—"

"Shh. Listen," Mrs. Lund whispered, placing her fingers on her lips.

Kerri frowned. "Let's be goin' in now before you catch your—"

"No, really," Mrs. Lund insisted, a smile spreading across her face. "Listen."

The girls stood silent, figuring Mr. Palmer could take her in hand when he arrived. Sound slowly reached their ears. An inordinate number of automobile horns seemed to be honking, and from several blocks away they could just make out the clear emotional voice of a newsie: "WAR OVER! GERMANY SIGNS ARMISTICE! TYRANNY DEFEATED! VICTORY AND PEACE!"

Kerri and Ina Bell looked at each other, then back at Mrs. Lund. The three women threw their arms around each other—laughing, cheering, and crying in turn.

When Mr. Palmer and Bib Randall appeared at the top of the steps, they could make no sense of the scene before them until Kerri turned her joyful face to them and yelled, "It's over, Mr. Palmer! To be sure! The war is over!"

* * *

Philomene Johnson was startled awake by shouts and cheers and the boom of a bass drum. As she rose from her bed and went to the door, a young couple raced past, headed for the main part of town. A trumpeter began playing "The Victory March," and church bells rang. *What in the world is happening?* she wondered, her mind still groggy from the abrupt awakening. Suddenly the bells spoke the answer to her heart—OVER! OVER! OVER! THE WAR IS OVER! She stood motionless, stunned into immobility by the weight of revelation. *It's over!* And somehow in that moment she also knew her dear Aunt Hannah was . . . *alive!*

Philomene turned into her house and shut the door. She dressed, pinned up her hair, shoved a hat onto her head, put on her coat, and grabbed her cane. She stopped briefly at the cedar chest to retrieve a precious standard, holding it tightly against her as she walked out into the cold November air. With tears of pride and relief, she hung the American flag on her front porch, saluted it, and then moved off with a halting but determined step to join the other revelers.

* * *

Postmaster Elijah Greggs stood in front of his war map, his head bowed in prayer, his hand placed within the crumpled little flags.

"Come home now," he whispered. "Come home and be at peace."

38

Eleanor drew back the hospital curtains and shoved the limp strands of hair away from her face. She retied her gauze mask and tried to swallow the anguish that sat in her chest like a rock. People were dying by the hundreds, and there was nothing she could do about it. Even with the war over, there were still so many doctors and nurses overseas that it fell to the medical students and Red Cross volunteers to care for the victims of the influenza. Medical classes were still being held periodically, but the majority of learning was practical. Eleanor had stopped her research, and for weeks she and Shawn had assisted Dr. Thorndike and the remaining healers attempting to contain the epidemic. The number of worldwide casualties reported in the newspapers was staggering—hundreds of thousands dying every week.

It was the end of November now, and the flu season should have been on the decline, but the pandemic continued to decimate communities the globe over. In Utah, the government had finally shut down all theaters, lecture halls, and political rallies, and many of the educational facilities, while the First Presidency of the LDS Church had joined other ecumenical leaders in suspending all religious gatherings. With those restrictions in place, the medical teams were beginning to see a slight decline in the number of new cases, but the total was still frightening.

Eleanor lingered at the window, looking up to the snowcapped mountaintops and watching the soft pink alpine glow fade from sight. She did not register the beauty of the scene, sensing only that beyond the pane of glass was a semblance of normalcy.

She turned back into the ward. Three rows of beds and cots stretched from one end of the long rectangular room to the other, and only eight of the forty beds were unoccupied.

The door to the ward opened, and Shawn came in with a tray of hot compresses. He distributed these among the volunteers and then moved to adjust the oxygen mask on one young man whose sickness had progressed quickly to pneumonia. She met Shawn at the bed of this critical patient, lifting the man's limp arm and taking a pulse.

Shawn looked over at her, and she could tell that under his mask he was offering her a weak smile. "Perhaps we should have gone into teaching or boat building," he said, his voice sounding rough and tired.

"Not bad professions," Eleanor returned, "but then we would have missed out on all this fun."

"Hmm," Shawn responded. "I'd hate to see what you consider work."

Eleanor noted the exhaustion in her friend's voice as she removed the cold compress from the patient's head, shook it several times, and replaced it. She caught Shawn's hand as he turned to help another patient. "Are you all right?" she questioned.

"You mean other than just plain worn out and my feet hurting?" he deflected.

"Shawn."

He took her hand and ran his finger over the promise ring. "I am fine, Miss Lund. Thank you for caring." He gave her hand a squeeze. "Now, back to work before Dr. Thorndike fires us for loafing. If you're a good girl, I'll take you to supper later."

This time when he walked away, she felt a sadness encase her. *Silly,* she told herself. *We're all just tired. We've been at this for months and it's wearing us out.*

A woman two beds over called out for water, and Eleanor went immediately to care for her needs.

* * *

Hours later, Eleanor found Shawn curled upon the divan in the doctor's consult room, shivering with fever. She had run down the hall frantically searching for orderlies and Dr. Thorndike, and now she sat by her friend's bed in the ward, stunned into silence and inactivity. *This isn't happening. Dear Lord, please . . . This isn't happening.*

She moved her chair closer to the bed, wrapping her hand around Shawn's arm and laying her head on the cool sheet. She thought of the time in spring when they'd attended the student art show together, of the day at Silver Lake—the summer sun shining on the water, the raccoon getting into their food—of their walks together on the temple grounds where they talked of deep medical and gospel subjects, of classes, and picnics, and . . .

She felt a hand on her shoulder and jumped.

"I brought you a hard roll with butter," Dr. Thorndike said, offering the bread to her when she looked up. "Did I wake you?"

"I must have dozed off," Eleanor said, yawning.

"Sorry, but there's no help for it. Here, eat this roll." He waved it by her nose.

"Oh, that's very kind of you, sir," she answered feebly, "but I can't eat."

The doctor pulled up a chair and sat beside her. "You must eat, Miss Lund. It takes energy to keep up a constant vigil." He offered the roll again, and she took it. "Good woman. I shall watch the sleeping boy while you eat."

Eleanor slumped back into her chair. She tore off small pieces of the roll, shoving the bites beneath the gauze mask.

"What was his temperature at last taking?"

"It was 102," she said, swallowing. A tear rolled down her cheek. "He can't be dying," she whispered fiercely. "He can't."

Dr. Thorndike was silent.

"Why isn't there more we can do for him? All these superficial treatments address the symptoms, not the disease." She calmed her anger. "I'm sorry. I just feel so profoundly helpless." She changed the compress on Shawn's forehead.

"Are you religious, Miss Lund?"

Dr. Thorndike's question took her by surprise. She hesitated. "Yes, sir. I am."

"Believing in an all-powerful Creator?"

She nodded. "Yes, sir."

"Then, the question we ask as scientists and as people of critical thinking is . . . where is He?"

"I beg your pardon?"

"Where is He, Miss Lund? If He is all powerful, can't His power overcome disease . . . stop wars . . . punish injustice?" He looked over at her. "Where is He?"

A warmth flooded through her body as she contemplated the question. "He's nearby . . . ready to comfort," she answered at last, her voice steady and sure. It was not the answer she had expected to give him, and she thought it rather trite. Her mind raced to find a more intellectual argument, a more profound treatise, but she stopped when she saw Dr. Thorndike put his head into his hands.

"Dr. Thorndike?"

"Oh, my dear," he said slowly, placing his hands on his knees and breathing deeply to control his emotions. "I could have rejected every other answer but that one." He looked at her. "I am not a religious man, Miss Lund, but I can attest to what you have just said."

"What has happened, sir?" she asked gently.

His words were marked with distress. "Mrs. Thorndike and I have received word that our son Miles has died in France."

Eleanor choked. "But, the war is . . ."

"Over . . . yes. He made it through the war only to succumb to the influenza while waiting to come home."

"Oh, sir, I'm so sorry," Eleanor said, tears pressing into her eyes. "I'm so sorry."

"Thank you, Eleanor. And thank you for your answer to my question. Margaret and I are devastated by the loss of our boy, but we have been comforted—sustained over the last few days by something we cannot explain."

Eleanor nodded.

"Is that God, Miss Lund?"

She felt the Spirit like an almost tangible fluid flowing from the top of her head to her feet. She nodded again. "Yes, sir." A Bible verse came into her mind. "'Peace I leave with you, my peace I give unto you: not as the world giveth, give I unto you. Let not your heart be troubled, neither let it be afraid.'"

"Is that scripture?"

"Yes, sir. It was one of my father's favorite verses."

Dr. Thorndike took out his handkerchief and wiped his eyes. "I would like to know the passage so I can share it with my family."

"Of course. I'll write it down for you."

Shawn groaned and opened his eyes. Eleanor and Dr. Thorndike were on their feet and at his side.

Shawn struggled for air. "I need . . . to . . . sit higher," he whispered.

Dr. Thorndike cranked the backrest to an inclined position. "I'll arrange for oxygen." He walked quickly away.

"What can I do for you?" Eleanor asked, trying to keep her voice strong and her manner efficient.

"Water."

She lowered his mask and helped him to drink. As she rearranged Shawn's pillows, she saw Dr. Thorndike standing in the doorway instructing Howard Burbage toward them. Eleanor raised her hand, and Mr. Burbage started forward, glancing nervously at the sick in their beds and making sure his mask was secure.

Eleanor leaned close to Shawn's ear. "Your father's arrived."

Shawn gave a weak nod. "My mother?"

"Not with him that I can see," she answered without censure.

"Eleanor?"

She leaned closer. "Yes?"

"Tell me something else. I like you whispering in my ear."

Longing and sadness gripped her heart, and she was thankful to have the distraction of Mr. Burbage's arrival.

"Miss Lund." He spoke to her, but his eyes were on his son. "How is he?"

"Holding his own, sir. He's a strong young man."

"Yes, he is," Mr. Burbage said, taking his son's hand.

Eleanor steeled herself against the poignant scene. "Shawn has told me that you've heard from all your soldier sons, and that they're safe," Eleanor said. Mr. Burbage nodded. "That's wonderful, sir. I'm so glad."

"Thank you, Miss Lund," he answered sincerely, glancing over at her.

Eleanor did not miss the note of unmasked distress in his voice. She nodded and turned her attention on Shawn. "Is there anything else I can do for you?"

"Aspirin."

She went to his bedside table and secured two tablets and a glass of water. When she lowered his mask, Shawn smiled.

"Efficient, isn't she?" he remarked to his father.

"She is," Mr. Burbage agreed.

Shawn took the tablets, and Eleanor could tell he had difficulty swallowing them. "I'll give you the powdered aspirin next time," she said, retying his mask.

"Are you staying with me?" he asked, his voice filled with an abundance of gratitude.

"Of course," she answered jauntily, attempting to deflect the pathos, "I take this promise ring very seriously."

"I'm glad," he answered.

"I will leave you two alone for a while," she said, turning to go.

"But . . ."

She frowned at him. "I do have other patients, you know."

"Of course," he said, lying back. "Don't go far. I feel better when I know your brilliance is nearby."

She rolled her eyes at him and walked away down the row of beds. Several patients asked for something, but she did not stop. She walked through the doorway and out into the long hall. She kept walking—walking, praying, and talking to herself. She shoved open the front doors of the building and ran out into the cold November night.

* * *

Three days later Shawn Burbage lapsed into a coma. Dr. Thorndike, Eleanor, Mr. and Mrs. Burbage, and Shawn's brother Steven stood or sat by his bed in deep contemplation and sorrow. Mr. Burbage and Steven had given Shawn a beautiful blessing that gave solace, but no promise of recovery.

"Is . . . is he suffering?" Mrs. Burbage asked.

"No," Dr. Thorndike assured.

"And it's pneumonia?"

"Yes," the doctor answered, "brought on by the influenza."

"And he caught the influenza from one of the patients he was caring for?"

"Mother," Shawn's brother said in a low, tortured voice, "must you ask these questions?"

"Yes, I must, Steven." She turned to the doctor. "Dr. Thorndike?"

"Yes, ma'am, it's likely."

"Greater love hath no man than this . . ." Mrs. Burbage recited to herself.

Eleanor started crying, and Mr. Burbage slipped his arm around her waist and gave her a fatherly hug. "How can we ever thank you for the tender care you've given our boy these last days, Miss Lund?"

"And the friendship of the last months," Mrs. Burbage added. "He esteems you highly."

Eleanor could not answer. She wanted to tell them how much their son meant to her—what an honorable man he was. She wanted to tell them how she loved his sense of humor and keen mind, but the words were trapped in her grief, and all she could do was nod her head and weep.

Mr. Burbage took Shawn's hand. "How grateful we are for the promise of eternal life, and for temple sealings," he whispered, his voice thick with anguish.

Dr. Thorndike looked over at him but did not comment. He also was suffering. As he looked down at Shawn's pale and drawn features, he could see his son Miles's face and imagine his final hours—frightened and alone in a distant land. Had his boy longed to see the faces of his family? Did he want his father there to heal him? Dr. Thorndike shuddered and realized that Eleanor was speaking.

"No. Oh, no. Oh, please . . . it's not possible."

He focused quickly on Shawn, sure that he would find him dead, but the boy was still breathing. He looked over at Eleanor. Her face had gone sheet white, and her features were twisted as though in pain.

"No, Lord, please," she mumbled. "This isn't possible." She moved numbly away from the group toward the gurney that was being wheeled into the ward. Beside the table stood a man with brown curly hair and a little boy of similar coloring. "Elias? What . . . Why are you . . . ?" Then she recognized the woman on the stretcher. "Oh, no."

"Eleanor!" Elias blurted out when he saw her. "It's Sarah. It's my Sarah. What am I going to do?" His face held so much suffering that it jarred Eleanor's sensibilities into detachment and professionalism.

"First, you and Zachery are going to leave the ward. You don't even have on masks."

Zachery started crying, and Elias began to protest, but Eleanor would have none of it. "Let the orderlies get Sarah into a bed. You two come with me."

The two men followed obediently. As they went down the hall to the masking room, Eleanor took in Elias's aggrieved condition. This was not the disdainful, intolerant person she'd met upon her arrival in Salt Lake City. The years of patient example from his sweet wife had wrought a change in Elias's heart—a heart that was now aching with fear and grief. Eleanor wanted to say something to comfort him, but he was talking without pause, releasing his anxiety in a rush of words.

"She . . . she just got sick yesterday, and she didn't want to come to the hospital. She told me to put the white flag on the house and to take Zachery to Mother Erickson's, but Mother is watching Grandfather while you're here . . . besides Zachery refused to leave his mother's side." The little boy's lips trembled, but his eyes held an uncharacteristic defiance.

Eleanor brought the masks from the supply room. "Is Alaina all right?" she asked. "I should have called, but I've been so . . . I didn't think."

"She's fine," Elias said quickly. "She and the children are fine." Eleanor handed Elias his mask and tied a smaller one on Zachery's face. She also replaced her mask, throwing the old one into a special covered bin. Elias immediately took up the thread of his conversation. "Everyone else in the family is fine, so I don't understand why Sarah is sick. And she went down so fast. Dr. Lucien came by today and insisted she come to the hospital. But, I don't see . . ."

"It's probably because I can look after her here," Eleanor said simply, walking them back toward the ward.

"Of course," Elias answered. "Of course." He put his hand absently on Zachery's head. "I . . . I need to get Father here to help me give her a blessing." His words were mumbled, and they trailed away as if his mind were distracted.

"That's a very good idea," Eleanor said, trying to keep her voice steady. She thought of the blessing that Shawn's father and brother had given him—words that connected mortality with heaven. *There is more than this earth life*, Eleanor said to calm her own frantic thoughts.

They arrived at the doorway to the ward, and Eleanor stopped and took Zachery by the hand. "We'll wait here for a moment while you go in," she instructed Elias. Zachery began to whimper, and his father turned to him. "We'll be fine," Eleanor said calmly. "Go in and talk to Dr. Thorndike about Sarah's prognosis." Elias nodded and went in. "Come on, Mr. Zachery," Eleanor said, looking down at him, "we'll sit over here on this little bench." The obedient child followed, climbing up on the wooden bench and sitting with his legs Indian-style.

"Are you hungry?" Eleanor asked him. "I think I might be able to find you a roll or maybe some chocolate."

"No, thank you," he said politely. "Daddy made me eggs for supper."

"Oh, that's good," Eleanor answered, trying to keep the poignant scene out of her imagination.

"Auntie Eleanor," Zachery said, picking at his shoelaces, "I want to be in by Mommy when my grandma comes."

"Is Grammy Erickson coming down to the hospital?"

Zachery shook his head. "No, my other one."

"Grandmother Eunice?"

Zachery frowned. "No Grandma Caroline, Grampa's wife . . . the one in the picture."

Now it was Eleanor's turn to frown. "Zachery, Grandma Caroline is dead. She's been in heaven for many years."

"I know," Zachery said brightly. "She's an angel, and I dreamed about her."

Eleanor felt a chill move through her body. "You did?"

Zachery untied and tied his shoelace. "It made me happy to look at her, and she said she was going to watch over my mother when she was sick."

The ward door opened and Dr. Thorndike stepped out. "Miss Lund, we need you inside."

Eleanor stood, her heart thudding in her chest. "Stay here, Zachery," she said numbly. She followed Dr. Thorndike to Shawn's bedside, where the palpable sorrow enveloped her. She took her friend's hand, noticing that his breathing was irregular. She prayed in her heart as she'd never prayed before that she could somehow make sense of this sadness—that she would not be angry with God . . . but, how . . . ? How could He take someone so precious and so good—take someone who's life would have been spent helping others? She ran her finger along the back of Shawn's hand.

"I'm not afraid," came his soft voice.

Eleanor smiled at him bravely as his mother, father, and brother moved closer. She relinquished his hand to Mrs. Burbage and stepped away.

"I'm not afraid," he said again, and his father and brother nodded. His mother looked away, tears streaming down her face.

Into Eleanor's mind came the images of her father's death within the grove of apple trees. His last words to her had been . . . *Nothing to fear.* Oh, how she longed to be back on the farm, walking among the beautiful trees—thinking about chores, and school, and gingerbread. *Why was she older? Why did she have to go through this hard experience?* She focused back on Shawn's face, amazed that he had come out of the coma. He looked at her.

"Dear friend," he whispered.

His jaw set and he closed his eyes.

Eleanor stepped back and touched Mr. Burbage's arm. "I . . . I have to go and care for my sister-in-law." The suppressed tears and anguish were making her throat hurt, and she knew she had to take her emotions away from her friend's side or she would lose any professional detachment—she would lose that calm façade she had to maintain for the sake of the other patients. "He is such a good man," she said as she backed away. "Such a good man." She bumped into the privacy screen.

Mr. Burbage looked at her with compassion and understanding, and she moved quickly around the side of the screen, brushing fiercely at the tears that coursed down her face.

Dr. Thorndike joined her. "Do you want to take a break?"

She took a deep breath and shook her head. "No, sir, thank you. I need to keep working."

He patted her back. "You let me know when you've had enough," he said bluntly. He turned back to care for the Burbages.

Eleanor lowered her mask and wiped her face with her handkerchief. She looked over to where they'd placed Sarah and saw that Zachery had snuck in during her absence and was sitting on his mother's bed, giving her sips of water. Normally children were not allowed in the wards, but for some reason the nurses and volunteers seemed to be ignoring the little man. *Were there angels near?*

Medical knowledge and spiritual awareness were clamoring for precedence in her brain, and she tried to focus on something simple and tangible that would untie the knot of fear and loss that sat in her chest. She took a step forward, and Zachery turned to smile at her. She stared at him in amazement. Sitting on the hospital bed with a doctor taking blood from his mother's arm, and a nurse fixing an oxygen mask over her nose and mouth, he seemed to be the picture of serenity and fortitude. He waved to her, and she walked to stand beside him.

"Is your friend going to be all right?" he whispered in a manner well beyond his years.

Eleanor gave him a hug. "No, sweetheart. I'm afraid he's too sick."

"I'm so sorry, Eleanor," Elias said, gently taking her wrist.

Sarah opened her eyes and reached up to touch her son's cheek.

"I'm glad to see you, Mommy, but you'd better sleep now. I'll wake you when Grandma gets here."

From the area of Shawn Burbage's bed came a sob of anguish, and Eleanor stiffened. "I . . . I need to get some things from the supply room," she said, turning quickly and moving toward the door. She pushed out into the hallway and stumbled to the wooden bench. Something had punched her in the chest and she couldn't breathe. She slumped onto the bench, clenching her fists against the pain. Dr. Thorndike came and sat beside her, taking her in his arms and saying nothing as she wept—wept as she once had in a grove of apple trees.

* * *

Sarah Erickson sat at a large table set up in Grandfather Erickson's front room. Her face was pale and gaunt, but a light of joy shone in her eyes as she looked around at her loved ones.

"Thank you for waiting on Thanksgiving dinner for me," she said simply.

Elias lowered his head to control his emotions.

"Vell, ve couldn't have Thanksgiving dinner vithout your famous rolls and apple cake," Grandfather Erickson said, patting her hand.

"I want apple cake now!" Katie called out.

"First prayer, then dinner, then cake," Mother Erickson answered. Katie started to protest, but her Grammy knew a sure way to keep the peace. "If you're good, you can have two pieces."

Katie immediately folded her arms and lowered her head, which made everyone laugh.

When a modicum of reverence was established, Grandfather Erickson prayed—a prayer of gratitude for Sarah's survival and the bounteous blessings of their lives—a prayer for the chaos and the suffering of the world to end—and a prayer that James Lund and Nephi Erickson would return home safely from foreign lands.

Every voice joined in a tender *amen.*

Dr. Thorndike stood at the front of the lecture hall, his hands gripping the edges of the podium, his head bowed. Slowly he raised his face to his students, looking attentively into their eyes, searching for youthful strength and resilience.

Eleanor Lund leaned forward.

"My dear students," Dr. Thorndike began in a tone of uncharacteristic tenderness, "I wish to address you before our leave-taking for the Christmas holidays." He took a breath. "We have lived through a bitter time of history. The Armistice is signed, the war has ended, yet in the four years its booted foot trod upon our neck, the world lost nearly thirteen million souls." His voice hushed. "Thirteen million souls. And countless others will sojourn through life maimed and broken. Many young men who valiantly survived that conflict returned home to find death waiting on their doorsteps. They either succumbed themselves to the influenza or watched family members taken by this plague . . ." his voice broke, "this plague of Biblical ferocity."

He lifted a paper off the podium. "We have lost many of our own membership to either that battle across the ocean or to the one here." His voice broke again. "Their sacrifice demands our utmost respect." Tears coursed down his cheeks, and Eleanor wept with him. He read from the paper, pronouncing each name clearly and with great reverence. "Nurses Viola Gray and Anna Marchant, serving with the American Red Cross, Glen Kimball, George Sainsbury, Grant Larsen, Shawn Burbage . . ."

Eleanor laid her head on her arms, the emotion coming freely and without shame.

". . . Frank Taylor, Milton Ivie, Miles Thorndike, Reed Holloway, John Holt . . ."

He had read his own boy's name with the same cadence and deference afforded all the others, and Eleanor raised her head to stare at the man and wonder at his greatness of character.

Dr. Thorndike lowered the paper onto the podium. "I am a doctor and a scientist, yet something other than fact and logic comes into play during the direst times of human struggle . . . qualities of faith, dignity, and compassion. I truly believe as Paul of old, 'Greater love hath no man than this, that a man lay down his life for his friends.'" He took out his handkerchief and wiped his face. Then he came out from behind the podium to be closer to them.

"And what of us left behind? How do we honor their courage and sacrifice? This is my word to you. Prove your mettle! Lay your offering on the altar of life and see how it compares, and if you find your gift lacking, press forward with determination. Consecrate to the good of mankind your precious lives. Be big, and active, and brave. What a grievous loss to humanity if you think small. The world does not owe you a living. You must use your gifts and resources to pull the world back from sorrow, and sickness, and loss."

Eleanor sat with the rest of the class in rapt silence. Her heart pounded in her chest, affirming each stirring sentiment.

"I am proud of you. Oh, so proud." His eyes met Eleanor's. He nodded once at her, and then looked away to the others in the room. "Be not vain in your abilities, but grateful . . . grateful that your work can lessen suffering and offer hope." His voice grew husky. "If those of us left behind will but do our work well, we will honor them."

With that, he quietly turned back to the podium, picked up his papers, and left the classroom.

40

Mother Erickson stood with her back pressed against the kitchen door. Through the tangle of thoughts in her head, she latched onto the one that held peace. *He's home. My son is home.* Then she looked down at the gold paper star in her hand and started crying. The star was simple and misshapen, and her son had fashioned it—her son the artist, her son whose skill on Christmases past had fashioned ornate and elaborate stars, snowflakes, and manger scenes. *Patience Erickson*, she scolded. *Be grateful. Be grateful for his life.* It was no use. Her mind wandered over several melancholy pictures until it fixed on the scene at the train station—*Alaina and Katie rushing to Nephi the moment he'd stepped from the train—his two sweethearts throwing their arms around him, laughing and crying for joy, while he stood motionless like a statue. He did not hold them or even look at them—Alaina stepping back, her face a mask of fear and devastation.* Patience Erickson wept and tried to wipe the heart-wrenching images from her mind. She remembered numbly walking forward and presenting the little wiggling bundle of blanket and child.

"Nephi, it's your son. Nephi Samuel Erickson."

But Nephi had backed away from the child—away from her and any show of tenderness. He was mumbling something incoherent and biting the back of his hand.

It was Nephi's father who had first recovered from the shock, and moved to take his son's arm. "Elias, go and get your brother's things. Patience, you stay with Alaina and Katie. Nephi and I are just going to take a little walk." He'd pulled Nephi gently from the crowd. "Come on, son. Come on. We'll just give you a little time to get settled."

Settled? A week had gone, and although her son no longer bit his hands or spoke gibberish, he wandered the house and yard at night, and still refused to let any of them touch him.

Dr. Lucien had come to visit and observe, and afterward tried to explain to Alaina a condition of soldiers called shell shock.

Patience felt the door push against her, and she wiped her eyes quickly on her apron and stepped forward.

Katie shoved her way into the kitchen. "Grammy, where is my star Daddy made me? I want to put it on the tree," she said, a note of impatience in her voice.

"Your star is right here, you little sweet potato. I was just getting string so we could tie it on." Mother Erickson moved to the drawer for string and scissors, praying as she went for strength to mask her broken heart.

Alaina came into the kitchen at that point, searching for her absent daughter. "So, this is where you disappeared to," she remarked to her twirling daughter.

Katie stopped spinning. "Grammy taked my star," she replied impudently, "and it's for the tree."

"I see," Alaina said, smiling as Mother Erickson handed her granddaughter the decoration and string. "Do you have everything now?"

Katie looked down at the articles in her hand and nodded.

"Good. Off you go, then." Alaina patted Katie on the head and sent her on her way. When the door closed, she turned to her mother-in-law. "How are you?"

Mother Erickson was taken aback by the forthright question. "I . . ." She stopped and stared at Alaina for a long moment. Unbidden tears leaked down her face, and she took out her handkerchief to wipe them away. "I'm not doing well," she answered finally. "Not doing well at all, little muffin."

Alaina came over and wrapped her arms around the dear woman. "He's going to be all right," she whispered.

Mother Erickson sobbed. "Oh, muffin, how do you know that?"

Alaina's voice was calm and soothing. "I've found out a little secret about Father in Heaven."

Mother Erickson stepped back and looked at her. "Is that so?" She smiled slightly.

Alaina nodded. "Yes, and what I found is that if you fast and pray enough, and read your scriptures enough, then a miracle happens."

Mother Erickson's lips trembled with emotion, and she nodded.

Alaina smiled. "Of course, you've known this secret for a long time, but I've just found it. You find that He's really there, and that He cares about every small detail of your life." Mother Erickson nodded again. "And even more," Alaina continued, "He gives you peace and guidance."

Mother Erickson spoke through her tears. "You've found all that, have you?"

Alaina grinned. "I have."

"I guess I've just been so miserable seeing my boy broken that I forgot," Mother Erickson confessed.

Alaina gave her a squeeze. "I think He knows that." Her voice softened. "I think our kind Father knows everything."

Mother Erickson took a deep breath. "He surely does. And our dear Lord takes upon Himself our sorrows and pains."

"I know it's going to be hard . . . maybe really hard for a long time," Alaina said, straightening her back, "but we can find a way through."

Katie burst into the kitchen. "Come see the star!" she yelled happily. "Daddy lifted me to put it up!"

"Your daddy lifted you?" Alaina questioned.

"Yep," Katie said, not realizing the importance of the act she reported. "It looks beumiful!" She grabbed her mother's hand and dragged her off to the front room. "Come on, Grammy!" she yelled back. "Follow me!"

* * *

"Merry Christmas, Miss Johnson," Edward Rosemund said softly. He stood on her doorstep, smiling and holding out a beautifully wrapped present.

Suddenly Jane, little Elizabeth, and Samuel came popping out from the side of the house. "Surprise! Merry Christmas, Miss Johnson!" they chorused.

"How lovely. Oh, how lovely," Philomene laughed, stepping back to catch her breath. She gave Samuel a hug. "Would you like to come in for some wassail?"

Mr. Rosemund looked solemn. "No, Miss Johnson, I'm afraid we can't," he said bluntly, and Samuel sniggered. "You see, we're on a pilgrimage."

"A pilgrimage?" Miss Johnson returned, a slight smile at the corner of her mouth. "I see. Well, Christmas is a very good time for a pilgrimage."

"Yes," Edward Rosemund continued, "we are looking for the Spirit of Christmas, and we were wondering if you'd like to join us in our quest?"

Philomene Johnson looked into their faces—rosy with cold and shining with excitement—and felt Christmas surround her. "You mean an adventure out into the dark, starry night?"

"That's the ticket!" Samuel blurted out.

Philomene looked shocked. "Mr. Rosemund, such slang!"

Samuel laughed. "Sorry, Miss Johnson. If I promise to mind my grammar, will you come on the pilgrimage with us?"

She looked down at him with an appraising eye. "Tempting, Mr. Rosemund. Very tempting."

"It's settled then," Edward broke in. "Take your present in, get your coat and gloves, and we shall be off!"

Moments later the little band was headed toward the main part of town, singing "Good King Wenceslas" and sharing Christmas cookies, which had somehow found their way mysteriously into all of Miss Johnson's coat pockets.

* * *

Bib Randall sat alone by the small fire in the servants' quarters. The house was still, and he heard the upstairs clock chime midnight.

"Mr. Randall?"

Despite the fact that it was a small voice, it made him jump. He turned to find Ina Bell Latham standing in the doorway. "Goodness, Ina Bell, you were quiet as a mouse." He stood to acknowledge her. "I didn't hear you at all."

She smiled shyly. "Would . . . would you mind if I joined you by the fire?"

"Of course not," he said, bringing another chair forward.

She sat down, making sure her legs and feet were covered.

Bib stoked the fire, added more coal, then sat back in his chair. The two watched the embers quietly.

Ina Bell finally broke the silence. "Are you still very tired from your sickness?"

Bib nodded. "I am. It's been over two months, and . . . not that I'm complaining," he added quickly. "I mean, I'm glad to be alive."

"I'm . . . we're all glad you're alive, too."

The clock upstairs chimed the quarter hour.

Ina Bell suddenly sat forward a bit in her chair. "It's Christmas then, isn't it?"

"It is," Bib answered.

"Merry Christmas, Mr. Randall."

"Merry Christmas, Miss Latham."

Tears were running down Ina Bell's cheeks. "I'm . . . I'm so very glad you didn't die, Mr. Randall."

Bib reached over and touched her shoulder. "Are you all right, Ina Bell?"

"No," she whispered, "I'm a goose, Mr. Randall. A frightened, silly goose."

Bib chuckled. "I have known you many years now, Ina Bell, and I don't think you're a goose. Hard working . . . kind hearted . . . and faithful, but not a goose, and not silly."

Ina Bell gulped down her tears and took a deep breath. She turned tentatively to look at him. "Well, how silly is it to love someone for a long time and never let him know?"

Bib stared at her. "Do you mean me?"

She nodded.

"But . . . but we've been friends . . . all these years . . . and I never thought that . . . never imagined . . ."

Ina Bell checked her embarrassment. "It's all right, Mr. Randall. I didn't expect you to share the same feelings. I just needed to tell you, that's all."

"No, Ina Bell, you don't understand . . . I just never thought anyone would ever have those kind of feelings for me. I'm a different sort of fellow, and not very good-looking—"

"You're very good-looking to me," Ina Bell interrupted.

"I am?" Bib spluttered.

Ina Bell nodded.

"Well, what a strange kettle of fish!" Bib said, sitting back in his chair and shaking his head.

Ina Bell smiled.

Suddenly he reached over and shook her hand. "Merry Christmas, Miss Latham!"

"Merry Christmas, Mr. Randall."

* * *

Hannah Finn was asleep on the one settee left behind by the German occupiers. On the small table nearby sat an unblemished china cup and saucer, and a half-eaten pastry. Pressed against her breast was a beautiful handmade Christmas card from her niece Philomene.

Claudine smiled as she gently covered her mistress with a worn silk coverlet. "Merry Christmas, madame. I wish you sweet Christmas dreams." She moved to the salon window and watched with wonder as the first flakes of enchanting snow danced lightly in the dark night.

* * *

Eleanor cautiously opened her bedroom door and peeked out. She tiptoed into the front room to place a special package under the small Christmas tree. She had only finished knitting the lap blanket ten minutes earlier, and although she was tired, she wanted to get it wrapped and placed before the morning. She hoped that Grandfather would love the Danish flag woven with tenderness into the blanket's design. She congratulated herself on all the ways she'd used to keep the project a secret from him.

As she bent down to place the gift, she saw a palm-sized present tucked back into the branches of the tree. She looked closer and saw many presents of about the same size and shape clumsily wrapped in butcher paper and string. Her curiosity overwhelmed her, and she reached for one of the gifts, looking quickly behind her to make sure Grandfather's door was shut. The writing on the paper was Grandfather's spidery scrawl, and the person to whom the present belonged was . . . *Patience*. She replaced that package and found another—*Elias . . . Alaina . . . Sarah*. She smiled and shook her head. Here she thought she was being sneaky with her present, when all along, the dear patriarch had, with difficulty, been wrapping heartfelt sentiments and waiting for the time when he could squirrel them away under the tree. She rummaged around in the back branches until she came up with another present . . . *Eleanor*. What had he given her? What had he given them all? She felt like a five-year-old creeping downstairs Christmas morning to peek into her stocking. Slowly she untied and removed the string and paper. In her hand was a carved wise man.

She opened them all.

Alaina and Nephi had been given Mary and Joseph; baby Nephi, a camel; Elias, a shepherd; Mother Erickson, the star; Katie, a flock of sheep; and

Zachery and Sarah, angels. Grandfather had given each of them a piece of the magnificent manger scene he'd carved for Caroline when they were first married. Clearly each piece had been selected to match some aspect of the receiver's life or personality. She looked down at the wise man in her hand, and a smile touched her deep emotions. *Does he think me wise . . . a traveler . . . a seeker?*

She looked up questioningly. *But where was the baby Jesus?* She nodded as tears fell in realization. The dear man hadn't given any one person the precious baby, because He belonged to all of them.

Eleanor jumped as a strong wind rattled the windows and door and came moaning down the chimney. A storm was coming, and she felt giddy about the prospect of new snow! She carefully rewrapped the gifts and hid them back in the branches, thinking all the while of the gift of life they would be celebrating. The message of the Savior was the message of life. Eleanor thought of Shawn, Joanna Wilton's mother, Dr. Thorndike's boy, and all the soldiers killed in the dreadful war. How could any of that make sense without a doctrine of eternalism? How could man ever find solace if there wasn't Christ's promise of life?

She smiled at herself. There were so many thoughts bumping around in her head. Most of the time she was glad she was a thinker, but not tonight. Tomorrow she and Grandfather were hosting the entire family for Christmas, and she knew the day would start early.

As she turned off the light and crawled into her cold bed, Eleanor had a picture come to mind of Katie sitting by the front door at Grammy's house in her red coat and boots, waiting for the rest of the family to wake up and start the Christmas celebration.

Scrimmy!

41

"And what about this?" Eleanor asked, holding up a somewhat large, nondescript piece of white cotton fabric sporting three oddly cut holes. She was on her knees in front of Alaina's bedroom closet going through a box of items. She wore an old patched skirt and a three-cornered cotton scarf around her head—perfect attire for the winter cleaning.

Alaina looked over. She'd been bent low pulling the dust mop back from the hardest-to-reach spots under her bed. She too wore an old skirt and a scarf. She frowned at the mystery cloth. "I have no idea what that is. Toss it."

Just then Katie came into the room—an exact miniature in dress of her mother and auntie. Her eyes flew open as she saw Eleanor aim the item toward the trash basket. "No!" she yelled, running forward and grabbing at the cloth. "That's mine!"

"Yours?" Alaina questioned. "Where did you get it?"

"I maked it," Katie said, hiding the article behind her back.

"Made it? Where did you get the cloth?"

Katie defiantly stuck out her chin and pressed her lips together.

"Katie, bring it here," Alaina said, holding out her hand.

Katie stepped back.

"Katie Eleanor Erickson, bring me that cloth."

The little girl's lower lip started to tremble as she shuffled forward very slowly. "Don' be mad, Mommy. I . . . I wanted to be like Zacry's mommy."

"I beg your pardon?" Alaina questioned. She saw Eleanor bite her lip to keep from laughing.

Katie brought the material out from behind her back. "Like Auntie Sarah when she was in the hospital."

Alaina took the white cloth and held it up.

"It's a hospital gown," Eleanor said, working to keep her voice steady.

Alaina's eyes widened. "Made from a pillowcase?" She pursed her lips to keep from smiling. "Ah, so this is where Grammy's missing pillowcase went."

"I only cutted it a little," Katie defended. "Zacry helped. He told me what it looked like."

"So you used scissors, too?" Alaina said.

"I didn't use 'em very good," Katie answered.

Eleanor snorted with laughter, and Katie turned to stare at her.

"Oh, you're a big help," Alaina scolded.

"Sorry . . . sorry," Eleanor said, trying to regain her composure.

"Is it funny what I did?" Katie asked hopefully.

Alaina sobered. "No. No, it's not funny." She kneeled and took Katie's hands. "You must never take anything that belongs to someone else without first asking permission. And you must never use scissors unless there is a grown-up to help you." She lifted Katie's chin. "Do you understand me?"

"Yes, Mommy."

Alaina handed her back the pillowcase. "Now, I want you to show this to Grammy and tell her that you're sorry."

"I don' want to," Katie said, scowling.

"You may not want to, but you will," Alaina said firmly. "When we do something wrong, Katie, we must say sorry."

"Why?" Katie asked.

Alaina stood. "Because saying sorry is another way of saying I won't do it again."

"That I won't take Grammy's pillowcase again?"

Alaina nodded. "That's right."

"But I won't, 'cause it's already cut."

Alaina took a deep breath as Eleanor turned her head away to keep from catching her sister's eye. "You will be telling Grammy you won't be taking any *more* of her things without asking."

"But, I was—"

"Katie Eleanor Erickson, that's enough! Now . . . do you know where Grammy is?"

Katie nodded. "Yes. We was cleaning the pantry."

"Then off you go. You'll feel better after you say sorry."

"I don' think I will," Katie mumbled as she turned to go out.

When she was gone, Eleanor laughed and Alaina sighed. "And she's only three!"

"Four in a couple of months," Eleanor reminded.

The women went back to their cleaning, content with the thought that they were nearly finished. The drudgery of the task was always diminished when two worked together, and the Lund sisters had been working together since they were little girls.

Eleanor pulled out the final box in the closet. It was pushed way to the back and hidden under an old drapery—a shredding piece of fabric that made Eleanor wonder why it hadn't been thrown away long ago. As she pulled back the box flaps, she had to pause for a moment before it registered what she was looking at—Nephi's marine uniform. She gently lifted it onto her lap and unfolded it. It carried an unpleasant odor of sweat, mud, and something else Eleanor recognized—blood.

"What's that?" Alaina asked.

Eleanor folded the jacket quickly. "Just Nephi's uniform," she said, attempting to settle it back in the box with a detached nonchalance.

Alaina came over and sat on the edge of the bed. "Here, let me see it."

Eleanor reluctantly handed it to her. It was threadbare in several places and stained, and the medals that hung on the left pocket area seemed a paradox. Across the shoulder was a dark smear that could only be blood.

Alaina swallowed hard as bile rose in her throat. "I . . . I didn't know he had this," she stammered. "I thought he'd thrown it away." She kept staring at the dark spot, transfixed by its gruesome revelation. "What else is in there?"

Eleanor looked back into the box. She brought out the uniform pants and looked down at a few scattered photos and the small pocket journal she'd give him before he left. "Oh my goodness," she said softly, reaching for it.

"What?" Alaina asked.

"It's the journal I gave him." Eleanor picked it up and stood. She moved over and sat on the bed with her sister.

The tan cover was frayed and mud-stained, but the small book itself was intact, and it was obvious that many of the pages had been filled with words or images.

"Open it," Alaina said, forcing her gaze to the window and the world outside. A January storm was dropping large flakes of snow; three inches were already on the ground, and the steel gray of the clouds indicated several more hours of accumulation.

Eleanor looked at her sister's profile. "Are you sure?"

"Yes," Alaina answered resolutely. Her gaze slid down to the book in Eleanor's hands. "Yes."

Eleanor opened to the first page. It was a sketch of Alaina and Katie, and Nephi had written underneath, "my sweethearts." Alaina ran her fingers over the page and smiled. Eleanor waited, then turned to the next drawing. It was a picture of the barracks in the training camp at Upton, New York. "Ah, look," Eleanor said, pointing to the adjacent drawing. "I asked him to draw the Statue of Liberty and he did." Another picture showed three smiling marines standing by a ship's railing: one was large and broad of face, one average with a jaunty smile, and the third had refined features and a thoughtful expression. The images continued—a harbor town, a French bakery, train stations, a French mail carrier, horses pulling a caisson, dead horses by the roadside, a small patch of flowers, a German soldier wearing a helmet with a spike on the top, a muddy wasteland, a tank, a dead soldier caught in barbed wire.

Alaina moaned.

"Let's stop," Eleanor said, starting to close the book.

"No!" Alaina said sharply. "I have to know."

Eleanor slowly took her hand off the picture of the soldier in the barbed wire, and they continued without comment. It was nearly impossible for their minds to grasp what their eyes were seeing—a soldier's face blistered and burned, soldiers standing in a trench with muddy water past their boot tops, a young man shot through the eye, a bloody hand holding a ruined pocket watch, the man with the thoughtful expression holding a dead soldier in his arms. Eleanor turned another page and both women gagged.

"What . . . what is that?" Alaina groaned.

Eleanor closed the book, stood, and paced the room.

"Elly . . . Elly, what was that?" Alaina pleaded, her voice wavering with hysteria.

Eleanor growled. "No, Alaina. No! I told you we should have stopped. I told you!"

But Alaina was desperate. "Those were bits and pieces of a man, weren't they? Bits and pieces of a soldier blown up into that tree!"

"What are you doing?" a soft, anguished voice came from behind them.

The two women spun around to see Nephi standing in the doorway, his face suffused with horrific pain as he stared at the book in Eleanor's hand. A howl of rage and suffering welled up from his gut, and he lunged for the book, ripping it from Eleanor. "No! No! You can't see that!" He threw the book with such force that it broke through the bedroom window.

Katie appeared at the bedroom door, screaming. "Daddy! Daddy! Don't!"

Mother Erickson was right behind her, her face white with fear.

Nephi ran to the broken window and punched it with his fist. The remaining shards of glass splintered into the snow. He turned and grabbed his marine jacket. "Do you see? Do you want to see that? That's Jimmy's blood . . . that's his blood from when I carried him to the grave detail."

Alaina didn't look at the jacket but at her husband's anguished face.

Nephi threw down the jacket and pushed over the side table. Eleanor jumped back as the lamp shattered. He pulled the covers off the bed and knocked a picture off the wall. The three women descended on him as one—his mother grabbing him around the waist and Alaina and Eleanor each grabbing one of his strong arms.

Nephi yelled and fell forward onto his knees. "No! Don't touch me! Don't touch me!"

The women held on.

Katie was screaming and sobbing.

"Katie!" Alaina yelled. "Check on your brother. Then run to the telephone box and call Uncle Elias. Tell him to come right away! Now!"

Katie turned and ran.

Nephi struggled and cried. "Don't touch me . . . don't . . . I'm disgusting." The women held on.

"Dear Lord, please give us strength," Mother Erickson prayed. "Send angels here to help us." Nephi sobbed. "And bring peace to one of Thy good sons." Nephi folded in on himself.

"Don't touch me."

"We love you, son."

"No!" Nephi screamed.

"Well, we do," Mother Erickson said, slightly releasing her grip. "Nothin' you can do about it."

Nephi rocked back and forth, and when Alaina and Eleanor let go of his arms, he wrapped them around himself. "I'm evil, don't you understand? I'm evil."

Alaina and Eleanor were stunned, but Mother Erickson responded with strength and clarity. "You are not evil, son." She rubbed his back. "You've had to walk through hell, and hell is a hard thing to scrub off your soul." Nephi wept. "You are a good man. A gentle man. How could you go through war without having it hurt ya?" Eleanor gently laid her hand on his shoulder, and Alaina placed hers on his head. "See there, now," Mother Erickson continued, "can't you feel how much we love you?"

Katie came tentatively into the room. "Uncle Elias is coming," she said softly.

Alaina looked up. "Good. Thank you, Katie. You were a big girl to do that."

Katie started crying. "Is my daddy sick?"

"No," Alaina answered. "He was just very sad, but he's going to be better now. He is. Come here, sweetheart."

Katie crept over to Alaina, never taking her eyes off the slumped form of her father. She sat on her mother's lap. After a time, she reached out her hand and patted Nephi's arm. "Don't cwy, Daddy. Don't cwy. You are safe now."

Slowly Nephi's hand came over, gently grasping his daughter's fingers.

Katie looked up at her mother, who smiled and nodded.

Outside the storm continued, covering the discarded book in softest white.

* * *

A week later, Alaina awoke in the middle of the night from a pleasant dream to find Nephi out of bed. He was pacing the floor and talking to himself, and she grieved. She took a deep breath, said a little prayer, and reminded herself that the healing would take time. She thought of a scripture she'd read that morning . . . *Be still, and know that I am God.* Be still. She lay quietly, closing her eyes and concentrating on what Nephi was saying. Maybe she would hear something that could give her insight to his anguish, or at least something to share with Dr. Lucien.

". . . and all of Cornell's brothers were named for universities, and his sisters were flowers . . . I think their names were Violet and Daisy. That's right—Violet and Daisy. Cornell talked about them in his last letter. Do you think if we had named our Katie after a flower she might have been a little softer?" He chuckled softly. "No . . . we like her just the way she is, don't we?" He paced to the moonlit window and stopped. "Cornell said he might come out to Salt Lake City for a visit, and maybe Jimmy could come with him." Nephi moaned softly. "No, no, Jimmy Gordon is dead. He was killed in the war. He . . . he was a funny man. You would have liked him."

Alaina was about to get out of bed and go to him when she heard baby Nephi's squeaky babbling.

"Shh . . . we don't want to wake Mommy," Nephi whispered. He stared down at his son, and in the moonlight, Alaina could see the corner of her husband's mouth drawn up in a smile. "You're a heavy boy, aren't you?" The smile faded, and it was several moments before Nephi spoke again. "I haven't held you, and I'm sorry about that. It's just that you were so pure, and I was . . ."

Nephi Jr. made a funny gurgling noise, and his father laughed softly. "You don't care anything about that, do you? Do you?" He brought the baby to his face and nibbled his tummy. Nephi Jr. squealed. "Oh no! Shh. Quiet." Nephi said guiltily, casting a glance over his shoulder at Alaina. She pretended to be asleep. "Shh . . . shh. We have to be quiet now, or we'll wake Mommy for sure."

Tears were making her pillow wet, but Alaina didn't care. Her soul was filled with gratitude and peace. She watched her husband's silhouette as he placed the baby on his chest, gently rubbing his back and whispering words she could not hear.

Be still, and know that I am God.

42

"I still can't believe the yield you got off of twenty walnut trees," Daniel remarked to his stepfather as he bent to pick up another forty-pound sack.

Fredrick Robinson grunted as he hefted a sack with each hand and carried them to the wagon. "It's been a good year. We've been selling off these nuts all through winter, and they might even last us till spring." He closed the back gate of the rig and retied his scarf. "It's going to be a cold drive to Martell."

"Come on, old man. Are you getting soft in your old age?" Daniel chided.

"I can still keep up with you, young pup."

Daniel grinned. "Well, I'm not much of a match now, am I?"

Mr. Robinson kicked the wagon wheel, and the horse shied sideways. "Sorry, son," he said in a miserable tone.

Daniel stopped him from going on. "Father, it's fine. I don't want you to have to worry about what you say to me." Mr. Robinson continued to stare at the ground, and Daniel's heart went out to the big bear of a man. For his mother and younger siblings, the grim reality of Daniel's mutilated form had been accepted and set aside, but Daniel knew his stepfather was still struggling with the experiences and injuries his son had suffered in France.

Daniel pulled himself onto the buckboard. "So, let's get these walnuts to the train before they grow into trees."

Fredrick nodded and climbed up beside his son.

Mrs. Robinson came out of the house carrying a small cloth bundle. "Pick up the post," she instructed, handing up a package to her husband. "Here's some warm spice cake for the trip."

Fredrick brightened. "I thought I caught a whiff of something wonderful. But where's Daniel's cake?"

"Very funny," Daniel said, slapping the lines on Angel's backside. "Walk on," he called, and the horse started forward.

"I'll arm wrestle you for it," Fredrick said.

Daniel laughed. "Now that's very sporting of you."

Edna Robinson stood on the front porch watching the rig pull away. She loved the two men—no question—and she was grateful to see a portion of normalcy returning to their relationship. Now if only her prayers would be answered about a young woman to catch Daniel's fancy. Her handsome son had been home long enough now to have a steady prospect. Her mind catalogued all the eligible girls in Pine Grove and Sutter Creek. Edna Robinson turned back into the house thinking that she just might invite Maddie Cross out for supper on Sunday.

* * *

Fredrick Robinson came out of the post office laughing and talking with Elijah Greggs, the postmaster. "Even though the kaiser's hightailed it to Holland, you could always put a picture of him on your wall and we could throw darts at it."

Mr. Greggs laughed and stamped his feet against the cold. "Good idea, Fredrick. I'll give it some thought, though I wish he'd face a much harsher penalty for his dark deeds." He checked his words when he saw Daniel's face. "Hello there, Daniel!" he said cheerily, coming to the wagon and reaching up his hand. "Your father said you two dropped off a good load of walnuts."

"Yes sir," Daniel answered, securing the lines with his foot and reaching down to shake hands.

"Now, I'm not being nosey or anything," Mr. Greggs said, grinning, "but, it seems that you got another letter from Salt Lake City."

"I did?" Daniel asked, turning to his father.

Fredrick Robinson smiled at his son's bright expression. He handed him the envelope and reached down for the lines. "I'll drive so you can read," he said, winking at Mr. Greggs. "Good day, Elijah." He looked over at his son, who was ripping away the end of the envelope with his teeth. "Daniel?"

Daniel stopped his activity to acknowledge the postmaster. "Thank you, Mr. Greggs."

"Well, I didn't write it, Daniel. I only delivered it."

"For which I'm grateful, Mr. Greggs . . . very grateful."

Fredrick Robinson gave the command to walk on, and Daniel went immediately back to the task of freeing the letter from its casing. As they moved onto the track for home, Mr. Robinson was content to sit in silence, snatching glimpses of his son as he read his letter. Periodically Daniel would chuckle out loud and share some amusing story or insight Eleanor Lund had penned.

"She says Grandfather Erickson gave her a carved wise man for Christmas, and that . . . well, here let me read it because she tells it better than I could."

He found his place.

Grandfather presented the family with beautiful pieces of the manger scene for our Christmas gifts. They were pieces from a

*crèche he carved over fifty years ago for his wife Caroline, and
you'll never guess what piece I received—one of the wise men!
Now, my question is, does he think me a wanderer, a truth seeker,
or a tomboyish person who's venturing into a profession that
should be kept the domain of men?*

Daniel and his father laughed, and Daniel read on.

*You know I'm only spoofing. Grandfather has encouraged me in
every endeavor. He is the dearest man, and reminds me in many
aspects of your good father.*

Fredrick Robinson coughed to clear the emotion from his throat, and
Daniel looked up. "She sends her love to you and Mother."

"I always admired those Lund girls . . . so bright and hard-working. Didn't
think much of James to begin with, but he's surely made something of himself.
Heard anything from him in a while?"

"Not since the letter about his injury."

Mr. Robinson moved the mare to a faster pace. "You boys certainly have
carried your share of burden," he said, his voice turning husky again. "War is
an awful thing, and none of us would wish for it, but when some madman is
turning the world upside down, then somebody has to stand up to him." He
swallowed to contain his emotion. "I'm proud of you, son."

It took Daniel several moments to respond. "Thank you, Father."

Both men turned to their own activities—Fredrick to his driving, and
Daniel to his letter.

*The flu season is over and we pray to never see such human devas-
tation again. We in the medical field have worked ourselves to the
bone. As I wrote several letters ago, I lost my friend Shawn
Burbage to the cruel disease, and I miss him very much. He
always encouraged me in my work. When I received word just
before Christmas from Miss Johnson of the deaths in your area, it
added to my list of sorrows: Mrs. Wilton, Victoria Rosemund, and
Mr. and Mrs. Regosi. Emilio and Rosa were part of my earliest
childhood memories. To think that they deeded the ranch to James
brings such tender feelings. I know he worked hard for them, and
they pulled him through a very rough time. He hasn't shared
many of his feelings in the few letters he's written from Belgium . . .
that's James, of course, but I know it's been hard for him. He says
a British doctor by the name of Robbins is helping him to get back
on his feet. I don't know if that's literal or figurative, because he*

won't inform us of his actual injuries. I suppose he fears I'll put
two and two together.

Daniel stopped reading and looked out at the passing scenery. He shook his head. He had no doubt that Eleanor Lund could put two and two together.

"Did she say something funny again?" Mr. Robinson inquired.

Daniel looked over at his father and grinned. "I just can't get over how smart she is. I mean, she's not stuck up about it or anything . . . In fact, she's pretty shy, but . . ." His mood sobered. "I bet there are not many men that can match her."

Fredrick Robinson noted his son's dejected expression. "Well, it's often best if a man and woman don't match exactly."

Daniel gave him a skeptical frown. "Really?"

"That's a fact," Mr. Robinson said with overstressed authority. "A plain and true fact. That way one can fill in where the other one lacks."

"I see. But, what if one lacks a whole lot more than the other?" Daniel responded. "Won't the one get kinda tired of always filling in?"

Mr. Robinson paused. "You have much to offer, son . . . much. I don't think Miss Eleanor would be sending you a letter a week if she didn't find much to admire."

Daniel scoffed. "We're just friends."

"Hmm . . . well, that's good, isn't it?" Mr. Robinson said, grinning. "Yes, sir. Yes, indeed. I'd certainly like to have Eleanor Lund for a friend. Smart girl like that sending me a letter every week."

"All right, that's enough," Daniel growled good-naturedly.

His father laughed. "Now you just go on and finish your *friendship* letter. Don't mind me."

Daniel found his place in the letter, trying to ignore his father's rumbling laugh.

It will take much for all of us to get over the scars of the war.
Nephi is still fighting demons of the conflict, and I don't know if
James is even walking yet. And I'm sure you're having to learn to
do things in a new way. It will take time, but we will see it
through. I admire all of you brave men.

Thank you for the questions from your reading of the Book of
Mormon. Isn't it an amazing book? I've sent along a separate
paper with comments and cross-references to the Bible.

Daniel was impressed by the "separate paper" filled on both sides with scriptures and Eleanor's insights. He loved sharing this connection with her and was beginning to understand the tender feelings and enthusiasm she had for every bit of doctrine.

And now to a more serious subject . . .

Daniel stopped reading. He thought he knew what serious subject she may be addressing, and his stomach clenched with the possibility of rejection. He and Eleanor had been sharing letters for months now, and although the pages of correspondence were filled with news, humor, and friendship, he had never pressed her for a declaration of her feelings, and she had never volunteered. He'd sensed the extent of loss when her friend Shawn had died, and now he wondered if the attachment between the two was stronger than he realized, or even than she realized. Perhaps her ties to Mr. Burbage made it unlikely that she would consider another involvement for a long time. And, of course, there was always the possibility that Eleanor had had time to evaluate the prospect of being courted by him and found it unappealing. He took a deep breath and read on.

> *I have thought often of those hurried moments at the train station before you left . . . of the feelings you expressed and your question to me. I answered impulsively at the time, but I think you deserve a well-considered answer now. I have searched my heart, Daniel, and prayed about it. In fact, I have fasted and prayed about it, and the truth is, I do have feelings for you.*

Daniel's heart jumped. He reread the last sentence.

> *. . . and the truth is, I do have feelings for you. As I look back, I realize I had feelings for you even when I was a silly girl of fifteen, but at that time I was a bookish tomboy, and I figured it was a just a crush on the town's most handsome fellow. I also thought you were only interested in Alaina, so my chances of catching your eye were slim.*

Daniel felt warmth flood his body as though the sun had just come from behind a cloud.

> *I would be honored to have you court me, dear friend. It will have to be through letters for the next many months as I must finish school, but come spring I may just have to jump on a train and come out to California.*

Daniel stared at the letter in his hands.

> *There is much that I cherish about you already, Daniel . . . your*
> *honesty and humility . . . oh, and of course, your sense of humor.*
> *It will be good when we can spend time together, although I'm a*
> *bit worried that you'll find out some of my foibles, and rethink*
> *your attachment to me.*
>
> *Grandfather is calling, and I have dinner to prepare, so I will*
> *close for now. I do believe we are embarking on a fanciful adven-*
> *ture, dear friend.*
>
> *With love,*
> *Your Eleanor*

"Stop. Stop the wagon!" Daniel yelled.

His father did so immediately, worried that his son had suffered some sort of shock from news in Eleanor's letter. "What is it, son? Are you all right?"

Daniel jumped from the seat. He ran out into the open field, his warm breath coming out in foggy puffs.

"Daniel?" his father called. "What in the world . . . ?" He leaned over to pick up Eleanor Lund's letter. Soon he was tying the wagon reins to the branch of a tree and joining his son in the meadow, where the two grown men whooped and hollered together like children in a snowstorm.

43

"Work! Work, you two dawdlers!" Edward Rosemund called out to Jane and Miss Johnson. The women had paused in their labors to sit on the porch steps of the Rosemund farmhouse and survey their handiwork.

Jane looked over at her father and waved. She leaned closer to Miss Johnson to share a confidence. "I've never seen a man look so uncomfortable with a shovel, have you, Miss Johnson?"

"I heard that!" Edward said, shoving the blade of his shovel into the ground and slipping sideways.

"And there's the proof." Jane laughed.

"You two mind your own business," Edward returned gruffly, straightening his glasses. "I'm breaking my back to get this ground turned so you can plant something—so plant something!"

Philomene stood with a chuckle. "My, Jane, he is getting cross. We'd better return to our labor." She placed the straw hat on her head and picked up the wooden tray filled with rich brown soil and periwinkle starts. "So, where did we decide these were going?"

"In the front of the bedding areas close to the house," Jane said, picking up her trowel. "I think they'll work well with the lily of the valley and daisies."

"Lovely." Philomene nodded.

"And do periwinkles have a meaning, Miss Johnson?" Jane asked, taking the box out of Philomene's hands and kneeling.

"They do, Jane. They mean 'sweet remembrance.'"

Jane was quiet, the trowel and work forgotten for the moment as she thought about her mother and brothers who were gone.

Over the months that Philomene had been privileged to draw close to the Rosemund family, she'd been impressed with Jane Rosemund's ability to carry her burdens with a maturity well beyond her sixteen years. She was composed and diligent while still retaining her youthful exuberance and sweetness. Philomene admired her and concluded that she carried many of her mother's admirable traits.

Jane took a deep breath, and Philomene waited respectfully as the young woman worked to regain her composure.

"'Sweet remembrance.' I like that," she said, gently picking up one of the starts and planting it in the turned earth. "And daisy . . . does it have a meaning?"

Philomene smiled. "Well, not a meaning exactly, but the giving of daisies is used to pose a question . . . 'Dost thou love me?'"

"That's a very forward question," Edward Rosemund remarked as he came up beside them.

Philomene jumped. "Ah! You frightened me, Mr. Rosemund."

They heard Samuel calling from behind the house, and Philomene was grateful for the distraction. She needed time to settle her unsettled feelings.

"Father! Father!" Samuel yelled as he came running. "Elizabeth is trying to throw rocks at the ducks!"

"Well, why don't you restrain her?" Edward asked, calmly laying aside his shovel.

"Restrain her? Are you kiddin'? I would have been glonked with one of those rocks."

Edward scoffed. "She's only four, Samuel. I don't think she can do much damage."

Samuel's eyes widened. "I wouldn't be too sure about that."

"Excuse me, Miss Johnson," Edward said, moving to follow his son. "I'll be back in—"

Jane interrupted. "I'll get her for you, Father." She stood, brushing the dirt from her skirt.

"But, I—"

"It's no bother," Jane assured. "I need to stretch my legs."

"But what if I needed to stretch my legs?" Edward complained.

"Ah," Jane said, walking quickly after Samuel, "now who's dawdling?"

"Impertinent young woman," Edward mumbled as his daughter disappeared around the corner of the house.

Philomene laughed.

"Well, we'll show her," Edward scoffed. "We'll just take our own holiday." He extended his arm to Philomene. "Care for a stroll, Miss Johnson?"

Philomene looked out to the pear trees already in lacy white bloom. She took Edward's arm. "I'd love a stroll."

"Wonderful!" Edward said. "We've worked hard and accomplished much this morning. We should reward ourselves with an adventure."

As they moved away from the house, Philomene looked back to assess their actual progress. They truly had accomplished much. The plantings had spaces between them now, but within a month or two those gaps would fill to create a beautiful carpet of greenery, color, and scent. There would eventually be winding pathways, a bench under the red birch tree, and perhaps even a white picket fence.

A cool March wind blew down from the higher elevations, and Philomene stopped to button the top buttons of her sweater coat. She took Edward's arm again, and he covered her hand with his.

"Are you cold? Shall we go back?"

"No, don't be silly. It's warm, actually, when the breeze doesn't blow. Besides, I've been hiking on far colder days than this." She paused. "Unless, of course, *you* need to go back."

Edward chuckled. "No. I think I can make it."

They walked through the meadow with its green grass and first hints of buttercup toward the path that meandered its way past the alfalfa field, then on toward the trees, sharing easy companionship and conversation.

"Edna Robinson was telling me the other day that Daniel had a letter from James Lund," Edward said.

"From France?"

"Actually, he's still in Belgium. It seems there's a physician who's taking very good care of him."

The trail angled up and Philomene slowed her pace. "It's such a miracle he's alive."

Edward matched her stride. "Indeed. He had more broken bones than any young person should have in ten lifetimes. But I guess he wrote the letter himself and said they may release him to come home in April."

"Next month?" Philomene asked, stopping to rub the stitch in her side.

Edward nodded. "Then we shall have two local war heroes . . . medals and all."

"Did the letter say if he was going to take ownership of the Regosi ranch?"

"Edna didn't mention that. Is the Trenton boy able to manage things in the meantime?"

"Barely. His older brother Joe is helping out." Philomene began walking again. "It doesn't seem possible that Emilio and Rosa have been gone six months . . . I miss them." Edward was silent. "Oh, Edward, I'm sorry." Philomene said with remorse. "How insensitive of me." She stopped and turned to him with a look of regret.

"No need to apologize, dear friend," Edward said evenly. "Life finds a way of moving along."

"Yes, that's true," Philomene answered evenly, "but, how are you doing?"

"Better," he said. "We've not spoken of this the times we've been together because the burden was not something to share, but now that the children and I have come out of the gloom, I shall confide in you." He paused. "The first few months were . . . well, a nightmare. At Christmas we distracted ourselves with service and the gaiety of the season, but that balm was fleeting. In the confines of our home, poor Jane cried all the time, Samuel was withdrawn, and little Elizabeth wandered the rooms looking for Victoria." Philomene looked stricken. "But we are better now . . . truly." He smiled and took her hand. "Truly. Haven't you seen us all smiling more and chattering away?"

Philomene had noticed a brightening of Samuel's demeanor at school. He'd even resumed teasing the girls and raising his hand in class, and Mr. Rosemund had regained his calm, purposeful expression. "Yes, it does seem your family is healing."

Edward smiled. "It is. And you've certainly been a part of that, Philomene."

She felt unsettled by the sentiment and his sincerity. "I . . . it's . . . I've been glad to help . . . in any way."

They reached the first grove, moving between the frilly sentinels to stand under the canopy of blossoms.

"I would rather sit on a pumpkin and have it all to myself, than be crowded on a velvet cushion," Edward recited.

Philomene nodded. "Thoreau. What perfect sentiments." She looked around at the splendor. "You should be proud of what you and Victoria managed." Edward hung his head, and Philomene felt a rush of remorse. "I'm sorry, Edward. Again, that was thoughtless of me."

He looked up quickly. "No, no, my friend, you're absolutely correct. This is a beautiful, productive farm. It's just that the credit does not lie in my pocket." A flicker of a smile touched the corner of his mouth. "We all know that Victoria was the astute farm woman." He ran his hand along one of the branches, his mood becoming reflective. "I could never run this farm without her."

Philomene was shocked by this pronouncement and tried to diminish its import. "Don't be silly, Edward, of course you can do it. You've learned much over the years."

"Yes, I have, but not enough. There is much that can go wrong on a farm, and what would I be able to do . . . stand out in the grove and quote poetry to the trees? No. It takes intuition as well as knowledge." He watched a dragonfly as it landed on a nearby branch. "Besides, my heart is not in it now."

Philomene turned to look out across the meadowland, attempting to hide her sadness and disappointment. "So, are you thinking of selling?"

"I am," he answered simply.

Loneliness surrounded her. The Rosemund family had settled themselves into her existence, and she didn't know if she could stand the breaking of those ties. "But . . . but we've been planting the flowers," she stammered lamely.

Edward smiled. "Yes. I needed to fulfill Victoria's wish, and I thought it would be welcoming for the new owners."

Philomene's heart jumped. "So, you've already sold?"

Edward came to stand beside her. "No, oh no," he answered. "Remember, I am an educated man, so it takes me a foolishly long time to make a decision."

"I can't stand this," Philomene said bluntly. Edward looked over at her and she stared him right in the face. "And I suppose you'll uproot your children and drag them back to the East . . . back to Harvard where you'll take up teaching again? You certainly won't be sitting on any pumpkins back there." She knew she was ranting, but it felt good. It released the pain from her chest and actually distracted her from weaker emotions and foolish tears. "You are aware, I'm sure, Mr. Rosemund, that there are many places a good teacher can ply his trade."

"Philomene, I—"

"It would be imprudent to not consider other options, Mr. Rosemund."

"I think that I—"

"And have you considered that your children may not want to move thousands of miles away . . . away from their memories and friends . . . away from . . . people who love them?"

"Miss Johnson."

"Yes?"

Edward smiled at her. "Do you not think I am considering everything? Do you not think I am considering the children's feelings for you?" Philomene stared at him, her mouth slightly opened as though to speak, but no words were forthcoming. Edward took her hand. "Yes, for you, dear Philomene."

"Then how can you take them away?"

"I have not said I am taking them away."

"But, if you sell the farm . . ."

"Are there no other houses for me to buy in Sutter Creek or Pine Grove?"

Relief washed over her, and she had to work hard to keep her emotions in check. "You *have* been thinking this through."

Edward nodded and awkwardly let go of her hand. "Ah yes . . . thinking and thinking . . . an abundance of thinking. Jane tells me that sometimes I think too much . . . that I should use my heart as well as my brain."

Philomene was perplexed by the sudden change in her friend's emotions. "Edward, are you all right?"

He took a deep breath. "I am . . . but . . . no, not really." He put his hands in his pockets and took them out again. "You are a brilliant woman, Philomene . . ." He swallowed. "And over the months I have . . . come to admire you . . . and care for you . . ."

Philomene was trying not to reason out the conclusion of his speech, not wanting to respond ahead of time to his intentions. Nevertheless, her palms were sweating as she waited.

Edward blew out a breath of air. "I am being a dolt here, aren't I?"

Philomene attempted to give him a smile, but it felt more like a grimace. "What is it you're trying to say, Mr. Rosemund?"

"Well, *ask*, actually," he responded. "Ask. I'm trying to ask for permission to court you."

Philomene felt like one of her students. In her whole life she'd never been asked that question, and, as she looked at Edward Rosemund's face, she was sure it was not a question that had ever passed his lips. Her mind was going through all the reasons for refusal, fear being the most predominant, but her heart was saying to go on and give it a try. She went with her heart. "I would be honored to have you court me, Mr. Rosemund."

He smiled and color came back into his face. "Thank you, Miss Johnson, but the honor will be mine." He offered his arm, and she took it. They walked back together to the farmhouse in the afternoon gloaming, an affable silence settling between them. Finally Philomene spoke.

"Edward, I have a recommendation concerning the farm."

He smiled, liking the idea that she was already providing counsel. "Don't tell me you want to learn farming?"

She laughed. "Oh dear, that would be a sight." She paused. "No, it more concerns the sale of the property. You haven't sent out any notices as yet, have you?"

He helped her over a ditch. "No, not yet. Why? Have you someone to recommend?"

The white farmhouse came into view, the front yard softened by the flush of infant plantings. Philomene smiled. "Indeed, Mr. Rosemund. I think I have the perfect people to recommend."

44

Dear sisters,

I am coming home! My friend and healer Dr. Joseph Robbins tells
me it isn't a dream, though I think it is. I will probably ship out
in two or three weeks. Dr. Robbins also leaves for his home in
Warwickshire at the end of the month. We certainly are glad to be
going home, I can tell you. His wife and children haven't seen
him for over three years. Won't they be excited? He is a grand
fellow, and I am grateful he was here to help me.

I have to tell you, dear ones, that I never thought I'd walk again. I
had many broken bones—some critical to walking—but Dr. Robbins
has seen me through this hard time in my life. I have been in a wheel
chair for the past two months but am now walking! I know you have
been praying for me, and that's been the ticket too, I'm sure.

My friend Wheaten Clune came to see me before he left for
Shrewsbury. He was able to watch me take my first steps, and
wasn't he proud of me! He is like my brother, and we will never
forget what we went through together. We two are sad because we
lost our friend Private Marcus Hill. He was killed in the same
explosion that took me down. He was a Mormon boy from Salt
Lake City, and I was thinking that maybe you could find his
family? He lived in someplace called Sugarhouse, and his parents
were Lois and Clayton Hill. Remember I wrote you about him? He
was the one that saved Daniel Chart's life. Small world, isn't it?

*It will be a wonderful thing to come home, but sad too. I have
decided to take charge of the Regosi ranch when I get back, but I can
tell you it will never be the same without Emilio and Rosa. Enough
of that. I can't think much about it without a fearful sadness.*

*I have written to Mother and Daniel Chart about my good news,
so now everyone who means something to me should know.*

*It will be strange to leave here. My life has changed so much—I
suppose that's because I've seen so much. All the different people I've
met and all of us wanting the same thing—peace and security. I
think that's the ticket for peace, for all the different sides to see that
we're all human. We all have families, lives, dreams, and fears. We
can all live together, but we have to appreciate our differences as well
as our similarities. Hear me going on like a statesman! I guess I have
to blame it on Dr. Robbins and the long talks we've had together. And
can you believe how this letter is just going on and on? Being laid up
has made for lots of time to improve my writing skills, I guess.*

*I won't be able to see you on my way home, little pals, as I'm traveling
on a hospital train with no stops between Denver and Reno, but I'm
sure there will come a time when we'll be together—so don't change
too much, hear me? Send a photo—especially of my new nephew.*

Your brother,
James

Alaina and Eleanor sat side by side at Grandmother Erickson's kitchen
table. Eleanor had been reading the letter out loud as Alaina did mending and
Mother Erickson fed Nephi Jr. his mush. The women looked at each other,
smiling with contentment and relief.

"There's a miracle," Eleanor said at last, folding the letter and putting it back
into the envelope.

"Bless that Dr. Robbins," Mother Erickson said, making a face at the baby.
The six-month-old giggled and slapped his chubby hand into the mush bowl.
"And the power of prayer," she finished.

"Indeed," Alaina agreed. She took her mother-in-law's hand. "I'm sure all those
times you put his name on the prayer roll at the temple might have helped a bit."

Eleanor smiled and continued to go through the post. "Ah, here's one to
you from Philomene Johnson," she said, holding the envelope out to her sister.

"That's odd," Alaina answered, breaking a thread with her teeth, "she normally
writes to you." She laid down the shirt to which she was affixing buttons and stuck

the needle into the pincushion. She took the letter. "Actually, it's addressed to both myself and Nephi. Is he still out in the back pasture with Katie?"

Patience Erickson nodded. "I think he's nervous about that job interview today."

Alaina took a deep breath and rubbed the top of Nephi Jr.'s head. "But Daddy's getting better, isn't he?" She looked over to Mother Erickson. "He held onto the last job for five weeks?"

"Almost six."

"So, see . . . we're making progress," she said, ripping open the letter and taking it out of the envelope.

Mother Erickson laid her hand on her arm. "You don't need to share it with us if you don't want to."

"Don't be silly," Alaina said. "A letter is much better if it's shared." She began reading.

> *March 20, 1919*
>
> *My dear Alaina and Nephi,*
>
> *I will come right to my main point so there will be no suspicion or gossip. I am being courted by Mr. Samuel Rosemund.*

"What?" Eleanor yelled, coming to her feet. "Our Miss Johnson?"

The women laughed as Alaina pressed the letter to her heart. "That's what it says. I didn't make it up."

Eleanor sat back down and leaned forward. "Well, go on! Go on! I want to hear the details."

Alaina smiled at her sister's enthusiasm and continued.

> *I know you will probably find this news surprising, as I myself would not have imagined such a thing. Mr. Rosemund is a fine man. He has many admirable attributes, and we share much in common. We had grown close over the months following his sweet wife's death, and I suppose this is just a natural extension of that friendship. I adore his children, and I believe they are somewhat fond of me.*

Alaina and Eleanor shared a knowing look. Every young person who'd had the privilege of coming within Philomene Johnson's magical influence was well aware of the breadth of that blessing.

> *Now, my dear Alaina, I come to the actual point of this letter. As all in the area were aware, it was Victoria Rosemund who was*

blessed with land sense (just like someone else I know), and with
her brilliance and the hard work of her husband and children,
the land flourished. With the untimely deaths of Victoria and her
two sons, the task of running the farm seems daunting to Mr.
Rosemund. Therefore he has . . .

Alaina came slowly out of her seat, her eyes never leaving the paper.

. . . decided to sell the property, and would like to offer . . .

Alaina sobbed.

. . . Mr. and Mrs. Nephi Erickson the first opportunity of purchase.

"Oh, dear Father," Mother Erickson cried, rising to hold her weeping daughter-in-law in her arms. "Oh, sweet miracles!"

Eleanor sat stunned, staring at her sister as though unable to think or breathe.

Alaina turned abruptly for the back porch door. "Nephi . . . I have to tell him! I have to find him!" She bolted down the back porch steps, yelling his name.

Mother Erickson picked up her grandson, and Eleanor shot out of her seat in a sudden rush of elation. "Wahoo!" she yelled, scaring Nephi Jr. He began crying in earnest, but Mother Erickson just kissed his little face, and his Auntie Eleanor patted his back as they ran to hear the good news being told.

As they emerged from the house, they saw Alaina running toward Nephi and Katie, who were coming back from a walk.

"The farm! The farm!" they heard her yelling. "Mr. Rosemund wants to sell us the farm!"

Nephi looked at his wife as if her words didn't make sense. She hugged him, shoved the letter into his hand, and picked up Katie.

As Mother Erickson and Eleanor drew near, Nephi came to the critical moment in the letter. He looked over at his wife in disbelief, and Alaina nodded, an unabashed look of joy on her face.

"Is this possible?" he asked, staring at Alaina in wonder.

"We have enough saved for a small down payment, and the rest we'll—"

Eleanor hooted with laughter. "I don't think he was asking about finances, you silly goose! I think he's wondering if it's a dream."

Alaina laughed. "No, it's not a dream! It's not! It's right there in the letter."

"What's in the letter?" Katie asked. "What is it?"

Nephi's eyes flooded with tears. He hugged his girls so tightly that they both grunted with laughter. "We're going to buy a farm, my little Katie. We're going to buy back your mommy's farm!"

45

Elizabeth Lund stood on the platform of the train station in Martell, waiting to welcome home her hero son. Her stomach was taut with nervous anticipation, and she kept glancing over at Kerri McKee for reassurance. Miss McKee smiled at her and winked. Mrs. Lund took a deep breath, feeling grateful that the servant girl had agreed to accompany her on this trip, grateful for her positive strength in helping her past so many fearful situations.

Kerri moved a little closer to her mistress as another Sutter Creek neighbor came to shake her hand and extend congratulations. The platform was filled with half the citizens of the surrounding area, as well as Mr. Turner's brass band, two dogs, and the mayor.

During their days in town prior to James's arrival, Kerri had been introduced to Dr. McIntyre, Elijah Greggs the postmaster, Pastor Wilton, his daughter Joanna and her husband Mr. Peterson, and Philomene Johnson and her fiancé Mr. Rosemund. Today she had added to her list of acquaintances Mr. and Mrs. Robinson and their son Daniel, and Mr. William Trenton—the young man left in charge of the Regosi ranch until James returned home. It was like meeting old friends, as she'd heard Eleanor Lund speak of these people so often in their times together.

Kerri's mind was brought to the present as the brass band struck up a rousing song. The April day was warm, not unpleasantly so, but with the crush of bodies on the platform and the added noise and excitement, Kerri figured that poor Mrs. Lund was having a hard time not bolting from the mad scene.

"It shouldn't be long now," Kerri said confidently.

"I hope not," Mrs. Lund returned, fanning herself with a train schedule she'd secured from inside the depot.

Kerri was proud of her. She'd come far since those terrible months of addiction and isolation. Slowly she'd moved into fellowship with the servants and simple outings away from the house, then to accepting a few visitors, and most recently to doing a bit of charitable work. The staff was heartened to see her making such progress, yet they were stunned when she announced her desire to be present in Sutter Creek when her son came home from the war. Kerri couldn't even imagine the courage it took for her to packs her bags and return to a place that held such poignant scenes of her life, both sweet and bitter.

"Here she comes!" someone yelled, and all heads turned toward the direction of the train. The band played more vigorously, and people waved their little American flags.

Mrs. Lund took Kerri's hand and leaned close to her. "Oh, Miss McKee, perhaps this was a mistake. What if he's not glad to see me? It's been several years."

Kerri put an arm around her shoulder and gave her a squeeze. "Now, enough of that. 'Twill be a grand surprise. There's not a person in the world he wants to see more than his mum."

And then the train was there and people were disembarking—most just attempting to melt away unnoticed through the crowd, a few smiling bashfully into the attendant faces, and one man lifting his hat and waving as though the celebratory greeting were all for him. The crowd laughed and clapped at his antics. Then came the true purpose of their attendance. James Lund, in his military uniform, came haltingly down the steps of the train, a cane in each hand. When he reached the platform, a cheer erupted from the crowd that made him look up in wonder. He, like his father, was a self-effacing man and did not enjoy being the center of attention. Nevertheless, he smiled at people as he made his way forward, thanking them quietly on behalf of all the soldiers of the war. The people were respectful of his healing body as they reached out with tender touches and handshakes.

When James came face-to-face with Daniel Chart, he put his canes into one hand and held his friend fiercely with the other. Another cheer went up from the crowd as men and women alike reached for their handkerchiefs. The two soldiers embraced for a long time as the newspaper men snapped photos.

Philomene Johnson gripped her cane tightly, and Edward Rosemund gave her a reassuring hug.

"Welcome home," Daniel said.

"Thank you, friend," James answered. He looked up and into the pleasant face of a young woman with whom he was unfamiliar. It puzzled him, because she held the arm of someone whose face he knew like his own. "Mother?" he said softly. He steadied himself with both canes and hobbled forward. "Mother?"

Elizabeth Lund moved to her son. She was shaken at the sight of him, not because of his halting step or stooped body, but because of how much he resembled his father—the same handsome, lanky frame, dark hair, and green eyes. It was like seeing her Samuel when they'd first met. She thought the vision would cause her grief, but an unexpected calm washed over her and she smiled. She grabbed the sleeves of his jacket, and he leaned over, gently putting his forehead onto hers. "Hey there, little soldier," he said.

"Hello, son."

"Did we make it through our battles?" he whispered.

"We did, son. I think we did."

"I love you, Mother."

Elizabeth Lund wept.

James handed her his handkerchief. "I can't believe you're here."

Elizabeth Lund patted his face to calm her emotions, then stood straight. "Well, I had the help of a remarkable traveling companion." She turned. "Miss McKee?" Kerri stepped forward. "This is my son, Mr. James Lund. James, this is my traveling companion—and friend—Miss Kerri McKee."

James smiled at her and nodded. "Miss McKee."

"Mr. Lund."

He was impressed with her straight carriage and self-assured manner. "I can finally put a face to the name, Miss McKee, as your name has often been in my mother's letters. Thank you, for all you've done."

"Well, sir, we mostly did the encouragin'. 'Twas herself been doin' the work, and we're very proud of her."

"Well, it's . . . it's very nice to meet you, Miss McKee."

Kerri straightened her jacket. "The same sentiments apply, Mr. Lund. Though, I must say, I feel as though I know ya too, as I've been reading your letters out loud to your mum."

James blushed. "*My* letters . . . out loud?"

Mrs. Lund laughed at her son's flustered expression.

"To be sure, and to the other servants as well," Kerri added, seeing how it unsettled him.

Daniel Chart laughed at that, and soon James joined him. The mayor barged in at this point, gushing out a verbose welcome and shaking hands with thoughtless vigor. There were pictures taken of him with James and his mother, and then of him with Daniel and James on either side.

"Pompous showboater," Kerri said in an aside to Daniel's parents. "Looks to me like a skunk between two lions."

Fredrick Robinson roared with laughter and took a closer look at Elizabeth Lund's traveling companion.

After another half hour of band music and well-wishing, the crowd began to disperse, leaving James alone on the platform with his mother, William Trenton, Daniel, Mr. and Mrs. Robinson, and this new acquaintance from his aunt's home in San Francisco.

He was feeling awkward and unsure when William Trenton stepped forward. "Are you ready to head for the ranch, sir? I have the carriage at the front."

"Really? Well, that's the ticket, William. Thank you," James said with relief. He patted the young man on the back. "Thank you for all your hard work." His voice caught. "And . . . for being there with Rosa and Emilio, when they were sick."

William nodded. "I'm just glad you're back."

James turned to the group. "Let's be on our way, then." He frowned suddenly at his mother. "But where are you staying?"

"At the hotel," she answered. "It's very nice."

"Well, you're not staying there anymore," James said decisively. "We'll go and pick up your things and you'll come out to the ranch with me." He hesitated. "Of course, I don't know what shape it's in."

Edna Robinson spoke up. "No need to worry there, James. Mr. Trenton asked me last week to come out and do a cleaning of the place. I also went out this morning and cooked up a big supper. Sort of a welcome home."

James lowered his head for a moment to get ahold of his emotions. He finally looked up at her and smiled. "Thank you, Mrs. Robinson. Now . . . I have only one question."

"Oven pot roast with carrots and potatoes," Mr. Robinson volunteered with a laugh.

"That wasn't my question," James countered, "though it does sound good. No, I want to know if you made enough for an army, because I want you to join us. It'll be more of a celebration if we're all together."

"Sounds good to me," Daniel said anxiously. "It . . . it will be a good time for me to tell you some news about Eleanor."

"Our Eleanor?" James questioned, moving toward the carriage, his mother on his arm. "What in the world would you know about Eleanor that we don't?"

Fredrick Robinson gave his wife a squeeze and laughed. "Oh, you're in trouble, son. Eleanor's big brother is home now to look out for her interests."

James grinned over at Daniel. "Do I need to be looking out for her interests?" He poked his friend with one of his canes. "Have you two been keeping secrets about the time you spent together in Salt Lake City?"

Daniel laughed. "So . . . the Yankees have started out the season strong, wouldn't you say?"

"Don't try to change the subject," James threatened.

The whole group was laughing at the men's antics as they reached the front of the depot. James stopped short when he saw the horse in the staffs of the Regosi's best carriage. He looked gratefully at William, and then moved to the animal, running his hand along the head and neck and speaking in low tones.

"Ah, Tuck, you good fellow . . . good ol' fellow." He laid his head against Friar Tuck's shoulder, thinking sadly of the thousands of beautiful animals killed in the war. Tuck whinnied softly, and James's heart released a measure of darkness and doubt. *Perhaps I will be able to heal, old friend, and find a purpose in life.* When he looked up, Daniel and his mother and father were climbing into their wagon, and William was helping his mother and Miss McKee into the carriage.

"Are you driving, William?" James asked, laying his canes at the feet of the women.

"No, sir," William answered. "I thought you might want to be doin' that. I brought along Moccasin to ride."

James chuckled as he pulled himself onto the driver's seat of the carriage. "You always did like that Appaloosa."

William untied the mare from the back of the carriage and swung up into the saddle. "Yes sir, ain't she a beauty?"

James smiled at him as he picked up the lines and took a deep breath. He hadn't handled a rig in over six months. "Why don't you all head out to the ranch while we pick up the ladies' things. Heaven knows how long it'll take 'em to get organized."

The men laughed.

"Beggin' your pardon," Kerri said, "but *organized* is me middle name."

"Is it?" James said, turning to look at her. "Well, we'll see, Miss McKee. Let's say I time you when we get to the hotel?"

Kerri's eyes flashed. "A bet is it, Mr. Lund? I'll have things together and back to the wagon in ten minutes flat."

James scoffed. "And I say you're going to go way over that. But even if you're one minute late, Miss McKee, you lose."

"You're on," she said. "And what's the bet?"

"The loser does all the cleaning up after supper."

"It'll be a pleasure watching ya scrub pots," Kerri said, settling back in her seat.

James grinned and gave Friar Tuck the command to walk on, grateful when his body relaxed naturally into the feel of the lines in his hands and the motion of the rig.

* * *

After James lost his bet at the hotel, there was one more stop he needed to make before heading out to the ranch. He now stood by himself in the Methodist Church cemetery looking down at his father's grave. "I miss you," he whispered. He reached over and touched the headstone. "I think you'd like me a lot better now, Father . . . I think I've . . . grown up a bit." He fought back tears. "You might be proud."

The new oak leaves rustled overhead, and James looked up. Dappled sun played on his face, and he smiled. "Maybe you are proud. Maybe you've been watching over me all along." He looked around the cemetery. "Wouldn't that be something if there really is a place we go to after this one? I don't know . . . maybe. My friend Marcus Hill was a Mormon boy, and he shared some amazing things about what heaven's like." James leaned on his canes. "Makes me wish I'd asked you more questions."

James's back hurt, and he sat down on the stone wall beside his father's grave. "My doctor, Dr. Robbins, said I'll be able to ride again. I'll probably always limp, and I'll be bothered with some arthritis, but everyone says it's a miracle I survived . . . Maybe so. Seems we're surrounded by miracles. Our teacher, Miss Johnson, is engaged to Edward Rosemund, the man who bought our farm, and Philomene told me today that they've sold the farm back to Alaina and Nephi."

James turned his hat in his hand. "All that was quite a surprise, I'll tell you. It seems like all my mail missed me on the way home." James swallowed hard. "Home. I'm back home now. That's the ticket, isn't it?" He couldn't stop the tears. "I'm sorry, Father . . . sorry I didn't appreciate the beauty of what I had. Sorry you and I weren't closer." He wiped at his eyes with his sleeve. "I know now what a good man you were." He blew out a big breath of air.

"So . . . the farm . . . is back where it should have been all along. That's something of a wonder now, isn't it?" He was silent for a time, absorbing the sensation of quiet like medicine. "I'm heading out to the Regosi ranch . . . well . . . my ranch, actually. Can you believe that? After all they gave me . . . To give me their ranch, it's just . . ." He clenched his teeth and took a deep breath.

"Mother is with me. She came to greet me home." James shook his head. "She's been fighting her own battles . . . but, you probably know that." Tears pressed at the back of his eyes. "I promise to take better care of her. I didn't understand before." He heard Friar Tuck's whinny from the street. "Well, I'd better be going."

He stood, wiping his eyes again and picking up his canes. "I'll be back soon to visit. Oh, if you bump into Emilio and Rosa sometime up there, will you tell them I said thank you? And warn Mr. Regosi that I have a lot of war stories to tell him . . . one good one about a German soldier and some carrots."

As James left the cemetery, he heard the comical croaking of a frog. To him it sounded very much like an old man laughing.

46

The month of May brought the rest of the Lund women back to Sutter Creek. Eleanor arrived the first of the month and stayed with Miss Johnson. The two women found it amusing that they were being courted at the same time, and they often found their beaus chatting together on Philomene's front porch.

While Philomene viewed her companion with deep respect and mutual affability, Eleanor was completely smitten with her partner. Each time she was in Daniel Chart's presence, she found something more that tied her heart to him. When they worked together on the Robinson farm, she admired his thorough and uncomplaining manner; when they went into town for supplies, she liked his easy way with people and his ready humor. And as they talked about the scriptures and the gospel, she was heartened by his openness and sincerity. She was also happy that he did not find her odd, and that her intelligence did not intimidate him. And, of course, she liked his face. Though permanently scarred on the one side, it was a good face, and she knew that when she smiled at him he would always smile back.

* * *

The middle of May brought Alaina Lund Erickson, Nephi, their two precocious children, and a surprise for everyone—Mother Erickson!

The dear little woman had overcome her misgivings about riding on a train, deciding that helping her children get settled, seeing the beautiful apple farm she'd heard so much about, and being present for her sweet Eleanor's wedding was far more important than a little fear.

When she'd stepped off the train in Martell, Eleanor had squealed with delight and jumped up and down for several minutes. After hugging her tightly, Eleanor scolded the little woman, stating that if she'd let her know ahead of time she could have made a Utah flag to hold up in welcome.

Eleanor moved immediately out to the farm to help with the work and to ready things for the wedding, and James brought his mother and Kerri McKee out to lend a hand as often as work on his ranch permitted. He and his sisters were touched to see their mother walk the land and make peace with her past. She reached out to her children, and old wounds were healed, and new attachments woven.

Alaina and Nephi, assisted by James and Daniel, moved their few pieces of furniture into the house, assessed the orchard, and attended to things around the farm. The rest of the "work detail," as Eleanor referred to herself and the other women, washed windows, scrubbed floors, polished woodwork, tended the garden, cooked, and organized. Alaina and Eleanor shared their pleasure in watching their mother and Mother Erickson working happily side by side, and although it was no surprise to Eleanor, Alaina couldn't believe how much cleaning Kerri McKee could fit into one afternoon. The sisters also whispered and giggled together about how often it seemed their brother James was nearby when Miss McKee needed assistance with something.

The luminous May days ambled by as Bartlett pears set and apple trees leafed and blossomed. Titus was returned to his home paddock, yellow buttercup and blue lupine flourished in the meadow, and Mother Erickson sewed Eleanor a beautiful and simple wedding dress. It was soft gauze cotton, with ivory ribbons and a pleated satin sash around the waist.

When Alaina saw her in it, standing in their childhood bedroom, turning in a slow circle as Mother Erickson pinned the hem, she broke down with emotion. She thought of times when they roamed the farm together, gathered eggs, cleaned out the root cellar, rode Titus and Friar Tuck up to Miller's Bend, and held each other tightly the day she and Nephi had left the farm for Salt Lake City. Alaina had told her frightened little sister that their separation would not be forever. And now, in ways beyond her simple understanding, the swirl of time had brought them together to share this moment—back on the farm she thought never to see again.

A soft spring breeze danced in through the open window, and Alaina dried her eyes on her apron.

"Well, good thing," Mother Erickson chuckled. "I was about to offer you the hem of your sister's dress."

Alaina laughed and blew her nose into her handkerchief. "Oh, Elly, it's perfect," she said, regaining some of her composure. "It looks just like you."

"It's more than I could have dreamed," Eleanor answered, bending over to kiss the top of Mother Erickson's head. "Did you have any idea you'd be doing this?" she asked, helping her to stand.

Mother Erickson beamed at her. "I was hopin', little angel."

Eleanor checked her image in the mirror. "I wonder what Philomene will look like on her wedding day?"

"Are you going to miss not having her here?" Alaina asked.

"A little," Eleanor admitted. "But how can I not be thrilled for her? A wedding in Brussels! How romantic. Her Aunt Hannah has written every week with plans and possibilities. She will be so pleased to have them all with her. And did you know that while they're away from Sutter Creek, workers will be expanding Philomene's little cottage to fit her new family?"

Alaina smiled as she thought about something her father used to say. "*Things change, Fancy. They change all the time.*"

Patience Erickson shook her head. "Brussels, Belgium. My, oh my. I could never imagine such a trip. Of course, I never thought I'd get on a train or see California."

"Or visit Lake Tahoe," Eleanor slipped in.

"What?" Mother Erickson said. "Who's goin' to Lake Tahoe?"

"We are," Eleanor said, a twinkle of mischief in her eyes. "After our time here, on our way back to Salt Lake City, Daniel and I will be stopping at Lake Tahoe, and since you'll be with us, you'll have to come along."

Patience Erickson sat down in a chair. "Oh, little muffin, I wouldn't want to . . ."

"Ah, none of that. The rooms at the Tahoe Tavern are already rented." Eleanor knelt in front of the tearful woman and took her hands. "Daniel and I want to share that mountain splendor with you."

Mother Erickson looked over at Alaina. "You knew about this?"

Alaina laughed and hugged her. "I did, and I think it will be a glorious adventure for you."

Mother Erickson looked stunned. "Well, who would have thought?"

They heard the front door crash open and the sound of Katie's little footsteps pounding down the hallway toward the kitchen. "Mommy?" she called.

Alaina smiled and called down the stairs. "We're up here, Katie!"

The footsteps returned to the front of the house and were soon tromping up the stairs. "You will never believe what I just seen Miss Titus do."

"I think our little Katie likes this place," Eleanor said as she stood.

"She loves it," Alaina answered. "A new wonder around every corner."

Mother Erickson chuckled. "And a big enough space for all her energy."

Katie kept talking as she headed for the sound of her mother's voice. "Mommy, that big Titus horse likes me. He came over to the fence, and—" She stopped dead when she saw her Auntie Eleanor in her dress. Her eyes grew big, and her little mouth formed a perfect O.

"Do you like it?" Eleanor teased.

"Oh, Auntie Eleanor . . . you look like a fairy queen."

Eleanor curtsied. "Thank you, fair maiden."

Katie giggled and moved forward to touch the dress.

"Ah! Don't touch!" Alaina called out just as the grubby little hand was about to grab the soft fabric.

Katie jumped, and embarrassed tears filled her eyes at the reprimand. Grammy moved to her and picked her up.

"Ah, not to worry, fair maiden," Eleanor said, cupping Katie's hands in hers. "Thou shalt touch my dress when thy hands are clean."

Katie looked over at her mother, who smiled and nodded. "Of course, when your hands are clean."

Katie turned back to her auntie. "When are we getting married?"

"Three days," Eleanor whispered, holding up three fingers.

"Hooray!" Katie said, clapping.

"Hooray?" Alaina questioned, looking at her mother-in-law. "What happened to scrimmy?"

"I think she's growing up," Mother Erickson said. "I hear less and less baby talk every day."

Alaina looked over at her daughter's cherub face and felt a little tug in her heart.

* * *

The day before the wedding, Kathryn Lund arrived from San Francisco. She stepped onto the train platform complaining that it was far too hot and she didn't feel well.

Eleanor and Alaina hugged her until she smiled, James commented on how much she'd changed—physically—and Nephi and Daniel put her suitcases in the carriage and made her ride in the wagon.

47

As Daniel Chart and Eleanor Lund became husband and wife, a front door opened on the rue de la Montagne, and Philomene Johnson was gathered into the arms of her kinswoman. Edward Rosemund picked up little Elizabeth and moved Samuel forward for introductions, beaming at the elegant woman and feeling the warmth of her greeting. Claudine swung wide the large door, and Hannah Finn held out her hand to Jane, leading the family inside for a meal of rabbit stew and dark bread.

In the servants' quarters of the austere Victorian home at 238 Beacon Street, Bib Randall was playing tag with Ina Bell Latham around the kitchen table. Miss Todd swatted at them with her wooden spoon as Mr. Palmer pretended to be above the whole thing, burying his head in his newspaper and scolding when one of them bumped his chair.

And, in Salt Lake City, Grandfather Erickson sat on his porch watching Zachery as he wrote his numbers for his mother. The gentle patriarch hummed a little Danish song as he thought of the meandering passages of life. His few apple trees were at the end of their bloom, and he smiled as a gentle breeze scattered snowflake-white petals across the front drive.

He missed his Eleanor but contented himself with the knowledge that in a few weeks she would be returning to his little house escorted by her fine husband. Eleanor would return to her medical studies, and Daniel would be helping Elias at the hardware store.

"Må gud give dig fred i stormen, elske at overcome fare, og tro til at føre dig hjem," he said softly, and Zachery turned to him.

"Was that Danish, Grandpa?"

"Ya, Mr. Zachery, dat vas Danish. A Danish prayer for Eleanor and Daniel on their vedding day."

The little boy moved to him, placing a hand on his arm. "What's it mean?"

With a chuckle, the patriarch laid his hand on his grandson's head. "God grant you peace in the storm, love to conquer fear, and faith to lead you home."

Zachery's face brightened. "Grampa, you just gave me a blessing!"

48

The wedding guests sat on the front porch or out in the garden laughing and talking of memories, weddings, horses, farming, and future events. Some snatches of conversation were brief and shared by only two or three people, while other topics enveloped the group and made for a rousing interchange.

Alaina sat on the porch steps with Nephi, enjoying the chatter of family and friends, amazed at her husband's easy involvement. He'd come far in the last few months. Dr. Lucien and Eleanor had both been great helps while they were in Salt Lake City, investigating the newest theories about the malady of shell shock, and staying right by Nephi's side during some of his darkest times. Of course, priesthood blessings from his father and grandfather were powerful instruments of healing and hope.

Alaina looked over at Elly and Daniel standing in the garden and sharing secrets, and thought again of the dream she'd had in the night. She was inside a beautiful building that held the feeling of heaven. She walked the rooms, admiring exquisitely crafted carvings and hoping no one would ask her to leave. She heard someone call her name and looked up to see Eleanor. Beside her was Daniel, and on her other side precious Katie and Nephi. Nephi was holding their baby and smiling. She looked down and discovered that she was wearing a beautiful white summer dress. Everyone was wearing white. As she moved down the hallway it opened into their apple orchard in full bloom. She walked among the trees and heard her father's voice singing hymns. She searched the grove until she found him.

"Hello, Fancy."

"Hello, Father."

"Don't you look beautiful in your summer white."

A breeze rustled her dress and sent a swirling cascade of pink and white blossoms around her.

"Is everything well with you, daughter?"

"Everything is wonderful." She laughed and continued walking toward the crest of the hill.

The dream had faded, but the feeling of peace had seeped like rain into her thirsty soul. Alaina patted her skirt pocket wherein lay her husband's war journal. No one knew that she'd run out into the snowy night to save it from ruin and forgetting. Normally it resided with her father's journal in the bottom of her quilt trunk, but today she wanted it near. She wanted to remind herself that life was joy and pain, ease and hardship, laughter and tears—and that God was over all. She sighed and wrapped her husband's arms more tightly around her.

The afternoon rolled on with talk, and lemonade, and gingerbread. It was decided at one point that the Yankees would again win the pennant, that Mrs. Robinson was the best cook in three counties, and that Eleanor Lund had been a beautiful bride. Of course, the bride herself declared that she was only standard, and glad to be so, at which Mr. Robinson laughed and gave her a hug. He then declared loudly that his new daughter-in-law was surely the brightest young woman in California and Utah combined. The company agreed. Joanna Wilton Peterson announced that she and her husband were going to be parents in about six months, over which she and Alaina spent some time crying and gossiping. Baby Nephi had been passed around like a contribution basket, ending up in the arms of Grandmother Lund, where he fell comfortably asleep. Mother Erickson and Elizabeth Lund sat side by side in matching rockers, talking about and watching their families in turn.

Eleanor had changed into a simple day dress, affixing her hair in a braid down her back. She was now out in the front garden dancing with her husband to the sweet music of an imaginary orchestra.

Kerri McKee sat in the porch swing, gently swaying forward and back. She sighed. "Ah, 'tis Wee Larkin magic for sure."

Katie stopped poking at a spider's web. "What's that?" she asked, coming to stand beside Kerri.

"Well, there's a special fairy by the name of Wee Larkin, and she only comes to gatherin's where every heart is happy, and she flies about with her magic thread and sews all the hearts together."

"Like my heart and Daddy's heart?" Katie asked.

"Yes, and baby Nephi's heart with his grandmothers', and Joanna with her dear friend Alaina, and Eleanor with her handsome Daniel."

Katie giggled. "And can I see her?"

"Oh, I don't know, Miss Katie. She's a wee small thing. But I suppose so, if you're very very happy."

James watched Miss McKee for several moments, then pulled his eyes away to take in the grove of apple trees on the hillside. He knew that all the men who'd been in the war were finding peace in this Eden place, and he breathed in the scent of honeysuckle, smiling at his surroundings. He found it odd, though, that in all this glory, his heart still knew a small shadow of discontent. "So, Mother . . . you, Kathryn, and Miss McKee return to San

Francisco in a few days?" he asked, shifting his weight and trying to make his voice sound nonchalant.

"Actually, son . . . no. Kathryn and I will be returning, but Miss McKee is no longer in your Aunt Westfield's employ."

"What?" James barked. He turned to Kerri, a shocked look on his face. "She dismissed you?"

"Well, no," Kerri admitted. "I quit. Ya see . . . it's rather hard to work for two households at the same time."

"Two households?"

Nephi decided to put the poor man out of his misery. "Well, there's no way Alaina and I can run the farm without help with the house and the children . . . so, we thought we'd hire her on. Room and board to begin with until she proves herself a competent worker."

The company laughed.

"You're staying . . . here . . . on the farm?" James stammered, staring over at her.

"I am, Mr. Lund."

Katie squealed with delight and launched herself into Kerri's arms. "I will be liking that!"

Mother Erickson leaned over to Elizabeth Lund and whispered. "From the look on James's face, I think he will be liking it, too."

Elizabeth Lund nodded and smiled.

Nephi stood, stretching his back and holding out his hand to Katie. "Come on, Miss Fancy, let's go for a walk."

Alaina started at the use of the pet name, and Nephi smiled at her. "I didn't think you'd mind sharing."

Katie jumped off Miss McKee's lap, running over to tug at Kathryn's arm. "Come go for a walk with me. We can look for Wee Larkin in the apple trees."

Kathryn hesitated, then stood and took her niece's hand.

Alaina stood too, edging her way toward the front of the garden. "And I want to know what woman wants to race me to be Queen of the County Fair?"

Suddenly Kerri was on her feet and leaping off the front porch as Eleanor turned abruptly from Daniel. The three women jostled their way down the garden path to the wagon trail, the family laughing behind them.

"Careful of the flowers!" Mother Erickson called with a chuckle.

"To the fence by the apple grove!" Nephi yelled. "Go!"

There was laughter and mayhem as each woman grabbed a hand, or an arm, or a piece of clothing, attempting to cheat and hold the others back. Suddenly Kerri broke free and Eleanor and Alaina raced after her. They ran with joy and strength past the alfalfa field, through the meadow with its yellow buttercup and blue lupine, and on toward the grove of apple trees.

The day greeted them, embraced them, and sent them on their way.

Historical Notes

1) The estimate of military and civilian lives lost in the Great War is 13 million.

2) There were over 500,000 horses and mules killed in the Great War.

3) The estimated worldwide deaths attributed to the influenza pandemic of 1918–19 are 26 million.

4) The World War I letter from Kate Gordon to her son is actual correspondence (used with permission from Mrs. Gordon's granddaughter, Patricia Nicholson). The letter is printed in the masterful book, *War Letters,* by Andrew Carroll. Kate Gordon sent three of her sons—Luke, John, and Jimmy—off to the war. Jimmy gave his life fighting to make the world safe for democracy. John and Luke returned home to the states in 1919, but Luke passed away three years later from medical complications due to a mustard-gas attack he initially survived in October 1918.

ABOUT THE AUTHOR

Gale Sears grew up in Lake Tahoe, California, and spent her high-school years in Hawaii. After graduating from McKinley High School, she went on to receive a BA in playwriting from Brigham Young University, and an MA in theater arts from the University of Minnesota. She lives in Utah, where she celebrates life with her husband George and her children Shawn and Chandler.

Gale would love to correspond with her readers. She can be reached through Covenant email at info@covenant-lds.com or through snail-mail at Covenant Communications, Inc., Box 416, American Fork, UT 84003-0416.